my Ride or Die

ALSO BY LESLIE COHEN

This Love Story Will Self-Destruct

My Ride or Die

A Novel

LESLIE COHEN

WILLIAM MORROW
An Imprint of HarperCollins*Publishers*

This is a work of fiction. Names, characters, places, and incidents are products of the author's imagination or are used fictitiously and are not to be construed as real. Any resemblance to actual events, locales, organizations, or persons, living or dead, is entirely coincidental.

HarperCollins books may be purchased for educational, business, or sales promotional use. For information, please email the Special Markets Department at SPsales@harpercollins.com.

FIRST EDITION

Designed by Diahann Sturge

Window illustration © robuart / Shutterstock, Inc.

Library of Congress Cataloging-in-Publication Data has been applied for.

ISBN 978-0-06-296678-0

21 22 23 24 25 LSC 10 9 8 7 6 5 4 3 2 1

For my daughter, Leyla.

Whatever life brings, may you always walk through it with friends.

my Ride or Die

Amanda

"Did you know that, in French, the term 'bachelorette party' means 'the death of a young girl'?" Sophie said as I entered her apartment to pick her up for her bachelorette party. *"Enterrement de vie de jeune fille!"* she cried, staring at me, unblinking. "You're about to throw me a funeral."

I was in no mood to be driven off course. We had discussed this thoroughly, in the same manner Sophie and I discussed everything.

I pointed around the room. "Let's go. Shoes. Bag. Game face."

"Remind me again why this event is not optional?" she said. She was wearing a short-sleeved dress the color of a red rose. It hugged her body down to her knees, which seemed like a rather conservative choice, until she turned. The dress had a slit on one side, exposing a thin column of her tan, bare skin. Conservative, with just a hint of being completely naked.

"Because we live in a society," I said, "and you have to be a part of it sometimes."

"I really object to that whole premise," she replied as she inserted her feet into a pair of sandals. A gold bracelet dangled over her thin wrist.

I'd tried to stop it, but it was a force much greater than I was: an email chain with eight other women on it. I'd managed to stop them from planning a big weekend trip to Vegas or Miami or (gasp) Nashville. I wrote a very polite, carefully worded email about the kind of wedding that Sophie wanted. Low-key. Bohemian chic. *Not* like all those other weddings. There would be *no* bridal shower. The bridesmaids would *not* be matching. There would be *no* monogrammed napkins or sappy speeches or posed photographs of any kind.

Sophie did agree to one night out in the city with her friends. Dinner. A few drinks. Of all the cliché wedding things Sophie was against, dinner wasn't one of them.

"It's just one night," I said, standing near the door. "We won't even use the word 'bachelorette.' No sashes or tiaras or frilly underwear. No gifts of any kind."

"No gifts?" She looked appalled. "Just kidding," she said. "I can buy my own underwear." She grabbed her wallet off the bed. "May I suggest a drinking game, at least?"

"Okay. What are the rules?"

"Drink every time somebody says 'so cute.'"

"We can't do that."

"Why not?"

"Because we'll be sloshed before appetizers."

And then we were off, headed downtown to meet the rest of the group at a trendy restaurant in Nolita named Comma or Curve or something elusive sounding that started with a C. Whatever it was, Sophie's childhood friend Zoe seemed extremely proud to have secured a 9:30 reservation. She had created a minute-by-minute agenda for the evening, as if it were a military operation.

We shuffled out of the taxi on a quiet part of Kenmare Street, passed under an unmarked awning, and entered a dark room with a double-height ceiling. We were immediately hit by the sounds of roaring soul music and chatter. There were rounded banquettes of brown leather and a few tall, cylindrical lights coming down from the ceiling. The walls were painted with cherry blossom branches and each table held a tiny votive candle. A staircase at the back of the room went up to a second floor, where we could see nothing but red, bell-shaped lamps.

As we made our way through the restaurant, the crowd seemed to part, as it usually did whenever I was with Sophie. With her dark, wavy hair that fell almost to her waist, a layer of straight bangs that fell almost into her eyes, and perfectly curved lips, Sophie was beautiful to the point where almost everyone looked quickly and then looked again for a long time.

We spotted Zoe standing at the bar wearing a black corset and fanning her face with a menu. Her chin shot up immediately when she saw us. She was standing in a circle with Sophie's other friends, next to a vase of cherry blossoms.

This was Sophie's artistic crowd—friends she'd made in college as an art history major or while bouncing from one assistant job to the next in studios all over the world. They ranged from being an amateur watchmaker with nothing but an attic in Saint-Germain to being very famous and photographing Kate Moss for French *Vogue*.

Sophie and I met freshman year of college. At first, she was just a name on a piece of paper. *Sophie Warren. Escola Americana do Rio de Janeiro.* That was to be my roommate. Even though it's been over ten years since then, I still, somehow, always think of us this way. It was a vulnerable time. We were thrown together into a hot, empty room in an unfamiliar city, and it bonded us for life. It gave me the feeling that I was closer to her than anyone.

"Where are your earrings from?" one of Sophie's other friends asked me. I held on to my ears with both hands and realized I didn't have a clue. I worked at a law firm with a bunch of men, so not only would nobody ask me about my earrings, but sometimes, just for fun, I'd think about walking into work and saying, "Bad hair day, am I right?" knowing nobody would respond.

I started talking to one woman, a curator of Russian art, who crossed and recrossed her arms as she spoke about the emergence of womanhood during Soviet times. Another woman was wearing a glorified bra as a shirt and talking about how she was jet-lagged, how she'd just been to a show in Paris with "the porniest paintings." A guy named Hans was chatting with the bartender—Sophie had insisted he be there because his family owned half the lighting stores in Manhattan. And she didn't have to worry about sleeping with him, since he was gay.

We were shown to our banquette, Zoe motioning madly to the waiters, which resulted in a tray of pink martinis as soon as we sat down.

"Congratulations!" Zoe squealed. "Now. Let's go around the table and say what we like most about Sophie."

"That's okay!" Sophie said. "Really!" She took a sip of her drink. "Let's go around and say what we like most about vodka."

Everyone laughed.

Sophie's friend Cassandra arrived at eleven, claiming she had "lost track of time." I wasn't a huge fan of Cassandra, but only because when I asked her what her occupation was, she said (get this) "muse."

A new round of drinks arrived. "Congratulations!" Zoe repeated, and our crew clinked together chalices of pink something or other.

"I tried to reach Abe so that we could play the newlywed game, but he didn't respond to my *many* emails . . . ," Zoe said. Sophie shrugged.

Zoe straightened her back. "Oh! I know! Why don't each of us share our craziest Sophie memory?"

There were "ohhhhh's" and "ahhhhhh's." Sophie was silent.

"I'll go first," Zoe said. "Sophie and I were snorkeling in the Parrachos de Maracajaú . . . that's in *Brazil,*" she said, with an accent. Zoe liked to mention her and Sophie's childhood, two American transplants growing up in Rio de Janeiro, as often as possible. It was her not-so-subtle way of reminding us that she had been there first. This kind of event almost always turned into a competition over who could win the most favor with the bride-to-be. Zoe was less than pleased that the role of maid of honor had gone to me. She had asked Sophie, in an attempt to regain some control, "But if you had to rank the bridesmaids, I would be, like, the top one . . . right?" Sophie recounted this to me afterward, adding, "In what godforsaken scenario would I have to rank my bridesmaids?" Despite growing up in Brazil, Zoe embraced American traditions. Possibly to a fault.

"We forgot to put on sunscreen after snorkeling all day and then the next morning, we drove up to Morro Branco in my cousin's old, shitty car. It had no shocks, no seatbelts. It was *the bumpiest ride* and I've never been in so much pain in my life. We were supposed to go camping but instead, we checked into the fanciest hotel we could find, and demanded they deliver us ten bottles of aloe!"

Another girl talked about going to Spain with Sophie. "We met this drug dealer on the beach and invited him back to our hostel. We gave him *all* our information. *Real names.* Address. Phone numbers.

Not a single hesitation came to mind. But then he actually showed up and we got scared, so we pretended not to be there, and he kept banging himself against the door! Do you remember that, Soph? *What were we thinking?*"

Sophie's mouth was in a straight line. "He seemed very trustworthy," she said. "He had a really nice tan . . . He owned his own business . . ."

"Don't worry," the girl added. "Even though single Sophie is gone, the memories of her will stay with me forever!" She held up her glass.

Sophie whispered to me, "I don't know. This is starting to sound *a lot* like my funeral."

Before I could reply, Hans started his story about how he and Sophie once took a taxi into a national park in Bosnia, but the cab got stuck in the snow and dropped them off in the middle of nowhere and left, so they had to hike out of the park, which took hours.

"We had the cabdriver's number, but he didn't speak any English. So we called someone else to pick us up and they said, 'Oh yes, it will be much more crowded when the park actually opens next month.'" He touched his forehead with his fingers.

Zoe and the rest of the table turned to me, ready for my contribution. I looked at Sophie and inhaled deeply. The tenseness of trying to keep both Sophie and Zoe happy was lodged somewhere at the back of my throat.

"Well, it's hard to choose just one . . . I mean . . . there are so many . . ."

Zoe sighed audibly. I told them about the month in college we spent throwing water balloons out the window at guys we were interested in. "It actually worked one time! Remember those two guys from the swim team? I guess the water didn't faze them."

Sophie smiled, so I kept talking. I told them about how we almost burned down our dorm when Sophie made ramen without adding water. About the guy in our anthropology class who examined Sophie's head and then told her she had "the most magnificent skull." How we went shopping for Halloween costumes and Sophie couldn't decide if a costume made her look like a hot cowgirl or like she was straight out of *Toy Story*. How we used to go to Whole Foods, tipsy, on Saturday nights, and once fell into the pasta aisle. How we rescued a porcupine from the side of the road and thought we were great champions of animal welfare. Until the next morning, when we realized it was a pinecone.

But Sophie's smile had faded. She had gone back to her sullen daze.

Zoe flagged the waiter, and he returned shortly with a tray of pastel cupcakes. Each cupcake had a little flag in it that read *Sophie & Abe*.

"Wow, Zoe! These are *so cute*!" I said, and then smiled at Sophie, before taking a long sip of my drink.

"Oh my God thanks!" Zoe said. Sophie barely looked at the cupcakes.

"Okay, Zoe. What's next?" Hans said.

"How about penis piñata?" Cassandra suggested in a mocking tone, eyeing Hans.

"What if we just get wasted and flirt with twenty-two-year-olds?" he responded. "Zoe! Consult the agenda!"

"Are there any bachelorette games that are actually fun?" one of the women asked, and everyone laughed and said no.

"Well, I was going to keep these to myself, thinking that Sophie, you'd kill me, but . . ." Zoe handed out pieces of paper. It was a checklist. Things for Sophie to do throughout the course of the evening.

Lick a stranger's abs.

Take a photo in the men's bathroom.

Ask a guy to help you practice walking down the aisle.

"Oh, I don't . . . ," I started to say. I looked at Sophie, who now seemed to be totally disconnected. Hans even snapped his fingers in her face.

Luckily, Cassandra chimed in. "She's not doing these," she said, shaking her head as she scanned the piece of paper. "Sophie is *way* too hot for these kinds of antics. Unless we run into Basquiat, in which case we'd have to make an exception."

Hans rolled his eyes. "He's dead, so unlikely."

"Okay, Alberto Giacometti!" one of the women said.

"Also dead. And gay," Hans replied.

Another of Sophie's friends shot up her hand. "Ah! I know who Sophie would go for! In a word: *Modigliani*."

More "ohhhhh's" and "ahhhhhh's."

"He's *long* dead," Hans said. "What is wrong with you guys?"

Cassandra shrugged. "Absence makes the heart grow fonder."

"Death is such a turn-on!"

"Yes! They're just slightly out of reach."

"Slightly?" I said. My only contribution.

They launched into a discussion of which male artists, living or dead, were the most fuckable. Then artists got compared to food. Who would be the kale salad of lovers? Good for you, but ultimately unsatisfying. I watched as the suggestion of Richard Avedon made Cassandra gasp.

On a normal basis, I think Sophie would have quite enjoyed all this. If the party were being thrown for somebody else.

After the check was divided among a pile of credit cards, Zoe insisted we go to a club called Gold Bar.

I took Zoe aside. "I don't know . . . Maybe we should call it a night?" I said, as I watched my friend slump farther and farther down into her velvet chair.

"It's her bachelorette party!" Zoe shrieked in response. "She has to kiss a stranger! And it's right next door!"

So to the club we went, where everything was made, perhaps unsurprisingly, of gold. The dance floor. The ceiling. The walls were lined with rows and rows of gilded skulls.

"I'm going to find someone for you to kiss, Soph!" Zoe pronounced, and then marched into the masses.

Sophie sat in the corner, silent and scrutinizing the crowd. I went to sit down next to her, as the others danced around us.

"Okay," I said. "Out with it."

She shook her head. I stood up. "Bathroom," I leaned down to say to her. She followed me.

I locked the door behind us. "You have to tell me what's wrong," I said. She stood against a black marble wall. There were mirrors everywhere. Ten sinks and ten Sophies going in every direction. "Not in the mood to kiss a stranger?"

"Don't be ridiculous. I'm always in the mood to kiss a stranger." She smiled at the mirror.

"Then what is it?"

She hesitated, stared down at the ground, and then looked directly at me for the first time all night. "Everyone is acting like my life is over."

"Nobody is acting that way."

She gave me a long look.

"Okay. Maybe a little. But this is just what people do at bachelorette parties! It's a send-off."

"Which is exactly why I didn't want one! I know my life is over. I don't need a bunch of people calling attention to it."

"Sophie. Your life isn't over."

"It is, actually. I may not be dying, but a part of me is."

"Really? Which part?"

"You know."

The thing about it was—I did know. It was the part that charmed everyone in sight. When we ate breakfast together in the college cafeteria, Sophie would work her magic on the guy behind the counter, which often resulted in a free bagel with extra cream cheese. If she went to a bar, she somehow convinced the bartender to give us drinks on the house and then asked if anyone had ever left anything interesting behind that she could use in her class the History of Found Objects in Art. When she dated a bike messenger, he gave her one of his bicycle wheels for a sculpture she was working on. I remember lying in my bed, looking up at her in total awe, and saying, "You know . . . if you were ugly, you would be the most annoying person on earth. Like, literally every guy at every bar and restaurant would be like—SECURITY!"

She looked oddly exposed to me now, as she examined herself in the bathroom mirror, her thoughts visibly wandering.

She said, "You know that feeling . . . when you meet someone new . . . and you don't know whether they're going to change your life or be a total jerk that you have to swear off with crystals and voodoo dolls?"

I nodded.

"It really is one of the greatest parts of life . . . to meet new people . . . to have new experiences . . . that we have this ever-evolving cast of characters in our lives that we can talk to and potentially have sex with . . . don't you think?"

"*Our* lives?" I laughed. "You mean *your* life. Nobody else lives quite like you do."

When we were in our twenties, Sophie traveled the world with no plan, no real direction. Just a few phone numbers and a passport. She was in London for a while, then Paris. She lived on the water in Croatia for two months. There was something about a guy with a boat. She became obsessed with sailing. Once she lost interest in the boat (and the corresponding guy), she went to see the dessert in Namibia. She lived in Zermatt, a ski town in southern Switzerland, and learned how to snowboard. She spent a month in Rajasthan, taking photos of leopards in Jawai, and then traveled south to see the elephants in Kerala. She lived with a crew of skateboarders in Soweto, Johannesburg. She never had her own apartment anywhere. She just set up shop with various friends (i.e., guys who were hoping to sleep with her) and took jobs working somewhere unplanned. Then she came back to New York and lounged around my apartment, half-clothed, flirting over Skype with former lovers in other time zones and sorting out visa issues while taking a bath, her laptop perched precariously over the water.

"You know what I mean, though, right? And there's this suspense over whether they'll ask you out and then they *do* and before they come over you're so excited you could throw up and you think maybe you're about to have this epic night or maybe they'll show up late and you'll say something stupid and they'll tell you that they just got out of a serious relationship or some shit like that?"

I laughed. "It's sort of like us. I mean, did we know that the gods, and whoever was in charge of housing at NYU, would create a lifelong friendship when they put us together freshman year? No. We could have just as easily been tearing each other's hair out."

"Exactly!" she yelled. "I just . . . I don't want to be done with that feeling."

She wasn't quite the same girl she used to be. But there were elements that remained.

"You're not done meeting new people. You're just . . . done . . . sleeping with them. Are you talking about anyone specific?"

"No. I'm talking about everyone. Generally."

I smiled, shook my head slowly. "I can't believe you're getting married."

I'd gone with her to all the appointments. The fact that we'd planned anything at all was the result of the fact that I was an attorney with finely tuned interrogation skills. We chose Vermont in the fall, an inn that was cozy and rustic, but relaxed about it. Sophie agreed to get married in October, but she didn't want anyone getting overly excited about the prospect of leaves. We selected whimsical floral arrangements and then asked the florist to create a circle of flowers that Sophie and Abe could stand inside, so the ceremony wouldn't feel so formal. We decided upon place cards with crescent moons and indigo blue for the table numbers. Sophie tried on a thousand ivory dresses. We were at the store for so long that a sympathetic salesgirl brought over a bowl of almonds and I looked at Sophie, all red-cheeked and standing in an explosion of ivory lace, and said, "Great! Do you have any hamburgers?"

I'd seen it all firsthand, and yet I still couldn't *really* see it.

"I know," she said. "Mainly because I think getting married involves a lot of being normal for most of the day."

I nodded vaguely and then perked up. "That's not true! Look at Ethan!"

Sophie laughed. Ethan and I were in a relationship, of sorts. Technically he was the hiring partner at my firm, so, my boss, but we were sleeping together. He was divorced. Or recently separated. I was a little fuzzy on the details.

"That's right!" She put her hands together in prayer position. "Let him be an inspiration to all of us." She paused. "I'm kidding."

"I know."

"Ninety-seven percent of mammals do not pair up to rear their young! It's the triumph of hope over experience."

"Did I miss some sort of nature special?"

"There may have been a TED Talk. About the brain in love. You know me. I'm nothing if not a scientist."

"But you love Abe, don't you?"

Her face changed, and it was like a light had switched on.

"You know what I love about Abe? I love watching him read a menu at a restaurant. I love the degree of seriousness with which he takes it. It's the same care and examination that he applies to pretty much everything he does. He lives with intention. He never says anything he doesn't mean, never does anything for show. 'For show' means *nothing* to him. He gives me book reports on books I haven't read and I pretend to fall asleep and he laughs and I think to myself, '*Yes*. I've found it. This is the thing that everyone wants.' But do I have to marry him?"

I wasn't sure how to answer her. "Well, no, I guess . . . but you said that . . . you would."

"We hadn't been together that long! We were obsessed with each other! He was the first normal guy I'd ever dated. The first guy . . . able to buy a plane ticket without going into debt. We were on the coast of Australia! He was teaching me how to surf! I was full of garlic bread! I would have said yes to anyone in that state!"

"Well, maybe you should talk . . ."

"It's not as if I don't want to be with him. I just don't want to get *married* to him, or to anyone, really."

"Why don't you tell him that?"

"I have. He wants to get married. It's important to him. He thinks I'm being too technical, and I just want to tell him, *I'm never being technical!* I'm either being sarcastic or wildly exaggerating."

I laughed. "That's true."

"You know what? I don't want to talk about this anymore. Get me a tequila shot!"

I followed her out of the bathroom and back into the real world. On the dance floor, Zoe was encircled by a group of guys and was interviewing each of them, ostensibly to find one suitable enough for Sophie to kiss, but it was unclear.

"We found a bachelor party!" Zoe shouted, and removed a tiara from her handbag. She was drunk now and seemed to have been waiting for the right moment to place it atop Sophie's head. "They're going to a strip club. Should we go with them?"

"I don't know," Sophie said. "Maybe."

Cassandra eyed Sophie in her tiara. "You look *so cute*."

Sophie looked at me with a wry smile and raised her shot glass in my direction.

I looked back at her and saw, in that instant, all that we'd been through together. Sophie wasn't just my friend. She was a person I'd been in almost constant contact with for over ten years. Someone I had talked to on the phone for an ungodly number of hours—as she combed the streets of Paris for the perfect white leather jacket and I walked to CVS to take a break from studying and stock up on candy. She was the person who came home to Connecticut with me when my grandfather passed away, then drove us around while we wore dinosaur masks we'd taken from my brother. We rolled up to red lights. Windows down. Just casually looking out at the driver next to us. So creepy and hilarious to us at the time that it made me forget all about my grief. Hers was the voice that stayed with me on the phone after a tense lunch with a friend, after a bad moment at work, while (questionably) on the way to an ex-boyfriend's apartment, while silently breaking down in the office bathroom after conducting my first deposition. I listened while she vented about her clients, her impractical boyfriends, her father's obliviousness. I sat next to her when an accidental pregnancy landed her in the doctor's office, awaiting a procedure—"Be With You" by Enrique Iglesias playing through the speakers in the waiting room, each of us trying hard not to cry. We had seen each other through everything, and I mean *everything*. The people in our lives, and the ups and downs that we had with all of them, were more bearable, because we had each other.

She downed the shot.

"Let's get out of here," I said. "You're not happy. And this is supposed to be for you."

She gave me a pleading look. "I think it's for Zoe."

"So let's go."

"We can't just walk out."

She looked at Zoe and then back at me. There was a strange energy in her eyes. "When we were in the bathroom earlier, did you happen to notice that window?"

"Are you serious?" I said, and then flashed her a mischievous look. "We'll never get past her."

Thirty seconds later I was hoisting Sophie up and over a gold-plated sink.

"You are the only person I would do this with," she said. We pressed the window open.

"Full-service friendship," I said, as I adjusted the sole of her sandal so that it cleared the windowsill.

Once outside, we found ourselves in an alleyway, surrounded by black garbage bags. Sophie took the tiara off her head and tossed it onto the pile triumphantly. We walked carefully, on top of the bulky bags, from one to the other, treating them like stepping-stones, on our great journey to get to the street.

Then I looked down, and screamed. There was a giant black bug on my shoe. I kicked it off and shouted, "RODENT! RODENT!" which caused me to lose my footing and fall backward into the trash pile.

Sophie yelled back, *"RODENT?"*

"Oh. Sorry. Wrong word. I meant, INSECT! INSECT!"

"Jesus!" She came over to me and gave me a hand.

"What's the difference?"

"There is a very big difference!"

"He was moving so quickly," I said, catching my breath, one hand on my chest.

"He probably heard about the freakin' cupcakes next door."

I laughed. "I am now officially frightened."

"Well," she said. "That makes two of us."

2

Sophie

They say that once you move in together, what you love about someone becomes exactly what you hate. What was once an adorable feature of a person transforms, somehow, into something more akin to a finger tapping repeatedly on your shoulder. You stop looking in the mirror before they arrive. And it wasn't that I was attached to that particular ritual per se. It was just that I enjoyed the buzz that came along with it. Was this all true or not? I wasn't dying to find out. But now that it was happening, I told myself to focus on the loveliness of two bodies coming together in space, rather than the handcuffs. Living together is an art. A beautiful art. *Água mole, pedra dura, tanto bate até que fura.*

Basically: Try something until it works. That was my mantra. *Secret* mantra.

I'd been putting the move off and off, because really, why? When everything is just fine and actually better because you have your own space to grow and prosper and if necessary get the fuck away from each other. But the wedding was within view, so it was time for the merging of our lives and our sock drawers. I was doubling the number of socks at my disposal! What an exciting time to be alive!

Apparently, you have to do this *before* the wedding. As a precautionary measure. This is what one does, or so I was informed by the person that informs me of everything: Amanda. She said, and I quote: "If you don't move in together before getting married, people will think you're a virgin or just plain stupid, and you are neither." I couldn't disagree. I didn't dare disagree. Amanda had always been my home base, so to speak—ever since she walked into my dorm room freshman year, with her blond ponytail and her strategically ripped jean shorts, and changed my life forever. She knew how to reel me in from the abyss. Even though, in my opinion, the abyss isn't such a bad place to be. I enjoy the occasional abyss.

So I was moving into his apartment. Despite my sentimental attachment to mine and its relative cuteness. I was *leaving the past behind,* which meant a cheerful residence in Chelsea, where I'd had countless cups of coffee, impromptu photo shoots, and love affairs. Abe had carted out some complicated algorithm that boiled down to: he had the nicer place. More valuable not in terms of romanticism but dollars.

Abe worked in finance doing something . . . involving . . . inexplicably . . . pie charts? And numbers. Yes. He was a chart maker/number organizer. I met him when I was dragged to a fancy restaurant in Midtown by the only person who would drag me to a fancy restaurant in Midtown—again. Amanda. She needed to blow off steam, to take off her (both literal and metaphysical) cardigan. When I met him, Abe described the small town in Montana where he grew up. I learned that Chinook winds form when the Canadian Prairies and Great Plains meet in the mountains. He spoke slowly about the land and how it was so peaceful and undisturbed, and I was ready to move there by the time he was done. Maybe. I don't know. I had a few questions: Would I be able to get interior design work, and if I did, what were the chances I'd get paid in cows? He had just spent the past year working in finance in Tokyo and Southeast Asia. He told me about climbing a 6,000-meter peak in Northern India and his trek through the Annapurna Circuit in Nepal, which, he explained, usually takes twenty days, but he did it in thirteen and without a guide.

"So, you're an artist, huh?" he'd said.

"I'm an artist. In the sense that I paint. But I also have a day job. I had this weird thing about wanting to see money . . . at some point."

"Makes sense."

"It's green, right? You work in finance."

"Yup. I learned that in business school. Money is green."

I gave him a quick high-five.

"Ohhhh, business school." I rolled my eyes. "I'm going to ruin your life."

He'd looked a little tired just then, but said, "Tell me more."

Whatever it was that he did with all those pie charts afforded him an apartment on a tree-lined street in the West Village. So I wasn't opposed to the idea of moving into his place . . . really. The problem was what Abe had done with it. It was all brown and maroon and leather. So much leather. Sign of extreme maturity on my part: I somehow managed to fall in love with Abe despite all the hideous furniture that came along with him.

And then there was the futon. If you could call it that. This particular piece of furniture gave other futons a bad name. And futons don't really have a good name to begin with. But this one . . . it was that elusive combination of maroon and brown that really tied the whole apartment together. There were pictures of hearts and spades and clovers embroidered all over it.

"You know how I feel about this futon," I said, standing in the corner with bubble wrap and a roll of masking tape.

"It's poker-themed," Abe said proudly, as I surveyed his place on our designated move-in day, wondering which items I could safely remove from the premises.

"It's really . . . something," I said.

"Oh, come on. If you found this at some secret flea market in Rome, you'd be all about it."

I held up my hand. "Don't insult the Italians that way."

I went outside and called Amanda. "I know you said to move into his place . . . But he has this futon."

"Sophie. It's just a piece of furniture."

"Right. You're right."

I went back inside. Feeling a little nonsensical, but also: it wasn't just a piece of furniture. Not to me. I spent a lot of time in other people's apartments. And no, I was not a prostitute, thank you. I dislike the term "interior designer" because it makes me think of old women and floral prints and pastel colors and Palm Beach. I preferred Swedish minimalism and bohemian-meets-French-modern. Floor-to-ceiling windows. White walls. Wild architecture that feels like a spaceship. Yes. A perfect blank slate. People paid me to fill their spaceships with furniture, art, tchotchkes. A crucible. Cowhides over base rugs. A midcentury console table. The quintessential mirrored table. They never saw it coming together, but then when I was done, they felt very bohemian. French. Invincible. This design job gave me something that working on my own art did not: the ability to eat. More valuable not in terms of romanticism but dollars.

"Please let me sell the futon," I said to Abe, with my biggest, most innocent eyes, the ones that said, *I promise I won't do this with all your belongings. Just this one.*

"I don't understand what the big deal is," he said. "Fine. Go ahead."

But then I couldn't actually sell it. Nobody would take it off our hands. Abe posted it on Facebook and all his friends seemed to think he was joking. I called Habitat for Humanity and Housing Works, and they both responded that the futon was far too majestic, that they would feel guilty taking it. I eventually found a guy from Jersey who wanted the frame but not the cushions. A girl from Brooklyn wanted it, but her boyfriend said, "I don't know if we're ready to introduce this piece of furniture into our lives." I was able to schedule a pickup with the Salvation Army, until they asked me to email them a photo at the last minute, and then I knew I was screwed. "Oh no. We couldn't possibly allow you to part with such a unique piece."

As the wedding got closer and closer, fights about the futon led to fights about everything else.

"There's nowhere for me to put anything," I said, searching for a drawer. "What are these?" I gathered three squishy, brightly colored balls in my hands.

"Those are my juggling balls!"

"Your *juggling balls*? Since when do you juggle?"

He took them from me. "Since always." And then, he juggled.

I cackled. "Okay . . . but can we maybe put them in a less conspicuous place? At least until we get invited to a children's birthday party?"

"No. I need them."

"Readily accessible?"

He nodded. "Yes. Readily accessible."

"Fine." I bent down and ripped open a box filled with my plates and silverware. "Then where should I put these?" I asked, smiling and gathering a fistful of knives. "I'm going to need them. Readily accessible."

Abe shook his head. "Do you have to be so morbid?"

"I was *joking*. I would never stab you. At least not with a butter knife."

I began unwrapping two large sepia-toned photographs of surfboards in the trunks of cars, which I'd taken in Australia.

"What do you think of these?" I asked him, examining them.

Abe replied, "I think they're beautiful. Are you going to try to sell them?"

"No . . . I don't think so."

He gave me a puzzled look. "I thought you wanted to be an artist."

"I do."

He grunted.

"What?" I said, even though we'd had this fight before. "These are photographs. I'm a painter."

"What's the difference? This is still *your work*. You should be trying to sell *your work*."

"'*What's the difference*'?" I said. "I can't start out my career by selling random photographs of surfboards."

"What does it matter how you start?" he said, flapping his hands at his sides like a bird trying desperately to take off. "Just *start*."

"Because that's how I'd be known! That's what people would associate with me. It would be . . . confusing."

He knew nothing about how the marketplace worked. He didn't care to learn. Just to yell and flap his wings. He thought I was afraid. But this wasn't about fear. Well, actually, yes, I was afraid. But that was a separate issue. About this, he was just . . . wrong.

He said, "Are you always going to talk about how you want to be an artist without actually doing anything?"

My head was suddenly throbbing. I put my fingers against my forehead gently and closed my eyes. "I don't tell you how to do your job. Can't you accept the fact that you might not know everything?"

The aggravation lingered, even hours later, as we ate dinner at his kitchen table. I attempted to make peace by making him a salad, which Abe loved. I think it said something about him. This lack of wanting of bread. The discipline. Anyway, we were eating the peacekeeping salad and we started talking about our honeymoon. It felt like safe territory. The future seemed bright. I said I was excited to go to Costa Rica and stay in a two-dollar-a-night hut on the beach and eat *patacones* and learn to scuba dive. Abe said he was too, that Tamarindo was supposed to have the best waves, knee-to-chest-high surf.

"And we can go to that national park, with the volcano," he said.

"Yes! And drink fresh coffee and appetizers made of corn!"

Then I suggested we move into an RV if we ever need to save our marriage. Which inevitably led to a fight, and Abe having to save our engagement.

"Heading off to Wyoming is not going to save anything! Why don't you at least *try* to listen?"

"I am listening! I just don't like what I hear! And then I start to yell!"

"Then *change*. Let it go. Don't be so *driven by emotions*."

"That's just code for '*be like me*.' Isn't it? But I can't. I can no sooner do that than I can change an apple into a desk lamp. You and I are different objects. To hold me to your standard is impossible. And I don't *choose* to be this way. Believe me. I would *love* to be like you, Abe. What you don't understand is that these things that bother me—*really* bother me. I don't find them fun or exciting! I am *bothered*!"

"You *choose* to be the way you are."

"You mean three-dimensional?"

"It's not a matter of dimensions. Not everything has a thousand layers that you need to pore over and dissect. I'm not one of your girlfriends. I'm not . . ."

"What? Smart? Interesting?"

"You don't even like your friends."

"I don't *like my friends*?"

"You always say this one is too boring and that one is so condescending . . ."

"I'm just *discussing* them. That doesn't mean I don't like them."

He laughed. I stared at him as if he might not be real. I said, "*Every time* I see a news story about a couple where one person murders the other with a paddle in a canoe on their honeymoon, *I think of you*!"

The stress of the wedding, or maybe all the dust in his apartment, was clogging up my brain.

While Abe was away at work the next day, I focused my attention on his kitchen. I figured if I could get that right, maybe we could solve everything. I thought, instead of this black box of a microwave, it might look nice if there was additional shelving that matched the era of the apartment where we could put some cute *objets de kitchen*. Neither of us used the microwave anyway, due to a documentary we'd watched about the dangers of radiation. I thought I'd surprise him. A peacekeeping slight-demolition-of-his-apartment? Yeah. I know. It took longer than expected. It was all day before I could pry the appliance from its socket, but eventually, I did, and it lay on the floor.

"What is the point of that?" he asked, when he came home to find a giant hole where the microwave once was.

"The point is, it'll be more beautiful."

"You can't just tear things out of the wall and hope for the best!"

"Actually, I can. I've learned a lot about construction over the years."

"I'm not putting any objects out that don't have a purpose," Abe said.

"The point is style."

"Ohhhhh, call the pretentious police."

"Excuse me?"

"I'm not one of your desperate, phony clients."

And then, because I couldn't stand his bossy, condescending attitude or his bossy, condescending hair, I reached down, hefted the microwave, and threw it in his general direction. It landed about a foot from me and didn't even shatter because *nothing was going my way.*

After the throw, I was sapped of energy and suddenly calm. We stood there in silence. Staring at the floor. The damaged appliance. The sad electrical cord swimming next to it.

"I wish I could get rid of you," he said, finally, leaning down to pick it up. He took the precious black box in his hands and walked over to the door to set it outside.

"So glad we're getting married next weekend!" I hollered, loud enough that he could hear me out in the hallway. "You know, I functioned perfectly well before you came along!"

"I doubt that," he said. "I doubt that very much."

I went into the bedroom and slammed the door and wrapped a pillow around my head. I started playing "Sounds of the Rainforest" on a white noise machine. Squeezing my eyes closed, my ears muffled by cotton, I looked at the clock: 7:52 P.M.

I called Amanda. As soon as she picked up, literally as soon as she uttered the word "Hey," I felt the tension inside me fall.

"Where are you?" I said.

"I'm at work," she said, sounding tired.

"Oh . . . sorry."

"It's okay. I just googled 'Mafia rubouts' so clearly I'm doing some important work here." She added, "It's . . . mostly work-related."

"Altercation with that Italian guy on Tenth Avenue who makes your sub?"

"It's like there are no surprises between us anymore." She sighed. "Anyway. What's going on?"

"I think Abe should marry his microwave," I said.

The rain, on the sound machine, was falling a little harder now. There was the slight rumbling of thunder.

"I need more information."

"He talks about it all the time. I think they should just *go to City Hall and get it over with already*."

Silence on the other end, and then: "That's really unfair."

"What?"

"I mean . . . City Hall? What if the microwave wants a proper wedding? How dare you deprive her of that."

I lowered my voice. "I'm kind of . . . I'm kind of losing it here."

"What happened?" she said.

"Abe has this uncanny ability to speak very forcefully about topics he knows nothing about."

I went on. And on. I told her how he comes home late, turns on all the lights in the bedroom, and gets on the phone with customer service at Delta. "I was sleeping!"

I told her how once, he came home from a work trip to Norway and I thought he was about to tell me something intense like "I cheated on you" or "We have to move to Norway for the rest of our lives." "But instead, he was like, 'Today I finished a ChapStick that I've been working on . . . for *ten* years.'"

I told her how he couldn't go to the grocery store unless I'd made him a list organized by department, how he refused to throw anything out, even though he didn't *need* ten pilling navy cardigans with brown buttons. "I mean, is he planning to move to Oxfordshire to live with an antiquarian sheet music dealer?"

She laughed.

"I just think there's something inherently unsexy about a person who is around all the time . . . You're not like, *come closer.* You're like, *go farther away.* Also, he says I'm inconsiderate, but I always write messages to him on the bathroom mirror, like these really cute, loving messages and drawings, and he's the one who never responds. He says he didn't see it, that the steam erased it."

"Well, steam does . . ."

"I KNOW WHAT STEAM DOES."

"I don't know," she said, sounding hesitant. "These sound like run-of-the-mill annoyances. Just problems inherent to living with someone."

"A man. This is what it's like to live with a man. This never happened to us."

"But maybe these are the cute fights that you always hear about! The differences between men and women! It's all so amusing!"

"I know. I've seen a sitcom. But here is the difference between men and women. Are you ready for it?"

She sighed. "Go ahead."

"Women *think*."

She asked, "Is it possible that you're just comparing Abe to the men of your past and he's . . . less exciting?"

I was silent for a moment. "There may be an element of that."

"Sophie. Those men were vagabonds. *Literally,* in some cases."

"Yeah, but maybe that's just your perspective."

Amanda woke up every morning at six fifteen and didn't ever hit the snooze button twice or lie in bed unnecessarily. And then she morphed into a successful attorney at a prominent New York firm, all fresh-faced and quick-witted, hair bouncing just below her shoulders, swinging her bag over her shoulder with an air of *I've got this.* So for her to call someone a *vagabond,* well, let's just say it wouldn't take much.

"It's not *my* perspective," she said. "It's reality."

I'm sure you think so, I thought but did not say.

"Possibly," I said, because she wasn't without a point.

I used to find the most worthless freak shows and fall head over heels for them. Seriously, the men I dated could not have exhibited more red flags, and yet I was like, *I love you tell me more.* In college, I was obsessed with this musician who exclusively wore turquoise polo shirts—I'm *convinced* because they matched his eyes. We went back to his apartment. We made out. He filmed it. I don't know. I was confused! Maybe-ish. Secretly, I wanted to see what it was like. Would it be different? You never know until you try. I didn't think anything was so wrong until I told Amanda about it. Every one of his actions caused her to get upset, and that's how I knew that I should be, too. When I was in his room, I was all, *Maybe filming us on the first date is hot and extemporaneous?*

When I was twenty-three, I lived in the French Alps for a bit and dated a semiprofessional skier. He was addicted to heroin, or used to be, but I shrugged it off because we were about to have sex in an abandoned construction site, and I didn't want to ruin the moment. He said, "I was addicted to heroin," and I, in my infinite wisdom, had no further inquiries. My late twenties was the ultimate. A photography MFA student who cheated on me with a Swedish lingerie model named Lykke. Twice. But I think part of me felt like I could do whatever I wanted with these guys, because I had Amanda to fall back on. She was part of the problem.

I heard the sound of Abe leaving the apartment, the front door slamming. My whole body recoiled in response.

After he left, I asked Amanda questions, questions, questions, like: "Do you think it's that I love him less? Or just that he annoys me more?"

My dependency on Amanda began in college, when she organized my class schedule because I had a tendency to disregard deadlines. She helped me get financial aid because my parents had a tendency to avoid bills. She pointed out when my conspiracy theories were too far off base. It wasn't long before I couldn't get on a train or buy a pair of shoes without her approval. And my first winter in New York . . . *How shall I compare my lack of preparedness for a winter's day? Thou art* . . . Okay. I didn't own anything appropriate. I grew up in Brazil, and in Rio, it was only cold for a couple of weeks per year, and by cold, I mean in the seventies. I didn't have money for quality sweaters or thick scarves. And the things I could buy ended up being all wrong. I layered sweatshirts, which doesn't work. Amanda, like some sort of fabric mathematician, had explained that cashmere is more expensive than wool, but one cashmere sweater will keep you warmer than multiple wool ones. When a pea coat with a faux-fur collar that I bought at a thrift store left me shivering, she told me I had to get a down jacket and presented the choices on a website. The prices of these jacket-shaped sleeping bags! But she convinced me it was a worthwhile investment piece, and I believed her. When my pathetic attempt at winter boots resulted in not one but two bruises to my tailbone, Amanda stood behind me in the bathroom and covered the purple-green bruise in cool ointment. I remember exactly how it felt, to have her standing there, literally soothing my pain. I remember looking down at my soaked feet, which I had covered in two layers of socks and Ziploc bags, because my boots were essentially sponges.

Well, once you start wearing Ziploc bags as footwear, it is safe to say that you no longer trust your own decision-making abilities. Amanda trudged with me through a snowstorm—her in a winter cap and me in a bandana—so that I could buy boots that had soles with traction. Traction is a thing everybody in America knows about. I never really got over my own foreignness, during that period of my life. I felt it all the time. But Amanda helped. To have a point of reference.

"I'm going to have to ask you something now," she said. "And you're not going to like it. But you're going to have to actually answer me."

"Okay."

"Do you *want* to marry him? Because that seems very unclear to me."

"Damn you."

"I know. But you're already asking yourself."

"Damn you."

"Sophie. Focus."

"I don't know! I mean, I'm a grown-up now. And I should be able to . . . I don't know . . . keep my commitments. I've always broken the rules . . . but what does that say about my . . . emotional maturity, if I keep doing it? I've let people down in the past . . . I think . . . and I want to be someone who people can . . . can count on."

"You are someone who people can count on. I count on you," she said, in that soothing voice of hers.

I took the phone with me into the bathroom and started reorganizing Abe's medicine cabinet. "It's fine. It'll be fine. I just feel improperly dressed for the occasion. Or something."

"When have you ever been properly dressed for *any* occasion?"

I whispered, "A psychic once told me I was going to kill my husband on our honeymoon."

"What kind of prediction is that?"

"I know. I know. But it was a reputable place! Like it was this cool beauty store in Tribeca."

"Sophie! The last time you went to a psychic, she told you that you had to have an exorcism to get the demons out of your apartment, and all that happened was you ended up paying a lot of money for cleaning supplies."

"This woman used tarot cards and spoke quickly . . . Okay, maybe she was a little kooky. Clearly, I was impressionable."

"Why didn't you tell me about this psycho?"

"Psy-*chic*."

"Okay," she said, in a way that made me laugh. "I would have stopped you."

"I know. I didn't tell you *because* you'd stop me."

She sighed. "In a few days, there is going to be a wedding in Vermont with light linens and earthy details and a variety of whimsical floral arrangements, some of which will incorporate sage. There will be place cards with crescent moons and table numbers printed in indigo blue and gemstones from Brazil that will direct each guest to their seat. And it will all combine your relaxed-but-imaginative aesthetic with Abe's rural farming roots to create a celestial, magical, pastoral vibe. But none of that matters if you're not in love."

"I am *in love*," I said. "But what does that *really mean*? Does it mean I should structure my life around it? Does it mean that we should live together and lose all sense of autonomy and start to hate each other and pretend that none of that is going to happen even though it pretty much always does?"

There was silence on her end.

"Have I stumped you?" I asked.

"Kind of," she said. "What the hell is that *noise*?"

"Sounds of the Rain Forest" had become a crescendo of frog sounds.

"Just some frogs. Ignore them."

As I lay there, I couldn't stop thinking about the night Abe proposed. We had driven from Sydney to a small town on the ocean filled with turquoise-jewelry shops and whale watchers and backpackers. We were exploring the town, and it started to rain, to actually pour, so we ran to this little shack along the water that had clear plastic covering the entire operation. It was a restaurant, as it turned out, and we felt bad because we were soaked and taking up space, so we ordered this seafood stew that came to the table piping-hot with a piece of garlic bread covered in butter, and it turned out to be one of the most delicious things either of us had ever eaten. Afterward, still in our damp shorts, we left our flip-flops behind and ventured out toward the water, where I discovered, wrapped in a towel, a small velvet pouch with a little tag attached to it that read *Adventure Partner.* And I said yes. Of course I said yes. Because inside this surfing investment banker was a person that I very much loved. Afterward, I didn't cry, didn't question my decision, just sat there on the porch of our hotel room, listening to the sound of Abe in the shower, surrounded by a lush rainforest, thinking: *We will be different. Our marriage will be different.* And yet here I was, just a short time later, just days before our wedding, thinking: *We are just like everybody else.*

"What are you going to do?" Amanda asked.

"I'm going to get married. That's what I'm going to do. I just think it's time for me to . . . to . . . age out of my craziness."

I heard the front door open and the sound of Abe's keys hitting his desk. "Shit. I have to go," I said.

"Where?"

"Back to the rain forest."

3

Amanda

I took a yellow legal pad into bed with me. The light from the street was the only thing illuminating my bedroom. A thousand stories filled my head, as I sat with my knees pulled to my chest, the pad resting against my legs. The trouble was, none of the stories were particularly parent-friendly. I jotted down a few words to describe Sophie: *curious; good with people; impulsive; maybe should have thought this through more?* All roads led to disaster. But what did I know about marriage? Maybe they'd live happily ever after. Part of me worried their marriage wouldn't work out, and part of me worried it would. Would Sophie leave me behind? Maybe we wouldn't be as close anymore. I heard sirens in the distance, and felt a pang of mourning for something I had not yet lost. The sound of sirens always made me feel more alone. Rain and sirens.

Sitting there, I found myself staring at my phone, lying at the foot of my bed. I stared at it the way you stare into the refrigerator, looking to satisfy an ambiguous craving. I reached for it. The familiar glow lit up the palm of my hand.

My mother once told me never to call a man to make you feel

better. "You will always be disappointed," she said. I texted Ethan anyway.

What do you say when you have to give a speech at a wedding, but you recently helped the bride sneak out of her own bachelorette party?

I forced myself to hit send, quickly, before it dawned on me that I could have spent the whole damn night in peace. But now. I pushed the phone back to the edge of the bed with one foot, my theory being, if it's just out of reach, it projects a certain laissez-faire attitude toward the person I've contacted.

It dinged, and I sprung up.

You have to give a speech?

I smiled. This *ridiculous* smile. At nothing. I was smiling at nothing. Except his reply. That was all. It was there. I was now engaged in a dialogue with Ethan Hayes. I said his full name, even in my own head.

I could feel my strategic brain booting up. Ethan Hayes was credited with single-handedly bringing my firm into the upper echelon of New York law firms. In the halls of the federal courthouse, he was labeled with the most coveted of terms: *rainmaker*. "That Ethan Hayes is a real rainmaker," they'd say. When he turned his attention toward me, it gave me a high like nothing I'd experienced before. He was good-looking, but he didn't have to be. I would have been hooked. Just from the power.

I typed and deleted several sentences. Ethan once said that a trial was like a chess match. You had to think several moves ahead. I felt the same way about texting him.

Of course . . . I'm the mistress of honor.

I smiled. *Got him.*

I met Ethan when I came to the firm for my second round of interviews ("interviews" in law school being a fancy word for digging for Xanax in my most corporate-looking purse). As he greeted me in the pristine, sun-filled reception area, I was struck first by his impeccable physical appearance: tall, sharp features, dark hair, coffee-colored eyes. His glasses were rimless and expensive-looking. I felt sure that one of his closets must contain ten more of the exact same suit. In his office he had a framed photo of a locker room, with words written above the cubbies holding the helmets and jerseys: *Everyone wants to win. Not everyone is willing to prepare to win.*

Upon entering, I was hit by the distinct smell of Chinese food, confirmed by the chopsticks and soy sauce packets scattered over the table. Ethan apologized for the mess, explaining that they had been up until all hours the night before.

"Things got a little out of hand." He smiled. "We started making jokes . . . God. Some really bad jokes. But you know how things always seem funnier at three in the morning?"

I smiled. I knew. He opened a blue folder on the table and proceeded to ask me questions. I rolled through my accomplishments in an unhurried, flat voice. Then I decided to go for broke.

"As you can see, I have the credentials to succeed here," I said to him. "I wouldn't be here in the first place if it weren't for that. But what you see, on those papers—pure numbers and grades—is not what you need to know. What you need to know is that I have a long history of fighting my way into places, and of not taking no for an answer. And *that's* why I would be an asset to your litigation team."

He smiled. "That fighting instinct, huh?"

I glanced up at the photo of the locker room.

I said, "I'm basically a girl from a small town who played too many sports with her older brother and now considers everything in life to be an epic battle to the death and went to law school so that she could fuel her incessant need for competition, but professionally." I smiled. "With a side of nonsensical neuroses."

He laughed. "I'm probably not supposed to say this, but . . . I like you, Amanda."

I received an offer letter one week later, and I was sure Ethan was the reason why. I accepted right away, because the ultimate job out of law school, the one that everyone wanted, was a job at a firm, working with someone exactly like Ethan.

After I'd started working there, Ethan would come by my office with sandwiches or cookies, whatever was left over from a meeting.

"I don't have an excuse this time," he said once. "I just wanted to talk to you."

It was a welcome distraction from the tediousness of my job, once the reality of it set in—the mindless shuffling of money between corporations, the tallying up of billable hours, the competition between associates for work, my anxiety rising each time I heard somebody's phone ring, the sound emphasizing the silence of my own. I wanted to be in court, to exercise my own judgment, to craft arguments myself, but there were years of grueling associate work ahead of me. The difference between what you think it will be like to work at a law firm and what it is actually like is the difference between a casino commercial and a casino reality—not nearly as shiny as advertised.

Ethan's emails became the highlight of my day. He asked me about my dating life. He claimed to want to know what it was like to be single nowadays. His interest stemmed from a purely sociological place. So I told him about all my nonsense dates throughout the city. He seemed to enjoy saving me from the guys at our firm who flirted with me over four-dollar happy-hour beers. He became a protector of sorts, at work and when I spoke about other men. Until one day, when I told him about a bad date, and he didn't laugh. He growled.

I showed his emails to Sophie. She stared at each one like a detective, attempting to crack the case. With my phone about two inches from her face, she issued her verdict: "He one hundred percent wants to sleep with you." She smiled. "Sleeping with your married boss . . . what could go wrong?"

"What should I do?" I asked her.

"Just be *fun*. Be clever. Act like you want him, but don't need him."

Secretly, I was enjoying my role as femme fatale for once. Sophie disliked all my prior boyfriends, especially the last one, a highly educated, highly unyielding corporate lawyer. Sophie always reminded me of this one time he told me he had a lot of work to do and "didn't have time to be bogged down by smooching." He worked as general counsel to Burger King and broke up with me at two o'clock in the morning after I'd come home from a night out with Sophie and admitted we'd made a drunken pit stop at McDonald's.

Ethan started talking to me about problems with his wife. "It's *okay*. It's always *okay*," he said to me, as our coworkers surrounded us, devouring nachos. He made it clear that he was lacking something, something that I might be able to provide.

The emails went flying, especially late at night, both of us stuck in the office. At firm events, he would find a way to stand next to me. I was pretty sure his hand on my back was all I needed to be satisfied in life. Except it wasn't. My coworkers only knew that he paid attention to me. They would say, "Ethan always treats you like he just had a dirty dream about you last night," and I'd pretend not to be *shattered* by the possibility. This is going to sound stupid, but: I didn't expect him to leave his wife. I was fine with him staying with her. I just wanted him to love me more. But then it began to dawn on me that maybe he would. The hope was alive.

Then, late one night at the office, while I was reading document 41,112 of 70,934, it actually happened.

Hi. We broke up.

That was all the email said. Five minutes later, before I had a chance to really process what was going on, Ethan and I had agreed to meet one flight up in the firm library on the twenty-fifth floor. A book. We were looking for a book. Could the information be found online? Probably. We didn't work too hard.

It was a kiss so good that I felt fundamentally changed afterward, like I might now be a different sort of person, the kind who was magnetized to him for the rest of my life.

"You guys broke up? Really?" I said, not quite believing it. *Was it because of me?* I thought, but was too afraid to ask. He nodded, his eyes half closed and books falling behind me.

Sophie was enthralled. She came over with a framed photograph of two leopards fornicating in a field.

"You deserve this," she said as she hammered it into my wall.

"It's not like they have children," I said. "They've been together since high school! And only married for three years!"

"You don't have to justify this to me!" she said. "Who do you think you're talking to?"

After the incident in the library, I didn't hear from Ethan for a few weeks. Then I saw him during an HR presentation on equal opportunity workplaces, and as we listened to this presentation in the dark, I watched him standing against a wall and fell a little bit more in love, as everyone else fell a little bit more asleep. Eventually, his eyes found mine and I knew that he felt it, too. It was a perfect moment of understanding, a perfectly even exchange.

The next morning, he sent me photos of his new studio apartment on Eighth Avenue with a message that said:

Will you still hang out with me if my apartment screams "creepy motel"?

A.D.B.D., I texted back, which was shorthand we used at work when somebody was down about a case. It stood for "always darkest before dawn."

He wrote back: thanks, baby. I didn't hear from him for two weeks after that. Then one night he called me from a hotel phone. He was in Philadelphia for a trial.

"Where are you?" he asked, his voice distressed. "Are you out? It sounds like you're out."

I flung myself away from the dance floor and sat in the corner next to a pile of coats, covering one ear with my hand. I was at a bar with my friends in the East Village, somewhere with a disco ball and zebra-print wallpaper.

"I can't stop thinking about you," he said. "I'm coming to get you."

"You're in Philadelphia!"

"So? I'll be there in two hours."

Two hours later, he was outside the bar in the driver's seat of an SUV.

I was thrilled, but also a little unnerved, because he was driving like a maniac. He was making sharp turns without the slightest care. He seemed disoriented. In a trance. Angry. It was at this point, while barreling down the West Side Highway at an alarming speed, that I thought: *Sleeping with your married boss . . . what could go wrong?*

Our relationship became a combination of long nights on the phone, hookups at my apartment, and confusing periods of time when I didn't hear from him at all. But I pushed aside my losses and relished my victories, riding high on each of them. Like last week, when he came into my office at night after we'd exchanged a slew of emails. I was staring at his last message when he came in, startling me, so I tried to be fun and clever and pretended like I had my life together by opening a package of Post-its. He crouched down beside my desk chair and ran his hand along the back of my leg and said, "I've never wanted anyone in my life as much as I want you."

That alone could hold me for a month. Maybe more. I blocked out the rest. I tried to enjoy the present, the simple fact of lying in my bed and waiting for a text from Ethan Hayes, deep into fantasy mode. Who needed a wedding date?

I stared at the pad of paper in front of me and added to my list about Sophie: *Sophie makes up words . . . Sophie doesn't care what people think.* My phone started chiming away, as Ethan and I went back and forth, our thoughts taking the form of chirps and beeps.

What are you doing? Do you have a date tonight?

I don't. Do you?

Very funny. I'm at a steak house discussing tax law. And considering a drinking binge.

Don't! You'll end up facedown on the table.

Good point. What are you wearing?

Seriously?

I'd like a visual.

A giant button-down shirt. Pink socks.

Sweet.

I put the pad of paper down on my night table and pulled the covers up. I closed my eyes and pictured myself with Ethan, my head lying near his chest. When Ethan wasn't around, my imagination worked hard. I could almost get there. He gave me just enough. This was exactly the type of game that should have ended once I entered my thirties. But there was a part of me that liked it. It was like parsing a complex legal issue—difficult, but ultimately satisfying. Otherwise, dating in your thirties could be rather straightforward. It didn't seem to matter who was standing beside you on that cliff in the south of Spain, so long as there was good lighting and an epic dance party—all reflected in the photos, of course. It was more like a race to star in your own movie. But my interests lay elsewhere.

My phone chimed once more.

I hate the idea of you being in Vermont alone, he wrote, and I smiled, stretched my legs out, rubbing my sock-clad feet together. I put down my phone, momentarily satisfied. I thought: *He wants me. I win.* And took the pad of paper back up and got back to my speech.

But then I had an idea. I realized: Sophie wasn't the only impulsive one. And maybe I wasn't so cautious. Maybe, after all these years, Sophie and I met somewhere in the middle. *Sophie is fearless. Sophie is witty. Sophie is . . . the one who taught me how to play this game.*

I grabbed my phone and smiled that sly, mischievous Sophie smile as I typed: So come and get me.

AN AVENUE OF TREES led down the road to a small red barn, covered in tangled vines. The rehearsal dinner was inside this barn, with an open kitchen and a wine cellar. After the five-hour car ride with Sophie's parents, talking about poverty in Brazil and the difficulties of marrying into "Kentucky families" (Abe's family was from Montana), I was greeting everyone in a slightly high-pitched voice. Sophie's friends were crowded around Zoe, who was talking about how she'd just been to a mineral spa. I nodded along as they spoke about people I didn't know, delighting in "oh, he's way too demanding" and "her nipples are visible in *everything* she wears!" They discussed books, but only books written by Europeans. They talked about an artist with an exhibit at the Guggenheim and called it pretentious.

"It was brilliant, in some ways, but how much can we *really* trust someone who refuses to wear shoes and has a 'lucky cauliflower'?" Sophie said, and everyone laughed.

When we looked to sit down, Sophie's mother grabbed me and pointed at the chair next to hers. "So I don't have to sit next to someone from Mississippi!" Sophie's father had cornered Abe's parents and asked them about the weather in Kentucky. He gave up eventually, unimpressed by Abe's farm-boy roots, and turned to his friends to (presumably) bad-mouth them in Portuguese.

Zoe set up a photo montage. After a few sips of wine, I checked my phone under the table. I didn't expect Ethan to show up in Vermont, but I was hoping for some sign of life from him. I had texted him earlier, and now I waited. On the weekends, Ethan always disappeared. What do you do when someone disappears? Sometimes Sophie would disappear for a few weeks, and I'd sit up in bed at night with my laptop and google "what time is it in Ethiopia?" I'd write her emails and texts and receive no response. Eventually, I'd hear from her: Sorry! I was moving flats! which was evidence that she was not only alive, but also now British.

Abe sat with his arm around Sophie, his long fingers fiddling with her hair. She was wearing a white dress with tiny red flowers all over it. It had thin straps that kept falling. It was different from her usual uniform—a black blazer, light jeans, and white Converse high-tops—but she looked glowing as she whispered something in Abe's ear.

I checked my phone again, getting increasingly irritated. This man claimed I was rocking his world and yet couldn't answer my texts on weekends? Halfway through dinner, while Abe's friends were toasting him in finance references, I slipped outside the barn. I stood near the lake, watching the ripples. I closed my eyes, in the stillness, and called him. It started off innocently. *Just one tipsy phone call.* That was all. If nothing else, Ethan would appreciate the gesture. This younger girl, slurring her words. But he didn't pick up. I had the overwhelming urge to hurl my phone into the lake. Just hearing the *clunk* of it hitting the water would be the most satisfying thing I could imagine. I went back inside.

I sat at the table and tried to focus on Sophie and Abe. But *where Ethan might be* kept creeping in. Maybe he was on the phone with a client. Maybe he was at dinner in a basement restaurant with no service. Or maybe he was back together with his wife. A tidal wave of paranoia was attempting to drag me under. I sent him another text. Cutely worded. No pressure.

Our party moved to an outdoor patio, where fire pits were surrounded by blankets and wooden chairs, all set up for relaxing under the stars. Yes, there, amid a sea of fleece and s'mores, I started to go a little crazy. Okay, very crazy. Though, was I crazy, or was I just now becoming sane? What started as a desire for attention became a fanatical need to confirm what Ethan and I were to each other. Hunched behind a stone wall, I called him several more times. And when he didn't answer, I did something I'd wanted to do a thousand times before but hadn't had the guts: I typed his wife's name into Google.

There was an Instagram account. I clicked on it, holding my breath. Maybe it would be a private account, and I'd wasted all this time wanting something I'd never have.

It was public.

Jackpot. Or whatever the opposite of that is.

A flood of pictures appeared on-screen and I felt dizzy. I sat down on the grass and stared at the phone as if it were the open gate to a castle. The miso-glazed sea bass I had just eaten was coming up slightly in my throat, but I clicked. And clicked. And clicked. The screen shifted in and out of focus. I felt an incredible rush of heat behind my ears. I spotted Ethan. Pictures of them together. One each week for the past year. How did I know? Because she labeled them.

Sundays <3.

Each Sunday, a new picture. *Sundays.* I suddenly realized why I'd never spent a single one with him. The photos were posted each week up until present day. The most recent Sunday post was a video of the two of them on a camel. I looked at the location tag: *Bronx Zoo.*

I stood up and went to Sophie, who was sitting next to the fire, away from the rest of the party, wrapped in a white blanket. She was lazily moving a stick through the flames. Abe was across the patio, trading stories with his friends.

I heard him say, "My uncle took the train all the way here from Idaho, which I didn't know was possible."

"Is he scared to fly?" somebody responded.

"No, he just *loves* the train."

I knew it was wrong to divert Sophie's attention the night before her wedding. I knew that the more pressing concern was the expression on her face, and the fact that she was alone, but I sat down next to her and whisper-screamed:

"Ethan was on a camel in the Bronx."

"Come again?"

"Ethan told me that he and his wife broke up, but he was *with her* last Sunday. In the Bronx. On a camel."

"Okay," she said, turning. "What?" I showed her my phone. She put it down and looked up at me.

"There are camels in the Bronx?"

"They're at the Bronx Zoo," I replied. "Not walking along Pelham Parkway."

"I thought camels lived in the desert?"

"It's a zoo."

"So they get them in?"

"Yeah. They get them in. Sophie!"

"Sorry." There was a brief period of silence. She picked up the phone again. Then she yelled, "What a fucking fuck!"

The entire party turned to look at us. There was silence. I broke into a smile. Elbowed Sophie. She smiled too.

"We're just joking around!" I shouted.

"Women!" Sophie echoed.

They went back to their conversations.

"Wow. Wowwwwwww." She put her fist under her cheek and looked at me. "*Não acredito!* So, they never broke up?"

"I don't think so."

She slapped her hands against her legs.

"I want to put his testicles in a blender. We should put his testicles in a blender! I want to throw him through a window. Let's throw him through a window! Amanda. Why don't we just throw him through a *fucking window*?"

I felt tears coming. "Why is it that even when you expect something bad, *fully* expect it, based on common sense and prior experience, you still hope for a good outcome? I mean, even when you have *absolutely every reason* to expect that something won't end well, there's still a part of you that hopes . . . you're wrong? For once, I'd like to go with the odds."

"Well . . ." She shrugged and looked at me with affection. "You wanted to believe him."

"He blatantly lied to me."

"People fucking *lie*."

"I feel so deceived."

"That's because *you were deceived*!"

"I don't know why I believed him."

"Yes you do."

"Because I was so in love?"

"Ehhhh. Try again."

"Because I'm an idiot?"

"Getting warmer."

"Just say it."

"Because you *love* this." She motioned to the space between us. "You love the push and pull. You're a sucker for the drama. It interests you much more than a regular relationship."

"Maybe in sports and in work, but I don't want it in my personal life!"

"Are you sure? Why the married man, then? Why the married *boss*?"

I paused. "He wasn't *married*. I thought he was separated and . . . in love with me. I didn't know the whole thing was a sham. I would not have thought him capable of something like this. Sometimes I feel like I'm longing for a version of him that doesn't even exist."

She shook her head. "I know. He should be so lucky, actually, as to be seen . . . the way you saw him."

I was silent, thinking it over.

"Look on the bright side," she said, reaching into an open bag of marshmallows. She popped one in her mouth. "You could be getting married tomorrow."

4

Sophie

My first thought, on the morning of my wedding, was about the light coming in from behind the window shades. It seemed wrong. The wrong color or something. Too bright. Not bright enough. Not right for the time of day. Something artificial must have been coming in. Something amiss. So I went to the windows, lifting the shades slowly, expecting to see I don't know what. Fire trucks? Ambulances? But outside, it was peaceful. Fine. A nice morning. Walk it off? The solution to many ominous feelings before this. And that's how I ended up walking the hotel grounds in my nightgown and rain boots at six o'clock in the morning. I knew that the more I walked, the less I would feel.

Ferrada. Ferrada. Basicamente, eu estou simplesmente ferrada.

Loosely translated: *I'm screwed*. But it's much prettier in Portuguese.

On my way out of the hotel, coffee pots were being rolled out on carts. Chairs were being assembled into rows. I pretended it had nothing to do with me. I turned my back on everything and went toward the evenly manicured lawn that stretched out until the mountains began. The tapestry of red and orange leaves all hanging very still. The outside world seemed to have been brought to a halt for the sake of our events. I stood in the center of the lawn, squinting, my hand shielding my eyes from the sun, as my nightgown blew around me. The light streaked the horizon, creating an orange stripe of trees.

My friends and family would be just waking up now, getting dressed and focused on the occasion. We're all in this together, aren't we?—not only do we want it, we *need* it. I mean, there's nothing like choosing between twelve different types of tablecloths to distract you from more serious issues like whether you'll ever become the person you want to be or whether you'll fail and end up needing life insurance to protect the plants growing in your studio apartment, once you've kicked the bucket.

I kept walking until my feet were sore, until it was getting to be time for me to go back, but I still wasn't ready. Would I ever walk enough to be ready?

I kept looking to Amanda for guidance. But the problem was: I don't walk into a wedding the way Amanda does. She looks to cooperate. To give herself over to the moment. To clap and smile and say congratulations and mean it at least as much as everyone else. She looks to impress people with her dress, painstakingly picked out from a sea of rejected dresses that fit her just as well, were just as nice, but weren't 100 percent perfect for this moment. Yes, she'll occasionally meet a guy and wake up with a champagne hangover and some tale of the dirty thing they did in the coat closet. But that's not what *drives* her. For better or for worse, I walk into the event and I am almost always in the mood to fuck shit up. I mean. Not *really*. I won't do anything. But I'll *feel* it, this little sense of rebellion, for pretty much no reason, bubbling up inside me. I find it difficult to stand among the crowd, the other mere mortals, gaping at this overly used, overly emphasized way of proclaiming love. Generally, I'm a pretty top-notch person, ethically speaking, but I get this way sometimes. My otherwise good sense drifts into the background, replaced by shifting emotions, a taste for excitement, some theater. I become a bit, a *bit,* like a woman possessed. But today, I couldn't think any of that.

I had to go back there. I had to go back to the hotel and be compliant. The hotel that was chaos. The hotel that was guests calling to ask me about the dress code and how to get to the hotel, despite the instructions I'd given everyone and the existence of Google Maps.

My mother and I fighting because she made some derogatory comment about Abe's mother wearing socks with sandals.

My father insisting on going over his speech with me and handing me a CD of bossa nova music to give to the band.

"The vocals should be minimal with a sort of breathy delivery," he told me, in case anyone was interested in adding vocals to the guitar beat, which they were not.

It was Zoe wearing her silk robe, something she brought from when she was a bridesmaid at another wedding to remind everyone that she'd done this before and also to say, *I'm missing a robe here.*

Eventually, I went back. I had to.

In the bridal suite, everyone was in full-blown getting-ready mode and the air was filled with the sound of Zoe talking, as she sprayed the room with something "cleansing" that came from a purple can and smelled like motor oil. She squealed when she saw me.

"How are you feeling?" She grabbed my hands with both of hers.

"Pretty nervous," I said. I held a water glass and my hand shook. I could hardly hold it.

Zoe eyed the glass. "Oh, that's normal! It's *so many people.* Honestly, if it weren't for all the people that see you get married, nobody would ever *stay* married!" She laughed, and I thought: *Is she right? Is* that *what a wedding ensures? That you stay married? Just because going back on all those vows would be . . . embarrassing?*

As soon as Zoe left the room, Amanda shut the door behind her.

"Problem solved," she said, and then brushed her hands together.

But the problem was not nearly solved.

THE REST OF THE MORNING was filled with the sound of hair dryers blowing and makeup brushes clacking together and cameras snapping and there was silence for about thirty seconds as the dress went on. Then it was right back to the preparations—the bottles opening and dreary sandwiches with sticks in them. I kept eating turkey, because of that theory about turkey making you sleepy—I thought a turkey sandwich might save me. That's what it had come to. In the bathroom, Amanda held up my dress so I could pee.

"You know," she said, "you don't have to eat *quite* so many turkey sandwiches."

"I know. I know. I thought they might relax me."

"Why?"

I snapped back, "I don't know! I'm not a doctor!"

Everything was a blur. A fuzzy sort of rush. One moment Zoe was running in with two tiny cups of water to save the flowers that were already dying in our hands; the next, a groomsman couldn't find his tie. I watched my mother down half a glass of gin at the bar, the sound of the ice cubes clinking stuck in my ears . . . Then, suddenly, the string quartet was stringing its first note. And that's when I knew. It caught me by surprise, somehow, as if the preparations would go on and on and it would never actually happen. I took a deep breath.

I was the girl in the dress.

The handsome but kind husband.

The sun was setting.

The guests were inside. Ready to participate. Cry. Envy.

"You two look like the top of a cake!" Zoe exclaimed, as our group shuffled together down the hall to the ceremony room. Abe would leave me behind soon, to head to the altar, but for now we were walking together, like two people about to face a firing squad. I had to remind myself that this was a positive experience. That what was happening was supposed to be *good*.

I let Abe go ahead. My pace began to slow. The photographer snapped a photo of me and said, "Smile! This is the best day of your life!" And I stopped moving. Something inside me froze. I couldn't go any farther. I thought: *This is the best day of my life?*

I couldn't take another step, which was ironic, because I'd waited until the precise moment when all I had left to do was walk.

Most of the wedding party had already left the room. It was just Amanda, my father, Abe's best man, and Abe's niece, the flower girl. I started babbling to her, since she was the only one standing next to me. "What do you think? Should I do it?" She giggled in response. *The bride wore white. The flower girl was useless!*

I saw a sign above the door that read NO EXIT.

I was suddenly aware that something was very wrong inside me. It all looked good from the outside. That's the funny thing, isn't it? How you can almost never tell. I grabbed Amanda's hand and led her across the room.

"I don't think I can do this" was all I could say to her.

"Really?" she said, with wide eyes. "Are you sure?"

"What should I do? Just tell me what to do. You know me better than anyone."

She was quiet for a long moment, and then nodded. "You need to make a decision."

"I just—I don't know."

"It's too late for that. I'm sorry. You need to decide."

I felt a tightness in my throat. "I can't."

"Listen. Sophie. I think that this, right here . . ." She pointed at the ground. "This is the most important decision you will ever make in your life. I truly believe that. The person who you spend your life with affects . . . *everything else*. Your future is anchored here."

"Perfect!" I glared at her.

"Well! I'm not going to push you to do something that you're unsure about just because it's printed in script on a thousand pieces of paper. So, decide what you want. And if it's not this, then it's not this. This isn't an obligation. Or a Jane Austen novel. You can do whatever you want to do. And it won't be a tragedy if you don't marry Abe or if you don't ever get married to anyone. It will be *your choice,* whatever it is. You should be celebrating. You should feel . . . celebratory."

What were my options, again? I wanted to ask her to list them. Instead, I stood there staring at her.

"Have you talked to Abe about how you're feeling?" she said.

I shook my head right away. "It's easier for us not to talk than to understand each other."

Once I said that, I knew, based on the way she looked back at me, that it was over.

It was late by the time most of the guests left the hotel. That night, Abe and I were supposed to be camping in Costa Rica. But instead, I was camping out in a hotel bathroom with Amanda.

I was sitting in the bathtub with a bottle of champagne. I wasn't drinking it, but I kept hold of it, just in case. Amanda was sitting on the floor, legs crossed, picking at a container of monogrammed almonds. She was still wearing earrings—dangling and turquoise—

but she had a navy sweatshirt on over her dress. We were waiting for the wedding party to change clothes, gather their things, and head to their respective rooms. And it was better for them to do that without me there, fielding questions.

"I am done with the world," I said. "I am *checking out* for a while. You know what sounds really good to me right now?"

"Almond?" she said, and then held up the tin.

"No. Total isolation. Do you think I could rent a cabin somewhere in the Alaskan wilderness?"

"You'd get lonely. And I would imagine quite hungry."

"I'd have snow cones."

"Snow cones? They live in the snow so they're also eating it?"

"You're right. Okay, so I would need you there. Or someone more skilled at acquiring meat. Maybe I'm just done with the men of the world. I don't want to be alone, but I don't want to be with 'them,' either."

She laughed. "You say *them* as if they're aliens."

"Aren't they? I mean, every time I visit them on their planet, I think, 'That was fun, but it seems like you guys aren't making much progress here.'"

"How do you think Abe is taking it?"

"I think he was relieved. He'd never admit to this, but I think he was more concerned about the logistics of breaking up than anything else. I could tell he was dividing up gifts and doing the math in his head. He was so detached about it, which I'd always suspected might be the case, but you never really know someone until you break up with them. I swear—if you could know, ahead of time, what someone was going to be like during the breakup process, I doubt most couples would stay together."

"What *are* you going to do about all the gifts?"

I shook my head slowly. "Abe had everyone buying us towels." I sighed. "Maybe I'll just take a really long shower."

"You do like your showers."

"Can I ask you a question? Why do we always end up in the bathroom together?"

"I know," Amanda replied. "It's like bathrooms are our official headquarters for plotting world destruction."

"What's wrong with me? I want to be the type of person who is in a mature, committed relationship but . . . I also want to seduce a stranger. Have a threesome, maybe."

"You could never have a threesome. You don't even like it when the guys you date take a call on the other line."

"That's true. I need all the attention. But it's not just about sex, really. I want . . . so many different kinds of love. I want the love that feels protective and maybe reminds me of my father. I want the love that is talking talking talking and you don't even want to sleep with the person, because why ruin the talking? I want the love between two people who have absolutely nothing in common besides an overwhelming desire to have sex. I want to completely forget about someone, have a dream about them, wake up missing them like crazy, and then call them and say *come over*. And I don't expect to get all that from one person, or from different people at one time. I want to sway from one love to the next, and to have the freedom to go back and forth, depending on how I feel, in the moment. I just think that's the most truthful way that I can live. Otherwise, I'll just spend a lot of time lying to people. And myself. Is that greedy? Maybe. But I don't just want that for myself. I want it for everyone. Like, there was this one time that Abe was eyeing this gelato server in Spain and I thought, *He should have that*. She has twenty-one flavors. Imagine the possibilities."

"How much champagne have you had?"

I took a sip. "Not nearly enough."

She said, "I think, for me, I just don't want to go through . . . the pain of it. I remember when my parents were breaking up, it was all so excruciating. Because I was surprised. I don't want to be surprised like that again."

"Ever," I said. "I agree."

"So what's the solution?"

We could hear a loud *whoosh* through the pipes. Somebody flushing a toilet in the room upstairs. Amanda looked at the wall.

"We should consider expanding our headquarters. Maybe move into a bigger bathroom and . . . invest in other rooms."

I put my feet up against the wall, ran my toes against the marble. The exhaustion of the past few days was setting in. Or maybe it was relief.

"It would certainly be more convenient," I said. "To have more comfortable chairs. A refrigerator. Some snacks. Our options are limited here. And we've done such good thinking together! Imagine what we'd be capable of with other rooms."

"So basically us," she laughed, "living in a house."

"Exactly."

And then, I had an idea. In my shattered state, I was finally starting to think clearly.

"Wait a second . . . what if we did move into a house?"

"A house?"

"What if we . . . lived together?"

"Like roommates?"

"Yeah, but it would be more than that." I took my legs down and sat up straight. "What if we formed some sort of alliance?"

"That would be very *Star Wars* of us."

"I'm serious! Think about it for a second. What if we eliminated the task of vetting every guy we dated for marriage? What if we could just live life together?"

"Then I'd have to spend a lot less of my time explaining myself to idiots."

"Exactly!"

She gasped. "But what would I do with all my charts and diagrams?"

I smiled. "Seriously, think of how much happier we'd be and how much we could accomplish with all that extra time. We wouldn't need men as such a critical part of our operations. And we wouldn't need to choose one. Forever."

"I'd consider it."

"Wait a second." I stood up in the bathtub, as I always do when I'm onto something. "This is actually brilliant."

"It would never work."

"Why the hell not?" I held my hands out into the air. "It's too hard! To find one nonexhausting male human to wave it all away and say, 'This will be perfect.' It's not factoring in reality. And at this point in my life, I'm not prepared to ignore reality. I'm not going to pretend it doesn't exist for the sake of having a *wedding* and pleasing everyone."

She stopped moving and looked very calm for a second.

"You're right."

"Do you realize that there's no reason we couldn't do this?" I started to get excited. "It's not illegal."

She shook her head. "It's not illegal."

"We definitely love each other. We support each other. We're the perfect match. You're the brains, and I'm the . . ."

"Floozy?"

"I was going to say the *imagination,* but sure."

"We'll need men, of course."

"Of course."

"For sex," she added.

"For sex."

"And plumbing."

"And plumbing?"

"Well, you know, to fix things around the house."

"So this idea is both cutting edge and incredibly old-fashioned?"

I laughed. "Exactly! The only thing we have to do is set aside other people's judgments. That's literally the *only* thing standing in our way. And let's think, for a second, about those theoretical other people and their judgments. At least half of them aren't happy themselves . . . in their own . . . situations . . . that they've created in accordance with the standard rules that supposedly make everyone happy."

She said, "But we'd have to have rules. Our own rules."

"That's true."

"What would they be? We can date and have sex, but not fall in love?"

"No! You can fall in love! Of course you can fall in love. You just can't decide to live together or get married. The love has to be without structure. It has to be without a long-term commitment to build a future together . . . because we'd already have one."

"Well, the men will be thrilled," Amanda said.

"Maybe, but it's not about them. This is about what we've decided to do. For us. For our own best interests."

"Correct."

"We'd have to be firm in our decision."

"Absolutely. We'd have to commit to not giving a shit."

We looked at each other with knowing glances, slight smiles creeping in.

"Do you feel like you could do that?"

She looked up at the ceiling for a few seconds, paused, and then said, "I do." She held out her hand, palm open. "And you?"

"I do."

We shook hands as Amanda pulled me up and out of the bathtub. We pressed our ears to the door and heard nothing. The coast was clear.

"I feel good about this," I said, looking around at a room full of debris. The scattered wreckage from #SophieMakesAbeHonest. Crinkled dresses strewn across the couch, flowers on the cusp of wilting tied together with ribbon, crumpled tissue paper and dry cleaning and blow-dryers and makeup left behind. "And I haven't felt good about anything in a long time."

"We'll set fire to the world," she said.

"Honestly, I'm not in it for the fame or the glory. But if some should arise . . ."

And that's how I created an alliance with my best friend. It was that simple. It was *easy.* It was time to start again. To fix up our lives. No more disappointment. No more wasted time. No more struggling to create a peaceful union of opposites. We were done pretending that the relationships we were in with men were always enjoyable, never miserable, a steady torrent of amazing sex. We were tied together now. We had established rules. A plan. We were saving our lives. We had figured out something that nobody else had the guts to do.

And the potential for all this to blow up in our faces? Almost infinite.

5

Amanda

The realization that my life was something malleable, that it could be rearranged, was at once calming and like the jolt of a sledgehammer. Having demolished one part, it seemed easier to look around at the others with a slight glimmer in my eyes.

Perhaps that's why, on the Monday after returning from Vermont, I shot out of bed before dawn. I left my apartment, the city quieter without the signs of life that accompanied me at my usual commuting hour. I called Sophie on my walk, breathing heavily into the phone. "I'm getting out," I said. "Of the firm. I'm sick of being miserable and acting like there's no way out, when there is. I want to be in court, so I'm going to ask for Ethan's recommendation for the US Attorney's Office. He's always telling me I have a great instinct for litigation. Let's see if he meant it."

"*Finally,*" she said. "Get out. Get out. Get out."

"I feel disloyal, like I'll be letting people down. Abandoning them in their time of need, or something. Is that crazy?"

"Yes. It's a law firm, not a puppy. And believe me, once you do this, you will quickly realize how very replaceable you are. No offense."

"You're right. If I can get this job, Soph, I would have control over my own cases, *finally*. I'd be running my own show, but I'd also have to, you know, run my own show. There would be nowhere to hide. And nobody to hide behind, which is great, but also scary, you know? It's all in."

"So *go all in*. I know this seems obvious, but you'll never become what you want to be . . . if you don't actually try to do it."

"I know. *I know*. Yes, my current job feels much safer than other things . . ."

"You shouldn't make any decisions based on fear," she said. "There's this expression I learned . . . somewhere . . . between Split and Dubrovnik. A ship in the harbor is safe, but that's not what a ship is built for."

Well, that cracked something open inside me. I *got* it. I repeated this sailing manifesto to myself as I walked into the lobby and headed through security, putting my index finger down on the monitor the way I did each morning, with just the right amount of pressure. There was something eerie and robotic about it, but I used to think it was better to work at someplace that scanned me with a laser beam and possibly radioactive materials than at some rinky-dink one-room operation. I used to think that this lobby—teeming with marble and abstract art and a fountain with water shooting from the mouth of a fish—was meant to be the spoils of victory. *But this is not what I was built for.*

I went into Ethan's office, uninvited for the first time. I found him sitting at his desk. There was an empty cup of coffee next to his keyboard. He was rattling a bottle of Advil.

"I have to talk to you," I said. He smiled, as if we were about to have one of those conversations, the twists and turns of how far I'd fallen for him.

"Shut the door."

"It's okay." I looked back at the door. "I just wanted to tell you that . . ." I took a deep breath, listening to my exhale wobble. "I want to leave the firm. I want to focus more on litigation, on public service. And I'm asking you to help me." I could tell that he was about to resist, to offer up an excuse, but what I was asking was not unreasonable, not unearned. He had no way out.

There was a slight flicker of despair in his eyes. He started fidgeting with the cap of the Advil bottle, taking it on and off, circling the rim with his index finger. "Are you sure that's what you really want to do?" He cocked an eyebrow at me.

"Yes. I'm sure." I hoped that it wasn't visible to Ethan how much the waters were churning underneath this particular ship.

"It's a tough gig to get," he said. "And an even more difficult one to keep."

"I'd like to give it a try." I stood up a little straighter. "I have nothing to lose."

"Okay," he said, nodding, his eyes downcast. "Okay. I'll see what I can do."

"Thank you," I said, with emphasis. Our eyes locked. A few years of my life were right there, in that space between us—that very unremarkable-looking space between where he sat behind his desk and where I stood. I felt a slight unclenching in my body when I looked into his eyes, because I still wanted him, despite everything. I still loved him, and I didn't want to let go of whatever possession I had of his eyes, his body, his attention. With each passing second, I felt like I was falling—but it wasn't just about him—it was me. I was plain tired of this. *My* body wouldn't do it anymore. My brain could probably go on like this forever. But my body had gone through enough torture, and it was done. I was stepping out of the seemingly endless loop of pleasure and disappointment. The alliance with Sophie was a new direction.

I turned and walked out of the room. I knew if we stared at each other a moment longer, my hand would be on that doorknob.

By the end of the day, Ethan had put me in touch with an assistant US attorney. In the following weeks, I went through three rounds of interviews. At the office each day, I avoided Ethan. I made my way to and from my desk briskly and then pressed the elevator button as if a bomb were about to explode behind me. And then one day, I got the job. I looked around my office, and it felt strange. I was free to go.

On my last day at the firm, I felt inexplicably drawn to his office. He was in court, but I couldn't resist the urge to pass by one last time, to feel that rising feeling in my chest as I got closer and closer. I peered inside. It was dark. I left a thank-you note on his desk. It was direct, grateful, and emphasized how much I had learned from him. And then, on my way out, I noticed something new. There was a framed photograph of his wife perched on the windowsill among his awards and trinkets, angled toward the door so that everyone who entered could see. It was an up-close shot, the perfect picture of a pretty woman on the beach—her head cocked to the side, sunglasses on, a few wisps of hair in her face. A strategic move? I had zero doubt.

I walked across the street to the Forty-Second Street library, a place I went sometimes to take a break from the office, to immerse myself in a universe unconcerned with admissible evidence and nonexempt assets. To get my mind to slow down, I would read English novels like *Women in Love* and *Jane Eyre,* books that were full of the torment I felt. I would miss these reading sessions. I wanted one more.

I sat with a book under a green light, ignoring my phone when it buzzed. Calls from Ethan. Apparently, he'd received my thank-you note. Ignore. Ignore. Ignore. The repeated calls made me feel like I was in a horror movie, with somebody warning me to get out of the house. But the far scarier option would have been picking up. I had just escaped. There was no way I would pick up now. I wasn't even close.

I stayed until the library closed, until I felt more okay, inside, and then I called Sophie.

"I did it," I said, as I walked to the subway. "I feel *unbelievably* good right now. Well, I'm nauseous and didn't sleep at all last night . . . Actually, I feel pretty terrible . . . but I'm also pumped!"

"I'm excited for you. Our plan is *working*! Come over? Let's celebrate by finding a place to live."

"Already on my way," I said, and hopped down the stairs to the subway thinking: *I have a new job and I'll never be alone again.* Why hadn't I thought of this sooner?

When I got to Sophie's apartment in Chelsea, the door was open. She was sitting on her bed—laptop resting in her lap.

"Okay, so, to really get this idea off the ground, we need to establish a base of operations," she said. She was wearing the shortest of shorts and her hair was in a messy bun, a silver hoop hugging one side of her ear.

"I agree. But before we start looking, can we figure out dinner?"

Sophie nodded. "Of course. We have to be true to ourselves, and our truest selves can't do anything on an empty stomach."

She opened her oven. A stack of menus came pouring out over her feet, covering the small Brazilian flag on her flip-flops.

I said, laughing, "You know? I've never lived in New York without using my kitchen for storage. I've stored shoes in an oven, winter socks inside pots. I once filled an entire spice rack with different forms of medication."

"It doesn't get more New York than a spice rack full of pills!"

"The only downside is that if I ever get the spontaneous urge to cook, there is a decent chance I'll set my apartment on fire."

Sophie picked up her phone and ordered for both of us. She knew exactly what to get. There'd been a lot of sushi dinners over the years—taking out, dining in, occasionally concerning ourselves with the possibility of mercury poisoning. I listened as she ordered her rolls cut into eight pieces, not six, and asked for less rice, "for symmetry."

While we waited, we looked at a few listings. Sophie's lease was up soon, and I knew I could get out of mine early because I'd helped my landlord threaten to file a restraining order against her ex-boyfriend in my most professional-sounding legalese.

Her buzzer rang, signifying the arrival of our sushi. She went to get the door, crossed her apartment with a brown paper bag, and emptied its contents onto the kitchen counter.

"I have this idea," she said hesitantly, "and it's probably going to sound crazy."

"Okay . . ."

"What about . . . a house." She mimed a box.

"Yes, I'm familiar with the concept."

"You know, unlike the crappy temporary apartments of our past, this would be . . . a real home."

"I mean, of course, *in theory* . . ."

When I was in law school, I lived in the basement apartment of a townhouse, where the carpet was shaggy and brown and all my furniture was plastic, *but* it was in a very fancy part of Georgetown. On my street, I was surrounded by houses with single-car garages, their front doors adorned with brass lanterns and whimsical doormats. I developed a habit of walking by, as my parents were in the midst of their divorce and the only home I had ever known was being destroyed, and I looked up at the heavy curtains and warm lighting—the sheer *permanence* of it—and felt something wrenching inside. "But . . . is that realistic? How are we going to afford a real home in the city, even with our salaries?"

I arranged the food on the table, sat down, and began poking holes in my dumplings with a chopstick so that the sauce could get inside. Sophie had showed me how to do this. She placed a small flake of ginger down gently on each piece of sushi. Afterward, she breathed a sigh of relief.

"Now it's much more pleasing," she said. "Aesthetically."

When we were halfway finished eating, we turned one of her canvases into a blackboard of sorts and hung up a highlighted map of the city next to it. Was "Eye of the Tiger" playing in the background on repeat, or was that all in my head?

It was a puzzle that we were determined to solve. We would outsmart the system. If we had one strength as a couple, I would say that outsmarting the system was it.

We had each saved up a good amount of money, and one of the benefits of our alliance was that, together, we could afford much more than we could separately. Six years at the firm had left me with a flush savings account. Sophie had bits and pieces of income from her design business, some pieces quite substantial, dispersed among a wide variety of savings accounts tied to credit cards both foreign and domestic. You'd think she was trying to hide assets from the authorities, but really, she was just disorganized.

"Don't make me say it. *Don't even* make me say it," Sophie said as she ran an edamame bean through her teeth and tossed the shell into a bowl.

"But it's the elephant in the room."

"Fine. We can discuss it. *Briefly*."

The suburbs. It felt strange not to consider it. My concerns were mostly food-related.

"It's not that I *can't* cook dinner every night . . . ," I acknowledged. "It's just that . . . I don't want to."

Sophie was worried about what the commute would do to her social life.

"What if I become one of those people who texts their friends with inane nonsense at six thirty A.M.?" She gasped. "What if I become one of those people who knows what a podcast is?"

We started searching. A "house" in our price range yielded few results.

"I have to tell you," I said, laughing, "I really like what fifteen million dollars can buy you in the West Village."

She pointed a chopstick at me. "Don't look at those."

We were flipping through pictures and floor plans and street views and maintenance costs. I sat on the floor and Sophie lay on the couch, folding and refolding the edges of a chopstick wrapper. I went into the kitchen and got out a package of Oreos. I took two, and then handed her the rest. I ate mine slowly, methodically. She went through a whole row.

"I should forget about this alliance and just marry a baker," she said, chewing. "I would make such a cute round person."

I rolled my eyes. "Nobody bakes these."

Sophie emailed her friend Jasper, who was a real estate agent, to see if he could get us into the places we wanted to see.

"He can get us in anywhere," she said. "He represents half the NBA."

"And that helps us *how*?"

"They're also thinking about filming a reality show about him," she mentioned.

"Oh." I smiled. "Okay." Sophie didn't need firm credentials; just the abstract fluff would do.

"I have a pit in my stomach," she said after she sent the email.

"You do?"

"Either that or I just ate a lot of raw fish."

Over the next few weeks, Jasper took us to see a dozen places. We set aside the idea of a "house" and looked at anything we could afford. Sophie liked seeing what other people had in their homes. What books were on their shelves. How they organized their closets. There was no end to the intrigue. She'd see a framed photo of a man in the shower with his two naked sons at his feet and there went her day. What would possess someone to frame *this* photo? She had to fill in the blanks.

She didn't like any of the places we saw. They produced a reaction within her so violent that the volume of her voice multiplied by ten. And it wasn't that I disagreed. One apartment had dead cockroaches in the bathtub. Another had a shower stall in the kitchen. One smelled like fried chicken, which seemed very mysterious until we stumbled upon an empty bucket. There turned out to be a small problem with that apartment, which was: there was a homeless person living in it.

We went to see more places. It went from bad to worse. One had a black stain, which, after much questioning, we discerned was where a cat had decomposed into the wooden floorboards. There was—finally—a beautiful apartment available on the Upper East Side, but the two elderly women who had lived there before had committed a double suicide inside it.

"No," I said, shaking my head at Jasper as we walked out. "We can't live here. Sorry. Bad vibes."

Sophie scoffed. *"You think?"*

"Maybe we should just take that place on First Ave," I said, exhausted. "It was kind of dark and looked right into another building, but at least it was . . . spacious?"

"No. Absolutely not," she said, with a dejected look in her eyes. "I can't do anything with that place."

"I know it wasn't ideal . . ." My standards had fallen. Perhaps it was the cumulative effect of so many foreign hallways and clunky elevators and cluttered living rooms. Four walls? Good enough for me!

"It's just an apartment," I said.

She shook her head. "It's not *just an apartment*. Brâncuşi's studio was just as photographed as his work. I went to see Agnes Martin's home in New Mexico, and it was a negative for the positive that was her painting."

"Okay," I said. "We'll keep looking. But there'd better be somebody photographing this place someday."

She cheered up. "That's the plan."

THEN, VERY LATE ONE NIGHT, we saw a listing for a brownstone. No pictures. Only a floor plan.

"There's a place within our price range on Convent Avenue," I mentioned hesitantly.

"Well, that's appropriate," Sophie said, looking over my shoulder.

We examined Google Maps. Convent Avenue turned out to be not a nunnery but a tree-lined street in Hamilton Heights, a pretty corner of Harlem that we'd never been to before.

"No pictures, though," I said. "That's a definite red flag."

"Yeah, but that may be perfect!" Sophie had her nose to the screen, eyes wide like a mad scientist. "That means it's a wreck! All we need is good bones and we can throw a stick of dynamite in there. I've learned how to do everything. We can do it all ourselves!"

She emailed Jasper in a hurry, and then stared at her computer awaiting his reply, as if it might come immediately.

"Do you think he's in the office?" she said.

"It's two A.M."

"Yeah, but what time is it *there*?"

"IN MIDTOWN?"

Sophie didn't believe that regular business hours applied to her. And it was hard to argue. Because moments after she sent that email, Jasper, somehow, miraculously, replied. He set up an appointment for us the next day.

"WHERE ARE WE?" I said, emerging from the subway and shielding my eyes from the sun.

It was serene and peaceful. We were surrounded by trees and three-story brownstones.

"It's so nice here."

"Yes. The sky. It's visible," said Sophie, with a slight head tilt, hand on her hip. I caught her posing in front of Jasper more than once.

We walked down several cobblestone streets. There's something nice but very unsettling about being in a part of New York where you don't feel like you're on the verge of being trampled.

We stood on the street in front of the brownstone, looking up at a set of stairs covered in moss. The stone facade was a brownish pink with two round golden doorknobs. We climbed the stairs, with a rush of adrenaline, and then opened the door. We stepped inside, slowly.

"The broker for the apartment warned me that he hasn't done any showings here recently," said Jasper, "so it might be a bit unkempt."

There was a convention of wooden furniture, a piano, rugs in red-orange, faded yellow pillows with embroidery and fringe. Tapestries hung from the exposed brick walls. There was a rocking chair that was so tiny, it could only have been meant for a doll. A duck-shaped urn was placed next to a TV remote, as if this renegade porcelain duck had been watching TV without us. Basically: it was a smorgasbord of random crap. All coated in dust.

"Is it just me, or is anyone else thinking about Miss Havisham?" I said.

"Forgive her." Sophie smiled at Jasper. "Amanda was an English major. She thinks everyone knows about Miss Havisham and muses about her on the regular."

He laughed. And then we heard a rustling sound from the other end of the apartment. We froze.

"Hello?" Jasper called. Silence. He looked back at us, and then asked, "Is anybody home?"

We heard the sound again, like someone crinkling something in their hands.

"Is anyone still living here?" I whispered.

Jasper shook his head and furrowed his brow. "Shouldn't be."

The three of us crept toward the origin of the noise, which seemed to be the kitchen. We peeked inside. Next to an antique silver serving set, a pigeon sat atop a pile of old newspapers on the kitchen counter, cooing. Staring back at us. The window next to it was open.

Sophie and I jumped back, accidentally ramming into each other. Jasper reached for the first thing he saw, which was a silver soup ladle.

"Don't kill it!" Sophie yelled, with a startling degree of seriousness.

"I'm not going to kill it! I'm just going to guide it toward the window."

"You can't *guide* a pigeon with a spoon!"

Jasper laughed. "Are you sure?"

As we discussed our options, the pigeon took flight in a circle around the kitchen, its wings beating frantically. Sophie and I screamed and took cover as the bird made its way around and around the kitchen and then eventually out the open window. Jasper put down the ladle.

We stared at him. He shook his head and closed the window. I shivered.

"This is nothing," he said. "I once walked into an apartment for a showing and the tenants were hosting a day care. It was supposed to be vacant, and there were eighteen babies sitting in the living room."

We went up to the second floor, examined the two bedrooms, then the third floor, which was being used for storage, and where a group of once joyful patio furniture had apparently come to die.

Jasper kept trying to put a positive spin on everything, but the problems were plain to see. Loose floorboards. An uneven staircase. Paint and wallpaper that was either chipped or peeling. Everything was discolored. The windows were filthy. There were cracks in the doors. In the windows. Cracks everywhere, actually. But underneath it all, there was *so much space*. And that alone had Sophie enchanted.

"And it has fireplaces!" she cried.

Jasper's spirits began to climb. "It's a real fixer-upper. Needs some TLC," he said. As he watched Sophie, there was an increased smugness to his voice, a knowing smile: he had, somehow, against all odds, hooked Sophie.

"We could have your contractor come in before the contract is signed. It's priced very well for something with this much space and potential. It's priced to sell."

"Really?" she said, blowing dust from a cracked lightbulb that had fallen from its fixture. "I think it's enormously overpriced."

Jasper and I stopped moving.

"There's a ton of work to be done," she said, her voice suddenly different—matter-of-fact.

"Well . . . not much . . . really. It's all cosmetic," he replied.

"Cosmetic?" She stared him down. "To start with, we'd need to upgrade the HVAC. All the mechanicals need to be brought up to code. We'd need to replace the roof entirely and the windows with double-paned thermals. We haven't seen the basement yet, but I can pretty much guarantee you it needs waterproofing and a check for termite damage, and let's not forget removing all the asbestos. I'd like to live here, not die. The drywall needs to be brought up to fire code. Not to mention the sprinkler system. The fireplaces have to be inspected and cleaned. And then, only then, can we focus on anything remotely cosmetic."

Jasper was speechless.

"And let's talk about the cost of those so-called cosmetics," she went on. "This whole place is probably . . . about . . . twenty-eight hundred square feet? New floors will be close to fifty thousand. Three bathrooms . . . that's ten grand a bathroom, depending on the finishes. Fifteen for the kitchen. Plus, we need a new water heater. That's ten grand, easily. A furnace. Also close to ten. A new roof. Let's figure on twenty-five thousand, conservatively. We'll need a contractor. And to go through the city. Thirty grand." She smiled.

"Listen. I'm sure you know all the tricks of the trade . . . 'That dog never barks. The ceiling never drips. It doesn't smell to me.' But I know exactly what I see."

She grinned so widely at Jasper, who now looked at Sophie as if she had transformed into the most beautifully competent butterfly. He must have thought it impossible, based on the way she looked, the high pitch of her voice, that she might actually know something.

As I listened to Sophie talk, swelling inside me was this feeling that we could *do* this, that this was our place to conquer. Since we were making a habit of having everything the way we wanted it, and not settling for anyone else's creation, why shouldn't our kitchen and bathrooms get the same treatment? I looked around and felt more and more certain that this house was a mess, but a mess with a lot of potential.

We walked around the basement, removing our fingers from spider webs, as Jasper, rendered useless, trailed behind us checking his emails. Sophie used the flashlight on her phone to inspect everything. I took notes.

"I feel like this basement is where someone would hide before killing us."

Sophie sighed. "You always think everyone is going to kill you."

"That's not true."

"Yes. You always think you're just a hop, skip, and a jump away from a *Dateline* special."

We went through each room again, floor by floor. When we got to one of the bedrooms, Sophie started to smile. "There is a distinct absence of a stripper pole in here," she said. "We'll have to fix that."

Jasper raised his eyebrows.

"Oh, how I wish she were joking," I said to him.

"Will you be sharing a bedroom?" he asked, as if he'd been waiting for this moment. I didn't want to crush his dreams, so I just said, "Absolutely not," and smiled. "Sophie doesn't like making the bed in the morning."

Sophie shook her head. He looked to me for further explanation.

"She finds it too firm a commitment to being vertical all day."

THE NEXT DAY, we put a bid in and beat out all the competition that didn't exist.

"We got the apartment!" Sophie shrieked through the phone.

"We did?" I shrieked back, in a state of sheer exhilaration, or maybe amazement that this was actually happening.

"We got it!"

"Oh my God!"

"Did . . . did anyone else want it?"

"I don't think so!"

Once the paperwork was signed, we decided that we had to tell people about our arrangement. A not-so-minor detail. We didn't want to do this in secret. Telling people was key, so that they'd stop trying to fix us up, stop pitying us at weddings and dinners and whatever other events required a partner.

We told our parents first.

"I'm not giving up!" I ended up yelling at my mother within the first thirty seconds of the call. "I just want to try something different! Look at what happened with you and Dad!"

"So this is what we've driven you to?"

"Kind of, yeah! But in a good way!"

She was silent.

"Mom. You're always telling me not to make the same mistake over and over again," I said. "So at least if I make a mistake, it'll be *new*!"

She was not consoled.

My father was surprisingly supportive and told me that I reminded him of Virginia Woolf. He put me on hold to find a book—the sheer number of physical books scattered around his house cannot be overstated—and then started quoting a letter that she had written to a friend about throwing over a man. "'We'll go to Hampton Court and dine on the river together and walk in the garden in the moonlight and come home late and have a bottle of wine and get tipsy, and I'll tell you all the things I have in my head, millions, myriads—They won't stir by day, only by dark on the river. Think of that. Throw over your man, I say, and come.'"

As usual, his commentary sounded very poetic and also like he had somewhat lost his mind. When your father is a teacher, you are never really out of school. I saw him teach once, *once,* and that was enough for me.

"I'm not gay, though, Dad."

"I know that."

"Just to be clear."

"I know. I drove you and your friends to multiple Backstreet Boys concerts."

"That's the sign?"

"That's the sign."

My brother was skeptical. "It's never going to work," he said. "You're just doing this because you get sad and lonely at the grocery store."

"I do not get sad and lonely at the grocery store."

"Yes, you do. I've seen you at Whole Foods. You're all, 'Should I buy these cashew-free nuts? Should I call him on his birthday?'"

"This from the guy who once dated a girl for two years who he *didn't even like* and then prepared to break up with her by reading an article in one of my *Cosmo*s titled 'How to End a Relationship Nicely.'"

"I couldn't just break up with her! I had . . . left a coat at her apartment."

"I'm sorry. You're right. You're the picture of maturity."

My friends seemed to think I was kidding, or going through a temporary malaise. Sophie's friends, on the other hand, considered it an artistic experiment that was actually a bit mundane for their taste. They wished her the best on her journey, and then turned back to arranging tea boxes or torching motorcycle tires.

One of her friends was a contractor. Colin. Sophie felt it would be wise to at least bring him in as a consultant. "He's very sweet, and the best part about him is that he always answers the phone."

I knew that he wanted to sleep with her because he took her call while clearly in the middle of his son's birthday party.

"I can call back another time!" she assured him.

"Na . . . n-no. It's okay. It's okay."

We could hear them singing "Happy Birthday," the song fading farther and farther into the background as Colin left the room.

He said that we would have to get permits from the Department of Buildings before we could do anything. He would help us file the applications, but it would probably take a few weeks to get them approved. And that was being ambitious.

"I'll talk to them," she said. "I can be very persuasive."

He laughed. "They don't respond to charm. Just bribes."

But charm she did. The architect, the electrician, the mechanical engineer who did the drawings. We had paperwork certifying we were asbestos-free the day after placing the call. When she got off the phone with Colin, she turned to me and said, "I was thinking . . . I want to spend the money on *us*."

"What money?

"From Vermont."

"You got the money back?"

She nodded, smiling. Sophie had been determined to get her money back for the wedding that wasn't. I told her that she'd probably lose the entire deposit. But she hadn't accepted that. She fought for it. She exchanged maybe fifty emails and phone calls with the events manager.

"I want to celebrate *something*. We just bought a pretty large chunk of property, without a man. We should celebrate. We're single. We're alive. We're not living in Westchester."

I laughed. "All true . . ."

"We should just go to Mexico for a week. While we wait for our permits."

"Yeah. Sure."

"No, but really, we should."

"Mexico? Why Mexico?"

"*Por qué no?* You're not working right now, and we haven't properly celebrated our alliance," she concluded.

"So, is it a honeymoon without the wedding? Or a destination wedding without the guests?" I asked.

"It's none of the above."

"You know what . . . surprisingly . . . that's not a bad idea."

Sophie sent out joke invitations to our friends:

Done Searching for The One

We're Going to Cabo to Have Some Fun!

We told our friends that they could come, thinking that nobody would. But do you know how many thirtysomethings are in the market to relive the carefree fun they had in their twenties? Turns out—quite a few. I arranged for all our belongings to be shipped to our new place while we were gone. Colin had another job in our neighborhood, so he agreed to oversee the movers and some initial work that had to be done.

"Can we live there during the construction?" I asked Sophie.

"Definitely! We'll just get sleeping bags or something."

I glared at her.

"I'm just kidding. Sort of. The bedrooms were in relatively decent shape. We'll have our beds and confine ourselves to a few rooms while we fix up the rest. It won't be that bad."

We gave Colin our keys and scheduled appointments for people to go in and out, evaluating and inspecting, fixing a few windows. And then we did what anyone would do when faced with a little extra cash and several weeks of life at a standstill—between the crappy apartments of your past and the real home of your future—we went to Cabo.

6

Sophie

As soon as we got on the plane, I thought: *You know, sometimes I am a genius.* That's how I felt whenever I got on a plane, actually. Like, *has anyone ever thought of this before?* A change in location is a perfect remedy. It is always there for you, and it works. I like that in a remedy. This was the ideal way to start our alliance. *To a lifetime of ever-shifting adventures!* I thought, as the plane shook and the ground dropped away below. The only constant in life being change, or however that one goes.

"I am *so* excited," Amanda said, leaning back into her chair as we were propelled skyward.

I turned to her. "Is that so?"

My newest adventure partner had just spent the past twenty-four hours trying to bail. First, she pretended to be sick, then she talked about how much work she had to do (at the new job she hadn't started yet), and then, finally, she popped half a Xanax in the airport bathroom.

She said, "Oh, come on. You know I've never planned a vacation I didn't try to get out of."

I rolled my eyes. "The thermometer on your bathroom sink was a nice touch."

She laughed. "I thought so."

"As if I were going to believe you had a one-hundred-and-sixteen-degree fever. How did you even get it that high?"

"I *may* have used the water I made your coffee with."

"You mean *boiling* water?"

She smiled and shrugged.

"Why don't you do us all a favor and go straight for the Xanax next time?"

"Because I don't like to take Xanax. It makes me feel insane."

"And pretending to have typhoid fever makes you feel, what? Normal?"

An hour into the flight, Amanda was asleep next to me in her high-heeled lace-up boots, one chunky heel jammed up against the seat in front of her, skinny jeans, and a giant black poncho with the words MAISON VALENTINO written on the back. I was always a little bit proud to be seen with her. Yup. There she was. My better half. Comatose in her fashion poncho on the lowest possible dose of Xanax.

With Amanda passed out, I looked out the window at the endless blue. I leaned back and closed my eyes and began to think of everything that had once bothered me with a sudden fondness. There was so much to look forward to. Love. Several loves, God willing. Suddenly I felt incredibly calm and at peace with the world. A sense of goodness toward everyone. I hoped Abe would find happiness with someone new, and quickly. I hoped that the poker-themed futon would find a lovely home. Somewhere nice, in the country. With room for it to roam.

Then I felt a shove from the large man sitting on the other side of me, who was trying to find a place to plug in his phone charger. He was bald, dressed pretty well, with a gray beard and a heavy accent. Like Larry David, but with a tan. And Mediterranean. And about a hundred pounds heavier. So not that much like Larry David, actually.

He was clearly drunk from the moment we took off, and kept referring to the flight attendants as the alcohol police. I asked him if he was all right. I plugged in his phone for him. We got to talking. Generally, I have to befriend the person next to me on airplanes. *Have* to. There is a kind of intimacy between people who sit next to each other on planes and trains and any form of transportation where you're trapped next to each other in a sort-of-uncomfortable, fear-inducing situation. I once stayed with a woman in France whom I'd met on the plane ride over, which solved the problem of me not having anyone to stay with in France. It only got shady for me once, and that was on a flight from São Paulo to New York when the guy sitting next to me talked about his wife and children and then suggested we get a hotel room for the night. Anyway, this Mediterranean Larry David was harmless. I was 84 percent sure. I told him all about Abe.

"The thing is . . . I never really wanted to get married . . ."

I talked and talked. It was cathartic. What he got out of it, I don't know. To talk to a cute girl? Was that anything? I felt like the more I talked, the more I left behind. We were somewhere above Texas when I shared my agenda for the weekend with him, which Amanda had forced me to put together and I had to admit wasn't a terrible idea. Inviting this guy to join us—*that* would have been a terrible idea.

"And then tomorrow night, there's going to be a jungle-themed party on the beach! I grew up in Brazil, so I've never met a beach party I didn't like. I mean, Brazil isn't famous for its economy . . ."

In no time at all, we were beginning our descent into Mexico, at which point the Mediterranean Larry David tried to order another drink and the flight attendant brought him to the front of the plane to be questioned.

Amanda awoke, squinted at me and then out the window. "Where are we?"

"So cute when disoriented. They'll put that on your tombstone."

"I feel weird," she said, her voice low and scratchy. "And *so thirsty*."

"Oooooph," my tan friend interjected from his location near the cockpit. "Call the alcohol police!"

She looked at him and then back at me. "Huh?"

I handed her a water bottle from my bag. "I take it back. 'Death by dehydration.' That's what it'll say on your tombstone."

She looked at me with only one eye open. "Did we die?"

"Yup. You overdosed on Xanax." I started to laugh. "I told you to cut that pill into fourths! *What were you thinking!*"

AND THEN GOD SAID, *Let there be light*. There is no other way to describe the transition between the dreary gray fog of JFK and then six hours later finding yourself in the middle of a vast galaxy of turquoise. It more than just heals you. It is a religious experience. But for atheists.

We caught a taxi at the airport and within minutes we were cliffside, looking out at rocky beaches, boats dotting the aqua-colored water along the coast and farther out, that deep ocean blue. The Sierra de Laguna mountains were in the distance, these high, high mountains that dropped down to the ocean. We looked out at the palm trees and white stucco houses with orange roofs, big bundles of red flowers spilling over the walls. The road to our hotel was less a road than a sandy path. It led to a clearing by the beach where the hotel lay.

We emerged from the taxi and entered an airy and sunlit lobby, all white with open archways. The man who checked us in also walked us across the room.

"This is your home for the next three days," he said proudly, and we had to adjust our eyes to take in the whole glorious scene: The pool, surrounded by beige lounge chairs under beige umbrellas. Behind it, a grassy hill lined with palm trees, and behind that, white sand and the ocean gently breaking. Sunbeams coming down through low clouds, hitting the water and creating a spotlight over certain patches of blue.

He looked us over. "Are you part of the group?"

I shook my head no.

"What group?" Amanda asked.

He smiled. "We have a big group staying here. There's a wedding this weekend, on the property. You look about that age, that's why I asked."

"Nope!" I said. "We are on our own."

There is an instant relaxation that happens in a place like this, a physical unwinding of your body, an unclenching of muscles and jaw and hands. A softening of everything. I think it's the air. And a combination of sounds that your brain recognizes. The warm, humid air, the gentle rustling of palm trees in the breeze, the sound of water—somebody swimming smooth laps in the pool and, of course, the ocean waves. Your brain says: *I am going to take it easy on you for a bit. Thank you for bringing me here.*

We went up to our room. We had two bedrooms within a larger suite. All facing the ocean. We tore off our pants and sneakers and ponchos and put on bathing suits and shorts. *Pantsless at last,* I thought, as I threw my New York clothes into a corner of the room.

"Isn't there something about pants?" I said to Amanda.

"There is."

"This is why I do my best thinking in my underwear."

At the pool, Zoe and her husband, Giff, were lying on lounge chairs, two glasses of ice water on the table between them. Giff's hair was slicked back from having just been in the water, his Ray-Bans on, the crinkly lines of his abs out for all to see. Gordon Gekko vibes. He had a body, though. I had to give him that. "Not like some other dads!" Zoe had pointed out many times.

Zoe was sprawled out next to him in a belted white-polka-dotted one-piece. When I saw her from afar, dark sunglasses on, shoulders pushed back, propped up on her elbows, her thin chin jutting out, I thought she looked like a movie star.

"Remind me of Zoe's latest venture?" Amanda whispered as we walked over.

"She's a wellness coach."

"Oh. Right."

I smiled. "She started with just a blender and a dream."

We hugged hellos, and then Giff announced that he was going for a swim.

"You're going *now*?" Zoe eyed him.

"Yeah? What's wrong with now?"

"Stay and chat for a minute! Sophie and Amanda just got here!"

"But I just got hot, babe. I'll burn if I stay out any longer. I do twenty minutes front. Twenty minutes back. And then I have to go in the water. I have a system."

"Why don't you just wear sunscreen?" She rolled her eyes. "I swear, getting Giff to wear sunscreen is worse than getting it on our toddler."

"I don't need it, babe." He shook his head vigorously. "I have a system."

"What *system*? You burn on every vacation we ever take!"

"It's fine! We'll be here all weekend!" I said. Where was the exit sign for the sunscreen conversation?

Zoe waved her hand in his direction. "Fine. Go." When he was barely out of earshot, she turned to us and said, "I think Giff has an emotional blindness disorder."

When they got married, she said Giff Foley, *investment banker to the stars* (probably . . . no, definitely not a thing), was the most easy-going, unruffled person she'd ever met. Delightfully simple, but stopping just short of dense.

"I thought he was delightfully dense?" I said.

She then explained that he *used to be* delightfully dense. But five years and one baby later, and she was secretly diagnosing him with an emotional blindness disorder called alexithymia. She rattled off the symptoms. Difficulty identifying feelings. Limited understanding of what causes feelings. Constricted style of thinking.

"But couldn't we say that about every guy we've ever met?" I replied.

We waited, put in our time with Zoe, and then Amanda and I slowly tiptoed away and found two chairs across the pool from them.

"I have to admit . . . it's good not to be Zoe right now," Amanda said.

We looked at the pool, where Giff was swimming laps, vigorously, unabashedly, water splashing everywhere. Each time he turned to the side, he opened his mouth and gasped loudly.

"In a word: grace," I said, and we laughed into our towels. I turned onto my stomach, wrapping my arms around the lounge chair.

"What do you think Zoe thinks about our alliance?"

"I don't know, but I think she's in Mexico to find out."

"A spy!"

"Five years ago, Zoe would never have indulged me in this kind of thing. But five years with Giff has changed her into not a more empathetic person generally but definitely more empathetic to the cause of marriage not being all it's cracked up to be."

We took a walk on the beach. The ocean looked powerful. I'd done my research. The water coming into Cabo hasn't seen land since Antarctica. It's gone all the way up the whole coast of South America. Just like me. I felt it healing me. The sun, above all else, was melting away the stress of the past few months. That's what the sun does. It dims your senses a little bit. You become . . . a little dumber. Also more thoughts about getting naked. I was already craving it. Sex was like a watermelon daiquiri to me. I didn't *need* it, but actually it would be very revitalizing yes please. What were my options? A not-so-insignificant detail.

At dusk, we got ready for dinner in our room. I showered. Through the steam I could see Amanda fiddling with her outfit in the bathroom mirror. She had on a black tank top tucked into a long flowy skirt with tassels hanging off one side. Espadrilles that tied around the ankle. How did she do it? How? She was all legs. That helped.

My stomach was growling. "What do you think would happen if we found out that avocados weren't the good kind of fat?"

She paused. "Western civilization as we know it would crumble."

"We all *think* we have our shit together, but if that happened . . . the very fabric of society would come apart."

"So, in your opinion, society is being held together by avocado?"

"I think so, yes."

"Okay. It's already six o'clock. You need to get out," she said, and hung a towel over the glass shower door. "We don't have time for this!" She stomped out of the bathroom.

"All right. All right. Don't be the shower gazpacho."

She stomped back in and stood next to the bath, where my wet bathing suit lay drying.

"The shower what?"

"Gazpacho," I yelled back, and then turned off the shower, wrapped the towel around my body.

"Don't you mean . . . gestapo?"

"Yes, of course. Gestapo."

She gave me a long look. "You thought it was gazpacho . . . didn't you?"

We entered the restaurant through a blue archway surrounded by mosaic tiles, a star-shaped light fixture hanging from a tree. Inside, a narrow hallway with pink stone flooring led to the main room—which had a thatched roof. We were led to our table, which had colorful blankets folded over each chair, just in case any of us wanted to take a mid-dinner siesta. Everyone was already seated—Zoe, Giff, Amanda's friends Olivia and Allie, Andreas, Hans, Cassandra—all chatting away on their rattan chairs. Andreas was Mexican, lived in Mexico City now. We met in New York, when he was training to become a chef, but now he was in Mexico going to cafés. He started his own magazine about coffee called *Bean* or . . . *Drip*. I wasn't sure. We used to sleep together and I remember wanting to get to the point as I said *oh yes beautiful* to a thousand photos of cappuccino foam.

I met Hans and Cassandra at a studio a few years back and we had remained friends since, crossing paths at various locations across the globe. Cassandra used to be the girlfriend of a well-known photographer. Some called her his muse. Some said sex pet. It depended on how much credit you were willing to give her. Hans and Cassandra were here after a four-day shoot in Tulum, photographing Miley Cyrus.

Everyone seemed mellow as they looked over their menus. Amanda stared at a couple being serenaded across the room.

"Tell them to hold the mariachi band!" she whispered to me, mildly hysterical.

"I can't tell them that! In Mexico, that's like saying hold the . . . band."

"But what if they come over here and start singing to us?"

"So? Who cares?"

"I don't want to be serenaded!"

"Relax. You're not being serenaded!"

"I am . . . relaxed," she said, and then made a face. That Amanda face that says she's annoyed. Preemptively. The band didn't have to arrive.

Vacationing with anyone—men, women, boyfriend, friend, chiropractor—there is always a point of tension. I've done this a lot, and it is unavoidable. It's too much time in close quarters, and the result is almost always a vicious fight over something like the lyrics to a Third Eye Blind song. The key is to let the issue come to the surface and then let it go. When it happened with Abe, I used to *beg* him to change the subject. I would say, "So what are we thinking for lunch today?" But he would never bite the line. He felt the fight needed to be "resolved." I would say, "What should we resolve, exactly?" The issue would snowball from something stupid into this colossal thing and then we were both just being stubborn. But Amanda understood this.

I pointed at the next table, at a woman dressed in a formal blue evening gown.

"I feel suddenly underdressed," Amanda said.

"This outfit brought to you by the color blue," I added.

And then we got distracted by baskets of taquitos and bowls of guacamole arriving with startling frequency. Soon enough, Amanda was finishing off her first margarita and laughing again.

"When I was little, I wrote a story about an avocado called 'The Ugly Avocado,' and keep in mind this was before the avocado craze. His name was Do."

"What happened to him?" Hans smiled.

"Well, he was traumatized because instead of sending him to vegetable school, where everyone would have been ugly just like him, they sent him to fruit school, and all the fruits were so beautiful!"

Everyone laughed. There were several pitchers of margaritas. I toasted to our alliance, and started babbling about Amanda, how she used to wear these clear-framed glasses and sat at her desk in the same faded T-shirt for a week during finals.

"She would also study with a hoodie on over the T-shirt, because she claimed that it blocked out distractions, and not just her peripheral vision."

"You knew back then that she was the one for you, didn't you, Sophie?" Hans said.

"I did. I did." I pretended to be all choked up, which I semi-was. "I saw her in that T-shirt and I thought, I'm going to live with this girl . . . forever."

Amanda teared up from emotion. I also teared up from emotion, I think, but also there was a lot of habanero sauce at my disposal. As I looked around the table, I thought: *Friendship.* I had been searching for just such a deity.

The sous chef came over to talk to Andreas. He brought a live lobster that he put down in the middle of the table and we watched as the antennae moved. The chef shucked corn and just casually chatted with us about the weather and the spices native to Mexico and how to get the smell of turmeric out of your hands as everyone continued to eye the freaking lobster in the middle of the table.

When he left, Olivia, who had been quiet this whole time, turned to us and said, "Are you sure you guys aren't doing this because you're afraid to be alone?"

Amanda stared at her. "We don't see it that way. I mean, I'm afraid to be alone, but who isn't? Isn't that the number one thing that binds humanity, that we're all terrified of being alone?" She smiled. "I fear choking . . . not infrequently. I think about it *all the time.* Almost every time I eat something in my apartment. 'What if this chicken has an unexpectedly large bone? What if I don't have enough water to wash down this peanut butter cracker?'"

"Here's what you do," Cassandra said. She had a very specific opinion about everything. "It's called immersion therapy. For example, I'm afraid of flying, so I sat at the airport and watched planes take off and land safely for two hours. I was afraid to be alone in my house, so I went outside in the middle of the night and stood there."

"Did it help? Did you feel safer?" Amanda asked.

She hesitated and then smiled. "Compared to being outside? Yes."

"It's not about that, anyway!" I interjected. "I have no problem being alone."

"That's not *exactly* true, Sophie," Andreas said.

I shrugged. "So, in our twenties, Amanda had panic attacks, and I sent out a lot of naked photos to this man," I said, cocking my head to the side. "I also spent a week wounded because he stopped responding and then I learned, via Facebook, that he was in a hospital in Thailand battling some sort of . . . tropical disease?"

"I'd rather not talk about it," he said, shaking his head.

"I was very offended until I realized that he was dead."

"I wasn't dead!" he said. "And by the way, you don't respond *all the time*."

"Yeah, but if I don't respond it's because I probably cut a jalapeño and then accidentally scratched my eye or something like that."

He said, "We'll be mid–phone sex and she'll be like, 'Oops, gotta go!' "

"Sometimes my phone runs out of batteries."

"That is such a bullshit excuse for 'I've already gotten off and don't feel like dealing with you anymore.' "

I shrugged and smiled. Everyone laughed.

Hans asked, "Is this whole thing just an excuse to be slutty?"

"Yes and no," I answered. "It's about variety. It's about being as slutty as human beings were meant to be. Like, this dinner is great, but if I told you that you had to eat these same taquitos three to five nights a week for the rest of your life, you'd grow to hate them, wouldn't you?"

Hans said, "So, yes."

"But this is exactly what your twenties and thirties are for!" Allie chimed in. "Experimenting. I mean, good for you if you marry your high school sweetheart or find the perfect career for you right away . . ."

"Good for you?" Hans said. "Don't you mean . . . fuck you?"

Allie laughed. "Did I say that wrong? I'm sorry! I meant fuck you!"

"And what if . . . ," Olivia said. "What if one of you falls in love?"

Olivia and Allie were Amanda's friends from law school. They were always making plans and then canceling on each other, with excuses like: "Ladies. I don't know if I can do dinner. I'm exhausted and in excruciating pain from life." To which the others responded: "Okay! Feel better!"

When Amanda's friends heard about our alliance, they were curious but mostly concerned with how it would affect them. *What does this say about* my *marriage?* they were all thinking. When we sent out the invitations, we got a lot of calls. Mostly from Olivia. *No, we're not sleeping together. Nothing sexual. No, we're not actually getting married. Nothing legal. We are just making a decision to live our lives together.* I heard her say it a thousand times.

"We probably will fall in love with various men . . . at some point," Amanda said, looking down at her hands. "And that's fine."

"It's more than fine!" I added. "It's encouraged!"

"We just won't get married. Or live with that person."

A hush fell over the table. I tried to lighten the mood. "We are best friends. With benefits. The benefit being that we can sleep with other people!"

Everyone got back to laughing, high on a combination of lime juice and tequila. There were steaming plates of chocolate clams, which Andreas explained were only called chocolate because of the color of their shells, which were shiny brown. We shared platters of shrimp tacos and squid seasoned with garlic. *Tamales fajados* and crabs steamed in butter.

A microphone appeared, and the staff at the restaurant began playing games with the crowd. Our table passed around pillow-shaped *buñuelos* and soaked pieces of tres leches cake. They requested the men come up onstage and flex their muscles, to be judged based on applause. Andreas and Hans went up there. We rooted for them with everything we had. But they didn't fare well against the others. Some big, bulky men with real muscles. Then the waiters called up the women of the room, and a few got up, did a dance for the crowd. I got up at the insistence of my table and because I had been taught from a very young age how to move my hips to music. I dragged Amanda onstage with me and we danced in front of the dwindling crowd. We were a hit, and by hit I mean, there was a loud round of applause and Amanda was only mildly traumatized.

After that, the microphone was passed around. Songs were sung in Spanish by diners with shockingly good voices. The woman in the blue ball gown, who was now wasted beyond imagination, got up there and swayed to "Lady in Red." She was completely off-key and whenever the chorus came on, she yelled, "Lady in *Blue*!" To personalize it, I guess.

She was clearly a regular, and before leaving, she told the waitstaff via microphone how much she would miss them. She was actually losing all of her shit. When she finished, she cried. Her husband carried her out of the restaurant. She cried more, waving a slow goodbye, as if standing at the helm of a ship, leaving her home country for good.

I looked at Amanda and, somehow, we knew. We didn't need a wedding photographer to tell us. This was a moment we'd remember for the rest of our lives.

7

Amanda

I awoke on our first morning in Cabo to the sound of the ocean and the thought of a thousand Instagram captions.

View from our room!

Good morning, Mexico

Never leaving.

Why don't I live here?

Average Saturday in #paradise

Sun emoji. Bikini emoji. Palm trees emoji. Desperate to seem tan and happy emoji.

I was being sucked into the kind of exposition that wasn't natural for me, or most other people, but it felt necessary. The longer I remained single, the more I felt I had something to prove. I was looking out the window at the swaying linen curtains, deep in strategic thought, when Sophie appeared next to my bed wearing a yellow bikini and flossing. A speck of her spit went flying.

"Must you be such a social flosser?" I said, rubbing my cheek with my fist.

"It's boring if you just stay in there. I like to explore."

"I know. I know." I looked up at her, a fluorescent green string moving in and out of her mouth. "Are you still using the GLAD kind? Didn't some report come out about how it causes cancer?"

She looked up at the ceiling. "Maybe. But . . . of all the things that could kill us, flossing seems really low down on that list."

She left to throw out the floss and then came back and tucked herself into my bed, under the crisp white comforter.

I had my phone in hand. "What should I post that casually conveys, 'Look, guys! We are doing this friend thing and it's amazing!'"

Sophie has always been against social media, so I was not surprised when she replied, "I don't know. I didn't major in marketing public relations." Then she started singing, *"If you're happy and you know it, post on Instagram . . ."*

"Clap along!" she said. I rolled my eyes.

"Ethan's on Instagram."

"Ethan's on Instagram?"

"Well, no. But his dog is."

"Oh. Then post a picture of a bone or something. Dogs are notoriously unimpressed by cute vacation photos."

I let out a sigh. "You know what I mean."

"Wait . . . so . . . his dog *isn't* the one running the account?"

I brought a pillow up over my face. "I hate myself."

"Can I ask you a question?" she said, with her hair, slightly frizzier than usual, streaked across the pillow.

"I've learned to fear your questions, but go ahead."

"Have you ever seen somebody's post and thought, 'Wow, they live such an interesting, beautiful life, I am *so* impressed!'?"

"No."

"Right. Because that's not what anyone thinks. They look at ugly photos and think, 'Thank GOD my life isn't like that,' or they look at beautiful photos and think, 'That bitch.' So, what's the point . . . exactly?"

No post, I decided. Independently. Had nothing to do with her.

"We have to be secure in our decision, remember?"

I nodded and silently deleted the app from my phone. "I am secure . . . I think."

"Well, then, secure people just *live.* They don't feel the need to tell everyone about everything all the time. They don't feel the need to say, 'Look, guys, I have great hair and went skiing in Switzerland!'"

I was grateful that she was there, that she would always be there, to set me straight.

"I know. I know," I said. "Sometimes, as I'm getting out of a cab, I think, 'I'd better make sure I didn't leave behind my phone . . . because if I did . . . that would pretty much be the best thing that's ever happened to me.'"

"Social media makes you feel bad because it puts you in the position of comparing your internal world with other people's external worlds, which is an inherently losing proposition. This is why I don't go on there. Unless someone is going to tell me what to do when you find out your ex is pickling his own mushrooms . . ."

We lingered in bed, laughing, reviewing the night, and then made our way to breakfast, where we split a waffle and imagined what one little cup on our table was saying about a bigger cup that they'd taken away to refill with coffee. Our waiter was from South Africa and Sophie talked to him about his grandparents and whether he liked Frida Kahlo and Diego Rivera.

We took a walk on the beach. A woman was yelling into her phone, "Sashimi, sashimi, sashimi!" And we started to laugh, just at the sheer hysteria in this woman's voice. We launched into a pastime of ours that involved making up the rest of the conversation based on the overheard snippet.

"If I've told you once, I've told you a thousand times—*sashimi, sashimi, sashimi*!" I said.

"She's always on a diet. I wish she would just get a fucking cheeseburger but instead she's all, *sashimi, sashimi, sashimi*," Sophie added.

She stretched her hands up and then out to the side. To see Sophie on the beach was to see her truly in her element. Even bundled in the wrong winter coat, she still did pretty well. But here, under the sun, in a bathing suit and jean shorts, her toes digging into the sand, I could see that *this* was where she truly belonged. I should have known. She'd been telling me for years. "I need a beach" was her favorite expression when something went wrong.

"What should we do now?" I asked.

"Maybe we should make ourselves truly useless and go to a spa or something."

"Allie and Olivia went to this place down the road yesterday," I said. "Olivia got some sort of treatment that made her feel like she was vibrating inside a space capsule."

"Is that a good thing?"

To the spa we went, to find out. The plan was to bond over cucumber-infused water. However, what we did not anticipate was a sign sticking out of the grass that read HOLISTIC AREA. PLEASE KEEP SILENT BEYOND THIS POINT.

"It's a *silent* spa?" I looked down at the grass and then up at Sophie for some direction.

"I'm sure we can . . . whisper?"

We went inside. A woman sitting at a desk between two orchids handed us robes, which we put on in a room filled with pink lockers, and then walked to the waiting area—an airy, spacious room, with a window overlooking a Zen garden. It was dark, with just a little bit of sun coming in from a skylight and a few candles. There was a sand-colored couch, a few guests lying under blankets. The room was quiet but for the jangling of wind chimes and the sound of running water coming from the middle of the room, where a large pool was being filled by water pouring from a slit in the wall.

We walked by two girls, one of them holding a phone.

"He makes the same expression in every photo," one whispered to the other. "He has no range!"

"I bet they're talking about a baby," I whispered to Sophie, and she laughed.

We discerned from their matching purple robes that they were bridesmaids in the wedding being held at the hotel that night. We sat a safe distance away from them, but close enough that we could still overhear a few things.

"I thought he was having an affair," one said to the other. "I got really deep into his texts with an international number. I thought I *definitely* had him this time." She sighed. "And then I realized that it was just his Uber driver."

"What were the texts?" the other said.

"I don't know . . . just things like . . . 'On my way down.'"

They laughed.

"I thought it could be a euphemism for something!"

"I *get* it," Sophie whispered to me. "Even the nicest, most honest guy is susceptible. Even *we* are susceptible. And men are just like us. But worse."

"I think that's why I liked Ethan," I said. "At least he was cheating *with* me. Little did I know that, too, could backfire."

"Well, we're winning now."

"I think so too."

We were enjoying the robes and slippers, the sound of the wind chimes. The blue lagoon. They gave us champagne, which was either an act of generosity or them confusing us for bridesmaids.

After our massages, after the rejuvenation aroma rose hiccup therapy or whatever it was, all the other spa patrons had left, and Sophie and I remained.

"How would you feel about me hooking up with Andreas?" she asked.

"Oh. Sure. I mean, do whatever you want!"

"Would you be mad?"

"Why would I be mad?"

"Would you feel . . . weird . . . about it? Since this is our trip and all?"

"Oh, believe me, I assumed you would find someone here."

"Really?"

"I just didn't realize we were starting already."

"It's not a competition!" she cried back.

"No. I know. Listen. Of course it's all right. I'm not sleeping with you tonight!"

"Because I don't have to! It's just, how often am I in Mexico? The last time I saw Andreas . . ."

"Sophie. It's fine. Totally fine. Do it. I insist."

"You seem mad."

"Why would I be mad?"

"I don't know," she said.

I just wanted her to admit that she *always* had to find a guy, that she wasn't as independent as she was in her head. Sure, she didn't need the Instagram captions, but she had her own ways of seeking . . . reassurance. She called it a love for sex, but I think it was a love for compliments. Maybe both.

In the late afternoon, Andreas took us stand-up paddleboarding. Afterward, we stopped at a taco stand on the side of the road, where I tried octopus for the first time.

"It's funny, because here, I feel totally comfortable eating roadside octopus," I said, devouring my taco. "But can you imagine in New York? If someone was selling octopus at the side of the street and you ate it? You'd face almost certain death."

We kept walking. There were cows along the back road. Fishermen carrying dark nets. We stopped at a few other stands selling decorative baskets, ceramic cups, bracelets with colored balls on a string. I bought a textile of colorful animals from a little girl who was no more than ten. We stopped at a stand selling ice cream and chips. When we got back to the hotel, the sun was still strong on the beach, and a few of our friends were lounging. Giff, wearing pink dolphin-print shorts, came by in a golf cart and was trying to initiate some combination of golf and tennis and Frisbee. Who gave him a golf cart? Among the many questions you couldn't ask, with Giff. He had taken a surfing class that morning, and when he parked the cart next to us, we could see cuts all over his legs.

"You're actively bleeding!" Zoe shrieked, and then went to find a water bottle and a few extra-large Band-Aids.

"I'm fine, babe!" he yelled after her. "Minor surfing accident!" He turned to us and said, "Unexpected detour to the hospital today." The gashes were bright red and dripping.

"Wait a second. You've *been* to the hospital?" Hans asked, staring at Giff's legs, horrified. "And they let you *leave* like that?"

"They didn't patch you up at all?" Sophie asked.

"They gave me Percocet and told me to get some rest," he said.

Sophie turned to me and covered her eyes with her hands, shaking her head, trying to disguise a smile. "Not an ad for Mexican healthcare," I said.

THE "PARTY ON THE BEACH" that night turned out to be part of a food and wine festival. So, we were crashing someone else's party, which I wasn't aware of, officially, until Andreas was sneaking us in. "Sneaking in" didn't require much, aside from getting us past a string of bamboo. All the men at the party were in white pants. The women were wearing white, semi-sheer dresses. There were tables filled with oysters and corn, and a band playing music none of us had heard before.

Our group separated from the rest of the crowd and went farther down the beach, toward a fire pit. We stood in a circle and Sophie and I said some nonsensical things about friendship while throwing sand into the fire. We gave each other necklaces made of flowers that Sophie had put together in the time it took me to go to the bar for a drink. The band turned into a DJ playing hits for the international crowd and even some numbers the lowly Americans had heard of. We were all dancing shadows on the beach, bouncing off the firelight. The sky was pink then purple then black.

Sophie stood behind the DJ booth in her clingy white dress that she wore not because it was *white* or because this was *her day* but because it made her look ridiculously hot. Cassandra danced by herself, holding a bottle of tequila. Hans was talking, talking, talking and probably on drugs. I say this not because he was the type of guy to do drugs but because he cried when he told us the story of not being named his brother's dog's godfather. Olivia and Allie were taking selfies together. Giff was shirtless and riding a bike in circles.

Sophie and I sat down at a table with everyone. We were sunburnt and tipsy. We met a couple from Tanzania and planned a group safari. On the makeshift dance floor, outlined with rocks in the sand, Zoe and Giff were making out like teenagers. Zoe was wearing a gold dress that left very little to the imagination. We chalked it up to parents away from their children. Sophie and I had our arms around each other for most of the night. We danced, only stopping to take big gulps of ice water, and make friends with the festivalgoers. There were once-strangers twirling each other. The waves were washing in the background. The ground was covered in nothing but bare feet and blowing spray. Our declaration of friendship seemed to be bringing out the best in everyone. There must have been something encouraging about it, about knowing that friendship wasn't just a side note to love.

Sophie leaned into me. "So, apparently, the security cameras caught Cassandra and one of the bellhops in the hot tub last night." She nodded along to her own story. "The guards confronted them and Cassandra ended up having to go back to her room . . . with no bottoms."

My eyes widened. "She couldn't find them?"

"Nope. But the cleaning staff *did* find them this morning, and they hung them on her doorknob."

"Oh my God."

"I think this may be adult spring break," Sophie said, laughing.

"The ironic thing is, I went on spring break when I was younger," I said, "and I didn't have nearly this much fun."

It was after one o'clock when I found myself drifting away, eager for a moment of solitude. I didn't want to walk on the beach because that seemed dangerous and too moody. You see a girl walking alone at night on the beach, watch out. She is doing some heavy thinking. I went toward the pool instead.

The wind had picked up. I heard music thumping from inside the hotel and someone on a microphone requesting that the bride and groom come to the front to cut the cake. For the first time that night, my mouth fell out of a smile and into a straight line. As I looked up at the lit windows of the hotel, I felt . . . left out. *Still,* at an event Sophie orchestrated for us, a small piece of me felt the way I always felt at weddings. And you can't talk yourself out of a feeling. You can tell yourself that the circumstances are different, that *you* are different, that you don't want what they have. You might even be right. But even after all the declarations, there was still a slight pit in my stomach that simply didn't care.

The alliance gave me the freedom to step back from it all, but there was a part of me that still wanted to peek through that window, at what I was missing. Maybe I wanted a little too much. What was I expecting, exactly? For life to be a constant stream of satisfying feelings? Life was closer to a ride that you couldn't get off of. And sometimes, the ride wasn't moving. Sometimes, you had to wait. But the stillness was precisely what scared me. Maybe it had something to do with my parents, the fact that they never argued, never showed the slightest sign of a problem, and then one day, it was over. The silence, to me, was the scariest part. A void wasn't nothingness. A void was something that needed to be filled.

I knew it would pass. So I let myself feel it. I let myself wander over to the pool and then look into the deep end, in a daze. The wind was loud. The palm trees were swirling against each other. I sat at the edge, pulled my dress up around my thighs, and let my legs dangle ahead of me. I watched a man across the pool roll up his suit pants and put his feet in the shallow end. He looked tired as he untied his black bow tie until its ends were hanging. The tails of his white shirt were no longer tucked in. He looked exactly like what he was: a wedding refugee.

The pool was lit up below the surface, but we were surrounded by darkness, a row of sleek hedges and empty lounge chairs, the occasional speck of a firefly. His black socks were lying at the edge of the pool, alongside an untied pair of dress shoes.

I examined his face in the blue glow. He looked a little familiar. Was he someone I knew, or just the guy who got the last of the cinnamon rolls at the breakfast buffet that morning? I couldn't decide. After a few more minutes of pretending not to look at each other, I got up and went toward him. That little bit of Sophie inside me needed to know.

He smiled at me, and then quickly looked back down at his feet. The faint sound of music from the beach and the music playing inside the hotel were blending together into one muffled racket.

"What happened to the rest of your fleet?" I said. He looked up at me. "Of groomsmen."

He smiled. "I escaped."

I smiled back.

I thought that might be the end of our conversation, but then he said, "It's been a long night."

I nodded.

"Between the reception . . . the ceremony . . . the pictures. I was up at five this morning! I think I played golf?" He squinted. "Then there was the bachelor party . . . the engagement party. What I'm saying is: Before these two got engaged, I was in elementary school."

"You look so familiar," I said. Because I wasn't quite there yet, with where I knew him from. What I thought was that's just how cute strangers with whom you have an instant connection look—familiar.

"Yeah," he said. "Actually . . . you do too."

I thought he was playing along with my game and that this was a great sign of our connection until it hit me. *Elementary school.*

"I think . . . we went to elementary school together," I said. I pictured his face but smaller, wearing round glasses. He was no longer skinny or blond. He had broad shoulders, and thick, almost black hair that was sticking up and leaning slightly off to one side. A few days of stubble.

"Oh God. I hope not."

"Yup! We definitely went to elementary school together." I laughed.

I pretended not to know his name even though, at this point, I did. He said his name—Nick Allen. And then he said mine.

Nick Allen. I have to think of him by his full name, because that's the way I almost always heard it. Said by the teacher. On official documents like the seating chart taped to the classroom wall, under the title of Snack Captain, written in crayon.

"I remember you! Of course, I remember you," he said. "Recess. You were in charge of the orange cones."

"That's right! And you were the . . . Snack Captain." Because these were the sort of random facts that you remember about people you went to elementary school with.

"Didn't you play on the boys' tennis team?"

"Yeah, but only because there was no girls' team."

"Oh yeah . . . why wasn't there a girls' team?"

I sighed. "I don't know. Connecticut in the nineties? We were behind the times." Nick played on the baseball and soccer teams, but he wasn't the star. He wasn't known for his athleticism. He was smart, but not known for his intelligence. He was the type of kid who helped people with their homework, who was friends with a few girls but only because they talked to him about other boys in class.

"Didn't you have glasses? The round ones?"

He looked embarrassed. "Thank you for bringing those up. I was *ahead* of the times. Harry Potter? Stole my look."

I laughed. "Didn't the class chinchilla have a thing for you?"

"It was more like I had a thing for him," he replied. "Even though he was actually pretty mean and violent."

"Ernest!" I said, with my hand raised. "That was his name!"

"Ernie . . . I called him Ernie, but yes, probably Ernest to you."

"He used to hiss whenever anyone played with him," I said. He nodded. "But you were very dedicated to him. Didn't you walk him around with a leash?" I asked. "Can you walk a chinchilla?"

"Not really, as it turns out." He smiled. "I tried to walk him, but he would run in the opposite direction."

I covered my mouth and tried not to laugh. It was all coming back to me now. This bespectacled little boy in a white turtleneck and khakis, trying to walk a chinchilla.

"Didn't he escape from the cage once and hide under the teacher's desk?"

"He had a bit of an insubordinate streak."

"And I remember you were so distraught when he ran away!"

"I had scratch marks all over my body," he said, and then exhaled as if thinking of something fondly. "He was a vicious animal, but he was all we had."

I was laughing and a little light-headed from all the mental time travel.

I thought about mentioning the khakis, but resisted making fun of his self-imposed uniform. Or mom-imposed, more likely. In high school, a male friend of mine once told me that you can't judge a guy by his pants because guys don't buy their own pants until college.

"How long are you here for?" he asked, and I snapped right back to the present. And in the present, Nick Allen was . . . kind of a stud. He looked like he might play the "bad boy" who drove a motorcycle in a movie, except for his eyes, which gave him away. They revealed everything. They revealed . . . his interest in me.

"I'm here until tomorrow. You?"

"Same. I thought a seven A.M. flight tomorrow would be just brutal enough. I'll miss the brunch." He gave me a look like, *kill me now.*

"Oh, there's always a brunch."

"I don't actually object to that part of weddings."

"I agree. It's the best part. The tension has been released."

"You know . . . I've discovered that there is a lot more that I'm willing to tolerate while shoveling eggs and bacon into my mouth."

"It's a whole different world."

Our conversation was easy. I was immediately attracted. Or maybe our conversation was easy because I was immediately attracted. It was a real chicken-or-egg situation.

"Where do you live now?"

"New York," I said. I told him that I lived in Harlem. He said he lived on Ninety-Sixth between Second and Third.

"I'm on the West Side a lot, though," he said. "I coach Little League in Central Park on the weekends."

My hopes sank. "Oh, do you have children?" I asked.

"No," he said, shaking his head. "I'm a doctor, and this kid came into the emergency room a while back and asked if I'd be their coach. Apparently, their former coach got hit in the face with a ball and never came back." He smirked. "What can I say? I'm a sucker for a kid with a bloody nose."

"Kids go to the emergency room for a bloody nose?"

"They do these days. When I was a kid and broke my nose playing basketball, my mom told me to sleep it off. She *may* have given me ice cream. Or a cough drop."

I laughed. "Do you remember how the school nurse used to give us Jolly Ranchers?"

"For basically any problem? Yes."

"I didn't question it."

"Oh no. Neither did I. I thought that was, like, sound medical judgment."

"And you know what? They did make me feel a little bit better."

He grinned at me.

It was a few minutes before I could figure out what was so great about this conversation. There was no awkward surprise at having run into him after all these years. No real strain because of the gap between then and now. Remembering the past usually made me cringe. But this had the strange effect of making me feel like I was talking to someone I was supposed to know.

I heard a loud burst of laughter and looked behind me, at my friends in the distance.

"I've got to say," he said, "your party looks like a lot more fun than ours. Is it a wedding?"

"No . . ." And then I felt a jolt inside me. "It's just a party. Well, not *just* a party . . ." *Should I tell him?* I decided against it. I'd probably never see him again. Why get into it?

"My friends are playing 'never have I ever' in the hot tub, and we're all thirtyish."

He laughed. "Oh yeah? Well, one of the groomsmen broke his arm at the rehearsal dinner last night doing a coordinated dance number." He raised his eyebrows.

I offered up: "I watched somebody start crying about not being his brother's dog's godfather."

"The mother of the bride kissed one of the groomsmen 'by accident,' then spilled soy sauce on her sister 'by accident.' Her sister then went around *wasted* asking if anyone was in the mood for sushi."

I laughed. He went on.

"The maid of honor spent her entire speech talking about a funeral, and she *still* gave a better speech than the best man, who spent most of his breaking down the plot of *Ant-Man*."

"*Ant-Man*? What's that? A superhero movie about insects?"

"See. You should have been there. You'd know the answer to that."

I laughed again.

"To the best sister!" He did a mock cheer.

"Ohhhh, everyone is always *the best*."

"Where are all the bad people? The shitty friends. The mean brothers. The siblings who missed your graduation or the friends who forgot to pick you up from the airport."

I smiled. "They're out there. They're just not the ones giving the speeches."

"Hashtag YourLoveIsLikeAFineWeinberg."

"Ohhhh, the hashtags." I didn't tell him about my glee at being the one to come up with #SophieMakesAbeHonest. But that was different. Being the bridesmaid who comes up with the cleverest hashtag? You can't put a price on that.

"There was a priest and a rabbi officiating and it was like a battle," he said. "Each one was trying to outdo the other, as far as jokes. The rabbi was winning, obviously."

"Rival officiants! It gets so confusing. I always leave the ceremony thinking I need time to figure out where I am, religiously."

"After the ceremony, they handed out these little triangles of paper that had butterflies inside that we were supposed to release. But the butterflies all went straight to the ground."

I opened my mouth wide. *"They were dead?"*

"No. They were alive. But traumatized from being trapped in a tiny envelope."

I shook my head slowly.

"It was more like a butterfly sacrifice than anything else."

Laughing, I said, "The worst for me is when the speeches go too heavy on the PR. 'She has a degree from an Ivy League school! Skis and snowboards with the greatest of ease! Is getting into rock climbing! Cooks healthful yet satisfying dinners every night!'"

"'Has been promoted three times in the last year at her job and volunteers at an animal shelter and still finds time to bring her friends chicken soup whenever they're sick!'"

"How does she do it?"

"'*How?*' . . . The very overqualified bride hyperventilated in the bathroom because she heard it might rain during the ceremony."

"What? Is that a joke?"

"I'm afraid not. It was the first time in history that someone has hyperventilated while seeing the words 'slight drizzle.'" He sighed. "What is it about weddings that fucks people up so much?"

I gave it some thought. "I think . . . it's the pretending that you have your shit together that does it . . . as a family . . . as friends. Weddings are like this singular chance to perform a play that you could never pull off in real life."

He nodded with an expression that was a little bit sad. "One night only!"

I thought of an old video I'd seen of my family at some cousin's wedding. I was three years old and my parents seemed so happy, so enthralled with me, their angel daughter, and my rambunctious brother, and the little family they had formed. But there was something dark about their happiness, knowing what was to come. Watching them, it was clear that they had no clue. Time did something to these moments. It changed what you thought was so totally fixed and unchangeable. I felt like telling him this, but I didn't. Because I didn't want to seem like one of those girls. You know, crazy.

Instead, I smiled widely and said, "Would you . . . want to come and join our party for a bit? Have a drink?"

"Sure," he said. I looked down as the water in the pool rippled. "I like you." And then, his face flushed. "I mean . . . *I'd like to.* Sorry. I mean, I do like you, but . . . I didn't mean to say . . ."

"It's okay. I've taken you back to elementary school! You were disoriented."

"That's right. Now, in true elementary school fashion, if you could please leave me alone here so that I can die of embarrassment, I'd really appreciate it."

"Come with me!"

He looked down and smiled. "Okay."

When we returned to the party, it was winding down. The hotel staff had removed all the tables and chairs. Our friends remained, sitting on blankets and towels. I left Nick at the bar, with one of his friends who'd ambled over, and found Sophie.

"Do you know who I just ran into? Nick Allen!" I blurted out, before she had a chance to answer.

She gave me a puzzled look. "Who?"

"We went to elementary school together!"

I found my phone and sat down next to her on a towel. I went on Facebook and showed her an old picture that someone had tagged me in years ago of our entire class. I told her that he used to look sort of like the kid from *Jerry Maguire*.

"He looks *exactly* like the kid from *Jerry Maguire*."

"I know!" I squealed.

"It's not a compliment," she said with a smile. "Just so you know, the iconic hottie from *Jerry Maguire* that everyone was talking about was Tom Cruise. *Maybe* Cuba Gooding Jr. But definitely not that kid."

"Hey! That kid was memorable."

"Yeah, because he was weird."

"How was he weird?"

"Didn't he know all these random facts about things? I don't like a child who's too omniscient."

"He was smart."

"Fine. Okay. *Be smart.* Just . . . like . . . keep it to yourself. Nobody likes a show-off."

"Have I never told you my Nick Allen story?"

I told her. I was in fourth grade and there was a field trip to the United Nations coming up. I didn't have a field trip buddy because of some sociopolitical situation I was navigating at the time, and I needed one. Desperately.

"It was just someone to sit with on the bus and maybe share lunch with and generally keep track of so that neither of you got kidnapped, but I was fairly panicked."

"Naturally. Wait. Who goes on a field trip to the UN when they're in fourth grade?"

I shrugged. "Private school."

"What were you supposed to get out of that?"

"Sophie! Focus!"

"Sorry. Go on."

"So I walked into gym class, and there was Nick Allen fiddling around at the jungle gym with nobody paying attention to him. I knew that field trip buddies were traditionally girl-girl or boy-boy, but it suddenly occurred to me, why? So I went right up to him and asked and he said yes. He didn't even hesitate. He wasn't weirded out. He didn't ask me any follow-up questions. He just went back to the jungle gym."

"God. Men are lovely sometimes."

"I know. With the girls, it was like you needed an application, a résumé, writing samples, at least three personal references."

"God. I love you."

"And then it hit me: *What have I been doing this whole time?* Clearly wasting my time with the wrong gender. There was a whole untapped market of field trip buddies out there!"

"And? How was his performance?"

I looked her over and beamed. "Sophie. He was *the best* field trip buddy."

"Really?" Her eyes were filled with glee.

"He was nice about sharing lunch and held my hand the entire day, even though it wasn't really necessary . . . you know . . . to hold hands. He only broke for bathroom breaks or when we ate our sandwiches or when we encountered, like, a lamppost."

"What does he look like now?" Sophie asked. And I widened my eyes. I motioned over to the bar.

"All right, then. It's official. He no longer looks like the kid from *Jerry Maguire*."

"What if he isn't even interested in me?"

"Women." She shook her head. "Ask not . . . what your country . . . or thyself . . . that fucking question. Ask yourself *this*: Am. I. Interested. In. Him?"

I must have looked a little wounded. But she sensed it, and went straight into recovery mode. "Listen. It doesn't really matter, does it? You're not marrying him, remember? You're just having fun with him for now."

"That's true. He'll be a crush! And I was thinking . . . we should call them crushes."

"Are all your ideas elementary school–themed today?"

"But that's the fun of it! Let's bring it back. Don't you remember that feeling when you love someone, but you can't quite have them? *That's* what makes the whole thing so delicious. That feeling before? *That's* the best part. It's the having that fucks it up."

"I like it! Now . . . let's go skinny-dipping."

"What? No. I have to go. I have to go talk to him."

"Come on! We're all going."

"Who is?"

"All of us."

"Are we allowed to do that?"

Sophie narrowed her eyes at me. "I don't care what you say." She smiled. "You've clearly never been on spring break."

"I told him I'd be right back . . ." I looked over at Nick. He was still talking to that guy at the bar.

"Just do this first with me. He'll wait."

"But . . ."

"Amanda. He'll wait."

I smiled. She was right. He would wait. He would have to.

And then there were a bunch of men in bathrobes and women with their dresses coming off running toward the ocean. I felt like I owed it to Sophie. She had planned this whole weekend, and in true Sophie fashion, I had to repay her by getting naked in front of strangers. Somehow, in the darkness, I found that I could do it, though I kept my underwear on, once I saw that someone else did, too. At first, there was the shock of delight. The idea was foolish until you hit the warm water. The rest of our group shouted at us from their spot on the beach. Sophie and I went hand in hand into the water. Or she dragged me in, depending on your perspective. What did it matter? All I could think was: *What would be exciting in this moment?* If history had taught me anything, exactly this moment was all we had.

I WENT BACK TO NICK with my wet hair coiled into a bun. He was alone now. The bar was on the top floor of a small hut on stilts, overlooking the ocean. We ordered two drinks with ice and rum, and drank them staring out at the black water. The palm trees had thin strands of yellow lights wrapped around them. The sky was sprinkled with stars. We ate banana cake. I kept thinking, *We should just be friends,* because as we sat there, I felt a little bit like I was talking to one of my brother's friends. We talked a lot about sports. The town where we grew up. We teased each other.

"I hate going back home," he said. "It's not the same town I grew up in."

I shot back, "What? Nicer?" His eyes narrowed on me in a moment of fake annoyance that ended in both of us smiling like idiots.

Yes, we should definitely just be friends, I thought, but then our knees grazed under the table and the rum started kicking in and I thought: *Maybe not.* My hesitations started sinking like sand. I was feeling blissful. Drugged. Maybe the beach, the sun, the alliance. I thought: *I can do whatever I want right now.* Did I want to end the night by exchanging numbers? By making a promise to meet again? Did I want to spend weeks obsessing over subtle signs? Analyzing the wording of texts and whether he really wanted to arrange another meeting? Phoning my friends? Bringing in a team of experts to decipher the evidence? *Maybe not.*

The bar had been empty for a while. The waiter brought us the check, sliding it toward us in a not-so-understated way. We stared down at it, sadly.

"Oh," he said.

"Yeah."

Neither of us was ready to end it. Our knees against each other wasn't the end.

"We could walk on the beach?" he suggested.

"Okay!"

It was pitch black. It didn't make any sense. We didn't care.

On our way to the water, his hand knocked against the outside of my hip once, twice, then stayed there. I turned and moved into him, to let him know that it was okay, that he could do more, if he wanted to. He pulled me in and blocked the cold breeze from whipping against my hot skin. I could feel heat coming from his cheek. Neither of us moved, until he leaned down to kiss me, soft at first, and then harder.

It was a bold thing, going out to the edge of that dock. But I had no fear, because I was so attracted to him, and that obliterated everything else in my head. The pressure was building as we breathed into each other in the dark. At the end of the dock, there was a table and a few chairs. What to choose? He sat down in one of the chairs. I got on top. His fingers were up my back and between my legs as I moved my mouth behind his ear. I don't know what came over me, but I stopped, suddenly. Unwrapped myself. Backed away from him a few feet. Stood there, staring into his eyes. I straightened my dress, pushed my hair out of my face, and slid down my underwear, so totally relaxed, as if we'd done this a thousand times before. I went back to him, so eager that I could barely walk.

He didn't seem surprised. His face grew serious and he took my hand. I got back on top of him and then cocked my head to the side so that I could kiss him very gently as he moved inside me. It felt so good right away. He held my hair, at the base of my neck. I started to move quickly, easily, with a complete loss of control. He stopped kissing me. He closed his eyes.

Once it was over, he wrapped me in his shirt. Okay, so he knew what to do. He had that air about him. The shirt was a nice touch. A good-looking doctor with a shirt-lending policy was unstoppable in this world. But I had one over him this time. We started walking back to the hotel.

"Maybe I'll see you again?" he asked. "In New York?"

I was lifting lumps of sand with my feet. As we approached the hotel, I handed him back his shirt and started walking away from him, backward. My hair was blowing in the breeze, and I was feeling light, carefree, like the star in my own movie.

"Maybe," I said, smiling, without hesitation. "If I see you, I'll say hi."

And then, I was gone, ending it on a high, with him only wanting more, as I'd always wanted to but never quite could. Until now.

Sophie

To dance and receive praise. That's how to spend an evening. I can't recommend it enough. Even Cassandra with her cigarette said the night was a wild success. She also told me I was a beautiful wanderlust girl with vision. And then there was some kind of fuzzy comparison to a sunrise. Or . . . a blanket? I don't know. Could have been noodles in a microwave, for all I could discern over the music. Amanda and I were dancing in the middle of the crowd of our friends and some lovely, wine-appreciating strangers who knew how to throw a damn good party.

"I don't know how this Spanish slow song morphed into Pearl Jam, but I'm into it!" Amanda shouted.

I shouted back: "Question: What's the best ratio of shrimp to tequila?"

I was as carefree as could be, except for the slight care of making sure Andreas saw me from where he was standing and that he was casually impressed or spellbound, if possible. Either way.

Beyond our dance circle, Andreas was watching, all right. I

started acting more animated than usual. More laughter. I was careful not to catch his eye too often. Only someone with whom you have an extraordinary connection can turn you on from across a beach. No hands. No mouths. This was chemistry. I thought I knew what attraction was, before Andreas. It was in bed. At night. While touching. Nope. It was on the subway. On the way to meet him. On a park bench. In broad daylight. In front of children.

I went up to him. He'd never have approached me. He knew how to play my games too well. I need men to be one-tenth asshole in order to get inspired. Sorry. It's just the way it is. Plus, I didn't want to leave Amanda and have this night be about him. If Amanda wanted to sleep on the beach, we would sleep on the beach. But then she went missing for a short period of time, and I can't be trusted when left to my own devices. So I walked over to Andreas and took his hand and whispered in his ear, *To com saudades* (I miss you), as I led him to the dance floor. Looking back over my shoulder, only briefly, I saw his face light up as though he'd won a prize.

We started dancing and soon my whole body was humming. I knew we would end up sleeping together. I knew this because I've shared cookies with Amanda before. She can eat two or three and then move on. Her approach to cookies was reasonable, contained. And it's not that I looked at her eating two or three cookies and thought, *Wow, something to aspire to*. I thought: *I have no idea how she's doing it.* I had to have the entire sleeve. And I'd like to say that I felt filled with remorse afterward. But I didn't. Because I really had no choice. When I got used to having a lot of sex, I needed it. Craved it. I was addicted to the point where I was mildly hysterical. But then, if I got through a few days, I felt fine. But then, the trouble was, when I had a little bit again, I was right back where I started. Wanting more and more. An addict in every sense of the word.

After we went skinny-dipping, I ran upstairs with a towel around me and my dress slung over my shoulder. I was vaguely aware that I had left Andreas behind without an explanation. I put on a fresh pair of underwear—strategically chosen black lace that was barely there—and then got into bed with my phone, knowing I had a text from Andreas to answer.

How nice when someone plays right into your hand. I'm still in the lobby, he wrote. Want me to come up? The sun was just starting to rise. I told him to come up.

I'll leave the lights on, I said, as a joke, since it was getting to be morning. My phone sex has color, dammit. Plot twists, different languages, layered metaphors, unexpected side characters. Some men are better responders than others. Andreas was top 1 percent. I got used to him and then other men became boring. "I'm going to need a scene partner at some point," I'd say, in my head.

I answered the door in my underwear and nothing else. He walked into the room wearing a sweatshirt with the name of the hotel on it.

"Oh, I'm sorry. Are you working here now?"

His hand was already extended, on the dent of my hip. "I bought it in the gift shop. I was pacing for so long. They kept the store open for me. I had to buy something."

His hands were wrapped around me now. We stood in the middle of the room while he got close to me and exhaled deeply into my neck and felt my whole body with his fingertips. In no time, I was floating, so high. The sun made my skin feel prickly and more sensitive to touch. What normally felt great now felt like firecrackers going off inside my bloodstream. I kissed him behind one of his ears as his fingers kept running. I could feel myself getting there so quickly that my heart was pounding, so I took a breath and led him over to the bed, where I sat perched, legs tucked under me. It wasn't long before his wrists were tied up above his head with the telephone cord and I was leaning into him with my breast in his mouth and I was coming hard, asking him to come for me. We lay for a few minutes in satisfied silence, and then tried to close our eyes, but the sun was too bright. I grazed his body "by accident" and he said, "I can't sleep next to you," and pinned my wrists down against the mattress for another round, which was exactly, gloriously, my intention.

I held his hand and walked toward the shower. I set the water on the hottest function allowable since we wouldn't really be under the spray but near it. His hands were on my breasts, grabbing them over and over, and then his tongue was doing the exploring, as we clung to each other tightly, my open mouth next to his shoulder, biting down. "Normally, I can stop," he said into my wet ear. "With other women, I can stop." He pressed me up against the glass wall.

"Mais forte," I was screaming, but what I did not account for was the copious amount of steam emanating from the bathroom. The fire alarm went off, blaring loudly. A voice through the speaker demanded a mandatory evacuation of the entire hotel. Jura? *Really?* I thought. But yes. The voice sounded quite serious. I wrapped a towel around me and ran, with Andreas behind me, naked but for his hotel sweatshirt. We ran down eleven flights of stairs because the alarm was so frighteningly loud, and post-orgasm, I have very little idea of what is going on in general. Through the wall, a man was saying, "Please evacuate the building," and I didn't even know whether this was about us, though, admittedly, there had been a lot of steam. But at least, to put a silver lining on it—as half-asleep guests grumbled about the time and the staff in their matching sweatshirts ushered everyone to the front of the hotel—at the very least, Andreas was in uniform.

It was a morning of recovery. We slept late and slowly made our way to the beach. Lying under an umbrella in the sand, we dove into a basket of croissants I'd stolen from the buffet. One of the Greatest Croissant Heists of our time, to be clear.

"God, I'm starving," I said, tearing one apart.

"I can imagine," Amanda replied. "All that sex and causing a hotelwide evacuation really works up an appetite."

I wolfed it down and then lay back and stretched my body out over the towel. I was thinking about not much except whether the fact that a cloud looked like a piece of cauliflower was interesting enough to say out loud.

"I feel very relaxed right now. I should start every day with multiple orgasms. The relaxation is palpable." I smiled.

"The annoyance is palpable," she replied.

"Don't act like you didn't have your own rendezvous last night."

She laughed. "I know."

"Well! I'm *waiting*!" I sat up and drank half a bottle of hotel water that tasted a little funny.

"Well, as you know . . . I've never had sex on the beach."

I sat up straighter. "AND?"

She scrunched up her nose. "I'd never done it before and . . . Well, sex *on* the beach seems dirty and sandy and highly impractical. I mean, I would imagine sand just gets *everywhere*. But last night, I had sex *near* the beach."

I gave her a round of applause.

"There was a chair. I don't know. It was just something fun to do in the moment. I wanted to have an *experience*, as you always say." She winced. "Are you judging me right now?"

There was a chair. God, I loved this girl.

"I am not judging you. I am full of pride and admiration for the monster you've become. How was it?"

"I feel sort of embarrassed about how forward I was."

"Don't be ridiculous. He probably loved it."

"No . . . I know. It's not that. It's just . . . I wasn't really myself. I think because I knew I'd never see him again. And because we made this deal—you and me. I was *completely* uninhibited."

"Ah-ha. Which is why the sex was so good."

She bit her bottom lip and shrugged, but a huge smile was peeking through.

The water was warm. We went swimming. Our hangovers eventually lifted. I started to have that dreaded end-of-vacation feeling. It came over me, usually the day before I left, when I thought about packing, the plane ride back, the lump of black travel clothes sitting in the corner of my hotel room, that I had tossed aside so triumphantly, as if I'd never see them again.

"I'm starting to think about reality," I said, as we lay on our towels. I was on my stomach, my head on top of my hands and turned to the side, facing Amanda.

She groaned and fell into her hands. "Not yet."

"No. It's good. I'm having a moment of clarity, actually."

"Oh. Tell me."

"I think I understand why artists are unemployed."

"What do you mean?"

"Well, not fully unemployed. They usually do something to stave off the . . . hunger. But I think I'm too busy at my current job to create art on the side. It's not that I hate it. I like it," I said. "That's the problem. It leaves me no time to create . . . and to feel the fear . . . of failure. And I think maybe I need to feel that fear."

I had so many pieces of art in my portfolio but nowhere to go with it, which made whatever I had feel like nothing. It was like having a *q* in Scrabble without a *u*. It's fine, but you can't do much with it. I had to make a change. What would I do, exactly? Hard to say. I had to put a new word down on the table. Why was I thinking in Scrabble terms? Again, very hard to say.

"Strangely, I think that's a pretty good idea," she said. "You used to be so afraid that you'd fail, before you got this job."

I sat up and crossed my legs under me.

"Exactly! Maybe I need to get a job that's . . . random. Like stamping papers."

"No. I think you should get a job in the art world. Right now, you're just avoiding it, which you've been doing for the past ten years."

"That's not true. I just don't want to put my art out there until it's good enough. Until I know it's good."

"Sophie. You may never know that. There are extremely successful actors who can't watch themselves act. I think you should get a lesser job, a part-time, less time-consuming job closer to what you really want to do. Get a job at a museum, or a gallery!"

"No. Not a gallery."

She gave me a long look. "The only way out is through."

"Damn you."

"You can't want to be an artist but be terrified of galleries! You can't afford to feel that way. I understand *why* you feel that way. But you have to face them. You have to get . . . in the game . . . a little bit. Right now you're standing on the sidelines, and I know you don't want to get in the game because you don't generally like playing games when you're not winning, but you're never going to win if you don't lose for a while."

I sighed. "This wisdom of yours . . . it's bothersome to me at the moment."

"You don't like other painters, especially successful ones. And why would you? Nobody wants to be around people who are doing what they'd like to do, but you *have* to. Because you have to learn from them. Instead of being intimidated, you need to watch them polish their trophies and figure out how to get one yourself."

"Your inspirational speeches are top-, top-level speeches. I can't imagine my life . . . without access to these speeches."

She lowered her sunglasses. "Luckily . . . you don't have to."

I felt something akin to joy. *When we get home, it'll still be like this. And it'll always be this way.* Us coming home to each other. This was a kind of comfort I'd never experienced. I'd been attached, in the moment, or for short stretches, but it was beginning to dawn on me what thinking long-term could do for a person.

We'd unpack in our new place, which would of course be a little drab, compared to life in Mexico. But in a short time that entire world would be ignited by possibilities, the wild and emotional story we planned to build, side by side.

Then she looked out at the water and said, "Are you sure we should go back? You who always needs a beach?"

"I'm sure," I said. I needed to get to work. And for that, I needed New York.

9

Amanda

The permits were taped to our front door. Beautiful, quickly issued permits. We took them down and unlocked the door feeling hopeful. Cautiously optimistic. We were tan and relaxed but by no means did we expect everything to look perfect. We were realistic. We knew what we had in store for us. Okay. *Slight chance* we burst through the door resembling one of those giddy couples in a home renovation show, prepared to *oooooh* and *ahhhhh* over their brand-new apartment. *Slight chance* one of us ends up crying tears of joy. You never know.

What we found was an amalgam of our old furniture and trash, sitting in the dark, under a leaking roof. Actual tears felt much more realistic.

I looked for a light switch, as a matter of habit. There was none. Just a sea of cardboard boxes and pieces of construction equipment with uses unknown to me. All I knew was that they were usually attached to an operator of some kind, and here they sat dormant. Waiting for us. A gift from our contractor. Some of the windows were covered by slabs of wood.

"What . . . the . . . ," Sophie said, looking up at a large tarp hanging from the ceiling, meant to be taped up to prevent the roof from leaking, but it had fallen—haphazardly placed masking tape being what it is—and so leaking was exactly what our roof was doing, all over a pyramid of our boxes. The peak of the pyramid was right under a stream of dripping water.

Sophie ran over and started hurling the boxes across the living room. I stood there, frozen. Literally. I couldn't begin to address the situation. It was only when I took note of things in more detail that I could see water seeping into cardboard. There were empty water bottles everywhere. A decaying apple sitting on top of a pile of crumpled papers. We stumbled upon a box of hair, which was unexpected.

"Is there no heat?" I uttered in a low voice, as Sophie began doing things that were actually helpful, like putting bottles into a garbage bag and shouting profanities.

I continued my role of standing in place in this dark and unknown house as Sophie surveyed upstairs. She returned to report that the showers and sinks weren't connected. Neither was the hot water heater. I went into the kitchen and ran my hands under the ice-cold water, in a pathetic attempt to confirm. At one point, I thought the water was warming, but my hands had just gone numb.

"I'm going to make some calls." She sounded severe.

"Sophie. It's Christmas Eve," I reminded her.

"And?"

I stayed silent.

She held her phone out in front of her and I heard the sound of ringing. "This place is supposed to be *habitable*."

"How . . . are we supposed to live like this?" I asked.

Well, all Sophie had to do was threaten suicide via voicemail, and miraculously, Colin called her back. I heard only her end of the conversation—Sophie starting strong, yelling what made sense and seemed logical. There were long periods of silence, then brief interjections, then mere syllables. Her speech began to slow. She looked at her phone. She pressed a button.

"I have no idea what just happened."

"What do you mean? What did he say?"

"He's a contractor," she said. "He makes up excuses for a living."

"What about all this garbage? The equipment? The apple? The water bottles everywhere?"

"He's blaming the electrician . . . the plumber. It's always someone else's fault. Someone else who, *conveniently,* isn't on the phone. We'll just . . . we'll have to manage. I'll fix the roof. We can get space heaters. Let's eat something and then reevaluate."

Three hours later, we were sitting in our living room, surrounded by space heaters and sweet potato fries.

"Let's think of the positives," she said. "We have our beds. It's not supposed to rain tomorrow."

We fixed the tarp. The space heaters kicked in. As the temperature in our apartment rose, so did our spirits. It was still damp-feeling, but not as bad.

"We can start tomorrow. We can do everything ourselves. I promise."

"We can? Are you sure?"

"No longer am I the girl you once knew," she said, "who struggled to do laundry."

"I can be pretty handy, too, if forced."

She began rifling through our mail, which was really just a stack of Christmas cards, soaked through from the rain. She was sitting on top of a pile of doors, which were supposed to be in their frames, but the hinges hadn't arrived yet.

"This 'from ours to yours' business is really not doing anything for me," she said, squinting and holding one of the waterlogged cards up to the light, as if there might be a hidden message.

"Maybe we should just send a picture of this apartment," I said. "From our mess to yours!"

Sophie sighed. "I think people are sick of us."

"Yeah." I looked around. "I'm not sure we have what it takes to participate in today's competitive holiday card market."

"I'm just glad it's our mail you're going through," I said, "and not the neighbors'."

Sophie loved to go through her neighbors' mail. Not actually opening it. No seals were torn. She would stare down from a safe distance. See what she could make out with a deep squint from above. And then she'd head into a tailspin about how her life wasn't as full as she'd once imagined.

"Oh, I'll get to theirs," she said.

I sat on something large and cube-shaped, covered in bubble wrap. Probably a dishwasher. All the cabinets and equipment we'd ordered were in the middle of the living room, creating a kind of obstacle course of kitchen appliances.

I went upstairs to the bedrooms and then came back down.

"It's not that bad. Secretly, I've always wanted an oven in my bedroom."

Sophie started to laugh. "Yes, and what little girl doesn't dream of a home with boarded-up windows!"

I laughed. "I mean, how many times did I, as a child, walk by a construction site and think, 'Wouldn't it be amazing to *live* like this?'"

"Exactly. Walls . . ." Sophie scoffed. "So pedestrian."

We wore our coats to bed that night.

For the next week, we drilled and thwacked and cooked on a camp stove that took twenty minutes to boil water. We called Colin for the occasional instruction at times, when we had absolutely no idea what we were doing.

"I think he said to flip a circuit," I reported to Sophie.

"You can't flip a circuit. You can flip a switch? Or blow a fuse?"

"Are you sure you can't flip a circuit?"

"Why were you even talking about a circuit?"

He talked us through installing our stove, until the bright blue flames came clicking through the holes in the burners.

I fixed a hinge on a door and felt very satisfied with myself until the entire door came out of the wall and crashed to the ground. "Son of a . . . ," I yelled.

One night, I turned on the water and the whole sink started rattling. I screamed for Sophie, and she came running in, half dressed and holding a hammer.

"I know I've said this a thousand times in the past week but . . . *What was that?*"

"I just turned it on! That's all I did!"

It kept rattling. I stood against the bathroom wall, backing away. "I don't know, Sophie. I'm scared. I'm really scared." The rumbling got louder, like a rocket ship about to launch. The faucet started sputtering brown liquid.

"Sophie!"

"Oh, stop." She went over to it and covered the sputtering with her hand, started yanking it this way and that. "What's the worst that could happen?"

"It could explode!"

"Good," she said, going at it with the hammer. "That'll save me the trouble of demolishing the shit out of it."

The noise stopped and the faucet let out one final sputter before shutting off for good.

The next night, I woke up to a repetitive creaking sound, which could have been any number of things, but I pretended that it was soothing. To lull myself back to sleep, I thought of the sound of the swings creaking outside my childhood home.

Then the smoke alarm went off.

"So this is the ONE appliance that's working right now?" I yelled from the doorway of my bedroom.

There was a brief silence, and then the sound of a comforter being ruffled.

"It's probably from soldering the pipes." Sophie stormed out of her room, sighed, and beat the smoke alarm to death with a hammer.

"Is that your solution to *everything*?"

A few nights later, I woke up convinced that there was a presence in the house.

"I feel like someone is *with us,*" I said, standing over Sophie's bed.

"Maybe you're a medium," she replied, groggy, rubbing one eye.

"Yeah, but they're not really telling me anything . . ."

"Oh."

"What if I'm a medium but there's some kind of communication issue or language barrier? So I just get creeped out but I have no information?"

"Like they keep trying to talk to you but you don't speak Spanish or something like that?"

"Yes!"

We started to laugh.

"Ah, the medium issue nobody ever talks about! Sometimes they don't speak English!"

"I'm going back to bed."

She rolled away from me. "Good talk."

On New Year's Eve, after we were done working, Sophie lit candles and put on music. I went to a bodega that sold cigarettes almost exclusively, and returned with a package of Hostess cupcakes. I tore open the cellophane and handed one to Sophie. We clinked the small black cakes together as if they were champagne flutes.

"Hey!" Sophie looked at me brightly. "Just think. People pay thousands of dollars to go camping and sleep outdoors under the stars. We are getting to do that for *free*."

"Who pays *thousands of dollars* to go camping?"

"You know . . . glamping? Isn't that a thing? Where it's basically like camping except you have servants and chocolate-covered strawberries?"

I rolled my eyes. "I have to go upstairs and do some prep for Monday." My first day at the new job. I gave my hair a dramatic toss and grabbed a candle. "When the servants arrive, tell them I'll take my chocolate-covered strawberries in the bedroom."

MY NEW OFFICE WAS WAY DOWNTOWN, by the Brooklyn Bridge. It was an area of the city renowned for its courthouses and City Hall and ten-dollar hand-pulled noodles. Despite being the most prestigious office of federal prosecutors in the country, going after Wall Street titans and corrupt politicians, I arrived on my first day to find that the place was by all measures a dilapidated dump. My desk was from at latest 1950, and every time I opened a drawer, there was a disgusting surprise inside! Fingernail clippings. A sticky umbrella. Mold from a forgotten piece of cheese. There was only one email in my inbox when I arrived, stating that they'd tested the water and it was not potable. There might have been some irony to the fact that I lived in one of the biggest cities in the world, yet neither my apartment nor my office had viable drinking water.

One Google search provided me with a *Wall Street Journal* article that was a deep dive into the smells of the building. My new coworkers shared stories with me about how somebody found a dead rat in the radiator. Bedbug infestations had occurred. One of my coworkers, when he got to his office, had found it so disgusting that he came in over the weekend to paint it himself. There were defendants who requested their next meeting be held in prison because it was more comfortable than our conference room.

"Just as a warning," I overheard a prosecutor say to a client before a meeting, "if someone had dinner in there the night before, it might be a little aromatic . . ."

At the firm, I had only a handful of cases at once, a first-year associate to help, plus an administrative assistant. Here, I was put on about twenty cases, and I had to do everything myself. I made my own copies, sent my own faxes. Yes, I had a very high-powered job at the US Attorney's Office, where I stayed late some nights because I wasn't sure how to use a fax machine.

About a week in, I was told to give away all my other cases. I was put on a big case about a sports agent accused of making payments to college basketball coaches in exchange for their help steering players to him as clients. The chief of the public corruption unit took me to court. "I'll supervise you to make sure you can handle it," he said.

"This is very confidential," he insisted as we walked. "We've started investigating. We have wiretaps on people's phones. And, quite frankly, we need help."

He immediately struck me as someone who was very into the

bravado of being a prosecutor. When we got to court, I took notes furiously. He turned to me and said, "Put your notebook away." Dramatic pause. "This isn't a law firm." At which point I wanted to turn to him and say, *But is it a movie?*

Of course, I didn't say that, because the truth was—*I* needed the help. In the courthouse, I was lost. I didn't know who to go to or how to get something filed or stamped. The wiretaps required a special sealing envelope and they needed to be left with the right person and sent to the right vault. But I always had the wrong envelope. And the people who worked there weren't exactly helpful, sending me down long hallways to various unmarked offices that turned me around in different directions and ultimately got me nowhere. Let's just say Operation Hoop Dreams (actually what it was called) was off to a rocky start.

I went home to Sophie and told her that I was trying to *be okay* with the mess, somehow, but it wasn't easy.

"Accept it," she advised. "Not everything can be neat and orderly," she said as she put down her welding visor and went at a piece of metal with a blowtorch.

"The only way I can do that is to either change my entire personality or become a Buddhist."

She stopped and lifted up the visor. "Relatively speaking, Buddhism seems easier."

So I dug into one of my boxes until I found a copy of *The Tao Te Ching*. A gift from Allie, who'd read it while trying to get pregnant. Somebody had given it to her, and she had passed it on because of some metaphor involving reciprocity.

I lay in bed and put my legs under a blanket. I opened the book. As I read, I could hear Sophie upstairs, the roar of her at work. To distract myself from everything, I thought of Nick, and felt a sudden rush in my chest. That moment on the beach. I let my memory take over. I wanted to hold on to every piece of it. It felt like a dream now. Crush number one had worked out quite nicely. What did other crushes have in store for me? *And why didn't I give him my number? Didn't I want to see him again?* The non-Buddhist inside me was chiming in.

I stopped. I tried to enjoy the fact that I had achieved a goal. I'd had fun, and now it was over. I picked the book back up, opened to one of the dog-eared pages. Sophie came into my room.

"Do *not* text Ethan," she said.

"What makes you think I would text Ethan?"

"Because nothing is working out and it's snowing."

"Because it's *snowing*?"

"I know how you get when it snows. All moody and emotional."

"I'm not emotional!" I said.

"What are you reading?"

"*The Tao Te Ching*."

"Great. It's worse than I thought."

I closed the book and put it under the covers. "It's fine."

"This is exactly what I was afraid of," she said. I could tell she was thinking about taking the book away, but she stopped herself. "Listen. Read whatever you want. Just don't text him. And . . . everything is going to be fine."

"I won't," I said. "And . . . I know."

"Venice wasn't built in a day."

"I think that was Rome."

"Okay. *Rome* wasn't built in a day."

"That's right. Italian contractors! Can you imagine?"

She started shouting in exaggerated Italian, with hand gestures to match, as she left my room. *"Bene! Sei magnifico! Sei fantastico! Cavolo! Boh! Che storia! Che figata!"*

I smiled, and opened the book again. Because I was an ADA now and also an aspiring Buddhist.

Just do your job, then let go.

One problem: How to quickly reverse thirty years of results-oriented thinking and go to this? It seemed like a good way to live. But the problem was the implementation and that teeny-tiny unnerving jolt of adrenaline that rose in my body whenever I thought about hearing whether I'd won or lost. I know. I know. There is no "winning" or "losing." To which I have prepared the following response: *Ohhhhh, come on.*

But I kept reading, as the radiator clanged, pumping out heat. There was a path, apparently. I came upon something that resonated, and I started reading it over and over again, to let it attach to me.

Things arise and she lets them come;
Things disappear and she lets them go.

I imagined myself grabbing something tightly, holding on, never letting go. Thoughts were bubbling up. Specific, nonvague, nonmeditative thoughts. I started to think about what could have happened with Nick if I had said yes to him, *Yes, I'd like to see you again.* There was a wave of guilt. *Not every night has to be followed up in a fantastically interesting way* is what I'm sure Buddha would have said, were he to modernize this little manifesto.

Calm descended upon me as I lay in my cocoon, taking deep breaths and picturing myself under a tree, Nick's mouth at my neck. I felt safe and secure. I had this *perfect* memory. *Enjoy it. Don't fuck it up.* I focused on breathing, on this moment now, and I felt free. When you didn't care quite so much, when you weren't hanging on to every interaction for dear life, you were free.

> *She has but doesn't possess,*
> *Acts but doesn't expect.*
> *When her work is done, she forgets it.*
> *That is why it lasts forever.*

Sophie

There is a way in which a home is like a body. It can be volatile. There's a history. A narrative. I'd been drawing a lot of bodies lately. I took photos of my own body, not because I was narcissistic but because I happened to be the only one in the room at the time. I am a great model. Always available. Extremely affordable. I overlay each photo with text. Some phrase that felt necessary and was funny to me, like: *These curves were made for walking just kidding I ran here.*

This brownstone needed a phrase, too, which is why I took charcoal to the wall of our living room and wrote: *Museum walls are so much whiter!*

It would be painted over, later on.

I sat on the floor in the middle of the living room. If this was anything like the projects of my past—the photos and paint and men that I clung to—it would have potential but be highly criticized. Too this or too that. Not realistic or spatially conservative. Okay. Analogy breaking down. But this place would be unlike the mattresses-on-the-floor studios. Because *this* would be the culmination of knowledge gained about design and home renovation and, of course, art. I would use both sets of skills, the interior design of my past and the art of my future. I looked around at the mess and knew it wouldn't be easy. There was no clear path to break through. I thought: *Challenge accepted.* Well, challenge a little bit frowned upon but ultimately accepted. Look out, world! Just kidding. *R-E-S-P-E* . . . Again. Kidding. *What you want! Baby, I got it.* Sorry. That song just goes so well with a project.

Amanda held an apple core between her fingers, eyeing it with disgust.

"Remember that one time in college you ate cereal instead of dinner and acted like it was a medical emergency?" I said to her.

"I don't recall." She tossed the core in the garbage.

"You said you felt faint. You didn't have your usual strength. And I watched as you sat on the edge of your bed, holding an apple, and then dropped it onto the floor, just to show me how ineffectual your hands had become in your hypoglycemic state."

"That doesn't sound like me at all."

"Oh yes, it does." I pointed at her. "Well, what if that apple has come back for you?"

She put her hand over her mouth.

"It's the ghosts of apples past!" she said.

"Everything here is a fucking ghost."

We tore down the kitchen cabinets first. Breaking down was the best version of therapy. Forget the shrink. Destroy something with your hands. In my twenties, I had a brief obsession with bones and the breaking apart and putting back together thereof. This led me to become friends with a series of butchers in Harlem who were also artists on the side. They gave me the bones and taught me how to cut with a steady hand. How to remove the spine from a fish. It was an exciting new skill that also ensured I'd be a vegetarian for life. I stained the bones completely white and made sculptures out of them and had all kinds of things to say about life fragmentation and purification and the space between body parts and how the body changes over time. And then one day, I got someone to break me into the cadaver lab at a hospital and I knew I had gone too far. I became that bird we found in the kitchen, desperate to get out.

As a knee-jerk reaction, I spent the next few years working in fashion photography, where the bodies were not fragmented at all and actually quite exquisite.

After the cabinets were done, we installed blue and white kitchen tiles. We pulled up the carpeting in the living room. It reminded me of pouring gesso over a canvas. A home, in some ways, was the deepest form of sculpture and art. In every place I'd ever lived, if I couldn't stand the wood, I painted it white. My apartment in London took me over a year to furnish. I finished right before moving out. It didn't matter. It was how I chose to spend my time. To me, the real art was how you lived, how you recycled, how you repurposed things in your home. It was art to have a coat hanging on the door. The right coat hung upon the right apparatus, of course.

I was looking to tame the wanderlust. To create a strong sense of place. The kind of place that I fantasized about—light-filled, authentic to the past and present. Colin helped me install the hot water heater. And put in new windows. Amanda picked out bathroom tiles, but I returned them in favor of black and white tiles Colin salvaged from an old house being demolished down the street. I used mortar and mixed grout to put them in. It was sort of like a puzzle. I actually dated a guy once who had a tattoo on his ankle of a single puzzle piece that had eluded him, in case you ever think *you* don't have your shit together.

We tried to make a ladder out of scrap wood, but it kept collapsing, which is really not the point of a ladder. We cleaned up the original sinks, the doorknobs, pulled up the shitty flooring upstairs and found these beautiful wood floors underneath. To be clear: there is nothing better than pulling up wall-to-wall carpeting and finding wood. I was scraping paint off a window and found glass. *Vintage* glass. With that slight distortion. What joy I felt, I can't explain. There was such treasure in something old, in dusting it off and bringing it to its former splendor. Everyone else overlooked it. The average person was lazy. But it was a certain type of person who delighted in the delicate nature of old Victorian pieces. It was saving something that was lost, like discovering a pyramid. In my closet, I pulled down a panel and found stained glass.

"Amanda!" I yelled. "Come here, please!" When she stepped into the room, I pointed at it.

"Why would there be stained glass in here?" she said, looking it over.

"Well, my novice friend. People used to believe that stained glass wouldn't bleach out your clothes, so they put it in their closets, but then they found out that it did, so they covered it up."

"Interesting . . . ," she said, even though she clearly found it less than, and went back to her room. She needed to gear up for court the next day. She had to get in the correct mind-set, and by that I mean lie on her bed and think of all the ways in which it could go terribly wrong.

We spent a few days painting our bedrooms, making them soothing, with Scandinavian hues modeled after this bedroom I saw in Stockholm once.

"I am invested in your bedroom being as comforting as possible," I said, as I rolled paint.

"Why?" she said, trying to flip her roller and getting paint all over the floor.

"So that I don't have to be on random noise patrol."

She laughed. Yes, in its finest moments, this was a labor of love. But it wasn't always dignified. It was sometimes accidentally electrocuting myself. It was frustrating roadblocks. It was scraping paint and inhaling the fumes.

"I just realized," I said to Amanda, on a day when the fumes had really gotten to me. I was wearing an oversize T-shirt and holding a scraper and feeling a little bit light-headed and delirious. "That if you took two porcupines to a fancy event, it would be hard because none of their clothes would fit."

She gave me a confused look.

"Seriously. Clothes wouldn't fit them. Would they go naked?"

"I think you need to open a window in there." She came over and shoved the window ajar.

"Also. Something about my childhood. I had an epiphany!"

"Okay . . ."

I pointed the scraper at her.

"So children just naturally follow their parents around and think they're right, right? Like, one time, I followed my mom across an airport and onto a flight to San Fran when *I knew* we were going to LA, but I just believed her and that she was right until we were actually on the plane and they said on the microphone where we were going and then she realized it on her own."

"Okay . . ."

She wasn't impressed. And neither was I, once I said it out loud.

"Also! My mother used to say all the time, 'I'm not myself until I've had my coffee!' But . . . she always drank decaf."

Amanda laughed. "Why don't you go outside for a minute or two? Get some air."

"Okay, but, thirdly, I think my bedroom needs a trick door."

"A trick door?"

"Yeah, you know, so that I can escape . . . if someone comes into my bedroom."

"I've got news for you. If someone comes into your bedroom, you are fucked no matter what."

"No. Not like, a serial killer. I could have men coming in and out of it."

"What would be the point of that?"

"So you *don't* like the idea of a trick door?"

"What's the trick?"

I had absolutely no idea.

AMANDA ACCOMPANIED ME to various hardware stores across Manhattan. Hans gave us a discount on sconces, an artichoke lamp from a Danish company, and a large ball lamp that looked like the sun. In exchange, we brought him a few dusty candelabras and told him that his new haircut made him look like Brad Pitt at the peak of his powers. We brought the pieces back to our apartment and I moved around the furniture while Amanda sat on the kitchen counter and ate crackers.

When our large, blue velvet living room couch arrived, which I had intended as a statement piece and used up most of our decorating budget on, Amanda had a small meltdown.

"It's *so* big," she said, with the most worried eyes. She walked around it, examining it from all angles. I thought it was a handmade upholstered masterpiece.

"Furniture always looks big when it first arrives. It's because you're used to nothing being there. Your eye is playing tricks on you."

"You don't think it looks like the couch that ate Harlem?"

"I do not think it looks like the couch that ate Harlem."

I heard her wake up at three A.M. to move around the cushions.

Other days were filled with us dancing and turning the volume on the music way up, so that we could hear it while we installed a washing machine and dishwasher. There is no more satisfying sound than the dishwasher you installed rumbling in your kitchen at night while you do other things. We ate sandwiches with pickles and cheese on the roof and then watched our clothes spin and rinse and listened to the water drain on our dishes and thought: *Oh, wondrous appliances.*

AMANDA WENT TO WORK AT HER NEW JOB. She made chocolate chip pancakes each morning, with whole wheat flour and coconut oil and whatever else made her feel okay about it. I was trying to tell my design clients I would no longer be taking on jobs. Mentally. I was trying to tell them in my head first. A critical first step. But it wasn't easy, particularly when a referral came in for a penthouse in Tribeca.

"Look at these casement windows!" I stretched my arm across the kitchen counter to show Amanda my phone.

She glanced quickly, in her work outfit—a white collared shirt tucked into a black skirt with buttons running down the side—and then shook her head. Went back to flipping. "Sophie. No."

"But . . ."

"Today is the day. Tell them. *Actually* tell them. And then start making progress in the right direction."

"I applied for a few fellowships last night, and funding at nonprofits, but that just feels like sending paper into a black hole."

"You never know." She presented me with a plate.

We stood across from each other at the counter. I sliced a pancake with the side of my fork. "I need to meet someone in person. Paper is too easy to ignore."

"Does anyone go around Chelsea with their portfolio anymore?"

"No. That's very old-fashioned."

"So what do people do?"

"I don't know, but I'm about to find out."

I know that as an artist, I should adore galleries, but I find them full of other people's visions and voices. Walking in, it was like there was a song playing too loudly and you either embraced it or had to get the hell out. I hadn't been to a gallery in two years, since an Anselm Kiefer retrospective in London where I stood before his *Black Flakes,* a 20-foot-long painting of a snow-covered field, for hours, silent and trying not to cry. Each time I opened the door to a gallery, I felt like I was pushing into my fear.

I'd done it all before, after college. It was what had led me to interior design in the first place. All these people sifting through my portfolio and in their most professional voices giving me polite reasons why not. Once again, I needed money, after spending all of mine on the apartment. I was eating popcorn for dinner.

I started doing it all again, going to events, openings, parties, and meeting other artists. I knew that they had to like what I did, but they also had to like me, so I focused on that. I popped into lectures to get advice about getting a job in the art world. Amanda came with me, if they were at night, and listened as if she might be quizzed later. I said nothing about my own art to anyone. Not yet. That felt like something I had to keep to myself.

One person led me to another. I was eaten alive by envy. I had interviews that went nowhere. But I was showing up. I was listening, occasionally eavesdropping. People in the art world didn't respond well to inquiries. It was like ordering gelato in Italy—one question, fine. Two and you're pushing it. Afterward, I went home and took a hot bath and tried to think positive thoughts. I painted a woman with her hands on her temples.

Still, I got up the next day and went to Chelsea. Soho. I walked into gallery after gallery. Warm, quiet places with cold women behind desks. Always a woman at the desk, skinny enough to look slightly ill, with her hair pulled back into a bun. She wore big glasses and layers of gold chain necklaces. She had a phone tucked against her shoulder and typed loudly. She would look up at me from where she sat in her white swivel chair, surrounded by stacks of thick art books. I would hesitate, and then tell her what I was looking for, which was, essentially, her job. You can only imagine how well that was working out for me.

Still, I found myself standing outside yet another gallery, this time in Nolita. I walked through a maze of fountains and sculptures, lying across a gardened lawn, inside a chain-link fence. Instead of going in right away, I stood there for a few minutes, to gather myself, or maybe because I'd been reading Joan Didion on the subway and I wanted to finish the chapter.

I watched a man and a woman haul paintings from a truck. The guy locked the truck and then went inside a bakery and came out with two coffees. He handed her a doughnut. She took a bite.

"This is pretty good," I heard her say to him.

"It's dairy-free," he replied.

"Oh." She gave the doughnut a dirty look and then tossed it in the garbage with such comedic timing. "That's disgusting."

I started laughing. The man went inside the gallery. The woman stood next to me, sipping her coffee and smoking a cigarette. I smiled at her.

"I'm impressed," I said.

She furrowed her brows. "With what?" She was wearing a button-down denim shirt, nails painted black, and blond hair, dark at the roots.

"With your ability to toss the doughnut."

"Oh." She smiled. "I'm getting a gut," she said, patting her stomach. "It wasn't worth it."

I shrugged. "I can't resist any of them, and I'm supposed to be a starving artist."

She smiled.

I looked up at the gallery. "But for now, I'm looking for a job."

She nodded and looked down at her feet. "Have you thought about becoming an art handler? A lot of artists do that."

"Oh, really? What does that entail?"

She raised her eyebrows and stood up from the wall. "How strong are you?" She looked me over.

I laughed. "Well, I've been hauling four-gallon tubs of gesso across town for the better part of my adult life." She looked at me as if she wanted more. I went on. "I once carried ten paintings thirty blocks. I've transported planks of wood that nearly stopped the functioning of my arms. And I carried a twenty-four-by-forty-two-inch painting from Chinatown to Midtown on my back."

She paused. "Let me see if the owner is here. Just remember—fifty-eight inches."

"What's that?"

"Eye-level center."

"Oh."

"Celine, by the way." She stuck out her hand.

"Sophie," I said. "Dairy enthusiast."

It took a bit of finagling, as my résumé does not showcase my ability to build crates or my knowledge of how pictures lay or when to use boots versus nails. But I did ultimately get the job. Because what I lack in experience I more than make up for in enthusiasm for mystery tasks.

The first thing I learned was how to build my own canvas stretchers. Then I did a lot of shipping and hanging. I fixed leaks and did some electrical work. I assisted with viewings and recommended lighting. I avoided edges and wore white gloves for matted works on paper. I used soft tissue over bubble wrap. Bubble-side up. Never bubble-side down. *Never.* I took shows down and put new ones up. I learned how to climb a 30-foot-ladder without fearing imminent death. It was manual work, similar to what I was doing at home, but I enjoyed it, handling the art and dragging (not the technical term) it around. It gave me a sense of what it might be like to bring my own work into a gallery someday.

I let my artistic aspirations leak, slowly at first, and just to Celine, but then much more readily to others. I found, once I was inside the walls, people were more willing to part with information. They told me to be delusional, be vulnerable, know yourself, steal from others, covet what you hate, and know what you like. They told me to ignore criticism but to recognize the grains of truth in it. To form gangs with other artists but not be weakened by them. Don't be embarrassed, but be humble. Don't be self-deprecating to a fault, but be realistic about your goals. Art doesn't have to be good, they said. Having a story doesn't make you entitled to have an audience, they said. I took inspiration where I could find it, and came to the following conclusion: I had to have a specific vision, a body of work that was connected in some way, and no fear whatsoever, except a modest amount.

At night, I was painting more than ever before. Our kitchen was covered in buckets of paint and gallons of gesso. Big tubs of black and white paint and smaller tubes of colors. Colors were three times as expensive, so I bought the little ones, and just went back to the store more frequently. I set up an easel in the living room with a table next to it, with cups of water and brushes in empty Chinese food containers. Being around art that I didn't necessarily like stirred up something in me—a feeling of *Why not me?* I had this idea about the different phases of life, the image of a woman as a puzzle being put back together and taken apart, and I was enjoying struggling with this bizarre-looking female. I turned it upside down. I tried to make the paint look more like flesh. The mouth was wrong. The hands were fantastic. I started on another painting of a bed in the midst of a forest, but I had too many feelings about how the bed should look. Drifting somewhere between confidence and insecurity, I was creating. And I didn't feel like such an amateur, once I got a better glimpse of what was out there. Art could be very shrewdly marketed. A handful of people could make something fashionable. It was a combination of style and business expertise. *Why not me?*

I kept working on a painting until the piece developed a heartbeat, until I felt like there was this invisible thump lurking behind the canvas. That's when I knew I really had it, when it seemed like something might open up within it. And within me. It was exciting and horror-film-like at the exact same time. I had study pieces and drawings tacked to the wall, pictures from magazines. I was constantly throwing out scraps of paper used for removing paint and adding textures. Our entire apartment smelled like sulfur from dirty brushes I'd forgotten to clean. Dead brushes now. That was the problem with acrylics. Brushes covered in oil, you could salvage. Acrylics forced you to stay on top of your shit. But the big advantage of acrylics was this: if the painting sucked, you could flip it and start over. I like that in a medium.

I made a few friends and began working with them in a large, questionably legal warehouse in Astoria. They all had a variety of jobs having little to do with art making. Painting apartments. Selling jewelry at Macy's. They treated those jobs like experiments, whether they needed the salaries or not. Security guarding at The Met was a study. So was driving a cab. Selling jeans. Cooking a steak. Buying two hundred pairs of socks on Canal Street. There were those living in squalor and those that had studios. We went to look at art. Everyone wanted the same thing—to sell art and to be recognized—but for nobody to know that they wanted that. To show your ambition was repulsive to them. There were concerts in the warehouse at night, a place that during the day got soaked by water from the elevated J train. But what I loved most was to hear about the work, the foam plantation or the sculpture using teeth and condoms. The unwritten rule was that you couldn't ask them about it. Not directly. You couldn't say, "What are you working on there?" They said art always sounded ridiculous when you described it, especially when it was in progress. It was only after the fact that it sounded okay, preferably once famed and celebrated.

I slept with one artist doing large-scale sculptures composed of old piano parts and shoelaces in a converted firehouse in Harlem. He let me share the space with him and I fell in love with him despite the way he said, "Did I tell you I'm doing a show with Pace? I didn't want to change galleries, but they were quite persuasive." I was lying on my back, with my skirt up around my waist, in a pile of shoelaces. "You know . . . your work is good," he said, buttoning up his shirt. "But you shouldn't do this unless you have to."

I looked him straight in the eye and said, "I have to." I said this instead of what I should have said, which was: "Shouldn't there be some sort of afterglow period here?" I mean, Jesus Christ. What if I had wanted to cuddle?

"Where do you find these men?" Amanda asked.

"His work is magnificent," I said, emptying containers of dirty water into the sink. It splattered and Amanda went at it with a sponge.

"Sophie. The fact that he makes magnificent art doesn't make him a good guy. The art will only serve to obscure the person, to not see them as they actually are."

"But does anyone see people as they actually are?"

"Yours is a question with many answers."

"I'm serious! I know that I project a huge fantasy, but don't we all, to some extent, see what we want to see and disregard the rest until we can't do that anymore? Is anyone really who they actually are? See. That's the problem with marriage . . . or long-term relationships . . . isn't it? People become who they are because they don't have the energy to keep up an artifice. And then the other person gets upset and says something like 'You aren't the person I married,' when really, they've always been this way. They just aren't trying as hard to be what you imagined in the beginning."

"So, in your opinion, we never really fall in love with a whole person?"

"No. We fall in love with a certain percentage of a person. We fall in love with the parts that we like."

"Or, alternatively, that person is just behaving badly because they like you less."

"*Or* they think the relationship is less fragile, so they test it more, once you're locked in."

"This came for you, by the way," she said, walking toward the front door and then returning with a small, tan envelope. "In today's mail." She handed it to me.

I knew right away, from the writing, that it was from my mother. I tore it open. There was a velvet pouch inside. I shook it onto the kitchen counter, and out came a necklace made from blue-green stones, set together in a row. My insides lurched. It was the color of her oval-shaped wedding ring. *That ring.* It was so unique. Nobody had anything like it. Paraiba tourmaline. A stone only found in this one mine in Brazil. Well, until they found it in Mozambique, but that's a different story. Anyway, it is the essence of the ocean in a gemstone. Very rare, too. Just one is discovered for every ten thousand diamonds.

Before my parents' divorce, my mother had a jewelry business, taking the topaz, amethyst, and aquamarine stones that my father used to export and making them into pieces to sell on the docks of Rio. I used to sit on the floor of her bedroom and sift through her jewelry box as if it were a fancy store, trying on necklaces and rings and bracelets, while she put on makeup, the fluorescent light illuminating her face. When I was in high school, my father's company took a downturn. My mother sold all her jewelry, except the ring. She wanted to keep it, to have this one ostentatious piece in her possession. But I guess she changed her mind. Because here was the oval-shaped wedding ring. Demolished.

"Am I supposed to wear this?" I said to Amanda. "This symbol of the breakdown of my parents' marriage?"

"Maybe you could think of it as . . . a symbol of . . . a new beginning?"

I shook my head. No.

My mother used to dry the sink after we used it. Because it was beautiful and copper, so she kept a towel next to it and patted it down. In case somebody came over. So you can imagine how she felt about the slight blemish of my father losing all our money. You can imagine how she felt about watching a strange man take our television. When I was fourteen, I had my watch stolen while I waited for my mother at a hair salon. It was the only jewelry my parents let me have, because it was practical. In Rio, there were over three hundred armed robberies per day. But I didn't have to worry, once I got older. We no longer had anything worth stealing.

I put the necklace in a drawer, intent on never seeing it again, and then went into the living room. I had an idea. It was coming to me in fragments. What if I were to do a set of abstract paintings, meant to look like gems? I wanted them to represent value, yet be some kind of visual pun. To look like a diamond, but actually be paint. Mere shapes hit by light differently to form various colors. I stayed up all night painting. I took out the necklace and placed it under a magnifying glass. The next day, I went out and bought a large crystal. I decided the paintings should have a graffiti-like element, so I laid down aquamarine first, then gave more distinct lines to a pink neon, covering it with a warmer edge. Using a technique called dry brushing, I slowly added translucent layers to make the form of the shapes, edging it out with a warmer tone. I wanted a set of blue geometric figures, with a pink neon outline, so I would do a fuzzy pink glow on the wall getting brighter toward the center. And then add to the aquamarine, blending for shadows and reflections.

I went to work feeling like I had a big secret, like I was doing something illicit in my home. As we washed rags in the sink, Celine told me that there was a summer show being assembled at another gallery she worked for. Summer shows were lower stakes, she explained, as the whole art world was on vacation. I said, what if I put together some pieces to show to the gallery owner? Within twenty-four hours, I had my portfolio in front of him.

"I see," he said, and then stared into space, as if trying to figure a way out of this. "I can see little connection here. It all feels like a gimmick. I just can't conceive of anyone wanting to look at these for any length of time."

The next day, I brought him my gem painting, which was almost done.

"Better," was all he said, before informing me that the group had already been selected. And then, about a month later, when I was totally preoccupied with painting, with the fractured and bright and kaleidoscopic nature of vision, my phone rang.

It was a 212 number. I both could and couldn't place the woman's voice, in the first few seconds of the call. Oddly enough, in that moment, she sounded just like my mother.

"Sophie," Celine said.

"Do you have bad news for me? Am I getting fired?" I blurted out. I don't know why.

"No . . ."

"No?" I said, in firm disbelief. "Really? It's not bad news?"

"I have good news, actually."

"You have *good* news?"

Good news in the life of an artist is about as rare as a shooting star . . . assuming that's rare . . . astrology-wise.

"Hold on." I took my phone outside the apartment and onto the street. I wanted to look around to make sure that the world was still functioning and that we hadn't entered some sort of apocalypse scenario.

"Are you still there?"

"Yes! Yes! Sorry."

I was silent and waited for her to continue. I didn't want to interrupt. I didn't want to say anything that might alter the course of events. I wanted to fully experience this moment.

"They want to show that gem painting, as part of the group show."

"They do? I thought it was already full."

"They have room for one more piece."

At that moment, I could hear the happiness in her voice. She too wanted to fully experience this moment. It meant something to her as well, and that made it all the more meaningful to me. She started talking specifics. Only one piece. Price. I wasn't really listening. Couldn't process past that first bit.

"They . . . they had someone back out, I guess?" It was one of those moments where you'd be better off not asking. But you have to know anyway because humans are a bunch of curious masochists. Is it the entire human race or just me? Often a question of mine.

She seemed reluctant to answer. "Yeah," she said, as if she were dropping the word down as softly and nonchalantly as possible.

"I'll do it, of course!" I said, I had to say, before it went away. "Thank you so much!"

"Great! The show is in ten days. Can you finish the work by then?"

"I can."

I ran inside to tell Amanda. Our dining room table and chairs hadn't arrived yet, so she was sitting on a pillow, at my old long table, pretending to be Japanese.

"They want my painting! I'm going to be part of a group show!" I looked at her triumphantly. She stretched her arms up to the ceiling and burst into a smile.

"It feels like such *validation*. To know that something I did is good."

She answered me by nodding profusely.

"I mean, I kind of know that what I'm doing is good, sometimes, for a short moment, but I'm also self-critical so when an outside entity that for some reason carries weight acknowledges it . . . it's . . . it's like the world is finally seeing it the way I see it."

She piped in with a string of: *It's amazing. I'm so proud of you. It's really so incredible. Wow. How cool. Congratulations!* It was all a blur.

"It's only one piece and a small gallery that nobody has ever heard of."

"Nope. No false modesty. I reject. *Sophie.* This is why you came to New York."

"And it's all happening because of you! Your advice. Your *orders.* I would never have been able to withstand all that rejection, if it wasn't for you and this brownstone and the fact that you let me graffiti the bathroom walls."

"I've always known that I was the key to your success," she said, in a haughty voice.

"Can you believe it?" I practically squealed. I went to her for a hug, but I had too much energy and it ended up being more of a tackle to the floor.

"I can," she said.

For the next few weeks, I painted every night, even once Amanda turned all the lights off and reminded me about the benefits of showering. I lit a candle. Until it was finished, it was like a song in my head, except instead of notes, it was the lines and colors that were moving. When I was done, I held it up to the light and Amanda said that it was so good that they should charge people just to look at it. I realized I loved it too.

"I'm going to go shower," I said. "My scalp itches."

When we walked into the gallery, on the night of the opening, I tried to absorb myself in the other pieces. I wanted to be less nervous, more cool, to have an appreciation for other peoples' work. Celine waved to me and Amanda from across the room and then gave me a strained smile, went back to her conversation. She wasn't calling me over, so I didn't go.

It seemed smoky inside, though I couldn't smell anything. The light was hazy and gray. I stood in front of a table full of small sculptures made of wire. I spoke to the artist about them. He nearly jumped on top of me, the way he spoke so purposefully, loud, close to my face, as if he hadn't spoken to a single soul in weeks. There were red stickers going up on the walls around me, plastic glasses of wine being clinked. There were handshakes and people passing beneath the paintings, and it all left me feeling strange. Unmoored.

I still wasn't looking for my piece, even though Amanda was. I'd experienced this a few times in college, with the faux art shows, and it was painful to watch people stand in front of your piece, and then keep walking. The keep walking was the worst part. The moving on. To the next thing. Something of such extreme importance to you. And yet a fleeting moment for them. Dropped cold.

But then once I'd made my way around the room and didn't see it, I got concerned. *Have they decided against showing it?* I scrunched my toes inside my shoes. The expression on Celine's face. Was she trying to hide the bad news? I went to the bathroom to collect myself. And then, as I hunched over the sink and doused my face with cold water, I looked up. There was my piece. To the left of the toilets. My heart was falling into my ribs.

I went back out and told Amanda.

"It's in the bathroom," I said.

"Is that a metaphor?"

"No. It's actually in the bathroom."

She disguised a small frown.

"Maybe that's cool though . . . in a way?" Her voice was high-pitched.

"Just so you know, there will be no Oscar given for your performance here tonight."

She looked back at me with an uneasy smile.

"It's okay. I'm fine. It's fine."

"Do you want me to get you a glass of wine?"

"Yes, please."

While she was gone, I started to drift from everyone. All the photos and sculptures around me seemed distorted, like the images could come to life, and come after me. I drank wine. I struggled to eat a carrot. My throat was so dry. I thought: *Great, maybe I'll choke on this carrot and then my art will be worth something.*

There was a spiral staircase on one side of the gallery. I wasn't sure if whatever was upstairs was part of the exhibit, but I decided to go up there and find out, before dealing with Celine and putting on a good face and telling her how pleased I was to see my piece. Once up the stairs, there was a display case, and a guy sitting on a stool.

He was wearing a gray sweater that was rolled up to his elbows, carrying a blazer in his hands. He had fair skin and short dark hair chopped sloppily. I could smell the mustiness of the attic, or maybe it was his cologne.

"Oh. Sorry," I said, and was about to descend the stairs when a set of earrings caught my eyes. He didn't say anything in response, just kind of stared at me. I went over. Inside the case, the earrings were irregular baroque pearls. I looked down at them, every now and then looking up at a mirror and catching him eyeing me.

"My parents were in the jewelry business," I said, to make an excuse for myself, which I didn't need.

"Try them on."

"Oh, I can't. It's somebody's art!"

"No, it's not. They're for sale. As jewelry."

"Oh." I took one pearl earring and inserted it into my ear. I leaned into the mirror.

He stared at me. He had long, thin eyebrows and deep-set brown eyes. He stepped back.

"Do I look like a Renaissance painting?"

He smiled. "Yes."

"In a bad way?"

"No, not in a bad way."

I glanced at the mirror. "Not really my style." I took the earring off.

"Julian Black," he said, with a short nod, and then stuck out his hand.

Julian Black? I repeated, in my head. As in, *Black Gallery*? He represented major artists. Expensive. Everything he sold. I'd flipped through a magazine with pictures of his art-filled apartment. Major dreamboat, assuming you were looking to spend the night at a rich person's gigantic art-filled apartment on Spring Street. And really, who wasn't? He was forty-two and single and his bachelor pad was far nicer than any bachelor pad had the right to be.

"What are you doing here?" I said. "Shouldn't you be on a yacht somewhere?"

He laughed. "Excuse me?" He had a smile that revealed lines around his mouth, his jawline, and a set of straight, white teeth. An actor's teeth. I could picture him reciting Shakespeare before a crowd. He would make a great Hamlet.

"Sorry. I meant . . . I read about your boat . . . in that magazine . . . how you like to be on the water?"

"It's winter."

"Not in the South of France! Or. Wait. Is it?" I looked up at him. "I used to live in Paris," I added, for no reason.

He smiled. "I believe it is also winter in the South of France. I have a friend who runs this place. What are *you* doing here?" he said, with a mock squint. Sherlock Holmes. He would make a great Sherlock Holmes.

"I made that piece downstairs," I said. I cocked my head to the side, put my hand on my hip, in a mock display of confidence. "To the left of the toilet."

"I was staring at that piece for a while. It's really beautiful."

"You think?" I said, trying to seem detached but ended up bordering on shrill.

"You mentioned the jewelry business. Is it meant to be the inside of a gem?"

"It is."

"And the graffiti outlines?"

"I'm from Brazil." I shrugged. "I wanted to portray some part of the graffiti art movement, since I grew up with it, in Rio. Art was something I saw on the streets, more so than anywhere else."

He nodded. "The contrast is perfect. The way you've done it."

"I thought it would be interesting to juxtapose graffiti art with these traditionally beautiful, traditionally valued jewels."

More nods. I went on: "To question the value of something that is so much less desperate for our attention. I wanted to put spray paint on canvas, create bursts of swirled color, and set it against something . . . solid seeming. Something that supposedly lasts forever along with what can easily be removed or painted over."

"Sure."

"It's diverse communication, but it's also very much vandalism, you know? A cry coming from the city's marginalized communities. When you see something written in black spray paint, a name or a word, at eye level on the street, it can stop you dead in your tracks. I wanted my art to have that quality as well."

"I get it. It's what Susan Shriver and Pamela Ruth have been doing for years, but you're going to do it better."

"I suppose. Sorry. Who are they?"

"You don't need to know. That's my job. So is it meant to be a commentary, then, on the art market itself? Since art, like gems, can be converted into a valuable asset strictly through speculation?"

"Sure." I smiled. "At least that's the buzz from the bathroom."

He rolled his eyes. "I actually think it's a good thing. At an art opening, everyone is always looking at each other. Not the art. To be alone with a piece of art is rare."

He spoke with a certain nonchalant authority.

"That's true," I said. "I just have this ridiculous fantasy about how I want my art to be seen . . . The lighting is perfect . . . There's silence, or just a low hum of voices . . . Nobody is hungry or thirsty . . . Everything else stops. Too much to ask, I think."

"Well, if it makes you feel any better, that's what it was like for me, when I saw your piece." His voice was strange, but familiar somehow. Soothing. "Listen. Nobody will come away from this and remember how bad the chardonnay was. But they might remember that quiet, intimate moment they had with your piece."

"That's nice of you to say." I resisted the urge to curtsy. "Thanks."

"Do you paint exclusively?"

"Yeah . . . I know. The notion that art is a paintbrush . . . It's like, where have you been for the last forty years? But I think the paintbrush is poised for a comeback. I've experimented with some crazy things, like using dry ice in my art. But then I couldn't figure out how to dispose of it. You can't throw it in the garbage! You're supposed to put it in a ventilated area until it evaporates, like a backyard or a balcony. But what do you do if you live in the city?"

"So, what did you do?"

"I threw it out! I took it out of my building, like I was smuggling cocaine. And then I ran into my doorman, and I thought, 'Great. Myron's a witness now.'"

"Myron would rat you out?"

"Oh, in a second. He was very judgmental. He would call me and say, 'Your *second* male caller of the day has arrived.'"

"He kept track of you. Well, I guess I can understand that." He smiled. "Do you have more of these . . . gem paintings?"

"Not at the moment. But I'm working on it. I was thinking of making it into a series. Using different stones. I think it could really be something."

He nodded. "I agree."

"I could call it Semiprecious," I said. "Or something less on the nose."

"I like it."

I felt like there was a 10 percent chance I was hallucinating all this. I didn't know quite what to make of him. It seemed too good to be true, so maybe he just wanted to sleep with me. Or maybe he genuinely liked my work. Too soon to tell.

"I'd like to talk more, but I have to run." He ran his hands through his hair. "Are you available for lunch tomorrow?"

What I did know was that these opportunities didn't come along very often. So whatever his intentions, I didn't really care.

"Lunch would be fantastic."

11

Amanda

"You know how, in your twenties, you wake up to drunken texts from ex-boyfriends or whomever?"

"Of course," Sophie said, while removing a rubber band from around a package of raspberries. Sophie and I had breakfast together every morning. She woke up earlier than she had to, just to join me in the kitchen, half-asleep, as we put fruit into a blender. We didn't discuss much, just sat there in contented silence, reading the news and our emails.

I shuddered at my phone. "Well, in my thirties, I wake up to anxiety-ridden Google searches."

I showed her. My last search, from around three A.M., was pms body hot no fever. She laughed, and then the sound of the blender took over.

At night, we took a great deal of time to talk about our days, sharing anecdotes from work and our dates. Sophie told me what she learned about glass cutting while eating caviar that she scored from a Russian artist in Brighton Beach. There was such a convenience to having the exact person you wanted to discuss everything with right there in your home. Often, I would still be wearing my work clothes and sitting on the sofa in our living room, spreading peanut butter and jelly on a cracker. And Sophie would be sitting in the window.

"I think my latest crush may be more of a friend," she said.

"That actor you met?"

"I don't really want to kiss him. I just want to hold his hand and sleep next to him sometimes."

"Doesn't he have a girlfriend?"

"He does. She's a yoga instructor and says things like, 'What's your favorite season? Mine's spring!'"

I mimed a person throwing up, then laughed. "Your hatred for spring . . . Just because *you* have allergies, must everyone suffer?"

"Yes. Everyone must suffer. She was surprisingly okay with me, though, which at first I thought was very mature of her and maybe a sign that she's at one with the universe and I was about to sign up for one of her classes, but then I realized: Wait a minute. I should be insulted! Am I not threatening?"

I gasped. "Of course you are. You're very threatening."

She drew her brows together. "If not me, who?"

"If not now, when?" I smiled. "But are you really *just* friends with this guy?"

"Are men and women ever *just* friends?"

"Yes, Plato."

"But not if you want to sleep with them. And have you ever had a male friend that you didn't at least *think* about sleeping with?"

"Of course!"

"I haven't."

"Well, I have," I assured her.

"That's just because you're lying to yourself. And myself, I might add. The problem is we only have so many words."

“Oh, that’s the problem?”

“Yes. We are limited by our lexicon. We say ‘friend,’ but ‘friend’ can mean so many things.”

“I’m iffy on my crush of the moment.”

“The Internet guy?”

“See. When you say that, I picture someone coming to our home to fix the Wi-Fi. He’s a web developer.”

“Sorry. Sorry. So, what’d you guys do last night?”

“We went to dinner and then back to his place to watch a documentary on the use of methamphetamine by Nazi soldiers during World War Two.”

“Cute. How did it end?”

“Well, it was kind of a pharmaceutical arms race, and the soldiers who took these drugs were really acting beyond the limits of what they would normally be capable of, which makes you think. I mean, think of the chemical advantage over a person without drugs.”

“I know how the war ends. I meant your date.”

She held her arm out, and I added a layer of jam before handing her a cracker.

“Oh. With a really long subway ride home. That’s the problem. I like him, but he lives in Clinton Hill. I can’t keep him on the roster. It’s too far.”

She shook her head. “It’s a shame that such a nice guy lives in such an undesirable location.”

“His bike is in the shop, so . . . that is also something that he deals with. I texted him this morning that I’d be busy working for a while but I’d let him know if my availability changes.”

“What’d he say?”

“Thanks.”

“That’s it? T-h-x?”

"No, he spelled it out."

"Oh. That's sweet."

"Right?" I laughed. "What's going on with your guy?"

"Which one?"

"John?"

"You mean Pedro?"

"No. John."

"Ohhh, that John."

"The one that you said 'had the best sleight of hand.'"

I was pretty sure that was a euphemism for something, though it wasn't beyond the realm of possibility that Sophie was dating a magician.

"He's a dancer, so the flirtation is second nature to him," she explained. "The promise of sex without the guarantee of it."

"I enjoyed hearing his tap routine on our floor last night."

Sophie had one budding romance after another that ended just as easily as they began. They never seemed to ask her about the future, but she was tapping (literally, in this case) into her circle of free-thinking, free-living artistic lovers who said things in bed like, "You're a restless soul who will never be lonely." Pale and skinny musicians with band names on their sweatshirts who hung out in our kitchen and said words like "vibing." They came and went.

"Ah, yes! He was teaching me how to soft-shoe."

I rolled my eyes. "I figured. I thought, 'They're either having wild sex or he's teaching her how to soft-shoe.' I'll take him over the knife thrower any day."

"He wasn't a knife thrower! He was a pilot, who just happened to have a spare room where he threw hunting knives at a target board."

"As one does. As a hobby."

We started laughing.

"What? You think it was a sign of aggression?"

"It's a sign of something!"

We were hysterical now, both of us lying on our backs on the sofa, laughing until tears ran down our cheeks.

"I wouldn't want to be on one of his planes," I muttered. "I'll tell you that much."

"Why? If the plane went down, I'd feel confident in his survival skills. We'd never starve."

"This is your dream scenario? How about avoiding a plane crash altogether?"

"Okay, so he was a little unhinged."

"A little?" I wiped a tear away, and then went upstairs to bed.

Our little life.

As Sophie became more immersed in the art world, she started spending more nights out, with Julian or with other artists. Being home alone left me in the strange, uncomfortable position of counting the passage of time, of waiting for her to return. Sitting behind my desk at work, there was always a great deal of activity and a ringing phone. I could lose myself in the bank records of the coaches, in scanning the list of money coming in and out, looking for big cash deposits. I would listen to my coworkers on the staircase near my office. In a slow moment, I could always focus on scraping gum from the inside of my desk with a plastic knife.

On Valentine's Day, my friends from work were going out for a Fuck Valentine's Day drinking session on Church Street, but I didn't feel like joining them. I was starving and exhausted from dealing with wiretap applications all day. So I ordered take-out from my favorite Vietnamese restaurant—a cavernous place a few blocks from my office—to pick up on my way home.

To get to the restaurant, I pushed through a crowd outside. Then, once I got to the restaurant, I had to paddle my way through something much less threatening: a sea of pink and red balloons.

"Oh, for Christ's sake," I said under my breath, pushing white strings from my face. The hostess was wearing a tight red turtleneck and red lipstick. I told her my name and waited as she went to the kitchen.

Suddenly, another face was in front of me. My oceanfront hookup. On dry land.

"You have to help me," he declared.

"With what?"

"I am on a date . . . from hell."

I rolled my eyes. "You're an emergency-room doctor! Surely you can handle it."

He looked concerned. "Don't be so sure."

Seeing Nick in New York, in such a different context, made it hard for me to process what was happening.

"Okay. Tell me. What is so bad about it?" I said, hands on hips.

"She's been talking a lot about her mother."

"Awww!" I tilted my head and gave him a wry smile.

"She FaceTimed her during appetizers."

"So sweet!" I looked past him to see if my order had emerged from the kitchen.

"She asked me if I thought there was chemistry."

"Between you and the mother?"

"No! Between me and her daughter."

"Well . . . is there?"

His eyes were in a fierce squint.

"She said that if all goes well, I could come and meet her mom after this. Apparently, she lives nearby!"

"How fortunate!" I started to laugh.

He was staring at me.

"I don't know what to tell you . . ."

"I didn't know you wore glasses," he said, at which point our eyes locked. The hostess appeared with my bag. I removed my glasses and rifled through my bag for my credit card. I handed it to her. "I'm sure there are a lot of things about me that you don't know."

He laughed. "Not as many as you'd think . . ." He looked at me and we had this brief psychic moment where we both knew that we were orchestrating this little plan, just so that we could talk afterward. "Please? This one favor? And then you'll be rid of me for the rest of your life."

I sighed. A faux sigh. "Fine. What do you want me to do?"

"Just come over and say you're my sister and that our dad died."

"Our DAD? Are you insane?"

"Dog?"

"Better." I paused. "Fine. Go." I motioned for him to go back to his table.

He went to sit down. First, I made sure that my brown bag of takeout was adequately protected. Priorities.

I spoke to the hostess. "Actually. Would you mind holding this here for me for a minute?" I lifted the bag. She nodded and took it from my hands.

I walked over to his table, looking over this poor girl that I was about to dupe. I took a deep breath.

"Nick!" I said, angrily, hitting his shoulder. "I have been calling you nonstop! Why aren't you picking up your phone?"

"I'm on a date . . . engrossed in conversation . . . with Jenny here."

"I had to track your location! We have to go to the . . . animal hospital. It's . . . Ernie."

He gave me a faux distressed look. "Ernie?"

"Yes . . . our family . . . chinchilla . . . Ernie. He's not well."

Jenny looked genuinely confused, for obvious reasons.

"Your . . . *pet* chinchilla?" she asked.

Nick, for his part, was just trying to pull off genuinely upset, but I had clearly thrown him.

I answered for him: "Oh, Nick just loved Ernie. He would put him on a leash. Take him for walks. The only problem was chinchillas don't take kindly to walks . . . but, you know! You do what you can!"

He stood up. "I'm so sorry. Do you mind if we call it a night?"

She was thoroughly freaked out, and more than happy to get out of this situation. "Of course."

I grabbed my bag of take-out on the way out. We lasted about a half block before the silence broke.

"You're officially a jerk," I said to him.

"*I'm* a jerk? You're the jerk," he said. "Our pet *chinchilla*? What happened to dog? We had decided upon dog!"

I laughed.

"Also, how dare you bring up Ernie at a time like this." He shook his head and tried to remain mad, but his smile kept breaking through.

"I'm sorry . . . I just . . ."

"No. No. There's no excuse. How dare you."

We stood on the street facing each other, our big coats between us. We were far from the beaches of Mexico. Here in New York, snow had begun falling, big, wet flakes the size of quarters, floating down. In the pause that followed, I put my hood on, my face half covered in the swath of my scarf. Only my eyes showing. He kissed my forehead carelessly, as if merely responding to an instinct.

"I'm not going home with you," I said.

"I'm not asking you," he answered.

"I'm going uptown."

"So am I. Where's your Valentine's Day spirit?"

THIRTY MINUTES LATER, he was reheating my soup in his microwave. The conditions inside his apartment were sparse. It had all the charm of a waiting room. There was one framed photo of what appeared to be a cherry tree covered in frost. A gray couch. A single wooden table with two chairs pulled up to it, one chair holding a stack of medical textbooks. The kitchen had an island with two barstools. I sat on one and ate my soup from a white bowl with his foreign spoon. I looked out the window at the snow falling against the red brick building across the street.

"I ordered the same exact soup an hour ago," he said. "We could be soulmates."

"I believe you mean . . . soupmates?"

"That's a *terrible* joke."

"You think?" I smiled.

"Really. One of the worst jokes I've ever heard."

"We didn't order the same soup because we're soulmates. We ordered the same soup because their pho is fucking delicious."

He shook his head. "It really is. I have to go about a thousand blocks to get it, but it's worth it. That's part of the reason I agreed to a first date on Valentine's Day. She had a reservation and I wanted the soup."

I smiled and lifted up the now empty brown bag and raised my eyebrows at him. "You don't need a reservation if you order for pickup."

"I see that. And it's noted."

"I was planning to eat it at home, while watching the Rangers game. I had a *big* night planned for myself."

My eyes naturally darted over to his television.

He went over to the TV, grabbed the remote off the couch, and put on the game. He made a grand gesture toward the couch.

"Are you sure?" I asked, lifting my bowl.

"Am I *sure*? I'm about five seconds away from asking you to marry me."

I sat cross-legged with my soup, staring at the television, pretending I wasn't interested in him. Nick put my glass of water on the coffee table in front of me, along with the napkin that came along with the take-out. He sat down next to me. A few minutes later, he tried to kiss me, and I batted him away, my eyes focused on the television, even though—the smell of him.

"I'm not kissing you right now," I said.

"Fine. I'll just kiss you." He came toward me. I batted him away again.

"Are you honestly turning me down to watch hockey?"

"I am honestly turning you down to watch hockey."

He paused. "This has never happened to me before."

"Oh my God. Just wait until the intermission!" I said, looking over to plead with him, and then he fell back onto the couch in mock despair. For the next fifteen minutes, I ignored every instinct I had, in order to stay true to my original stance. Priorities.

When the intermission came, I asked him to switch to ESPN so that I could see highlights from the Syracuse game. Just to mess with him. There is something about a guy who is just *too* used to getting what he wants.

"I have this tendency to think that my life is boring, and then I realize Jim Boeheim has had to watch his team play a two-three zone for forty years, and then I think, okay, my life isn't *that* bad."

"Wait, so will you marry me or no?"

I smiled and waved him off. "That's just the ESPN talking."

"I don't think it is."

I looked back at the screen. "Oh, please." I took the remote control. "Do you think the World Series of Poker is on? College bowling? Ooooo, look! High school volleyball!"

"Amanda."

I watched him lift the remote control and the screen go black. He threw it, and before the remote hit the other side of the couch, he was on top of me, his tongue in my mouth. I was pulling his T-shirt toward me and then taking it off.

We kissed slowly, deliberately. There was part of me that still had these two images of Nick tangled up—the sexy guy, the dorky boy. His hand glided over the top of my hand and then we interlaced our fingers. I looked down. I don't know why, but when I saw his fingers, I pictured the same hand, but smaller, returning from the cafeteria with a dozen packages of graham crackers.

"I should tell you something," I admitted. "I'm a little freaked out."

"What's wrong?"

"I don't know . . . it's a little strange, right? I mean, we knew each other as kids. Then we had that one night in Mexico. And now this."

"I'm all freaked out, too," he said, after he had taken my sweater off.

"Why?" I was sitting close enough to him that I could feel the heat of his skin.

"What if this doesn't live up to my fantasy? And what if it's not as good as the first time?"

"Really?"

"Nah," he said with a smile, and then grabbed me and lifted me up, took me into the bedroom.

His bedroom was a mess, clothes draped over every piece of furniture available. He put me down on what felt like a pile of dry cleaning, and then he shoved the cellophane-covered stack out from under me. His hands were unhooking my bra. He stopped himself. Then they were at the top of my pants, around the button. He stopped himself.

"Take them off," I whispered to him. "Take everything off."

He asked me if I wanted to be on top, like last time. I was embarrassed that he'd remembered. Usually, I did. As Sophie always says: "If all else fails, just get on top and get the job done." And that was advice I followed to a T. But this time, I didn't. I wanted to feel the weight of him. I wanted to look up at him. It wasn't pitch black with the sound of the ocean in the background. There were no rum drinks. Just light from the street.

Afterward, he told me that he saw sparks.

"Is that a line that typically works for you?"

"Honestly, I didn't think I needed a line," he said. "Given our current situation."

I laughed. "You're right. You have me. It's over."

"That's not what I meant," he said, with kindness in his voice.

"I know."

"I think we need some kind of catch up. Between then and now." He repositioned a pillow under his head and wrapped his arms around me.

"What do you want to know?" I asked, and then burrowed my head into the side of his body.

"*Everything,*" he said. "Now, *that* was a line."

I laughed and rolled away from him, pulling the covers with me.

"Hey! Hey. Stop. It's also true, in this case," he said. "Start with why you changed schools. I remember you leaving but I don't remember why."

"My parents," I said, and then something inside me broke down a little bit, so that I could keep going. "When they separated, we had to."

I turned on my side to face him.

"How was it?"

"It wasn't the easiest transition . . ."

"Because your fourth-grade field trip buddy spoiled you for life?"

I smiled. "Sure. If that helps you."

"Do you remember that field trip?"

"Vaguely . . ." I was careful not to look at him when I said this, which made it easier for me to lie.

"I should have asked you out back then."

"Asked me out? We were in fourth grade!"

"I know. But there were some serious couples, even back then. Remember Kaitlyn and Corey? They were practically married, by the laws of pipe cleaners tied into knots."

"I wasn't nearly ready for that."

"Oh, me neither. I just wanted to play baseball and watch cartoons and girls ain't nothing but trouble."

I laughed. "I hate to tell you this, but . . . it's true."

"I do remember being on the baseball team in high school, though, and this girl, who was I guess the girlfriend of one of the guys on my team, put a brownie through the fence rings of the backstop and I thought, 'Hm, maybe there is something to this whole girlfriend thing.'"

I smiled. "That's what did it to you, huh?"

"I was sad when you left."

"Really?"

"I mean, not *sad* sad. But I remember hearing about your parents and feeling sad for you, in that way that you feel when you're a kid and you hear about something happening to another kid that makes you sad for them."

I nodded, lay back on my pillow. "It was an ongoing issue. For so many years. They would fight and be so pissed at each other. My dad would leave. Then I'd see my mom get off the phone with him hours later, and she'd be smiling. He'd be gone for months and then leave a handwritten note at our door. Or he'd put Twizzlers in our mailbox."

"Come on. Really?"

"Yes! And she'd have this euphoric look on her face, like, I could have sworn they were teenagers. *Dawson's Creek* had nothing on my parents. But then, when we got older, it became much more of a hostile situation. There was a brief court battle. It became . . . less cute."

"Is that why you became a lawyer?"

"No . . . I don't think so . . . not really," I said softly. "That is why I had almost daily panic attacks in family law, though." I shot him a half smile.

He raised his eyebrows curiously. "Why in God's name did you take that class?"

"I don't know. I kind of wanted the information, believe it or not. I just couldn't handle the information. It's like every time I drive by a car accident, I cover my face with my hands. And then I peek. And then I spend half the day traumatized by what I saw."

He put his hand over his face. "I have to admit," he said, "I can't really picture it. You in a courtroom. You don't seem that . . ."

"Tough?"

"No . . . I meant," he broke in. "I'm sure you're plenty tough. I just meant . . ."

I smiled. "It's okay! I like having this other side to me that people don't see."

He was quiet for a moment. "Me too. Sometimes I feel like I have this normal life where I wear normal clothes, and nobody pays much attention to me, and then I get to the hospital and put my scrubs on and it's a big shift. Another world. This big rush of adrenaline. It's sort of like being a professional athlete on game day, in my mind at least. But often someone's life is at stake. I definitely want to help people, but I also like being in control. Does that make me sound like I have a huge ego?"

I smiled. "I *completely* get it. Being in court is so much about ego. As a prosecutor, you have a ton of power. You get to decide whether to bring the case. Then you call the shots. And the stakes are high. But on the flip side, somebody's liberty is at stake. I'm constantly waking up in the middle of the night thinking about how this person is or isn't going to go to jail because of what I'm doing."

"Yup," he said, nodding.

"A trial for me is just a mix of playing offense and defense. First, you get to ask the questions, and then when you're done, the defense gets to go, and suddenly you have to defend your witness and make sure they're not obliterated on the stand."

"So you're like the Scottie Pippen of the legal world?"

I laughed. "I am exactly that. My boss once told me to think about cross-examining a witness like a boyfriend that lied to you. You get to poke holes in his argument. I mean, if you're telling a lie, eventually it won't hold up. You can tell if someone is hiding something."

"I can't," he said. "A week ago, this twenty-one-year-old woman was in the ER for six hours. She said she had nausea whenever she ate. She'd had it for two months. And I was *racking my brain* trying to figure out what zebra diagnosis this could be. And then her boyfriend came in and said, 'Um, hey, doc, we're just here for a pregnancy test.'"

"I'd really like to see you in action at the hospital."

"You don't have to go to the hospital. You can see me on the street. Yesterday I walked past someone who collapsed and I had to initiate

CPR. I've been a doctor for years, but the bystander on the phone with 911 said, 'There's a medical student here doing CPR!'"

I gave him a sympathetic look.

"Can I come to court? Is that frowned upon?"

"Anyone can watch anything. It's just . . . a little uncool maybe. One of my coworkers had his parents come once. The defendant ended up writing a letter to the judge the night after opening statements, basically accusing the prosecutor's parents of heckling him."

"No."

"Yes! The judge read the letter out loud to the entire courtroom and then said"—I imitated the judge's voice—"'I've observed the so-called parents. They seem like lovely people.'"

He looked amused. "What if I promise not to say anything and come in disguise? Camouflage?"

"Camouflage?" I laughed. "What would that do for you? Question. When you picture me in a courtroom, are there a lot of shrubs and greenery?"

He rolled his eyes. "It must be cool, though, no?"

"There are some cool parts. The investigative part that people don't see. The wiretaps in real time. I like that. It's work that has a direct impact on people's lives. Just recently, my office went after a guy who was passing himself off as an attorney and essentially stealing people's money. And once he was convicted, people came up to us in court and said, 'This guy ruined my life. I'm glad that he's being held accountable.'"

He stared into space for a moment, and then looked at me. "I'm surprised you aren't married," he said, and I felt my body tense. He reached his hand around me, so that I would turn sideways, toward him. "I feel pretty lucky."

Was now the time to mention Sophie? Probably. But I liked the way he saw me—as something valuable that he'd happened to scoop up. I could see how delighted he was, as he got up and went about setting up the bedroom for us. I watched him go to the kitchen and return with two glasses of water. He put the shades down. He flicked off the lamp and threw a blanket over the comforter. He came over to me and tucked the covers under my body on all sides, to an exaggerated extent, until I resembled a burrito. It was actually sort of a cozy environment. His bedroom. I could see spending the night there. I worried that telling him about Sophie would make me seem undesirable, like at some point, I'd been out of options.

After he closed his eyes, I looked at him and could see the boy he used to be and the man he was, all at once. I liked them both. So I waited for him to fall asleep, and then I snuck the hell out of his apartment.

I pushed down the fold of the duvet and got out of bed slowly, carefully, so as not to allow the mattress to bounce or to pull any of the covers in my direction, and then felt around the floor for my clothing. I managed to locate everything but couldn't find my sweater. I thought about turning on the hallway light to help me, but it was too risky. And that's how I ended up slipping into a cab in the middle of the night in the most dignified way a person can: wearing a winter jacket and a bra.

As the cab moved quickly uptown, I closed my eyes and exhaled. The sky was just beginning to brighten. I heard a slight humming noise. It took a few buzzes before I realized that it was my phone.

I answered it.

"Where'd you go?" Nick asked, his voice scratchy but at full attention.

"I, um . . ." I was unsure how honest to be. And then I remembered: *What did it matter, anyway?* "I wanted to sleep in my own bed," I said.

"Oh." He paused. "You should have said something."

"I know . . . I didn't want . . . to offend you. And I couldn't find my sweater, so if you see it . . ."

"I would have helped you find it."

I didn't respond.

"What's the deal?" he said.

"What do you mean?"

"Are we going to see each other again?"

"Well . . . you do have my sweater." I looked out the window.

He laughed. "And you know what they say . . . one good bowl of soup . . . leads to another?" He sounded light, but uneasy. Something about not needing Nick had put him in a position of vulnerability. I could tell that he wasn't used to it, being the one to ask questions that might push the other person away.

I smiled. "That is true."

"Okay, then. Good night."

"Good night."

I OPENED THE FRONT DOOR QUIETLY and tiptoed inside, but there was no need. Sophie wasn't asleep. She was in the living room painting. She turned when she saw me and marched into the kitchen, which was covered in paint and brushes and canisters of water.

"Thank God you're home. I've been *dying* to eat an orange." She went over to the fruit bowl.

"Why didn't you just . . . eat one?"

"Because I didn't really feel up to eating a *whole* orange, you know?" She began peeling an orange over the garbage can.

"So you were dying for half an orange?"

"Exactly! I don't know. There is something about eating an orange in the middle of the night that I find very refreshing."

Her fingertips were gray, her hands streaked with blue paint.

"That's because . . . it's breakfast."

She took her time peeling, making sure the orange had every scrap of rind removed and was as perfect as possible. Then she handed me half and sat on the counter.

"I feel the same way about eating pretzels," I said. "But I wait for you to come home because I'm afraid of choking." I looked over at her canvas on an easel. "What are you working on?"

"Another gem painting. This one feels like it's about the small ways in which we avoid catastrophe each day. Were you at work?"

I shook my head. "Well, my news feels a little juvenile now," I said. "I'm sleeping with Cabo guy again."

Her whole face lit up.

"Tell me more."

If I had a great night, Sophie, more than anyone else, relished hearing about it. She lived vicariously better than anyone. She took such pride in my success. Sophie, who was always so chatty, suddenly got very quiet, very meditative, as if wanting to absorb every detail. It didn't matter what was going on with her. Her eyes were wide. Hungry. Ready to celebrate the upturn in our collective fates. *Ours*. Always. She was easily, without a doubt, the very best person with whom to share a victory. I told her everything—about the soup, the sex, the burrito.

"I love this guy for you," she said. And I felt an enormous sense of relief.

Sophie and I shut off the lights and went upstairs. I realized that I actually felt better than I'd ever felt after a romantic escapade. There was no spending the night in some guy's cramped apartment. No sharing the bed. No pretending to sleep even though I was uncomfortable, while he actually slept. No scrambling in the bathroom to look presentable the next morning. No pretending not to be hungry. No pretending . . . at all. And no worrying about the future.

"Vacation sex," Sophie said, shaking her head. "It always stays with you. I once fantasized about a Spanish dad that I saw while on vacation in Greece. I thought about him for like . . . a year afterward."

"Did anything happen between you two?"

"No. He was with his beautiful wife and their two beautiful daughters and we were staying at the same hotel, so we would lock eyes every now and then. His wife was always wearing these bathing suits with long, matching cover-ups. But, I don't know, there was something about this dad that just really got to me. He was hot, but also protective-seeming of his family. The only thing that happened, *slightly* happened, was—I was sitting by the sea one night and he came down and sat next to me and he sort of . . . touched my foot."

"He touched your foot?"

"He put his finger right there," she said, showing me. "You know . . . in the place between your big toe and your second toe."

"He didn't say anything?"

"No. It was a totally silent moment."

"This is what got you?"

"Yes. I told you. A year. And I don't even have a foot fetish."

"Well, Nick has done more than touch my toe."

"*Graças a Deus!* Thank God. I don't wish that kind of agony on anyone. So much fantasy. It was exhausting."

The only thing more fun than my time with Nick was telling Sophie about it afterward. And the one thing better than all that? I was home.

12

Sophie

I spent an extravagant amount of time on my appearance that morning. When Amanda is stressed, she refolds her clothes until her closet looks like a store that has never seen a customer. A color-coordinated sweater stack means she's breaking down inside. I'm more of a shopper. But in a way that nobody would ever know. The results were subtle. I had no interest in showing up in a contrived outfit with makeup or jewelry or anything exactly in place. The only way to dress up is to not be so deliberate. To not see a single pin. Julian, with his innocent invitation to an innocent lunch, would never know about the hours I spent trying to find the right outfit. About the extra time I spent on my hair to make sure it fell in a messy but ideal way. He'd never know the time I spent in the shower removing every hair from my body, then rotating earrings and pants and shirts until the best combination came together. To show the effort was to show your cards and essentially look worse. I wanted to not look like I was trying, and I'd never tried so fucking hard in my life. Why? Unclear. I didn't want to sleep with him. But I felt like he'd be more professionally useful if he wanted to sleep with me.

As I rode the subway down to Chelsea, I was warm but cool to the outside, in a black turtleneck and bell-bottomed jeans. Hidden under my jeans were a pair of biker-ish boots. Lies lies lies, all to convey that I was downright blasé about this business meeting. Lunch. Whatever. I was trying to talk myself down. Who was he? A gallery owner. Who was I? Besides desperate for his approval? I can't recall. These boots really needed a disclaimer. *Warning: Girl in boots may be significantly less tough than she appears.*

As I walked up the stairs to the restaurant, I could see Julian through the window, already seated at a table. He was staring at his phone with a frown, which immediately dissolved once he saw me. Red Cat was frequented by everyone in the art world. Located in the heart of the gallery district, it was the chosen lunch spot for dealers and collectors and gallerists galore. I'd heard about it many times before, dropped in conversation, but I'd never been. Red Cat was for those who belonged. It was just a restaurant. Anyone could eat there, technically. Sure. Tell that to the idiot inside my brain that was climbing the stairs and screaming, *Lunch at the Red Cat with an art person I am going to be so famous!*

Just being able to point to him, to the hostess, to this one man, made me feel a sense of snobbishness over the others, like my former self. Before this lunch.

Then I sat down, and immediately dropped my armor.

"I've always been too afraid to come here."

He smiled. "Really? Why?"

"I don't know if you know this but . . ." I leaned in, lowered my voice, conspiratorially, "there are many important people here."

"This is exactly where you should be."

"Perhaps we haven't been properly introduced. I'm Sophie. I paint in secret. Is that not . . . I mean . . . does that not sound like a crackerjack strategy?"

He smiled again, sat back in his chair. My confession appeared to calm him. Both of us.

"Sorry," I said, shaking my head. "Let's start over." I stuck out my hand and he shook it. "This is an average day, and this place means *nothing* to me," I said.

He laughed. "Why is it I don't believe you now?" he said.

The waiter presented us with a plate overflowing with tan beans.

"Tempura-fried green beans with a mustard dipping sauce," he said, as he placed the plate on the table.

Julian took one and said, "Addictive and terrible for you, of course." He popped one into his mouth. "Like all good things."

"Yes," I replied.

He nodded. "So, tell me a little bit about your training."

"Oh, well, my formal training is in acrylics. But a lot of my influences were muralists like Eric Grohe, Keith Haring . . . Diego Rivera."

"Eduardo Kobra?"

"I love his work. He made me want to be an artist."

"I see his color palette in your work. The checkered backgrounds."

"Of course, Tarsila do Amaral and Di Cavalcanti were certainly inspiring to me as well. I like to play with the combination of more formal, classical painting and something that is impulsive and casual."

"What have you done so far?"

"You mean in terms of art?"

He looked amused. "Yes. Art."

"I used to be really interested in exploring the theme of . . . I guess . . . voyeurism?" I laughed lightly. "I would take things that I'd find like a piece of mail and create a portrait of that person based on whatever I had. It would turn into a mixed-media piece, a collage of sorts. With paint and photos and maybe a cable bill." I rolled my eyes. "Perhaps the phrase 'invasion of privacy' comes to mind?"

"All's fair in . . . I don't know. I've seen collage artists do some crazy things. Anyway. How did you become interested in that?"

I cringed. "Doesn't it always start with an ex-boyfriend?"

"Oh," he said. "I suppose it does."

"There was a guy I was seeing in Paris and he broke up with me, very abruptly, over email. The email . . . kind of killed me. I couldn't get over it. The wording of it alone was so traumatizing that I created an entire piece based on this one email." I cringed again. "The subject line was 'Now listen.'"

He winced in response. "I once got an email from an ex-girlfriend with the subject line 'Frankly my dear . . .' and you know how the rest of that one goes."

"Well, I bet *you* didn't disguise yourself and follow her on a train from Paris to Provence, taking photographs, now, did you?"

"No . . . no, I did not."

"I'd say that I regret it, but it turned out to be one of my most interesting pieces. I used the email and photos from our relationship to create this collage of emotional dirty laundry that people really responded to. I was actually able to get it published in France in *Art International*."

"Wow. And what happened with the guy? Did he ever see it?"

"He did." I nodded, slowly. "He had some *slightly* incriminating photos of me that he then tried to get published in retaliation."

"You're kidding?"

"Two artists . . . probably should not sleep together. Unless you want to see broken plates scattered everywhere and then those plates later attached to a canvas."

He laughed. "Have you ever shown your work at a gallery?"

"No. The truth is . . . I'm scared of the girls."

"What girls?"

"You know the ones who sit at those desks near the front, looking mean?"

"Ahhh, the gallery girls."

"I think they do it on purpose, don't you?"

"I hadn't considered that."

"It's just a theory," I said.

He gave me a warm look. "Have you thought anymore about the gems?"

"I have, actually. I'm working on a second one right now." I took out my phone and showed him some photos of it.

"This is great. I think they should be big, big pieces."

"I agree."

"Like that one I saw in the bathroom, but on a larger scale. About sixty inches in diameter, even. Have you ever worked on anything that large before?"

"I have. I actually prefer it."

"This is something that would do very well at Art Basel," he said.

"In Miami?" I managed to say.

"No. The real one. In Switzerland. Miami is for cocaine and bullshit."

"Oh."

"I shouldn't say that. What I should more *politely* say is that I think the Europeans would respond better to your work."

I laughed. "Either one sounds great to me. Miami . . . Switzerland . . . Hey. Give me a call. Give me a hit."

He smiled with a slight hesitation in his eyes. "Listen. I'm not going to promise you anything. Art is such a fickle thing. It's about the market, the mood, and the dumb luck of who shows up."

"I know . . ." I hesitated, because a part of me wanted to shrink, to not ask him to do anything for me, out of sheer discomfort. But I pressed on. I knew that no matter what he said, this guy could give me the "luck" I needed. The luck was meeting him. The rest was a matter of maneuvering. First, he needed to know that I was putting in the work. "I think . . . at this point, I've created a solid body of work. I've shopped it around. I really wanted to hit the bricks as far as research goes, so I've been going to galleries and really doing my homework."

"That's good." He appeared lost in thought. "It's good to see what artists are selling. So you've accumulated some rejection letters?"

"I have. But it's okay." I nodded. "It's like getting a flu shot."

He laughed. "How so?"

"It's for the greater good! It always stings. You know that going in. But at some point . . . you feel protected . . . in theory . . . against the elements."

"Someone to add to your 'fuck-you' list."

"My what?"

"Every artist has one. It's the list of people that have rejected you. That you need to prove wrong, ultimately."

"I don't have a fuck-you list. I do have fuck-you boots."

He nodded, looked down at my legs. "You got that show where we met."

"I was in the bathroom."

"Oh, that's diplomacy, that's all. There is always a competition for who is the top dog between the gallery's stable of artists. A new younger artist like you comes in and poses a threat. Having actual pure original talent is a threat to everyone. A new artist paints with ease, creating something more accessible. You're attractive and young. I could tell immediately that you have a natural feel for color. Your piece was interesting. There was a sexiness to it, even. I could see many people being attracted to whatever you create."

I didn't know if any of it was true, but I liked the way it sounded.

He said, "Part of growing in this world is realizing your romantic idea of being an artist is different from the art world, which is basically about commerce. It's a business just like any other. It's about primary and secondary markets. You have to figure out, where do you want to fit in? Some galleries push on the trend aspect, which can be negative for an artist. In New York, there is a lot of opportunity but also a lot of dilution. You can easily get lost as an artist and feel like if you don't play the game, you're not going to get involved. And in a lot of ways, that's true."

He was saying what I already knew, but it felt good to hear him say it, like I wasn't imagining difficulties that weren't there, or that only applied to me.

"I just want to earn money from art," I said. "That's my goal. I've been a hostess, a waitress, a bike messenger. I've started my own design firm. But I want to be able to sell art, without having to supplement my income, which I realize is a very hard thing to do but *somebody* does it, and I want to be one of those people."

He nodded.

"I'm going to be poverty-stricken within six months, aren't I?" I said. "Just give it to me straight."

He was amused, eyes flickering on me all the time. "Well, do you have anything else anchoring your life?"

I knew what he was asking, in a roundabout way: Are you married?

"I have an arrangement. With my best friend."

"That's . . . cute."

"No . . . I mean . . . I set up a life with my closest female friend, just as friends, nonsexually, as opposed to forcing ourselves to live with one of the men we were dating. We're still *seeing* men, on the side. Just without the intention of marriage or a lifelong commitment that will strangle us in seven to ten years."

"Interesting . . . I understand what you're after. Everyone thinks they'll be the exception."

"Exactly. But I think that it's time for us, as a society, to face the reality of the situation, to look a little bit down the line."

"Artists are always at the forefront."

"Yup . . . that's me . . . At the forefront. Of nonsense and gobbledygook, *é foda*."

"Translation?"

"It's fucked."

And then he said, with perfect calm: "I'm enjoying your company. I think you're talented. I think you could have quite a career in front of you."

My heart was racing. I could hardly answer him. But I did. At least I think I did. My words were being obliterated by the sound of his words ricocheting around in my brain. Doors that had been slammed shut for so long weren't necessarily open, but there was a light on underneath. I could see that sliver of yellow light, just barely peeking through.

"I can introduce you to people, of course, but I think socializing can be damaging to young artists. I think it's more important to focus on the studio, on becoming a developed artist. Truly the best gift that you can get as an artist at your stage is the gift of time and resources."

"I've turned my apartment into a studio. Conveniently, my roommate just loves the smell of rotten eggs."

"Well, look, you have to be really inward and self-involved when you're developing your art. It's an autonomous action."

We finished our lunch in comfortable silence. And then, as he paid the bill, I said, "Why are you doing all this for me?" Because I had to.

He paused and thought it over. "Two reasons. One, I pride myself on my ability to recognize potential. And I saw potential in your piece at that show, which was confirmed in talking to you. And now I'm doing it because I'm an egomaniac who likes to be right."

I smiled. "Everyone likes to be right."

"Yeah, but I like it . . . a lot."

There was a flash of something to him just then. I wasn't sure what.

"Okay," I replied.

"What are you doing tonight?" he asked.

I smiled and said, "Absolutely nothing."

A lot of my questions remained unanswered. But I believe it was the great artist Zhen Wei Woo who said when the doors of promise open, the trick is to walk very quickly through them.

BY THE TIME I got back to Harlem, it was after six. My feet were most likely on the ground, but my mind was gone—high, high above me, in the clouds somewhere. The weather was warming, and Convent Avenue was being transformed into idyllic spring, with trees starting to bloom, set against ivied, historic townhouses. I trotted along, looking up from time to time, all high on promises. The turning of the seasons made me feel powerful, like I just might be able to accomplish anything. I burst into my apartment and, upon seeing Amanda, spat out:

"We have to go to a party!"

"Who does?" she said, looking back at me as she pushed green beans around a frying pan. She was wearing jeans and a dark green sweater. I went over to the kitchen sink and filled a glass with tap water. I drank it down.

"You. Us. Tonight. It's at a members-only art club in Chelsea. Julian invited me. Are you free? Could you be free?"

She emptied the pan onto a plate and took out a fork from the drawer and stabbed a green bean. "Are you sure that he wants me to go? Or that *you* want me to go?"

"The only person I'll know there is Julian, and I don't want to be too dependent on him."

She was unconvinced. "I'm confused about this guy," she said.

"Join the club."

"Is he interested in you, or your work?"

"I'm not sure yet."

"Are you interested in him?"

"No. I mean, yes, under other circumstances, sure. I wouldn't throw him out of bed."

"Sophie. If he's really as connected as you say he is, and he's interested in your work, you should *not* sleep with him."

"Which is exactly why I need you to come with me! As my friend. And bodyguard. *Come on.* Please. Amanda. This guy is charming and witty and just a little bit mischievous, and if you don't come with me, it's going to be a problem."

She moved her mouth back and forth, as if considering.

"I bet they'll have hors d'oeuvres," I added.

"You think?"

"Probably!"

She put down her fork and emptied the plate into the garbage. "Okay. Sold."

I followed her upstairs. "We don't have much time to get ready."

"Why do I buy green beans?"

"I don't know, but you always buy them."

"They taste like weeds."

A BLACK CAR ARRIVED TO PICK US UP. We examined it from the window. Amanda descended the stairs of our brownstone wearing a pink dress with a thin belt. Her hair was parted on one side.

"We could have gotten our own car," she said as she opened the door, confused and maybe even a little insulted. She didn't like anyone who did anything without good reason. She believed in an even exchange of goods and services. It was like she had one of those balancing scales in front of her and if something didn't measure out *exactly,* danger was afoot.

I shrugged. "I think he was just trying to make it easy for us to get there."

As we headed downtown, I watched cars whip by us on the highway in silence. I took rings on and off my fingers.

"I've never seen you this nervous," Amanda said.

"I've never *been* this nervous. Is this how you feel?"

"All the time."

"It's exhausting."

"You're wearing your big hoops," she said, glancing at my earrings, shaking her head. "But you're not encapsulating your usual 'big hoops' attitude."

I laughed. "You need to start writing these things down."

"I think, in retirement, we should have a stationery store."

"With funny expressions, instead of 'happy birthday'?"

"Exactly. That feels right to me."

We arrived at a five-story brick townhouse on Twenty-First Street. Music could be heard coming from inside the building. A red light was shining through the window on the top floor. We watched three girls in long coats *clip-clop* down the street, laughing as they rushed up the stairs. They used a key to unlock the door.

A key? Amanda and I looked at each other in a moment of panic, as if all our efforts getting ready had landed us right smack in front of a locked door. I could actually picture us fleeing the scene and making the best of it at one of the bars around the corner. "This is *much* better, anyway. A key. How ridiculous."

Then the driver handed us one.

"You'll be needing this," he said. We inhaled in unison and then walked up the stairs. I unlocked the door and a girl in a black strapless dress, blond hair pulled back neatly into a low bun, greeted us. Her name was Blair. Just kidding. I have no idea what her name was, but she looked like a Blair. I presented her with my key, unsure whether I needed to justify my presence. She played with her necklace and looked down at me skeptically as she asked, "What is your involvement with the creative arts?"

In response, I mumbled something about Julian Black.

"Julian? Of course!" She pointed her long bony fingers in the direction of the coatroom.

The entranceway was filled with framed prints. Various colorful images competed for my attention. An eyeball with legs. A doll with no legs. One picture was red and yellow and had the words *I fucking love you* written in black, dripping paint. A neon yellow sign read *Squeeze my Lemon* in block print.

We went up a spiral staircase. The room upstairs had red walls with black moldings, oversize chairs made of tan leather and red velvet. One wall was adorned with a floor-to-ceiling painting of a pair of lips. The chandelier was made of tree branches. It smelled like firewood. A tuxedoed man presented us with a large tray of champagne. We each took a glass. The room was a mix of young and old. Women in red lipstick and sleeveless turtlenecks. Men in tight black sweaters. There was a table in the center of the room with vegetables arranged in patterns and a large block of cheese with knives sticking out of it. I overheard a woman with a flower in her hair ask a man about his most satisfying accomplishment.

"Oh my God," I said. "That's Derek Lasher."

"Who's that?" Amanda asked.

"He's a really well-known artist. He takes those photos of famous people with butts on their heads."

"Come again?"

"With his fingers together like this, over their heads, so that it looks like a butt." I showed her.

"I don't understand art."

"I think it's kind of interesting."

"Are you sure it's not exceedingly stupid?" She raised her eyebrows at me.

I thought about it for a minute. "You're right. It's crap."

I started to look for Julian. As we passed through a room with a grand piano, I spotted him at the end of a long hallway in a navy suit and yellow tie. He was talking to a gray-haired penguin-shaped woman wearing gold earrings. The only word I heard was "Kaminsky." I wanted to snap up his attention immediately.

"Do you want to say hi to him by yourself?"

"Maybe."

"I can wander," she said. "If you need me, I'll be chasing down a tray of mini hamburgers."

Once I caught his eye, he stopped talking and let the penguin drift away.

"Hey," he said. "You clean up well." I was wearing a one-shouldered black dress and heels that made my legs look long. I turned so that we could kiss cheeks. "That was Helen Walker."

I stared at him.

"The chief curator at the Museum of Contemporary Art in LA."

"Ah."

He looked good. A question shot through my brain: *Can I sleep with him?* No. I knew the stories. The studio assistant who went to every single party and got himself a big show in Germany because he slept with his boss's curator. After that, nobody believed he received anything based on merit.

"Oscar!" he said. He introduced me to Oscar Gioni, director of the Serpentine Gallery in London, then I smiled along as he and Oscar Gioni discussed a party that took place years ago. These were all people I'd read about but never imagined existed in real life. Amanda came over and I introduced her. We all talked for a few minutes, then she excused herself to get a drink. I spotted her later playing pool next to a black-and-white drawing of Amy Winehouse.

Julian introduced me to a blur of people, always with one hand on my back, his free hand holding up a glass of champagne.

We were trying to talk to each other but kept getting interrupted by either a person he knew or a waiter carting hors d'oeuvres.

"Mushroom cap?"

"Um . . . no . . . no, thanks," he'd say. "Anyway, you know, the public is pretty sensitive, and if you look at what people were doing in the seventies or the fifties, it was so much more avant-garde, crushingly uncomfortable . . ."

"And people are so sensitive that you almost can't do anything . . ."

"Tuna tartare with a miso glaze?"

"No thanks!" I chirped.

"Especially female artists . . . but if you're a beautiful person that society wants to see, that will really help you . . ."

"Bruschetta with a tomato, caper, and garlic relish?"

We shook our heads. He smiled at me.

"Herb-crusted and grilled tenderloin of beef on bruschetta with a Dijon-pesto mayonnaise?"

"Oh, for the love of God," he said, and actually looked a little bit pissed. "Do you want to get out of here?" he asked.

"Sure."

I felt bad about abandoning Amanda, but then I remembered what he told me over lunch. *You have to be really inward and self-involved when you're developing your art.* I had his time and attention right now, but who knew for how long? I knew that Amanda would understand. And she seemed to be enjoying herself, talking to a guy in a plaid shirt and knit hat. When I walked into the room with the pool table, she immediately screamed, "Sophie!" She grabbed my arm, turning to the guy to say "One moment please!" as if mocking a prerecorded message.

"Interesting choice." I shot her a look as we walked to the other side of the room. "Didn't we formulate some sort of policy about guys who wear ski hats indoors?"

"Wait! Listen! He's a writer for *Art and Auction*!"

She introduced me to the guy—Max, apparently—and started rambling to me about how bad he was at pool and to him about how amazing my art was. She was clearly tipsy.

"I apologize for my publicist." I smiled at him. "She doesn't have any other clients. Can you give us a minute?" I pulled her away.

I had the distinct impression Max had no intention of rejoining the party.

"I was going to ask if you'd be all right if I left, but I can see . . ."

"You're leaving? With Julian?"

"Well . . . yes . . . but . . ."

"Are you sure that's a good idea?"

"Well . . . yes."

"But what about your bodyguard?"

"Believe me. I have no interest in fucking this up. It'll just be easier to talk to him if we go elsewhere."

"Okay. I believe you. I believe you."

"Max is hot, by the way. You should . . . do something about that."

"Oh . . . I'm not interested in him."

"Why not?"

"I'm just not," she said. She seemed, compared to her usual self, to not be saying enough words.

"Fine," I said, turning to walk away, "but you owe me an explanation!"

I FOLLOWED JULIAN to a restaurant down the street that I thought was him choosing a place at random but seemed to be the unofficial after party. He waved across the room at people we'd just seen. They came over. I did my best to say things that were not ordinary but interesting. To be just the right amount of naive. I was enjoying so much listening to their talk about the price fetched for the most recent Jeff Koons piece or the latest stunt that Banksy pulled at the Venice Biennale.

"That's why Warhol was a genius. He sold nothing at high prices," Julian said. "There was no intrinsic value to the items he was selling. It was a joke. It was making a joke of art and the art world. Everything was a photocopy. He didn't call his artist studio something intimate and small, like 'atelier.' He called it 'The Factory' and had his secretary and his mother signing things, just to make the point."

"Also great-looking stuff, by the way," I added, and then felt relief when Julian nodded and said, "Completely." Then the conversation turned to Egon Schiele and how he went to jail for painting prostitutes.

Julian seemed to like me, that much I knew, but what I didn't know was if that meant he'd ever show my work. Maybe he was waiting to decide. Talking to other people. I had no clue what was going on behind the scenes. All I knew was that I couldn't ask. Maybe I should have, but I was too afraid to push on something so fragile. He was smart enough to know I'd be curious where all this was going. But he didn't mention it. And why should he? Why lock himself into something for no reason? He had earned the right to, among many other things, keep me at a distance, dangling. What I told myself was to stick around, as long as possible, until I found out. My grandmother used to say, "You can get used to hanging."

Very late that night, I found myself walking with Julian toward Spring Street.

"Do you want me to get you a cab?" he said. For a crazy instant, I thought about saying no. *What would happen?* In my experience, sex really opens people up information-wise. But no. *Do not go that route. It will be better in theory than in practice. It almost always is.* Maybe we could have some affair down the line, once I'd won all the Grammys. But not now, while my status was precarious.

"That's okay. I can get one." I walked to the curb and held up my hand. "This was fun. Thank you."

"We could get a drink."

"We've already had many drinks!" I smiled. "Tomorrow is another day."

"That's right." A cab pulled over and he opened the door for me. "Until tomorrow."

I rolled my eyes and kissed him on the cheek. "You'll get sick of me. I promise." I slammed the door.

As the cab drove away, I thought: *I wish I hadn't said that.*

13

Amanda

I didn't plan on making any calls. The plan was to accompany Sophie to her party, and then return home, mildly buzzed. This was the arrangement in my head, anyway, and it would have all gone according to plan had there not been a game of pool that I was playing badly and a flask of vodka that some guy in a beret claimed was punishment for my every missed shot. Well, at some point after Sophie left, I ended up more drunk than was convenient and attempting to hide from the beret in what turned out to be the laundry room. The unfortunate part was not any of this, but that I had my cell phone.

"Hey!" I said, when Nick picked up, because at the time this seemed like a very spiffy opener.

"Hello," he said. And then, silence. That's when it dawned on me that I hadn't planned on what to say. *I just called to say . . . I don't know what, exactly.* My brain was still catching up to the decision to make the call.

"Are you . . . out?" he asked.

"I am *not* at a party."

He laughed. "Okay . . . So by process of elimination that would make you . . . Wait. Is this a drunk dial?"

"I am *not* a teenager."

"Quick. What's the capital of Indonesia?"

"I don't know that sober."

"Are you all right?" he said, in a low voice.

"I am *so great.* What are you doing?"

"What are *you* doing?"

I leaned back and accidentally activated one of the machines, which startled me.

"I am *not* drunk," I said, and put the phone up to the dryer. "See! I'm doing laundry!"

"Where are you?"

"I'm doing laundry at a party!" I said. "If that doesn't tempt you, I don't know what will."

There was silence. "I'm going to need an address, darlin'."

I told him where I was and then opened the door back into the hallway, where I found myself face-to-face with a champagne-toting waiter.

"Can I get you another glass, miss?" he said. I shook my head.

"That is *not* my boyfriend," I said into the phone, right before hanging up.

I got roped into another game of pool with the beret, but it wasn't too long before I saw Nick's face appear—smiling, but focused—lit up by lamplight. I didn't realize, until he showed up, how much I'd been counting on seeing him, how much I had just plain missed him since the last time.

He got my coat without asking. We wanted a taxi. One appeared right away. On the street, he twirled me under his arm and I landed at the exact place where my hand could reach for the door, like this was a goddamn musical. He told the driver my address, which was exactly what I wanted. We were pressed up against each other the entire ride home.

I was proud, a little smug, at having found the ideal crush. I wasn't afraid to call him. He showed up, upon request. He wasn't inclined to force a commitment. And I felt everything that I wanted to, everything that was the beginning of a relationship. That charge that ran between two people who didn't fully know each other and kept expanding with each piece of new material.

And so, I called. Over and over.

The spring was filled with nights at his place, waking up to Nick with a white towel wrapped around his waist and wet hair, his apartment smelling like coffee, me wearing a sweatshirt of his that was gigantic.

"I don't know why you like that one so much," he said. "You look like the thing that was eaten by the person who owns that sweatshirt."

It was hard for him to sleep beside me, he said. "Visiting hours are over," I would say, pushing him away.

He rolled his eyes. "Shouldn't there be some sort of screening process for these jokes?"

Our mornings became longer.

"What do you want me to get you?"

"Chocolate chip pancakes," I said.

"I was thinking something healthy."

I mimed a person throwing up. "We can get a sweet potato."

He appeared to think it over. "So chocolate chip pancakes and one sweet potato?"

"Well, I can't imagine broccoli in this scenario," I said. "Can you?"

He shrugged, and when the food arrived, we ripped open the containers and ate them while standing.

"We can sit down, if you want."

"I like standing."

"Date still counts?" he said, his mouth full.

"Oh, absolutely," I replied, running my knife through a pancake. "Date counts."

We went for walks around the city, not headed anywhere in particular, just deep in conversation, as the sidewalks became more or less congested and the sun peeked out between buildings. I never wanted to leave him, even once we'd been together for a long time.

At the end of one walk, we felt rain, and were standing right in front of a subway entrance. It looked dirty and bleak and I heard rumbling in the distance, a new storm coming in, giving the sky an electric feel. My phone kept buzzing with texts from Sophie. I said I should head home, and then we started walking in the direction of his apartment. I put my phone away. He wanted to cook me dinner. How could I refuse? I'd go home right afterward.

We got back to his apartment just in time, just before the sky opened up. While he cooked, I lay on his couch, watching television and playing with the fringes of a blanket.

"My Pakistani friend was right!" I sat up straight. "I can't believe it!" I said, responding to a news blip that scrolled across the bottom of the screen.

"What Pakistani friend?" he said, putting the fan on over the oven, as the smell of fish crept over his apartment.

"The guy at the bodega down the street from me."

"Ohhh. What?"

"He said that Andy Murray's career was over. I thought he was just out for the season! I had no idea that he was *done* done. But he said that with the specific type of back injury he has, there's no way he can come back from that, and he was right."

"And what's surprising is that he doesn't even specialize in orthopedics!"

I laughed. "Hey! This guy watches *a lot* of tennis. And not just Wimbledon or Australia. He watches, like, Barcelona and Indian Wells. *Deep* cuts."

And then we sat on stools in his kitchen, eating the dinner he'd made. I looked down at my plate, at what appeared to be salmon with some sort of stuffing.

"What is . . . the white thing? Is it . . . crab?"

"It's lobster," he said. "It's lobster-stuffed salmon."

Lobster-stuffed salmon?

I tried to eat it, but it was so rubbery that I couldn't put a fork through it. The concept alone. So I went for the lump of zucchini next to it, which seemed safer but was so salty that I could barely swallow it. I looked over at his plate, to see how he was doing. He had eaten his entire piece of salmon but seemed to be avoiding the zucchini. He kept scanning my plate. I kept trying to eat it. "I'm just not a vegetable person," I said, and when he didn't flinch, I scooped the zucchini and took a big bite. I started coughing. My eyes watered.

"All right." He stood, picked up my plate. "It's horrible."

"What did you do here?" I said, laughing. "Why did you get lobster-stuffed salmon?"

"I thought it was fancy!"

I gave him a long look. *"I'm fancy?"* His standards were unclear. I mean, he thought *lobster-stuffed salmon* from the grocery store was fancy, so anything was possible.

"And the zucchini?" I questioned.

"I may have used the wrong side of the saltshaker . . ."

I put my fingers on my forehead and looked down. "Well, this was really a very special meal you made for us."

"Shut up. Shut up. Shut up." He picked up his phone.

"No. Really. Truly. One of the great meals of my lifetime."

"Just . . ." He looked exasperated. "Tell me what you like on your pizza."

By the time it arrived, I was so famished that I ate two slices in a row without stopping.

"I have a great idea for a restaurant," I said.

"Let's hear it."

"Are you ready?" I held my hands in the air. "Because this idea is going to blow your mind."

"You're almost certainly hyping it up too much."

"I'm not. It's really *that* good."

"Go ahead."

"It's a romantic pizza place called Love at First Slice. And when you walk in, they play that song '*When the moon hits your eye like a big pizza pie . . .*'"

He laughed. "Is that their only song?"

"I guess there could be other songs. I haven't worked out all the details yet."

"I can see that," he said, eyeing me as I finished a piece of crust. He moved toward me and put his hand around my wrist.

"Can I ask you a question? Do you remember holding hands with me on that field trip?"

"I do."

"I do too. I remember it really well."

And then we were back in his bed, my leg crawling over his. He kissed me goodbye in the morning, at his door, with a pizza box full of cold pizza lying in the kitchen behind him.

On Sundays, I went to Central Park to watch Nick coach his Little League team, which was essentially just a bunch of kids in oversize green jerseys swinging and missing. Every now and then, one would hit the ball a few feet in front of him and wind up with a triple and delusions of grandeur.

Nick displayed a surprising amount of patience, unlike the coach of the other team, who rounded up his players and told them that they were an embarrassment to the league.

But even Nick got frustrated. "Kyle! You can't play third base the whole game!" He walked toward me, massaging his forehead with his hand. "He wants to play third base because his favorite player is David Wright," he whispered. "But he's got the worst arm on the team." He ran across the field.

After the game was over, we sat on the field in the sun. I watched Nick lying on the grass and thought how the summer has been good to him: his skin was browner, his eyes greener. I gave him a hand, lifting his body off the grass. We walked toward the tennis courts. We passed by the reservoir and walked downhill, the expanse of green clay courts coming into view, surrounded by high fencing on every side.

We sat on a bench and Nick changed from cleats to sneakers. I took two tennis racquets out of my bag. He applied sunscreen to his face as the sound of smacking tennis balls surrounded us.

"Just so you know," he said, "I already regret this."

"I haven't played in at least a year."

"Yeah, but I remember how good you were in elementary school. You had a reputation."

"I did?"

"Yeah. You had a reputation for being good at tennis and I had one for getting pantsed on the monkey bars."

He looked at me and his face was coated in white. "It's not *really* rubbed in," I said.

"It's not?" He tried to fix it, but somehow made it worse.

I dabbed at it with my fingers and he swatted me away. I started laughing. He looked like a mime. "I can't take you seriously like this."

"I don't want you to take me seriously."

"Oh, really? Why's that?"

"Because I'm the underdog."

We rounded the path to the courts, passing by the small house to sign in and find out which court was ours. The woman inside glanced down at Nick's shoes and gave them a dirty look.

"Those aren't tennis sneakers," she said. "You need white tennis sneakers to play. Sorry, kids."

I felt my hopes sink. She looked down at her phone, clicked, and a photograph of a dog flashed across the screen. I motioned her over to the side.

"He's too upset to talk about it, but," I said, pointing to Nick, "his chinchilla just . . . died. He was . . . very attached to him. And he needs this, to take his mind off, you know . . ." I winced.

She looked at me, hesitantly, but then let us go, with a warning. Next time. We bowed our heads.

"What did you say to her?" Nick said, as we walked to our court.

I put my hand through the throat of my racquet and spun it around my wrist. "Oh, nothing much. Just that I'm your parole officer, and this is your last day of freedom."

He took a tennis ball and tossed it up at me as we walked, so that it bounced off my back. I glared at him. "You're on probation."

"I couldn't have more fun with anyone," he said.

We started hitting and I was very careful not to smash any shots, to hit every ball evenly, to maintain the rally. We stood at the net and agreed to play one set.

"Loser buys dinner," he said.

"Fine."

"Don't go easy on me."

"Oh, believe me. I won't."

Once the set began, I hit harder, and shot out to a 3–0 lead.

"This is all happening very quickly," he said.

I rushed to the net, smashed a lob, and then called out the score with a smugness that was certain to bother him.

"This isn't fair!" he called out, breathless. "I'm not wearing the right sneakers!"

"Oh, *really*? So if you had tennis sneakers, the score would be different?"

"It can't be ruled out," he replied. We were both sweating, but he was in much worse shape, with wet splotches all over his shirt.

I threw a ball at him. "Serve, please. No excuses."

I made some errors. He won two games, and started to walk with a strange swagger.

I smiled. "I think that sleeveless shirt has really gone to your head."

But then I started to find my rhythm. The better I played, the harder he pushed back, and the more off-kilter his strokes became. Balls went sailing above the fence.

"This isn't baseball, you know? There are no extra points for that!"

The gap between our points widened. I won the set 6–2. The next one 6–1. The sun was going down. We brushed the courts, removed clay from the lines, and sat on a bench with our racquets, drinking water. He kissed me, with one hand on my back, touching the damp spot beneath my shoulder blades.

"Where do you want to go to dinner?" he asked.

I zipped the cover over my racquet, smiling widely. "Someplace where the food costs a thousand dollars."

He shook his head. "Boy, you really enjoyed yourself, didn't you?"

I nodded and looked at him brightly. "Very. Much."

He looked down at the grass and nodded. "Good."

I hooked my arm into his and leaned into him as we walked, and the whole world felt different. There was this person covered in sweat and sunscreen, and nothing else.

A FEW DAYS LATER when I was at work, he called to ask if I was available on Friday night. I said yes. He called several more times to confirm. To repeat the address. To see if I wanted him to pick me up. "I'm free and I'll be there!" I assured him, as I rushed to get to court. I looked the address up later and saw that it was a church on 121st Street and Broadway. There was a string trio to perform the music of *La Bohème*. I was a little wary of the whole thing, the lobster-stuffed salmon of dates.

"I'm just glad we're not going to his place tonight. He's the worst kind of cook," I said to Sophie as I got ready in the morning before work. "Confident, but with no skill or ingredients."

Sophie was sitting on my bed critiquing my outfit choices. I reached into my underwear drawer.

"Noooo," I said, examining a pair I'd been set on wearing. They were that elusive combination of sexy but also could be worn at work all day. And they were torn on one side.

Sophie stood up right away and went into her room and came back with a needle and thread. She sewed as I ate cereal. I heard her on the phone saying, "No. I'm free. Other than sewing my roommate's underwear, I've got nothing to do."

When I got to the church that night, there was a crowd of people already inside, waiting for the performance to begin. The church was beautiful, with stained glass windows and crystal chandeliers overhead. With its black-and-white checkerboard floor, it felt like Old World meets *Alice in Wonderland*. It was the first time since Mexico that I'd seen Nick wear a tie. There were candles everywhere.

"Wow," I said. "Very romantic."

He pumped his fist. His hair looked like it had just been washed.

I smiled. "You know, the very fact that you're so into this makes me question it entirely."

When the music began, I stopped talking, stopped moving. It was melodic and evocative and completely walloped me. I almost started praying. The music combined with the summer air gave it all a dreamlike quality. We sat in the back, near some elderly women who were openly weeping. "It's pretty, but *so sad,*" I heard one of them whisper.

Nick kept looking at the women, and then back at me. He put his arm around me and held me, a little closer than usual. Whenever I leaned toward him even slightly, he kissed me. As the performance ended and people began to shuffle past us to leave, we were still sitting there.

"I have to tell you something," he said. "And I'm going to need to ask you not to be sarcastic for five minutes."

"I don't *need* to be sarcastic."

"Yes, you do. But okay. Agreed? Are you ready?"

I swallowed. "No."

"I love you," he said. "I've loved you since the moment I saw you, or re-saw you, maybe sooner. Maybe always. I'm not a big believer in fate or . . . cosmic forces . . . or anything of that nature. But I don't know what's going on. You've got me seeing sparks . . . and buying opera tickets . . . and watching tennis tournaments that take place in obscure parts of the country . . ."

"Cincinnati?"

He eyed me. "Yes. Cincinnati."

"It's the second-largest city in Ohio."

"Yes. It's a city." He sighed. "Do you want me to stop?"

I smiled. "No. Keep going."

"*The point is,* I love you, and you know now, so feel free to make one of your jokes."

I pushed my lips together, as if they'd been unfairly sealed, and waited an extra second, until he was just on the edge of his seat, and then said, "I love you too."

Our eyes locked, and I leaned into him. We kissed, and I felt there was nothing separating us. I realized how restrained I'd been before, with others, how there'd always been a barrier of some kind. My heart was beating so fast that I could almost worry about it, but I didn't.

"All right," he muttered. "This won't work at all."

"What? Us?"

"No. I'm making out with you in front of half of the Upper West Side."

He walked me home, and as we walked, I started to feel an overwhelming surge of joy. Mixed with an avalanche of sadness. All my resistance was drowning. Because I realized that I wanted to live with him. I wanted to marry him, maybe. I wanted to build a future with *him.* He was exactly the person I'd always wanted. And I wouldn't be able to have him, because it was all happening just a little bit too late. I found myself wishing that *I* were a different person. Perhaps someone with the slightest clue what she was doing with her personal life. My hands were shaking. I felt sick. Why exactly had I blocked myself off from this?

"What's wrong?" he said.

"Nothing."

"Are you stunned speechless by all the romance?"

I didn't say anything back. When we stood in front of my place, a long period of quietness passed between us. "I should go inside," I said.

"You don't want me to come in?"

I felt faint.

"I do," I said. "It's just my roommate. She texted me earlier. She's not feeling well. She asked me not to bring anyone else home."

"Why didn't we just go to my place, then?"

I gave him a pleading look. *Please just let me go inside and don't ask me any more questions.*

"I feel like she might need me tonight," I said. "I'll call you tomorrow."

There was hurt in his eyes, but I pretended not to see it. I kissed him and then ran away, up the stairs. "Thank you for tonight!" I clapped my hands together. "Very romantic!"

Another wounded look. My heart sank.

When I got up to my bedroom, I replayed the evening in my head, an evening which now felt like a crushing disaster. There was a very strong part of me that wanted to wake Sophie up and tell her about everything. But instead, I walked from one end of my bedroom to the other, thinking of what to do in the dark. I paced and paced, looking to solve a riddle that had no solution. There was no line of reasoning that would hold up. It wasn't complicated. It was him or her. Still, I kept clinging absurdly to the notion that I could solve this, that there had to be a way, if I could only just find it.

When I woke up the next morning, I didn't say anything to Sophie. I didn't want to talk to her about him, at all. And when she asked me what happened last night, I said that I missed the concert, that I was stuck at work until very late. I said that the trial was killing me. I did something that I hadn't done in the history of my friendship with Sophie: I lied.

Sophie

It is rare, as a young artist, to find anyone who understands your vision, let alone someone who has the power to do anything with it. But I had found it. I didn't know what, exactly, to say about it, in concrete terms. I knew he was invested in what I might become. Every night, there was another art fair, another gallery opening. There was lunch before, dinner after. I felt like my professional life had taken a turn so severe that there was only before Julian, and after. We liked and disliked the same artists. We laughed about how everyone in the art world talked until you aggressively intervened. We agreed that art had become too commercial, but still, if you wanted to buy a truly beautiful piece, there was so much to choose from.

He told me that I was too quiet, that I had interesting things to say if I would just speak, if I weren't so hungry to listen. I was too busy being terrified, I admitted to him. I wasn't normally like this, I tried to say. He made it easy for me. He parted the waves of conversation so that I could be more assertive. He referenced the possibility of putting me in an upcoming group show at his gallery, where he would introduce me to his clientele. Did that mean I was one of his clients, officially? I wasn't sure.

And so, when he called one Saturday morning to tell me that he had a brilliant idea for me, I had wild hope about it.

"Why don't you spend a few weeks with me at my house on Long Island?" he began.

"Really?"

"I have a studio there that various artists have used, over the years. I'm sure you wouldn't mind a change of scene . . . ," he went on. "There's a huge artist-based community in the Hamptons. Jackson Pollock . . . Mary Abbott . . . Joan Mitchell . . . Elaine de Kooning . . . all had their studios out there. There's something special about the light . . . It's hard to describe. Or hard for me, as not an artist, to describe." He laughed. "You really have to see it for yourself."

"But what about my job?"

"The whole point of that job was to meet someone like me! And now you have, so . . ."

I had already said yes, in my head, from the moment I picked up the phone. But he didn't know that, so I let him continue selling me on it.

"It'll be like doing an artist's residency in the Hamptons."

"Sounds ideal," I replied calmly. Then, less calmly: "I mean, yes! Of course! I'd love to!"

"Great. I'll pick you up tomorrow night?"

"Tomorrow night?" I said. "Wow. Soon. Okay."

The thought seemed to have spontaneously come to him, yet there was also something urgent about it.

"Okay," I said. "Tomorrow. I can't wait."

As soon as I was off the phone, I went to tell Amanda. She was headed out for a walk around the North Woods, so I went with her.

It was at least twenty blocks before we got to the park, but it was worth it.

"I'm going to East Hampton tomorrow," I said, as soon as we hit green. "For a few weeks. With Julian."

We climbed uphill, in the most forested area. "You are?" she said, her arms flailing at her sides.

"He wants me to spend a few days at his place there. Something about the light . . . I don't know. I'm going to check it out. It's a great place to work, he says."

"But what about your job?" she asked, slightly winded.

We walked up a formation of rocks until we got to the top, where we stopped for a minute to rest.

"I don't know . . . I think I'm on the verge of something happening here, with Julian, and I really want to prioritize that. He told me he's going to put me in a group show at his gallery, which means he's taking this seriously, at least. I won't have time for anything else. He wants three pieces from me."

"Okay."

"You don't believe me?"

"I said okay!"

"You seem questioning."

"I'm not really *questioning*. Doesn't it seem just a little bit . . . odd to you?"

"No. It's really, probably, as an artist, the least odd thing I could do."

"Okay. Not odd. Maybe odd is the wrong word. It just seems a little obvious. He's an older, established guy. You're young and innocent and needing of things from him."

"Yes, I know. I'm not too naive to understand. I just . . . don't think it matters. He's interested in my work, and the attraction, whether it's there or not, simply doesn't matter to me. I mean, what is the difference between being attracted to someone and being attracted to their work?" I took a short breath before I could get out the rest. "It's an invisible line, in many ways."

She worked in a different industry. If her boss invited her to his house, it would be cause for a sexual harassment claim. They had such thick files of paper between them and what they did. There was nothing personal about it. In fact, it was deliberately impersonal. Judge. Your Honor. Witness. Your client. What your client is trying to say.

She wrapped her arms around me and pulled me in. "I trust your judgment," she said. "I don't know him at all."

I felt myself relax. "It'll be worthwhile, I think," I said.

"I'm not standing in your way."

What she didn't realize was that she *was* standing in my way, just by questioning it.

On our way home, we stopped for roast beef sandwiches with mustard and ate them at the counter of the shop as somebody's dog yipped at our ankles. We went to a bakery. I got a slice of chocolate cake. Amanda got carrot, but made me take a bite of hers because the piece was so large. Whatever Amanda got always tasted better to me. I could go to the same place and order the same thing without her, but it would never taste as good. I couldn't re-create it. We walked home, past the fruit and vegetable stands and a woman slicing mango into cups.

When we got home, we sat on our brownstone's front steps as a nearby car played Cat Stevens. A Mister Softee truck came barreling down our street at such speed, driving as swiftly and aggressively as an ambulance, and we laughed, as it went off to attend to some ice cream emergency.

I went into Amanda's bedroom a few times that night, while packing. And as we discussed it more, I could tell that she was warming to the idea, writing it off as a harmless and temporary few weeks on Long Island that could be easily rectified if it all went to shit.

Julian picked me up in an expensive car of some kind. I was more impressed, out loud, than I really wanted to be. It was as if there were some instinctual place inside me that said: *Be impressed by his car. He'll like that.*

"Is this yours?" I said, and he nodded but also, as he got out of the driver's seat to open the door for me, gave me a look, like, *who else's would it be?*

We made it out of the city quickly, but then began crawling along the Long Island Expressway—red brake lights dotting the highway as far as I could see. A steady stream of music played through the car's speakers. To pass the time, I taught him how to seduce someone in Portuguese.

"We say *gatinha,* 'kitty,' for girl, and *gatinho* for guy. *Gata* means cat, for a woman. *Gato* for a man. Yes, when we think someone is beautiful, we compare them to a cat, as in 'what's up, kitty'—'*e aí, gatinha.*' A conversation starter is usually 'How are you doing?'—'*Como você está?*'—then, you add '*gato.*' Of course it depends on the environment where the flirtation takes place, and the level of people. It's not that different from the United States, but instead of saying 'babe,' we say '*gata.*'"

"See," he said, "when I want to seduce someone in America, I usually avoid mentioning cats altogether."

I tried to picture it. Julian seducing someone. I wanted it to be me, but I also *didn't* want it to be me. Because I now knew, after attending countless events with him, just how many of the beautiful women of Manhattan he'd dated. He was always introducing me to someone, and then giving me the backstory. Part of me wanted to prove to him that I was better than all these women, just as an experiment. But a larger part of me said: *No, Sophie. Not this time.* I wanted to maintain our professional bond. I couldn't help but notice that none of the women he'd dated had become wildly successful artists, and that was the objective here.

Eventually, the large highway turned into a smaller one. We passed by luxury car dealerships, stores with lighting and bathroom fixtures, seafood shops. The roads got increasingly green. More and more manicured. More Jeeps. Rows and rows of privet hedges hiding country cottage–esque mansions. So many Jeeps. I didn't see the beach but I could feel that it was nearby.

We took a turn and entered the woods. Trees in every direction. Every now and then, a house. This street didn't have the grandness of the others. But it was quirky. Each house was either painted a strange color, or had a mailbox in the shape of a pig, or an iron gate meant to look like two smiley faces touching. Another had a sign over the driveway, THE LAST DUDE RANCH. It was as if a certain type of community lived on this street, as if the buyers of these houses had gotten together to make sure that their cluster of luxury developed differently.

"This is the more artistic side of the Hamptons," he said. "It's a little weird." He pulled onto an unmarked road, and then kept driving through the woods. "The Hamptons is very beautiful if you can ignore most of the people and the seventy-dollar lobster salad."

It was getting dark. I couldn't see anything anymore. I felt, suddenly, a little uneasy. *Where was he taking me?*

Finally, a house came into view. It was modern, with gray slate where natural wood shingles could have been. There was no driveway. Just a front yard with a single tree and blooming pink-and-white flowers. Slate stepping-stones led toward the house.

"De Kooning moved here from the city to get some peace and isolation," he said, as we got out of the car. "But then he painted a tempestuous sea with this active churning quality. Have you seen it? I'm not so sure he found the calm that he was looking for."

I smiled. "Maybe he had the lobster salad." When I got out of the car, the air felt different than in the city—cooler and slightly thinner.

He lifted my bag from his trunk, as well as his own, and we walked inside the house. He immediately started turning on lights and air conditioning. Meanwhile, I stood and looked around at his house, which was somewhat of a fantasy. It wasn't a house. It was an artist's loft, but with multiple levels, connected by a winding set of large concrete stairs. A sculpture under the staircase in the foyer filled the house with the sound of running water, reverberating off the ceilings and polished wood floors.

"That sound . . . ," I said.

"Oh, the waterfall? Isn't it great?"

"Yes."

"I wanted the house to be cleansing, and water is pretty much the most cleansing device we have. It's rebirth, spiritual, sensuous. I don't think there's anything more calming than water, how it renews us, and just clarifies something."

I smiled. "Sure. I like a good shower. I used to take baths every day after school. Even in elementary school, I felt like I needed to cleanse, from my very stressful day of moving blocks around and testing gravity."

"Exactly. It doesn't have to be anything big. A shower, pool, river, ocean. It all works. It is this perfect convergence of what is so powerful in art and in life."

"Oh"—I nodded—"I agree. I've had *many* stressful moments in my life washed away by jumping into the ocean. You get out and your outlook is completely different. Would you like to know my favorite Portuguese expression?"

He nodded.

"*Tempestade em copo d'água.* It means, literally, 'storm in a cup of water,' basically to make a huge deal out of nothing. Whenever I'm stressed about something, I think of the visual of this *tiny* cup of water with a storm inside of it and it makes me feel better."

"I like that a lot. I may use it myself."

"It's yours."

There were very few pieces of furniture, but the ones that were there were black. Marble and leather. There was a severity to the decor. All the black among white walls. But it was simpler, in a way, easier to see the beauty.

He showed me the rest of the house.

"I think of furniture as sculpture," he said, pointing out a chair from Germany. "I wish that I didn't. I wish I could just say 'Well, a chair's a chair.'"

"Thank you. My roommate does not understand this. I was deliberating between four different couches . . . for a long time. Even though, for most of my life, I thought couches were so pointless."

"More of a bed person?"

"Always."

I examined everything. It maybe wasn't the coolest, suavest thing to do, but I couldn't help myself. His bedroom had black satin sheets.

"How very Kardashian of you," I said, and he looked down, a little sheepish.

My eyes were feeling itchy. I kept scratching them, making it worse. I was hit by a wave of something. Tiredness, maybe? I felt a few layers removed from reality, but couldn't trace it to anything.

"Make yourself comfortable," he said, when we returned to his kitchen.

I took off my sandals. He broke the seal on a bottle of water and poured me a glass.

An hour later, two steaks and a pile of asparagus were out of the oven and on the table. I looked out the window above his sink, at the serene darkness.

"Your house is incredible," I said. "I noticed you don't have any art on the walls."

He smiled. "I haven't shown you the whole house yet."

"Is there more?" I asked, and then got up to take another tissue from a box in the bathroom. I had gone through half of it during dinner.

"Are you doing okay?" he asked.

"Yeah. I just . . . I think I might be coming down with something."

After dinner, we walked down an arched hallway that was so long, it felt like a monastery.

"This is what I'm most proud of," he said, and then opened the door to what I can only describe as a gigantic greenhouse. Gone wild.

"My living gallery," he said.

It was the largest indoor collection of flowers I'd ever seen in my life. He gave me a tour. There were large purple pom-poms with thick stems, something yellow called a licorice plant, a yellow and red flower called a sunrise rose. Thick leaves of green and purple, called sky hawk, apparently, and little yellow buds that looked like tropical fruit. There was an entire section dedicated to these large, circular flowers of red and purple and white that looked like pinwheels. I resisted the urge to spin them. There was lavender from Provence, something called tanzanite. Karma pink corona. Boom-boom white. He told me about Montauk daisies, how they were actually from a coastal part of Japan and not, in fact, from Montauk.

"I can't believe you have all this," I said, scratching my throat, as I examined a long tubular flower that was dangling over the edge of its container.

"Forty-five different kinds, from every continent," he said. I kept close to him. "This one is called nicotiana. They're not fragrant during the day, but incredibly fragrant at night because they're pollinated by night moths."

"Night moths, huh?"

He smiled. "My apartment in the city is my working life. That's where I have my Picasso lithograph and my photograph by Man Ray. This is my break from all that. I find it hard to relax while surrounded by the same things that make me money, if that makes sense."

I sneezed. "Sure," I said, and then sneezed again. "I can understand that."

He looked at me sympathetically.

"At least now I know why my eyes have been watering since I got here," I said, blowing my nose into a tissue.

"Are you allergic to anything?"

"Just . . . pollen. Grass. Flowers. Sunshine."

He looked at me with a note of sadness. "Most plants, though beautiful, have some toxicity."

"There's always a catch . . ." I sneezed, and then held up my palm, with the tissue crumpled up inside it. "It's okay . . . I'm okay."

I noticed something flying. I ducked.

"What is that?" I swatted at the space above my head.

"Oh . . . don't do that," he said. "Those are my bees."

He stuck out his finger and I expected a single bee to land on it, but it didn't. "'*Those are my bees*'?" I said, glaring at him.

"They've been bred at the Institute of Bee Health in Lucerne, Switzerland. Don't worry. They're pollinators and pose no risk to humans. They don't even have stingers. They're friendly."

"There is no such thing as a friendly bee."

"I keep them here to pollinate the gallery, so to speak."

I shook my head. "You are a few tweaks away from being normal."

He smiled at me from across his indoor garden. "Thank you."

He showed me the studio where I was to work. It was a converted barn next to his house with 17-foot-high glass walls, and some gently used supplies in a crate in the center of the room. Along one wall, there were framed pieces of art leaning against each other, still in their brown paper wrappings.

"Artists send me these things." He started rifling through the artwork. "I should probably get rid of them."

"No! Don't!" I saw how neatly his address was printed on each one. I imagined that I could have easily been the one addressing, terrified that it might not make it to him. That it might be the fault of a lazy mailman. Of all things.

"I don't have time to go through it all."

"But that seems like such a waste," I said, rather involuntarily, and then decided to use them as motivation. If these packages could talk . . .

I put down a tarp and built a canvas and spent the next few days in the studio, trying to work. I primed the canvas, laid out my colors, but my damn allergies kept taking me out of my own head and I mean that literally. There was me and there was where my head was and the two were nowhere near each other. What began as the sniffles turned into a faint headache, a low fever. My nose was a running faucet. My eyes were sore from all the scratching, but not as bad as my throat, which was in a perpetual state of itching where I could not scratch. In order to escape the pollen, I went out for runs. Just your average three runs a day. Totally normal. Each time I snuck out, I called Amanda from the middle of the woods, where there was non-floral air and shockingly perfect cell reception.

She said, "Just leave already. How long can you suffer?" To her, this was the only sensible thing to do. Show my cards. Head back to the city where I had not a single ally and I could walk the streets of Chelsea alone.

No. This wasn't suffering. *That* was suffering. No, I would fucking sneeze if I had to.

"I can't *leave,* Amanda. Last night, we ate lobster rolls with OSGEMEOS!"

"I don't know what that means, *Sophie*!"

"They're brothers and Brazilian street artists and I got to talk to them about art and São Paulo and what inspiration can be found from a matchbook and it was the most amazing dinner of my life."

It was odd to be on the other end of this type of call. Usually, Amanda was the one complaining about a medical condition and I was the one saying, "I wouldn't worry about it. I'm not the least bit concerned. Tetanus from a metal lock? Forget it. It was more like a scrape than a puncture wound? Well, that's the downside of googling things. I think it has to be a rusty nail. When are they testing you for it? Just relax, please, in the meantime."

"Well, then, keep your friends close and your tissues closer," she said.

"I just keep going out for runs."

"If that works, then . . ."

I lowered my voice. "I had to tell him that I was training for a marathon."

She laughed.

"You know how on those allergy commercials there is always some person running away from a giant flower? I am literally that person."

I was pacing within the trees, enjoying the sound of the crunch under my feet. I turned around every so often, to make sure a small animal wasn't behind me, also enjoying the crunch.

"Can't you buy some medicine on one of your trips into town?"

"*I have.* But it's not working. Because allergy medication is meant to protect you against the occasional stroll through a garden. Not living full-time inside one."

She was laughing.

"He keeps feeding me spaghetti and meatballs for dinner."

"And the problem is?"

"He thinks I need to refuel because of all the running! I had to hide some in my napkin."

"Are you serious? Why?"

"I can't eat it all! Based on the amount of running I'm supposedly doing, I should be consuming, like, eight thousand calories a day!"

"So you're hiding pasta in your purse?"

"Basically."

"This is the strangest version of *Lady and the Tramp* I've ever heard."

I sighed. "I sensed people were getting tired of the original."

I went on: "I took a two-hour nap on the beach because I can't sleep in there. I'm taking so many showers that my skin itches and I can't tell whether it's because of the showering or a reaction to the bees."

"What bees?" she asked, prematurely horrified.

"Oh. I didn't mention this? He's got Swiss bees. Living in his home."

"What do you mean Swiss bees?"

I yelled, "I mean *bees*! From Switzerland! Bees that would be neutral in a time of war!"

"You're making this up."

"I am not, unfortunately. I am, however, going to have to fake an injury when I get back to the city, just to explain why I'm not running the New York City Marathon this year."

I STUCK IT OUT. I developed some sort of immunity to the atmosphere over time. And my long days in the studio began to pay off. I sat in front of a bunch of dirty rags and a half-finished painting of an amethyst that was looking not half bad. I would only break for lunch, which I would eat with Julian. What he did all day, I wasn't sure. I asked him for a hair dryer once to speed up the drying process and he was conducting business at the kitchen counter with his laptop open, surrounded by espresso cups and a half-eaten croissant. His car seemed to come and go from the driveway. I didn't like to check because I felt lonely there, in the middle of the woods, without him. Whereas if I didn't check, I assumed that he was around.

It was the first time in my life that I had a proper studio, which meant the first time in my life I didn't have to worry about making a mess. I didn't have to think about annoying someone by washing my brushes in the sink. I didn't have to worry about the crud and residue and splatter when I poured out my buckets, about getting it on the walls or floor.

Julian and I took late afternoon breaks to go to the beach and talk about light—lake light versus pond light, Venetian versus Dutch, often surrounded by a pink and lavender sky.

"Long Island is based on an east-northeast axis, so the light bounces, because the sun comes up over the ocean and goes down over the sound," he explained.

"Refracted light," I said. "It has a softer quality. It mixes better in the eye, somehow."

I laid down on the sand and closed my eyes and heard nothing but the sound of the ocean and him turning the pages of his book. There was a Beach Boys song about vibrations playing in my head.

We went to a cemetery that dated back to 1911. Apparently, Jackson Pollock was the first artist buried there. A five-ton boulder indicated his grave. We walked around and saw the stones of Lee Krasner, Elaine de Kooning, and Alfonso Ossorio. The curator Henry Geldzahler. He told me about how Willem de Kooning refused to be buried there because he didn't want to be with the other artists.

"I understand. Brazilians take burials seriously. There are no flowers or food, and the mourning period lasts much longer. My friend's parents missed our high school graduation because a burial plot had become available in a very sought-after graveyard and they had to go put down a deposit."

"I just want to be set out to sea."

"Of course you do."

He took me on his boat. Came out of his bedroom wearing a jogging outfit that he explained was entirely wind-resistant.

"Do you want to borrow a pair of wind pants?" he asked.

"Can't I just wear my regular pants?" I looked down at my jean shorts.

"You can. This just enhances the experience. Takes away the encumbrances."

"Another eccentricity," I replied. "Are you sure you aren't an artist?"

We spent nights eating in town, at a restaurant by the beach, another next to a harbor, looking out at rows and rows of sailboats.

Some of those dinners were just the two of us. Others involved a seemingly endless stream of his friends—artists, critics, curators.

He came inside the studio one morning. He walked right up to the canvas. I couldn't stop him. It was too late.

"Well," he said. "This is coming along great."

"You think?"

"I do."

I told him everything I was thinking about. What I had expected and what it had become. He said, "Well, I think you're ready for your first show."

And when will that be? I wanted to say but didn't. He'd tell me.

"I think you may also be ready for a break?" he asked.

"Desperately. Where are we going today?"

"It's a surprise."

Town was quiet but for a pack of guys riding motorcycles in T-shirts. We drove through town and over a bridge and into another wooded section of the island. We turned onto an unmarked driveway and drove past a tranquil pond with a single swan swimming in it.

"Okay. The swan is overkill," I said, and he smiled from behind the steering wheel.

The house appeared. A little bit Asian. A little bit Mediterranean. A little bit the rustic barn not unlike the other houses.

"Just tell me! Where are we? Before I walk in and make a fool of myself." I raised my eyebrows.

"We are about to visit the studio of April Fisher and Stephen Bula."

April Fisher was a painter and sculptor. Neo-Expressionist turned New Old Master. She was married to Stephen Bula, a landscape artist. Maybe the best landscape painter of his generation. Together, they were an art world power couple. I'd studied them both in college.

They were so famous that they didn't seem like real people that might live in a house.

"Não acredito." I shook my head. "I don't know how to repay you for this week. And just . . . everything you've done for me."

"I do." He smiled. "Make a million dollars for my gallery."

"Sure," I said. "No problem." And for a brief moment, I actually believed that it was possible.

The first thing I noticed about the house was the steel-mullioned windows. So well done that, in a moment not influenced by my allergies, I felt like I might have stopped breathing. April opened the door and I think I said words but there's no way to know for sure. Inside the house, there were sculptures and plants placed sporadically. There was a library contained within a pristine glass box that hovered above the living room. I could see cast-iron shelves.

"Were those shelves by any chance designed by Stanford White?" I said.

"Yes, they were. You've got a good eye! Julian Schnabel restored a Stanford White house in Montauk after having rented Warhol and Morrissey's place there for the better part of a decade. I was just copying him."

We sat in their dining room, which had a crystal pirate ship chandelier above a long table of pine. Then they took us to their studios. We had to go outside, and up a series of stairs to a sunken platform flanked by two studios. A breezeway connected the house and the studios. In between, there was a cast bronze that I recognized, by Fisher.

"*Falling Woman,*" I mumbled. It was one of my favorite sculptures. I'd seen it for the first time in Italy.

Once inside April's studio, I took in rows of paintings, sculptures, some finished, some not quite, surrounded by crates of materials.

The view from the glass wall of her studio was of a garden, a small bird bath surrounded by stones. With Julian and Stephen on the other side of the room, April and I got to spend some time talking, just the two of us.

"I try to listen to the birds while I work," she said. "I don't like to have it completely quiet."

"Oh, I don't either," I said. "I'll keep a fan running, if I'm desperate. In college, I used to keep the show *Friends* playing on a loop on my computer in the background while I worked."

She smiled. "Really?"

"Isn't that strange? I just felt like it fed my brain this stream of brightly colored happiness, which freed me up, in a way, to go to as dark of a place as I needed to, on canvas."

She gave it some thought. "You know what? I understand that."

"Do you go back to the city often?"

"I do. I have to have a continually shifting environment. Either it's noise or color or some stimulus. I go back to the city every few weeks. I can't stay out here indefinitely staring at a garden. I need to have . . . unpredictable . . . social encounters."

Was that a fancy word for "affairs"?

"Do you have a studio in the city as well?"

"I do. It's extremely meditative, for me, to be in the country, but that's only because it's fleeting."

I nodded.

"Where's your studio?" she asked.

I smiled. "In my living room. It's always been my living room. Or my bedroom."

"Ah, well. You're young. You'll move around. You're not married, are you?"

"No. I came close! Bought the dress and everything. But no."

"Trust me. You're better off," she said, eyeing her husband. "I know it's so overly indulgent, but I always tell Stephen that I need to be able to pick up and get out of here. Luckily, I have a partner who is very supportive. He lets me be that person who can move, for the sake of having a deeper toolbox to work from. There's so much to inspire you, as an artist. The world is so limitless if you want to learn and see and grow. I think you almost need to be rootless, as an artist, which can be difficult for some people."

"I think a certain amount of root is helpful." I laughed, feeling very young, all of a sudden. "I've learned that I can't just travel the world without a place to hang my hat."

"True, but if you stay in one place, you'll find yourself empty. An artist needs to constantly refill that well. Traveling and meeting new people is one way to do that, but you don't *have* to travel, as long as you're having new experiences."

"Oh, I'm always wandering!" I said. "I've lived all over."

"That's great. You need to feel activated. Thinking about where you are, the need to make a living, corrupts the process. If you think too much about those things, you might not be as experimental or daring."

I turned to her. "I live with a friend. We have a good arrangement."

"Ah! That's perfect! You can come and go as you please."

But I wondered. *Can I come and go as I please?* Amanda would never actually stop me from going anywhere, but I could always tell what she wanted, and she wanted me at home. Unless she wasn't there. Then she was fine with me being wherever. She didn't like being in the house alone. It gave her too much time to think, to destroy herself from the inside out. And I told myself that wasn't my problem, but *wasn't it*? We never addressed the issue directly. I'd be thinking about going out and then she'd suggest a movie and the scones she'd picked up from the bakery, holding the white bag up triumphantly, and I'd just sort of brush it off and call her scone-dependent. But the guilt was what kept me there, more than a few times. *What had I missed?*

We heard a knock at the door and then a tall man wearing dark glasses came into the studio. He appeared Middle Eastern and looked somewhat disheveled but upon closer inspection, like his loafers might be Gucci.

"This is our gallery," she said to us, pointing to the man, and he gave us a thumbs-up from across the room. "We show exclusively with him. Much to Julian's dismay." Julian held up his hand to wave her off, as if he hadn't noticed. But clearly it bothered him. *Is this why we're here? To make a play?* If so, this man showing up definitely wasn't part of the plan. Suddenly, I felt foolish, thinking that everything was about my education.

"How was Istanbul?" April asked the man.

"It was okay. The show was kind of loose."

They continued to talk. I got distracted by a bookshelf with binders and books on it. Each shelf had a handwritten label on it. *Guggenheim. Works on Paper. Paris. Paintings. Exhibitions. Fiberglass. All Exhibit Materials.* The relics of a long career.

"Who is this?"

I turned to find the Middle Eastern man staring at me.

He looked at April and then Julian, and then me.

"She's an artist," Julian said. His eyes seemed to turn a shade darker.

"What kind of art?"

"She's a painter. Very personal. Conceptual. Provocative."

Very personal. Conceptual. Provocative. I made a mental note, stored his words away, prepared to recite them back to myself the next time I was standing in front of a piece of canvas that had gone horribly wrong.

"Can I take a look?" he said, and I looked at him without moving or speaking. He must have thought, because I was here, that I was of some value. The closer I stood to April, the more talented I seemed.

"Oh, you mean . . . photos? On my phone?" He looked at me as though, of course, that was what he meant.

I removed my phone from my bag and showed him my first gem painting, and then the second, and then the third, from Julian's studio. My eyes flickered up at Julian, who was staring at me. I explained the concept, briefly.

"I like it," the man said. "It's not overthought. You know, we have an upcoming salon, and we're looking for new talent to add . . . The last young artist who worked for me just got one of his pieces selected for the Rothschild collection."

"That's marvelous," April said.

"She's with me," Julian interjected. "I'm showing her work."

After that, Julian seemed eager to leave. In the car, he was quiet.

"He can't sell your work," he said. "He's pure talk." His voice was bitter.

"I wasn't going to . . ."

"The Rothschild collection." He rolled his eyes. "Don't worry about collectors. Collectors don't buy what they like. They buy what they're told. The Rothschilds are going to put that young artist's work in storage and never see it again. It's just a status point, for them. Billionaires trading trophies."

I was quiet, unsure of what to say.

"You don't want to be a part of that. You're pure and talented and you deserve a real audience."

"Oh, but the things I could do with a billion dollars!" I said. "I'm kidding. And you don't have to compliment me. He wasn't seriously interested in me or my work."

"Are you kidding? He all but licked his lips."

Again, I really liked the vision. I just didn't know if it was true.

When we got back to his place, he was rummaging around, pulling drawers open and banging them closed. I pretended to busy myself with undoing the straps of my sandals, removing a pair of gold hoops from my ears and placing them on the counter. I twisted my hair into a bun. I felt a flicker of alarm.

Amanda would have said at this point that I was being held hostage and beginning to develop positive feelings for my captor. And I did have this feeling of connection toward him that was at least somewhat based on fear. Each time I saw a trace of his anger, I never wanted to see it again, which left me in the uncomfortable position of trying to keep him happy.

Baixa a bola. Be less cocky, which, of course, I couldn't tell him to do. *Go for the ego,* that was all.

I smiled, robotically. "This is a nice place to come home to," I said, and then sat down on the couch.

He stopped moving. "You know what we should do?" He turned toward me.

"What?'

"Go take a shower. I'll take one too." He smiled. "And then let's reconvene here and smoke a joint."

"Okay . . . ," I said.

"Wait a minute," he said, and then left me standing there in his living room. When he returned, he handed me a bathrobe.

"Put this on after. No clothes. I know. I know. But it makes the effects of smoking feel so much more primal. Just . . ." He smiled. "Trust me."

I hesitated. "All right," I said, taking the bundle of soft, fluffy white fabric. It was folded tightly into itself. I don't know why but I suddenly found my eyes focused on his.

"It's nothing sexual," he said. "Don't worry. It's an experience. You'll see."

"I do love an experience . . ."

I went into my room and was careful to lock the door. I stopped and stood for a moment, staring at the ground. I started whispering to myself. *Okay. How do I play this one? Nothing sexual? Who does he think he's kidding? Okay. It's okay. I can handle this. Just remain composed.* I took my clothes off in the bathroom and turned the water on. There was steam emanating from the glass box. I went in, stood on the tile floor, and let the hot water beat down on me. But all my concerns were not drowning out, as they usually did. Instead, they were getting louder. *Julian. April. My alliance with Amanda.* All these conflicting thoughts were swirling.

It was the least relaxing shower I'd ever taken. As I got all sudsed up, I started to get all freaked out. *How close is the nearest other person to here? Is this how I get murdered? Oh God. Have I become Amanda? Should I call her?* No. My work. *My work.* I told myself to focus on what was real. My talent. My career. *I am going to go out there and I am going to ask him what his plans are for my work. Enough of this nonsense. If I had to, I could be tough in a bathrobe.*

I put the robe on and walked across his house, my hair wet and combed and tucked into the collar. He saw me and stared at the sash of the robe.

"Oh," he said. "Hold on a second. I just have to get the joint."

I was brutally aware of my own nakedness as I sat there, naked, in his living room.

While I was gone, he had opened all the windows and put on

music. I sat on the couch, my thoughts still running. I had no intention of sleeping with him, but something about this made me feel like I already had. Maybe that was the point.

He sat down next to me. I stuck out my hand, intending for him to pass me the joint. Instead, he held it. He kept hold of my hand and didn't move it away. He touched my palm, ran his thumb against the top of it. I was completely still. He didn't stop looking at me.

I looked around the room cautiously, and then said, "I don't want to go there." Our hands broke apart. A shot of adrenaline moved through me. "You've been really good to me, I just . . ."

He put his lips to mine, pushing me back into the couch. I turned my head so that his lips hit the pillow. I looked at him.

"Did you hear me?" I asked.

"Yeah," he said. He seemed surprised.

"I don't think you did," I said.

He paused. "Then why are you here?" he said, but the words felt like they had their own velocity, like they traveled into me at a speed far greater than anything he'd ever said before. He was now a person free-falling a thousand stories off the roof of a building—that was how fast my opinion of him was going. As fast as you could fall.

"I just don't want to complicate things," I said. "It's been really heartening, to me, to have your support, and I don't want to confuse that with something else."

He was silent, sullen. Then his mood appeared to brighten.

"What about if you painted something naked and I watched?"

And then, I started to laugh. And laugh. I laughed like I'd been holding it in. I couldn't stop. My eyes were tearing up. I don't know what came over me. The longer it went on, I felt all the tension escaping my body. I allowed myself to keep going, to forget who I was talking to, even once it was past the point of being funny, even once I had made my point, I still couldn't stop.

"I would stop," he said, "if I were you."

I turned to him. His form was the same, but his eyes had changed. There was a vacancy I didn't recognize. I covered his hand with my hand. "I was willing to put up with the flowers. The bees. The showers. I've wanted to be an artist since I was a little girl and there is a lot that this grown-up woman would do for that little girl." And then I said, "But not this. Because that little girl . . . would be so disappointed."

"I think maybe it's time for you to leave."

I smiled tightly. "I don't get it. Was I here just to have sex with you? Because I could have sworn there was another purpose."

He half opened his mouth, as if about to speak, but then closed it again. He stared off into space. Finally, he spoke. "Just go," he said. "I'm not interested in some girl painting rocks." And then, he looked at me, knowing that he'd gone too far. His voice softened. "I am absolutely sure that it is the wrong thing for you, and for me, to represent you without a clue as to what you're doing."

Everything inside me disintegrated. Gone. Gone. Gone. I had no ability to say what I was thinking, which was: *But . . . you did . . . have a clue . . . at some point?* It felt like the room was moving, and I had nothing to hold on to. All I could think now was: *Get out of here.* Get back to the city. Amanda. Our home. Something that was mine. I went into the studio, afraid to touch or even look at the canvas. I put it under my arm without so much as glancing at it.

A mere twenty minutes later, I was gone with the wind pants, standing at the side of the road with my suitcase and what used to be some very conceptually interesting art, waiting for a stranger to drive me back to the city.

On the drive home, I thought about my work. Why had I even chosen to illustrate a contrast? What was more bitter than the dualities of life, how a person could possess such charms, could seem so dedicated to you, and yet turn out to be such a magnificent jerk? They adhered to no principle, no law. From friend to foe. Just like that. How quickly it could happen, too. My neediness was what killed me. It was ugly. It was a big, black splotch on the canvas. Behind all those careful, careful words of mine, all so revering of him. Did he enjoy it, or had I lost his respect a long time ago? What else could I have done? My neediness was what weakened me. But I couldn't help it. I needed the fuck out of him.

The funny thing was—when I got a glimpse of the city skyline from the highway, I felt like I was seeing it for the first time. Seventeen years old, with my heart racing, my palms damp, sitting on a bus, a suitcase bouncing next to me. The skyscrapers weren't just the tops of buildings. They were hope that on this island, there would be beauty for me to collect, and that, after all and at once, I'd be able to make something of my own. I should have punched him.

15

Amanda

With Sophie away in East Hampton, I felt free to invite Nick over to our place. He came straight after work. We slept there every night, but I told him that once she returned, we'd be more reasonable about it. I didn't tell him what I already knew—we'd have to.

No part of me wanted to tell him about owning this apartment. I still didn't want to tell him about the alliance. I wanted him to see me in a certain way—young and available and all his for the taking, not hardened to some resolution that didn't involve him.

But that was all in the future. I pushed it out of my brain. I spent early evenings cutting up strawberries and drinking iced coffee and waiting for him to come over. When he got there, we would kiss all over the kitchen. It felt illicit.

"I'm glad we only started dating now," he said.

"Why's that?" I rested my head against his chest.

"Because I would have failed out of medical school."

And then we were upstairs, where my clothes were everywhere from nights of doing exactly this, then running off to work and not taking care of anything else. Sheets twisted. It was a spectacular mess. He pushed me backward slightly until I was down on the bed. And then, he got up.

He started to look around. I followed him.

"So, do you guys rent this place or what?" He walked around the area between our bedrooms, peeked into Sophie's room from the doorframe.

I felt a jolt of tension. My mind scrambled for an answer. "Sophie and Abe got it . . . They were going to fix it up. But then Sophie walked out, day of the wedding, and . . ."

I will still editing the story, in my head, even as I spoke, trying to stick the lies together with as much truth as possible.

"Seriously? Day of?"

"Well, it wasn't a runaway bride situation . . . actually, it was. So then they had to sell it, and Sophie was upset, because she loved this place so much. So I bought Abe's half. It was a great deal, and . . ."

"Wait. Hold on. So she left this guy at the altar?"

"Imagine!"

And then I realized: This was my way out. This actually made sense. These were my litigation skills, on full display. He was now consumed with Sophie and her escape at the buzzer. I gave him the blow-by-blow. He always said he wanted to see me in court.

"That's quite a story," he said, and then went back to examining. "It looks completely renovated. Did you fix it up?"

"Um, well . . ." I pretended to be busy making the bed. "Sophie and Abe renovated it, before the wedding." I swallowed. My throat was tight. "So, what do you think for dinner?" I said, fluffing a pillow.

"But you guys do own it . . . together?"

"Yeah . . ."

"That's a pretty big commitment, at this age, don't you think?"

I froze. "Is it?"

"It's nice! Don't get me wrong. It's a really nice place. I'm just surprised you'd still want to have a roommate."

I scratched the back of my neck repeatedly. "Financially, it seemed like too good of a deal to turn down. And I got to help my closest friend." I was suddenly sweating. "Okay. Investigation over."

He ignored me. "When did you buy it again?"

"Umm . . . November-ish."

"That's not that long ago."

"No."

He didn't say much after that. He didn't explore. Except when I felt a strange presence in the house and made him walk around, the way a burglar might, to see what it would sound like from my bedroom.

The bed became our entire living space. The night table a place where we stacked plates and glasses. Occasionally I sat in the window and dangled my feet outside and commented on the still-light sky, or if there was music coming from the sidewalk.

We ordered in dinner. A three-block walk to the bakery was our only outing. It was the last days of summer and the heat was at an outrageous high and left us with a kind of paralysis. Leaving the air conditioning to go to the sweltering streets or subway platforms felt impossible. The trash cans overflowing with cups and cans and bottles. Strangers saying "stay cool" to each other. When work was done for the day, we didn't have energy for much else. There's only so much "else" you can fit in when you spend all your free time under the covers, talking about childhood mishaps and whether chocolate is overrated. I traced his forearm with my finger, and I knew—I was brutally, brutally done for.

One Saturday morning, he brought over groceries from the bodega. "This should last us through the weekend."

"What about that concert in the park? With your friends?" I asked.

"Eh," he said, folding his arms across his bare chest.

"What about that street festival thing?"

"Maybe next week."

"Lawn party? Kickball league? Rooftop cinema club?"

"Have you lost your fucking mind?"

"Maybe we should have a picnic?"

"Feels like a lot of work for two people who just argued over who had to go to the kitchen."

I stretched, my hair in a ratty braid. "Maybe we should leave the house though, today?"

He looked at me skeptically. "You go take a boat ride around Manhattan. Report back. I'll be here."

"I ordered a pair of slippers," I said. "So those are coming today."

He nodded. "There you go. Booked solid."

So, we lay in my bed, well into the afternoon, watching baseball and then quietly reading. Or, at least, I was quiet. Nick kept sighing.

"Does anything ever happen in this thing?" I had given him one of my books. I felt he needed a break from reading books with titles such as *Humans: A Brief History of Mankind*. He really went large-scale with his selections.

"What do you mean, *happen*?"

"Well, so far it's just an old guy staring at a boy on the beach." My copy of *Death in Venice* fell to the floor.

"It's soulful."

"It's bo-ring."

"It's Thomas Mann!"

"So?"

"Oh, go watch something blow up on television," I said, grabbing the novel from the floor. "Philistine."

"I'll watch one of your movies, as long as it's not utterly ridiculous."

"That eliminates almost all of them."

"At least I don't listen to German audiobooks before bed."

"That was Nietzsche!"

"It's like falling asleep next to Hitler gearing up for a big speech in the morning."

I heard the sound of the front door opening. I grabbed Nick's arm.

"Did you hear that?"

"What?" he said.

"You didn't hear anything?" I said. We were quiet. Then there were footsteps.

"Yeah," he said, sitting up on his elbows. "I heard it. Do you have a weapon?"

"A *weapon*?"

"I'm sure it's nothing, but just in case. Do you have a bat? Or a knife?"

"I don't keep a *knife* in my bedroom."

"I guess that's a good sign," he whispered, as he stood and crept out of the room.

I heard the sound of a loud groan, downstairs. Sophie's groan. "Oh," I said. "Come back! It's just Sophie." I motioned him away from the door frame, but inside, I was still panicking. I went out to the hallway.

"Soph?" I yelled downstairs.

"It's me! Not a serial killer. Men are scum! But I've got dinner!"

Nick was still standing in the doorframe. I yanked him back inside.

"I'll be down in a second!" I said, and then closed the door.

"LISTEN," I turned toward him, finger pointed. "Just don't tell her that we're serious or anything like that."

"You think I'm going to announce, '*we're serious!*'"

"I guess not."

"Why does it matter?"

"I don't know . . ." I couldn't think of a single reasonable explanation. So I threw an unreasonable one at him. "Sophie is sensitive about people in relationships. Best not to bring up the topic at all."

"Why?"

And then, I panicked.

"She's Mormon," I said.

"O . . . kay," he said.

I didn't give him a chance for more questions. I ran downstairs in an inside-out shirt to talk to Sophie, who was cutting a tomato and dispensing the pieces into a salad bowl. There was a container full of chicken kebabs and a box from the bakery.

"Hey! So, I have Cabo guy here," I said, with my hands on my hips. Super casual.

She stopped chopping. "Oh." She looked at the stairs. "Do you want me to leave?"

She looked like she wanted to do anything but. She hadn't been home in over two weeks.

"No! That's okay. Stay. Of course, stay! We were just . . . you know."

"How was it?" She smiled conspiratorially.

I sighed. "Not now!"

"Ahhhh. Fine."

"Just . . . don't mention our arrangement to him, maybe," I said, motioning to the space between us.

"Why not?" Her eyes narrowed on me.

"I don't know. He's weird about this stuff."

"What stuff?"

I knew that she would be two eyes beating down on him no matter what I said. We would be under surveillance. There was no way my closest friend, the voice inside my head for over a decade, would look at us and not know that it was more than just a fling. So I panicked.

"He's Mormon," I said, attempting to make Nick into a funny story we'd discuss later.

"And he's having *sex* with you?"

"Or . . . used to be Mormon. I don't know. I feel like anything nontraditional might be weird for him to process."

I didn't ask myself why. I said: *Keep going until it all goes away. I'll tell Sophie at some point down the line and we'll laugh.* I could feel myself start to shake. My stomach lurched.

"But he's having sex with you?"

"I don't think this will be going on for too much longer . . . with him. I don't want to get into it and hear about all his 'beliefs.'"

She shrugged. "Okay."

Nick came downstairs.

"Hey!" I said, with a bit too much enthusiasm.

"Welcome," Sophie said, tapping her knife against the cutting board. "I've heard so much about you. You . . . and your people." She did a little half bow. I pinched her in the side.

"I wish I could say the same. Amanda's been pretty secretive about her roommate."

Drat.

"Has she?"

I laughed loudly.

"Well . . . you know me . . . attorney-client privilege." They stared at me blankly. "I mean. She's not my client. I just like to keep quiet about things. Nooooo need spreading unnecessary information . . ."

Sophie gave me a funny look. She appeared to ignore me and turned to Nick. "So, Nick, how do you feel about Greek salad and a lengthy venting session impugning the existence of the male gender?"

"Not much of a salad guy, honestly," he said.

She laughed but she was also scanning, gathering information about him, something I'd seen her do a thousand times before. Sophie was a formidable person. In her own way. And I was trying to fool her? I had this feeling that once she saw Nick, she knew everything.

"Your place is great," he said.

"Thanks! We did it all ourselves," Sophie replied.

"You did?"

"You didn't tell him?" she said.

"We did some things! Sophie always makes everywhere she lives look amazing, even if it's temporary! In college, she spent a month picking out a new rug for our lousy freshman year dorm room!"

When Sophie was finished with the salad, I carried the kebabs and we went up to the roof. Nick followed me, with his hand on my back. I tried not to flinch or walk ahead too quickly.

"So, you're a doctor, huh?" she said. "That means you can prescribe any type of medication?"

He smiled. "What did you have in mind? Xanax or something?"

"Oh," she said, shaking her head. "I am a woman in my thirties living in New York City. I obviously already have Xanax."

For a second, this seemed like it might all turn out okay. We talked about his job. Sophie asked him her standard one million questions.

I cut bread into thin slices, buttering them, arranging them on a plate, anything to keep my hands busy while they spoke.

I went back and forth to the kitchen for no reason.

"Which hospital do you work at?" she asked.

"Mount Sinai."

"Ohhhh, the Upper East Side. People with the fanciest diseases!"

"I wouldn't say my job is fancy. There are homeless people on the subway that I know by name."

"Is that right?" Sophie said, eyeing me.

He nodded. "I also do a shift at Elmhurst once a week," he said, which prompted her to inquire about the discrepancy in healthcare between different socioeconomical classes in the city. She wasn't talking about him, personally, but it came off as a bit of an attack. After a while, he looked cornered.

But then she backed off. "I was walking by a hospital the other morning, and it must have been before a shift change or something, because there were all these nurses and doctors all at once on the street, on their way to work, and I got so caught up in the spirit of it! I thought to myself, 'All these people are going to work to help people.' It's pretty amazing, actually. A totally unselfish thing to do."

Nick brightened. Typical Sophie. She could make you feel bad, and then so good.

"It's a collegial atmosphere," he said. "But that's certainly not unique. Amanda's office is like that too, right?"

"Yeah . . . ," I said, hesitantly. "It's a bit . . . like a family. I mean, you know, when the stakes are high, people help each other. Everyone wants you to win."

"Exactly. You're working toward a common goal."

Sophie was staring into space. Her eyes were glassy. "Well, I'm officially jealous of you guys," she said. "An artist is always by themselves. Artists, even when they're friends, are too competitive with each other to be true allies. I'd love a group mentality."

We were quiet. Sophie looked down at her plate.

"What's the latest with Julian?" I asked.

"Oh, we don't have to talk about that." She turned to Nick. "So, have you discovered a cure for Amanda's hypochondria?"

He smiled. "It's not that bad," he said.

She let out a snort of a laugh. "Well, I guess you haven't been around for that long."

"Actually, I've been around for quite a bit. Amanda and I met in . . . what was it . . . 1993?"

Sophie raised her eyebrows. "Oh yeah? Have you seen her stop a woman on the street for medical advice because she thinks she's a nurse but she's actually just a regular person wearing loose-fitting blue pants?"

I stood up and refilled all our glasses with water.

"I'm improving!" I said. "Growing! As a person. Isn't that possible?"

I regretted everything. Everything.

Nick's expression grew serious. "What you're talking about is actually a deep, dark hole that can go very deep and dark. There are people who live in emergency rooms because they are just terrified."

There was silence.

"Oh," Sophie said. "I guess you're right." She paused. "I guess she's not that bad."

I took a long gulp of water, crushing an ice cube with my teeth.

"What kind of art do you do?" he asked her.

I stared at a pepper shaker. I tried to change the subject, knowing that Sophie wasn't in the mood to talk about art. "Nick! Medical question! Does pepper really make you sneeze?"

Nick looked at me strangely. "In cartoons." He looked back at Sophie, waiting for an answer.

"Right now, I'm working on a sculpture of a penis," she said.

I choked on my water. Started coughing. *Good plan. Tell people Sophie is Mormon. That'll work. Sophie never talks about sex!*

"It's . . . mostly phallic in nature," she said, smiling.

"She's kidding," I said. "Tell him about the gem paintings!"

"I'm questioning value," Sophie said. "Like, what is it worth to you?"

His eyes were wide. "What is *what* worth?"

It was at this point that I decided dinner was over. I stood up and stacked dirty plates. I went into the kitchen and came back with the cake Sophie had brought home. I leaned over it and cut thick, haphazard slices, slapping them onto plates.

"It's from Butterfly," Sophie said, referring to the bakery in our neighborhood. Sophie and I had discovered it together in our first few weeks of living there. Sophie was always on the hunt for a bakery. The first thing I learned from her about Brazil was that there are no muffins there. "You eat fresh produce, juices, *tons* of salad . . . you hardly ever see a muffin, a brownie, a cookie. They're just not available," she had explained, as we sat in the college cafeteria in glorified pajamas and ate enormous bagels followed by Rice Krispies Treats in celebration of this being America.

"Oh yeah. Amanda's been dragging me there every night," Nick said. "It's good. They really put the butter in Butterfly."

Her eyes fixed on him. *Every night?* she appeared to be thinking, then said, "That's a pretty good joke for a doctor!"

He gave her a sideways look. "What do you mean?"

"I'm just kidding," she replied. She looked at her cake, but didn't touch it. "You know what? I think I'm going to go to my bedroom, actually, where I can really sink into the solitude of my existence, and you guys can just . . ." Her words petered out. She got up and left.

I felt a lump in my throat.

"That went well," I whispered, once she was gone.

"Are you okay?" he said, once we were alone in my bedroom. I was lying on my back with my eyes closed. An ice pack on my forehead. "You're acting a little nuts," he said, standing over me. "More so than usual."

I looked at him, peeking one eye out from under the ice pack. I could hear Sophie rummaging in the other room. "Let's go for a walk!" I said, sitting up.

"Okay . . ."

We walked around my neighborhood in silence. The sky was purple-streaked and surreally brilliant, the calm after the storm. He said, "What is going on?" He touched my elbow. "Just stop for a second."

I stopped walking. "I don't know," I said. I felt tears in the back of my eyes, my voice starting to falter. "I'm having a weird feeling. It's been happening to me a lot lately. I'm not sure what it is."

He sighed. "I'm sure it's anxiety. And I'm sure it's about the trial."

"It couldn't be a heart attack?"

"No."

"A heart *condition*?"

"No."

"A disorder involving a valve between the left atrium and the left ventricle that I discovered on Google last night?"

"I can perform all the requisite tests on you if that will make you feel better, but they will all be mildly unpleasant and they will all come back negative."

I shook my head at the ground. "I told Sophie that you were a Mormon."

"What? Why?"

"I don't know."

"But you told me that *she* was a Mormon, which I thought was really strange, considering that she's from Brazil, and they're mostly Catholic."

"I know. I'm sorry. That was . . . also untrue."

"Can I ask you a question?" He smiled. "Why does *anyone* have to be Mormon?"

I laughed nervously. "I don't know. I freaked out. Sophie can be a rather harsh critic of the men I date."

"Oh." He paused, staring at me, with his hands by his side. "You don't know what a Mormon is, do you?"

"Not . . . entirely."

THE HOUSE WAS SILENT but for the squeak of the stairs as I went to find her. Sophie was in her room, an empty beer bottle next to her bed. She was holding on to her elbows and watching television in the dark. Her shorts were lying at the foot of the bed. I could tell. She'd been crying.

"Nick left," I said. "I'm sorry if we made you feel bad at dinner."

She shook her head. "It's my own issues." She turned off the television.

"Are you all right? What happened with Julian?" I turned on the freestanding lamp next to her bed. She didn't respond. For a minute, I heard nothing but the hum of air conditioning.

"It is just occurring to me that I have nothing to do tomorrow." She kept staring at the wall. "Also, I haven't had beer in a while. It's really good."

"What happened?"

She raised her eyebrows. "You can guess, I'm sure."

"What did you do?" I asked.

"I laughed in his face."

I stuck my lower lip out. "Nice work."

She shook her head. "I know it hasn't been that long. But even in that short amount of time, I got used to him being there. And now it's hard to go back. To having nobody."

I sat down on the bed, near her feet. "I understand."

"It was more than sex. It was more than love. I would trade all those things for it, for what he was giving me, in a second."

"No, you wouldn't."

"I would. I can find a boyfriend. I can't . . . easily replace him."

"He wasn't the first person to like your work and he certainly won't be the last."

"It *has* to be about the work. Maybe some luck. Maybe some charm. But not sex."

I nodded. "I think you might be growing."

"I am so *tired* of being talked down to. Of being given 'advice.' Maybe I haven't sold a piece of art yet, but does that mean that I know *nothing*?"

"Of course not."

"Yes. It's true. I'm starting to believe." She paused. Her voice changed. "I am nothing. I have *nothing*."

"Sophie. That just isn't true. Think of everything you've learned. Think of the person you used to be. I understand how you feel but I also *don't* understand it. I can't understand how you can feel bad about yourself when I look at you and think, 'She is more beautiful and more accomplished than she has ever been in her life.'"

She looked up at me and cleared her throat. "Really?"

"Yes! I was looking at you, at that show in Soho, and I was thinking of you in college, and how all you wanted was to travel and to show your work at a gallery and to do things *differently,* and I thought, 'She may not be everything that she's ever wanted to be, but she's getting there.' You have to enjoy it now, Sophie. You *are* an artist now, and that's what you've always wanted. Just because it didn't work out with Julian doesn't mean it won't work with *someone else.* The fact that you got so far with Julian means that you are onto something. He's not nobody. He wouldn't waste his time. So now you have to just pick up and *keep going.*"

She leaned back against her pillow and threw her hands down at her sides. She was silent, and then looked up at me. "Is there still cake?"

I nodded, and we made our way into the kitchen. She didn't mention Nick until she'd taken a few bites. I knew it was coming.

"Can we be done with Cabo guy?" she asked, her fork hovering above her plate. "Please."

I didn't know whether she was concerned about our friendship, or she just disliked him. But I could feel it, that she knew he posed some kind of threat to her. Maybe she didn't want me to be up, while she was down. Sophie wasn't vindictive, but she was human.

It felt like the right moment for a confession. It felt like the time to say, *I am in over my head and I'm not sure what to do.* But I couldn't bring myself to do it. I didn't want to upset her further, maybe, but also . . . I wanted to protect him from her. I wanted to protect my relationship with him, from her.

"Yeah," I said. "We're done with him."

It was too late. I couldn't say, *Oh, lighten up. He's harmless.*

It was way too late for that.

After that night, I solved my problem by keeping them away from each other. I was strategic enough to do the dodging. I don't remember when lying became a regular part of my life. At some point, it just was, and I couldn't remember when it began, the way you can never remember the exact point at which you fall asleep.

Meanwhile, at work, I was in the midst of the biggest trial of my career. I was the lead prosecutor, and I was in charge, for the first time in my professional life. I was on top of my jury instructions, had prepared all our witnesses. I ate nothing but coffee slushies (coffee plus crushed ice) and the occasional lunch at Burger King with the guys on my litigation team. I told myself that I'd sort out my romantic life once the trial was over, once I'd successfully shined a light on corruption in the NCAA, once I'd achieved an adequate sentence, not overly harsh but a stern enough warning about taking advantage of student athletes on the verge of signing lucrative contracts. *Once the trial is over* became my mantra.

The problem arose when I had to leave court at the end of the day. My mind, at that point, was the mushy result of a day of racing thoughts. I was amped up in order to perform for the judge and jury, but then the second it was over, it all came crashing down. I had to prepare for the next day, the next witness. I had to move on the court's schedule. If I found something in a file that went against my theory, I had to scramble to make changes. I didn't have time for anxiety, but my anxiety found me anyway.

It started when I left court, with a nervous wrenching in my stomach that spread over the rest of my body like I had swallowed a bad pill. On the subway, the waves worsened. Around Port Authority, my heartbeat sped up and I felt like I might pass out. Or die. And then, just as my hearing and vision began to blur, the subway would rattle past the midpoint between work and home, and I would get very cold. I'd start to shiver, and hold my suit jacket closed, and rub my arms up and down, and by Columbus Circle, the feeling would subside. I didn't recognize then what perhaps I should have: there was an obvious problem in my life.

Once the trial is over.

Here's the thing: it didn't feel like lying. It didn't feel like "I'm maliciously deceiving the two people closest to me." It was about my fears and the priority I'd given them. Because if I ended up alone, as crazy as it sounds, I felt like I might not survive. And so, maneuvering around the situation felt like the only way to tread water.

And then there was that night that I crawled into Nick's bed very late and he asked me about living together and I thought: *What now?*

"Oh . . . You don't want to live with me," I said, shaking my head. I couldn't quite look at him.

"Apparently, I do."

"You don't," I said, lightly. "Trust me."

"Why not?"

"I don't know . . . I . . . I . . . I sometimes listen to my music a little too loud . . . and sometimes I take a shower that's a little too hot . . . and . . . Oh! I put my slippers on right after the shower because it makes me feel like I'm staying at a fancy hotel, which is . . . mildly delusional."

"None of that affects me."

"Wouldn't you rather us be together when we want to be? And then get some distance, some room to miss each other again. If we live together, we'll just get on each other's nerves. Isn't this a good arrangement?"

And then, I started really selling him on it. "*Imagine* having all the benefits of having a girlfriend without all the unnecessary chatter! Without the errands and the nagging and the questions about why your clothes can never quite make it straight from your body to the laundry bin without a stopover on the floor. *Imagine* not having to put the seat down and being able to go out with your friends without getting a thousand text messages harassing you to come home."

He moved toward me.

"Separate togetherness? Isn't that the dream?" I said.

"I don't know. You're confusing me."

And then, the solution came to me. "Also, I'm not sure I want to live with somebody, until I'm married."

There. That ought to do it.

"Oh. Why not? And if you tell me it's because you're Mormon . . ."

I laughed. *Why not? Why . . . not?* It was a valid question.

"I've had bad experiences." I shuddered. "In my past."

"Is it because of your parents?"

"Could be."

Was it because of my parents? I was confusing myself. Everything I said lately, to Nick and to Sophie, felt invented. And then I pretended to fall asleep, and he let me, because he'd just worked a twelve-hour shift, and because—he believed me. He was in love. This didn't make it harder to keep doing what I was doing. It made it easier.

Sophie

I may have lost sight of the road. Okay . . . the road was a speck to me. I went back to the circuit of exhibit openings, lectures, museums. I followed the man who lived in the house behind ours for a while—just, you know, casually. A casual stalking. But, in my defense, he was always home, had a wide variety of visitors, and a black curtain inside his apartment, so what was I to do besides assume he was a drug dealer or a masseur? He went outside onto his patio a lot, with his shirt off (very good solid body), and smoked a cigarette while talking to himself. I followed him to the store to buy lightbulbs. The anticipation loomed large when he went into a hotel, but then all that happened was he walked out with a crumpled jacket, rubbing the lapel between his fingers. I crashed some kind of feminist art tour that led me to The Met to see Gertrude Käsebier's photograph *Blessed Art Thou Among Women*. I stood in front of it, this black-and-white photo of a mother in a long, white dress, angelic and domestic, with one arm dangling around her daughter, as crowds of schoolchildren and tourists passed me by.

I went home and watched a documentary on Hannah Höch, a German artist who was interested in the representation of women for mass consumption, like dolls and mannequins. I went to see a retrospective on Ree Morton at The Drawing Center on Wooster Street. Her oil on celastic, gold with a flower, reading *Don't Worry I'll Only Read You the Good Parts* really killed me it was so good. A few years ago, I saw her piece *Bake Sale,* a table covered with cakes against a wall of bows, famously inspired by a male faculty member at art school who suggested that women on the faculty stick to baking. If only I could turn rejection into something so playful. When you see somebody who creates the type of art that you want to create, it is inspiring and maddening at the same time. It creates in you a kind of manic fury. I met a woman there who was a graduate student in philosophy. She showed me her engagement ring and I solicited her opinion on my career. She seemed qualified enough. She had a thesis.

I went to an exhibit at NYU's fine arts museum, where they were showing the work of Parviz Tanavoli, an Iranian sculptor. As I walked among the curvaceous bronze, fiberglass, and neon sculptures rising up from their pedestals around me, I was thinking of flowers and snakes and entwined lovers, and then I saw the Gucci loafers, and the man rising from them.

"I know you," he said, his finger pointed.

"Yes! I remember your shoes," I blurted out, and he smiled.

"You're Julian's girl."

I told him that I wasn't. "That didn't work out." I smiled. "Actually, it crashed spectacularly."

"I'm sorry," he said, but he didn't sell it. "I find Julian to be one of those 'if the sun shines on you' type of people.'"

"What do you mean?" Pretty sure I knew, but I wanted to buy myself a few extra seconds.

"I mean, if he happens to focus his attention on you, if he thinks you can do some good for him, it is a very warm experience. But he casts a long shadow. I don't know from personal experience, but I've heard from a few artists. Female artists."

"Yes . . . well . . . The unfortunate part was that I quit my job, because I was so naively sure that I was on the verge of making it." I rolled my eyes. I felt comfortable talking to him, because in one specific way he wasn't like Julian: He was gay. Pretty sure.

"What's been happening with your art?"

I forced a smile. "I have a lot of ideas."

"Are you still working on the Semiprecious series?"

"I've done three paintings, but lately, I've been thinking of taking the same idea and applying it to sculpture. Maybe something in glass and sand and mirrors. Three-dimensional, but still with the focus on light and how light affects color, and still with the theme of high and low. I'd love to work with sand. That's the Brazil in me . . ."

"You know what," he said, with his fist cupping his chin. "Do you know anything about Egypt? I was just speaking with someone about the artist residency in Cairo. At Townhouse Gallery? Have you heard of it?"

"I haven't."

"It may be a good idea for you, for an artist at your stage, or an artist at any stage, frankly. Townhouse is really an extraordinary place. It's located in the ruins of a nineteenth-century aristocrat's palace, in this delightfully decrepit alleyway filled with car mechanics and artisans who weld and cut glass and make mirrors. Yet it's one of Egypt's leading contemporary galleries."

"It sounds ideal."

"Egypt is also rich in minerals, which I'm sure you know."

"Yes, I recall something from middle school about Cleopatra using ground-up lapis lazuli as eye shadow."

"Lapis lazuli, that's right! The gold flecks are pyrite, I think? Set against dark blue. Like the night sky, all embracing and protective, one might say, if one were being poetic, which I think one should be, at all times." He smiled.

"Oh, certainly. Whereas turquoise . . . daytime. Clearly."

"Egyptian turquoise is more of a translucent color than turquoise from other places."

"Is that right?"

"But the main thing Egypt had was gold. An envious Assyrian king once wrote, 'Gold in your country is dirt: one simply gathers it up.'"

"Are you Egyptian?"

He shook his head. "Iranian. But I worked as a curator at Townhouse many years ago. I thought about that a lot when I was there, as the country is literally covered in dirt."

"I've never been. I'd love to go someday."

"It's magical and intense and inescapably charming."

We talked about geography as it relates to memory and fear, the colors specific to an urban environment. We talked about the idea of constant movement and our relationship with nature. He told me about the sandstorms in Cairo, about the yellowing of the sky.

"When's the next flight?" I joked, basking in the image of sand whipping off the desert.

"If you decide to send them your portfolio, I can put in a good word for you. I have a friend on the selection committee."

"Oh, wow," I said. "That's nice of you. Thank you. How long would it be for, do you know?"

"Six months, typically," he replied.

He took out a small, leather-bound notepad and handed me a piece of paper with his phone number. I put it in my wallet immediately, afraid if I held on to it for another second, it would disappear.

I SAT IN WASHINGTON SQUARE PARK for a while after that, looking at pictures of the gallery on my phone. I googled the essentials, like "residency Townhouse Gallery" and "Cairo friendly to foreigners" and "are Egyptian men good lovers?" People sat down next to me and then got up and I didn't notice, I was in such a tunnel. Pretty sure an unkempt man who smelled like alcohol started sketching me. I was deep in images of the alleyway where the gallery was located, and became immediately transfixed with this crumbling Ottoman palace that had blended so much into its environment that you couldn't tell the difference between the gallery and the street. It served as studio space. A place for performances. A refuge for protestors. When it first opened, ten years ago, the state forbid its art school students from going there. The newspaper printed articles condemning it. The premises were raided several times. It was partially demolished by the government. I was intrigued by the art that I saw on the walls, by the artists that had spent time there, who went on to have shows at places like the Tate Modern. I watched a lecture by a curator about working in a conflict zone, about the dangers of glamorizing risk. "Art is lawless," she said. "It is defanged when it is culturally used." I listened until my phone went dead.

This whole idea seemed a little wild, but not *not* something I would do. It felt natural, in a way, like a next step that actually might somehow make sense. I would have time and space to concentrate on my work, without having to think about another job. And I'd be surrounded by inspiration. But what about Amanda and our brownstone and the life we'd built in New York? She didn't like it when I left for the night, let alone six months.

The next morning, I threw myself at my computer and filled out an application, thinking: *I probably won't get in anyway.* I'd already lost control. It was exhilarating, a colossal rush, to be directed and moving toward something in a way I hadn't in a long time. Not dependent on anyone else's goodwill. Unconcerned with my relative cuteness or charm. I wanted, all of a sudden, to be deep in study. To define myself by what I did. I put together a portfolio with ten images I'd created in the last five years. I wrote a one-page letter of intent. I could have written a book. When I was finished, I called the man in the Gucci loafers to let him know I'd submitted an application. *I should think this through more.* That thought did occur to me. Several times. But I was moving too quickly. And then, once it was over, I slowly backed away from the computer.

I went for a run, my legs beating the ground extra hard, sprinting so fast that it seemed like everyone around me was moving painfully slowly. I came home and realized that I was starving and ate whatever leftovers were in the fridge, plus a block of cheese and an avocado that I doused with salt. I heard the sound of Amanda coming through the door.

"I hope you weren't particularly attached to anything in our fridge," I said. She didn't respond. I poked my head out of the kitchen.

She was pale and her hands were shaking as she locked the door behind her. I watched as she put her bags down and went straight to the couch, without looking at me, without removing her jacket. She lay there and held her arm over her eyes. She still had her shoes on.

"What's wrong?" I asked.

"Nothing. Just . . . give me a few minutes."

I heard her inhale deeply, slowly, through her nose and then exhale through her pursed lips.

"Can you bring me some ice water?" she asked. "Quickly!"

"Sure," I replied, and went into the kitchen and filled a glass with ice and cold tap water. I went back to her. My fervor from earlier had completely died down.

"I'm fine. It's fine."

She took a sip of water and then put the glass to her forehead.

"Is it the trial?"

"I don't know, I don't know," she said, as I peppered her with questions like "What's going on?" and "Did something happen?"

"My heart is beating *very* erratically. It's been doing that for fifteen minutes. Is that normal?" she said.

"You're asking *me* what's normal?" I replied. "Just take slow, deep breaths." I knelt beside her. "And let's talk about something else." She was curled up on the couch, and I lay on the floor, feeling the cold against my back. She said she felt dizzy, and had waves of pain in her stomach.

"Isn't Cabo guy a doctor?" I asked her. "Where's his hospital again?"

"No." She shook her head. "He's not on tonight."

"O . . . kay."

How does she know his schedule? I thought we were done with him. Were we not? Questions for another time.

I took her to New York–Presbyterian. In the waiting room, Amanda put her head between her legs and waited for certain death. On one side of us, just beyond the sheer white curtain, there was a man who had just electrocuted himself but couldn't explain his symptoms in any detail because nobody at the hospital spoke Mandarin. On the other side, someone was going through heroin withdrawal.

An hour later, the doctor told us what we already knew—she'd had a panic attack. We went home. Back at our apartment, Amanda started to shiver, and I handed her a blanket.

"Now. Will you please breathe, and let's talk about something else besides how you're feeling?"

She unfolded the blanket and covered her chest, pulling it up high so that her eyes and the top of her head were the only visible parts of her.

I turned on the TV and got into bed with her.

"We can watch one of your sports games, if you want."

She smiled. "It's not sports games. It's either 'sports.' Or 'the game.' But never both."

We settled on an old episode of *Parks and Recreation* on Netflix. She said that she still felt dizzy. I went into the kitchen and made us peanut butter sandwiches.

"I feel better," she said, halfway through her sandwich.

"Good."

"I still think it could have been a heart attack."

"No," I said, tucking myself under the blanket. "Heart attacks aren't solved by distractions and sandwiches."

"I'm sorry. I'm embarrassed."

"Oh, please. Who among us has not sent themselves to the emergency room for some nonsense?"

"You haven't."

"I would if I ever had insurance."

Two episodes later, I went to my room. I showered and changed clothes and then went back into the bathroom to brush my teeth. Written in the steam on the mirror, it said: *Thank you.* The words were inside a heart that either had an arrow strung through it, or a Band-Aid, a reference to her dysfunctional, overbeating, overflowing heart.

That's when I settled upon it. The realization that I couldn't go to Egypt. That would be completely bailing on her. A partnership meant being here. I could go, of course, she wouldn't stop me, would maybe even support it, but I would be going against the nature of our agreement. I wouldn't even be in this position if it weren't for her. The constant encouragement. The pep talks. The annoying but right things she said like *you're only beginning to learn.* If it weren't for her, I would still be trading furniture with Icelandic dealers on Craigslist. Whatever facts I could stack up in my favor, however good my intentions might be, the thought of bringing this idea to her made *my* stomach turn. It was a question, above all else, of loyalty.

Okay, New York. I will stick around. You won this round. I went to Amanda's room to check on her, but I opened the door, slowly, to darkness. She was asleep. I felt a small sense of pride, in having taken care of her. I didn't need to get on a plane and learn to speak Arabic and have an affair with an Egyptian. I needed to be a friend.

The next day, I stood on the sidewalk, a few blocks from our house, and called the program director. She picked up the phone with a slight British accent and her voice sounded so delicate and cultured that I almost started trembling.

"I'd like to withdraw my application."

I heard typing.

"Name?"

I told her.

"Okay! Withdrawn."

I felt a sunken feeling in my chest. "That's it?"

"That's it," she said, in a singsongy voice.

I thought it would be harder. I thought she'd ask me why. I thought, maybe, she'd try to change my mind.

Amanda

I agreed to meet Sophie after work. She wanted me to see Zoe, who, in her latest venture, was calling herself a healer.

"Maybe she'll be able to help you with your anxiety," she said to me. "Or maybe Giff will swing in on a chandelier. Anything's possible."

"A few points of discussion. What is a healer?" I asked, examining the glossy business card. ZOE T. FOLEY, NATURAL-BORN HEALER.

"I have no clue."

"No, but really. It has to be *something*. Does she do tarot cards?"

"I think that's what it has to do with, yeah."

"Is that something you can do professionally? And are tarot card readers considered 'healers'?"

"Yes and yes."

"Really?"

"I'd imagine if you have the audacity to call yourself a healer, then tarot cards might seem like a legitimate profession to you."

"Well, this has all been very informative."

"I'm a natural-born teacher."

"Maybe we should meet here after work and we can go there together?" Naturally, I was worried not about Zoe's diagnosis but about whether my anxiety would cripple me on the way there. "We could chat on the way?"

"Chat?" She looked at me. She said that it made no sense for me to meet her here, which, of course, it didn't.

When it came time to leave my office, my leg was shaking under the desk. I tried moving my foot in small circles and scrunching my toes, the way a therapist had once told me to. She said to picture my toes in the sand and to curl them under slowly. It wasn't doing much. I got up and marched the halls, seeking an accomplice.

"Anyone headed to Midtown East today?"

It was an odd thing to do. By no means was this normal protocol. *I was just in a social mood!* I was prepared to say to anyone who might ask. I received no takers. As I went out onto the street, I felt a tightness in my throat, a sense of impending doom for no reason. I told myself to keep going. It would unwind some, after a few blocks. I planned to walk for a bit, until I felt better, and then take a cab.

But it only got worse. Strangers on the street seemed dangerous, menacing somehow. *Nobody here can help you*, I thought, as I went farther and farther into a part of the city I didn't recognize. I thought of Nick, who was at work. If I needed to, I could call him. He would help me. Maybe bring me to the hypochondria section of the hospital where they dispensed chamomile tea and placebo pills.

As I reached the Thirties and Lexington, I started to feel stranded, like everyone who knew me was out of reach. I heard the sound of an ambulance wailing, and the sound attached itself to my brain. The ambulance was stuck in traffic on the street. A rising fear inside me was mimicking the rising warning bell behind me. Everything I saw made the feeling worse. A bunch of people in uniform standing outside a bus smoking cigarettes. A school janitor leering at a group of girls, his jacket bearing the school's name. A girl in a shirt that read MY DOG THINKS I'M COOL. There was a woman with her daughter walking next to me and I almost told her how scared I was. *She's a mom,* I thought. *She'll help me.* It was at that moment that I decided to call my own mother.

I said, "Mom? Can you stay on the phone with me for a few minutes?"

She said yes, and then put me on hold to have a conversation with her plumber about his tattoos. "But you have kids now!" I heard her say.

Somewhere along Third Avenue, I started to feel like I might pass out. I knew one thing and one thing alone: I had to get out. Of where? To where? I didn't know. I went to the curb and raised my hand. I popped a Xanax with the phone pressed between my ear and my shoulder. I tried to flag down a cab, but there weren't any available. There were cabs without their lights on, and nothing else. The traffic was murderous. I suddenly felt as if a cab stopping was the only way I would survive this, and I couldn't get one.

A cab passed by with its window rolled halfway down. There was a man in the back seat. It stopped at a red light.

"Excuse me, sir?" I said, approaching the car.

He gave me a confused look. He was wearing a suit.

"I'm sorry to bother you, but would you mind sharing this cab? I'm terrifically late for a meeting and it's just a straight shot uptown from here. I'll pay for the whole ride."

Before he had really committed to a positive response, I was opening the door and hurling myself inside. I started chatting away, attempting to charm my way into appearing normal. I got lucky. The guy was a lawyer. I talked through my rapid heartbeats, trying not to focus on them, to focus rather on the words that he was saying, to casually fumble through my purse and double down on my Xanax when he wasn't looking.

He got off at Fifty-Second Street and I took the cab a few blocks farther. When I got to the right place, which was a sophisticated-looking apartment building with a doorman, I took the elevator up and rushed through Zoe's waiting room, where incense was burning and it smelled vaguely of oranges.

"Why, hello there," said Zoe, opening the door in an uncharacteristically soothing voice. "Come in." Sophie was standing behind her.

"I can't breathe," I said.

Sophie looked me over. I was speechless, white as a sheet. They sprang into action. Zoe unfolded a massage table. Sophie handed me a bottle of water.

"Something happened on the street. I think it was a panic attack."

Zoe nodded placidly. "I'm so glad you're here." She pointed to the massage table and helped me get on.

"Have you experienced cranial sacral therapy before?" she said, as I lay down.

She began holding my head and humming. I closed my eyes. I tried to focus on my breath, but I kept sneaking looks around the room, eyeing a gold statue of three monkeys sitting next to each other on a log, various other tribal ornaments. *Where did she get all these things?*

"I'm feeling a lot of tension up here," she said, making a circle with her hand over my face and chest area.

"Yes," I said.

"You've been holding your own head up for a while, haven't you?"

"Yeah . . ." *Trick question?*

She inhaled deeply through her nose. "I can tell." She moved her arms, gesturing toward my feet in big movements, meant to transfer the energy in my body. "You're clearly a *vata*."

"Ohhh, *vata*. That's good," said Sophie. "Very model-esque."

"What does that mean?" I said.

Zoe said, "It means you have long limbs, are prone to anxiety, and don't like your vegetables cold."

I hesitated. "That *is* true . . ." *Is she actually onto something?*

As she talked, I started to feel better. Maybe cranial sacral therapy was working, or maybe it was the lying down, the deep breathing, the Xanax. The world was an easy haze.

"What's your blood type?" Zoe asked.

"I'm not sure."

"You're not sure?"

I shrugged. "It's never come up."

After that, she gave me three bottles of water to drink. "Drink these. Slowly," and I did, as Sophie and Zoe spoke about chakras. I think. I'm not really sure because I kept having to leave to go to the bathroom.

"You should come back. Twice a week."

"Twice a week?" I checked my phone and scanned my work emails. "I don't have time for . . ."

There was one from my boss. He asked if I could pick up some documents from one of our witnesses' offices at the United Nations tonight. He needed it tomorrow. He heard I was in Midtown East. *How did he know?* Oh. That's right. I had surveyed the entire office before leaving.

I asked Sophie, "Do you mind if we stop at the United Nations before we go home?"

She gave me a strange look. "Are we picking up an ambassador?"

"No. Just some documents."

"Bummer."

ALL THE LIGHTS WERE OFF when we got there, except for a single lightbulb coming from a security office. I told the guard my name and he pointed me to a side door.

"After-hours at the UN," Sophie said, following me down a dark hallway. "You take me to the coolest places."

"Some people would consider this cool."

"Nerds."

I laughed. "Okay."

"I'm just trying to figure out if there are any visas I need . . . Let's break into the gift shop and steal all the tiny flags!"

"Sophie."

"Just the Brazilian ones?"

"No."

"Fine." She sighed. "I'll settle for the Americans."

We could hear only our own footsteps. Then, at the end of the hallway, we saw a candle. A few feet past the first one, there was a second.

"That's . . . odd."

"Maybe there's a wedding here or something?" Sophie whispered.

"Who gets married at the UN?" I questioned. "On a Tuesday?"

She shrugged. "Someone *very* diplomatic."

We entered a door marked THE ASSEMBLY HALL. It was dark inside, when we opened the door, with rows and rows of seats, more candles. And Nick, down on one knee. At the end of his arm was a dark box with a diamond inside.

My immediate thought was: *That can't be for me.* Right after looking at me, he looked at Sophie.

On some level, I knew exactly what was happening. But I felt dissociated from my senses, as Nick continued to look at Sophie, willing her to disappear. Sophie examined Nick right back, awaiting an explanation.

I was hoping to disintegrate into the ground. All I could hear was Sophie say to me, "Wow. I guess you are good in bed."

Nick's jaw was clenched, face fallen. "I thought you'd come alone."

"This is an excessively random place to propose," said Sophie.

Silence settled in.

"We went on . . . a field trip," he answered her. He looked at me: "I told your boss to . . . I thought you'd come straight from work . . ."

All I could do was look down at the blue carpet. It was getting too difficult to look at him, to look him in the eye and pretend that I knew anything.

"Oh," I said. "We were in Midtown, seeing one of our friends. It's a . . . long story. I didn't realize . . . obviously . . ." And then I felt the blood draining from my face. A tingly sensation spreading over my eyes. I put my hands on a chair and leaned forward.

The next thing I heard was the sound of a ring box snapping shut and Nick coming toward me. "Are you okay?" I think he said. "Amanda? Amanda?"

Then Sophie was at the front of the room, slamming a gavel down on the table.

"What is going on?" she demanded. "Is this a game show?" She looked up at the ceiling. "I just want to state, *for the record,* that I was born here. I'm a citizen!" she said, looking around for security cameras.

I wanted to stay where I was, hovered over the chair—the jerk of vertigo still there—but I stood up.

"What's he doing?" she said to me, with such casual confidence, like she was ready to assume this guy meant nothing to me, that he was just some guy who'd clearly lost his mind.

"What does it look like?" he replied. I felt all my muscles tense.

"I haven't," I said to her. "I haven't . . . I haven't told him about us."

"About *us*?" he stammered.

"It's not what you think," I said, turning toward him.

"What *does* he think?" She stared at me for a long moment.

"Well, I guess he thought . . . we might . . ."

I was trying to speak but also despising myself, for being weak, for ever thinking I would end up anywhere but here.

She shook her head like she felt sorry for me. "Let me guess. Now you want out, right?"

"Out of *what*?" he said.

"Our arrangement," Sophie added.

"What arrangement?" he said.

"No . . . I don't want *out* . . ." I shook my head. "I'm just . . . wondering if we could maybe make some adjustments?"

She laughed. "Bullshit." Her fists were clenched.

"Sophie." I stopped a tear with the side of my finger. "This isn't easy," was all I could whisper.

She looked at me with disgust. "Oh, please. Cue the violins."

I swallowed hard.

"Can somebody *please* tell the man with the ring what the fuck you guys are talking about?" Nick said.

"Sophie and I made this decision," I said. "To live together, instead of getting married. To see men as something . . . on the side. And I didn't tell you because I was afraid . . . you wouldn't understand or . . . you'd lose interest in me. Right before we met, or, re-met, I made this deal with Sophie."

"Amanda *wants* what she *wants* when she *wants* it," she said, turning to Nick. "I was her backup plan. I just didn't know it."

"That is not true, Sophie. I wanted to move in with you. It's just that . . . this happened. And something changed."

"And now you want to move in with him?" She pointed at Nick. "Well, you'd better get something in writing, buddy. Don't make the same mistake I did, expecting loyalty."

"Sophie. Would you really want me to be loyal to you, in this scenario? Would you *still* want me to be loyal to you, even though my feelings have changed? I never pledged allegiance to you!"

I looked up. We were surrounded by flags.

"Actually, you did."

"But wasn't the whole point of our deal flexibility and to accept the fact that things change over time?"

"You're right. You didn't pledge anything to me. You kept your fucking options open!" She looked away from me. "You know what the saddest part is? I withdrew my application to a residency in Cairo for *you.* I eliminated a possible opportunity to figure out who I am as an artist for *you.* I could be having an affair with an Egyptian lover right now!"

I said, "I didn't know that."

"Would it have even mattered to you?"

I shook my head. "I don't know how you can even say that. Hasn't your career *always* mattered to me? You're acting as if you have no memory, as if this incident is *all you know* of me. Don't I get any credit for . . . the past? Haven't I built up a certain amount of goodwill?"

"Why did you make this arrangement?" Nick asked me. "And what do you mean, 'men on the side'? What does 'on the side' mean?"

"I don't know . . . exactly. I was sick of the pressure. To find one person, get engaged, get married. I hated the compulsion to do what everyone else was doing. I was sick of getting hurt and of . . . feeling like a failure when I wasn't even sure I wanted what other people wanted."

"And now?"

Sophie started laughing. This loud, mocking laugh.

"I don't know why you're laughing," I said, shaking my head. "You think you can say 'just kidding' a thousand times and disguise the fact that you hurt people? You can be so cruel."

"And you can be *judgmental as fuck*. The minute I do something that isn't exactly within your line of reasoning, you treat me like an offbeat lunatic."

"Sophie. I don't exactly have a strict *line of reasoning*. I spend most of the day second-guessing every decision I ever make."

"Bullshit," she snapped. "You're self-deprecating, but you always fundamentally think you're right and everyone else is wrong."

I was so angry that I could feel it in my eyes. There was heat emanating from my eyeballs. "Maybe I'm just a little bit exhausted by how *insanely superficial* you are. You and all your artistic friends who try *so desperately* for people to think you're unique, but the only things any of you really care about are fame and money."

She shrugged. "It's easy not to care about money when you have it."

I felt a rush of bitterness toward her. "I have it because I *work*, Sophie. You seem to forget about that. I earn money in exchange for *work*. It wasn't handed down to me from above. I'm not some . . . aristocrat."

She rolled her eyes, and said, in her most patronizing voice, "There are very few aristocracies these days."

"You think you're charming people? You're *using* them." I was shaking.

Nick stepped toward me. "I still don't understand. Why didn't you tell me? For all of our conversations . . ."

He was swept. I looked at him, but didn't say anything.

"*Pay attention,* Romeo. She said this already. Because if she told you, she might lose you. And how could she lose you? She can't function on her own. She can't even eat *pretzels* alone!"

"Huh?" Nick said.

"IT'S TRUE!" Sophie yelled, pointing at me.

"Sophie. I'm a federal prosecutor."

"Exactly! Grow up. You're in your thirties, and you can't be alone in an apartment?" She turned to Nick. "She doesn't need a boyfriend. She needs a babysitter."

"Look," I said, but my voice was beginning to falter again, "maybe I'm not the person that either of you fell in love with. Maybe, sometimes, I'm a much worse version. I give in to almost all my impulses and I'm afraid of . . . a lot of things. But Sophie." I looked at her, my voice breaking. "We have never spoken to each other like this. We have never . . . worked against each other . . . ever. I have always been on your side, and vice versa, so why can't we . . . work this out?"

But Sophie no longer looked like the Sophie I knew. I would have preferred for her to remain mad, to keep yelling, but instead she said, gently, "I made this arrangement because I thought relationships with men were fleeting, but ours was forever. I see now that that's not the case."

She looked resigned, but I couldn't give up.

"It's only . . . because of this crazy situation that we got ourselves into."

"No." She looked at me, shaking her head. "It's not. It's because of innate differences in our personalities that were only visible over time."

My mind was blank. I couldn't think. Couldn't speak. I was in some form of shock.

The anger was wiped clean from her face. She looked up at the flags. "United we no longer stand," she said.

I loved her now more than ever, for making the joke.

"Okay," Nick said, in a cool, flat voice. He was tired of getting treated as if he were secondary, and I couldn't blame him. He had proposed, and it looked to him as if nobody cared. I went to take his hand, but before I could, he said, face averted, "I'm leaving."

After they were both gone, I sat down in one of the many chairs in the room. I needed time for something to dissolve inside me, before I could go outside. A man wearing a nametag came in.

"Are you here for the island nations support group?" he asked, flipping on the lights.

I wiped my eyes.

"Have you lost your allies?" he said.

I was about to say no, but then shrugged. Because in some sense, it was true. I had lost my allies.

"Representing Mauritius," he said proudly, and stuck out his hand. "We have coffee and doughnuts in the other room. Come! Come with me!"

He seemed so warm and friendly, motioning me over.

I shrugged again. "Okay."

A guy in colorful African garb walked in.

"Oh, welcome, welcome! Someone new? What is your name, miss?"

The man turned to him and said, "Ah! Madagascar! My dear, dear friend."

I went with them. They were very persuasive.

"Which island are you from?" he asked me.

"Ummm . . ." I thought back to my Model UN days. "Greenland."

"Ah. Greenland. Very nice. Very good."

Twenty minutes later, I had eaten several doughnuts and knew nothing in this world but that I was Greenland.

"Nobody respects us," I started saying. "They think we're just a block of ice! But we have feelings, too!"

They nodded at me sympathetically.

"We thought we had a good thing with Denmark, but then *Canada* came along and promised us all these good things. And now we've overstepped our bounds and lost everyone. When I go home, it's going to be me, five Inuits, and a walrus."

I talked to a woman from Fiji for a while. She was very consoling.

"One country invaded us. Another tried to annex us. And did we have any friends to stick up for us? Noooooooo. I can't even count the number of times we've had pirates land on our shores. And has anyone helped us? Nooooooo. But we believed in ourselves. We knew we could do it. And here we are today."

"You cannot be dependent on *anyone,*" said the ambassador from Sri Lanka. "We used to be part of India. We didn't know if we could separate. We always relied on them. They were our partner! Nobody thought we could do it, but we did! And we survived!"

"You have to seek independence. That is the key. Independence."

I was shaking my head. "You're right. I know you're right."

Sophie

I've never stormed out of the United Nations before. You know what? Kind of fun.

But then I got back home or what used to be home and the reality of the situation landed on me like a ton of bricks. Literally. You know, the ton of bricks that was this brownstone and all the time and care it took to get it this way? It was, sadly, still here and—*ha-ha-ha-ha-ha*—mocking me now. It seemed like every aspect of this place that had been crafted in love and good cheer had transformed, while I was gone, into a point of fury.

I went up to my bedroom and prepared to leave, not unlike a child running away from home. I was many emotions, but I was mainly just embarrassed. I felt like she'd chosen him over me, which, I suppose, she had. And the worst part was—she didn't seem to think she'd chosen incorrectly. She wasn't saying, *I've made a mistake. I take it all back.* She was saying, *How unfortunate that I was caught.* I thought about Nick more than I thought about Amanda. I kept thinking, *That stupid guy Nick.* What was so special about him? That she was willing to risk everything? Also I was pretty annoyed at myself because *of course* that stupid guy Nick. Amanda was not going to pass up an elementary school crush turned doctor. There was *no way* she would pass that up. I just didn't realize she'd throw me quite so far under the bus to get to him.

I changed into a white T-shirt, tucked it into a silky, knee-length leopard-print skirt, and then reached into my closet and grabbed my boots. I packed a bag with enough to get by for a few days and then I was gone. Flying out the door.

Amanda. Could. Go. Fuck. Herself.

I am aware that technically, *technically,* this comes as much more of a threat when you are actually fucking the person, but I think it still applies here. What was I thinking? That our friendship was *so special.* I treated it like some sort of elevated, exceptional thing. Above a friendship. Better. Stronger. Well, I kept up my end of the bargain. I was so very inquisitive about what was going on with her. I sat on the floor of her room for hours and years consulting on text messages. And what did she do? She had some insights. She listened. Yeah. Okay. Fine. I'll give her that. I don't know how much *letting me go on a tirade* counts as kindness. Although I guess at the end, she usually said something wise and pointed out how nonsensical I was and that made me laugh and deflated my anger slightly. But is that really *doing anything*? Should she really get credit for that? Nobody in her right mind interrupts a person, mid-meltdown, and tells them, "Oh, actually, I have to go! I'm running late for a meeting!" But fine. Okay. Let's say we give her credit for this Mother Teresa–level act of generosity.

I was going to Hans's apartment because I recalled something about a Moroccan-themed dinner party. He and his boyfriend, Leonardas, had just returned from Fes. I called to confirm.

"Oh, and just FYI," he said. "The theme for the dinner is Hans."

"I thought it was . . . Morocco." I paused. "What does that mean, 'Hans'?"

"It means that everyone is dressed in a Hans-inspired way."

I looked down at my outfit. "I'm wearing my 'fuck you' boots. Is that anything?"

"Oh. Very Hans."

I needed to be around a bunch of artists. Artists were on the fringes. They heard the words but didn't always listen. You could say things to them like, "Sometimes I feel like a rabbit I saw once on a lawn, sitting in the rain, getting soaked, when there was a tree right nearby that it could have easily sat under," and they would understand.

Hans's apartment, for the night, had been transformed into a Moroccan cocktail lounge. His plush bohemian-style sofas were surrounded by pouf ottomans. The music was incongruously Latin. Leonardas was a trapeze artist, and he had brought his friends, so the party was a hybrid of circus performers and visual artists. Someone was building a 10-foot-tall puppet. There was a woman wearing a skin-colored body suit and people were painting organs on her. Hans showed me a grandfather clock, then introduced me to a clockmaker, who praised the clock's pendulum and knew that it was made in a specific region of France because of its curved lines.

Most people were wearing colorful clothing. There was a man in a gold jacket and a woman with pink eyebrows. There were tattoos, glitter, pirouettes, and break dancing. There were aerial rigs on the ground and a 15-foot-long snake named Anushka being passed around. Nobody wanted the snake to run away, for obvious reasons, so one person at a time was designated responsible for it. It was a nontrivial task, taking care of the 15-foot snake. But the snake didn't try to kill anybody. So that was nice.

I spoke to a contortionist with a Russian accent who knew how to breathe fire. It required very minimal skill, she insisted, other than the ability not to fear death. She told me about touring with a metal band, dressed up as a zombie. Her job was to spit blood onto the crowd. She said you didn't know from men until you lived with three of them in a van for nine months.

"I'm sure they were all in love with you," I said, because she was the most beautiful woman, with cherry-colored hair, green eyes, and a smattering of freckles across her nose.

"They were mostly concerned with nonsense like who could eat the most habanero peppers . . . Plus, I was dating this other guy who was obsessed with aliens." She raised her eyebrows at me. "We drove through Area 51."

"How did he like it?"

She appeared contemplative. "He was just so *anticipatory*."

We laughed and bonded over how isolating artistic pursuits can be, how something that looks so cool to others can sometimes require many arduous years of labor, and how much easier it would be to move to France, financially speaking. And then I thought: *Maybe Amanda can be easily replaced. Maybe this girl is the new Amanda.* But then she asked me about my work and I told her and she looked at me aghast.

"Why are you here? Why are you not working? You can't look sad. Don't ever look sad. But don't look happy, either! You can't show people weakness! People are animals! They'll eat you!"

A surge of sorrow. She wasn't Amanda. Amanda said a lot of things, but never that anyone would eat me.

I spoke to Hans and Leonardas for a while. They had just moved in together and were all high on it, which only made me feel worse.

"I came home and I saw something in a bag in my freezer that most definitely looked like a corpse. So I called Leonardas and I said, 'Leo, what's in my freezer?' He said, 'Don't worry about it.' And I said, 'No. No. You have to tell me. Is it a human body?' So he said, and I remember his exact words: 'It's a turkey but it's totally fine.'"

Hans looked at Leonardas, annoyed but adoring. Leonardas had his leg up by his ear and appeared to be stretching, which I would have thought strange were it not for the person doing splits on the floor.

Leonardas responded, "I found it dead at the side of the road." He shrugged. "I wanted to make something out of the bones and feathers."

Hans turned to me. "But he never did. And after a month or two, I made him take it out of the freezer. We gave it to Baxter," he said, referring to his neighbor upstairs who occasionally sold him drugs, "who woke up every morning and opened his freezer and talked to the turkey, consulting it as if it were an oracle."

Baxter, hearing his name, walked over. "I thought I was being macabre." He rolled his eyes.

Oh yes, living together is all fun and games until someone finds a dead animal in the freezer, I thought about telling Amanda. I wouldn't be able to. I would never go home, to our old home, to our old friendship, because it didn't exist anymore.

When Hans and I were alone together on the couch, we talked about Nick. The botched proposal.

"So what you're saying is . . . ," he said. "Your situation that was destined to blow up actually blew up?"

I glared at him.

"Sophie! You're against commitment, but you asked her for a fucking commitment!"

"But it was a commitment not to commit! It had layers!"

He sighed. "Amanda is just one of those girls. I love her, but she's in her box, and whenever she goes out on a limb and does something different, it's something different within the realm of the ordinary. At the end of the day, she wants a husband, and maybe they'll go to Budapest one time and fancy themselves very exotic."

As I listened to him talk, I thought about how all this was losing meaning to me. I no longer wanted to think or talk about any of this. I just wanted to work. I wanted to sit in a room by myself behind a closed door and work it all out on a canvas.

"Look. It's not just her," he said. "It's a lot of people. Everyone thinks that they're *so in love* that they're the exception. Everyone thinks their relationship is indestructible. But *everything* is fucking destructible. And that's what everyone realizes a few years after the beautiful wedding photos. But by all means! Take the beautiful wedding photos! If that's what you want, then do it. Eventually, we'll all be turkeys at the side of the road."

I smiled. "That's a lovely story."

He got up to pour me a glass of wine and then handed it to me. I downed it.

He shrugged. "Sophie. You're going to depend on people, whether you sign the documents or not."

"I know. I know. Do you think I was expecting too much?"

"You cleaned up Victorian doorknobs for her!"

"That's right! I nearly died inhaling paint fumes just to paint her room beige."

There was a moment of silence. The sadness again. Whatever else there was to say, I was going to lose my best friend.

"She should have told you," he said.

"Now say that I'm a ray of sunshine."

"You are always a ray of something."

"Thank you. Now. Who's here?" I scanned the room.

"What are you looking for, exactly?"

It was a good question. *What am I looking for?*

There was a man sitting in a corner of the apartment on a pillow, amid a bunch of other pillows on the ground. He was tan, with dark hair. He was wearing a dark green hooded sweatshirt under a blazer and definitely had that controlled-mess look nailed down—that slightly-rough-around-the-edges coolness where his clothes looked like an afterthought, like some happy, well-fitting accident.

I looked at Hans and then tilted my chin in his direction.

"Ohhhh." And then he said, "YoulllovehimhesItalian," as if it were one word.

"*Mi piace,*" I said with a smile, and then walked across the room.

I discovered that he was not just Italian, but a filmmaker. His latest work would be premiering soon at the Berlin International Film Festival.

He turned to me and asked, "So, what do you do?"

"I'm a painter," I said, completely unabashedly, for the first time. Too emotionally exhausted to say anything else. "But I'm thinking I might do some sculpture. I'd like to work with my hands. I'm having this weird craving lately to meld something."

He smiled.

I could barely look him in the eye on account of his handsomeness. I kept thinking: *What is this life-size cologne advertisement doing speaking to me?* He was so disarmingly handsome that he quite literally disarmed me, and I ended up telling him all about Amanda and the situation that had just transpired. I talked about freedom and optionality, and by the time I had finished, his hopes for the evening were visibly soaring.

"It reminds me of something. Have you seen the film *Juliet of the Spirits*?"

I cringed. "I'm a bit behind on my Italian film."

"Juliet, she's like a chain smoker with a short haircut and a wardrobe . . . very plain. She is moping around the house because her husband cheats on her. Her neighbor Suzy is this seductress dressed in colors and feather boas." He mimed wrapping a scarf around his neck. "Juliet visits Suzy to return her strayed cat."

"Naturally."

"And Suzy has this philosophy: Marriage is a life sentence for a woman."

"Go on." *Is this it? Is this the wisdom I'm searching for?* Would the clouds part? Would I finally have some answers? Just when I'd given up on the topic.

"Fellini and his wife shared a house, but they occupied separate floors."

"Separate floors. There's an idea. And what happened to them?"

"They stayed together. They had to. After *Juliet* failed, Fellini was bankrupt, and the government went after him for unpaid taxes."

"That's a lovely story." I smiled. He shrugged.

We left the party together and went to see a movie at the Metrograph, this indie movie theater on Ludlow. It was directed by Marguerite Duras, and was about the very glamorous wife of a diplomat in 1930s India. He whispered which scenes were done in one shot, with no cuts, and which scenes were clearly shot on three different days, because the light was different. Then he took me to a coffee shop with no name and easily the best coffee I'd ever tasted. But the sting of the Amanda episode had not lessened. Not one drop.

"You would be great company in Berlin," he said, sitting across from me, his coffee cup empty now but for a rim of foam. Under the table, he had a couple of his fingers hooked into the top of my boot. "Berlin is like a mecca for artists. The cost of living is low. It is one of the great museum cities of the world."

"Oh, I would love to but . . . ," I said.

I was tempted by his offer. Whatever was going on under my kneecap was coursing through my body. How many times had I springboarded a situation just like this into something more?

"I'm in the middle of applying for residencies, and I don't want to go anywhere until I get one," I said.

Apparently, in my caffeine haze, I had a plan. My second thought was that I wanted to tell Amanda, but I'd lost the tether between us; the elasticity that had been there for so long was now just a thud in my chest. I knew exactly what this feeling was. I just hadn't wanted to recognize it until now. I was heartbroken. There was only one person.

I finished my coffee, and he leaned into me and put his hand on the underside of my knee, just where my boot ended and my skin began. And then he whispered, "These boots are good, Suzy." He looked me over. "Very good."

"It's Sophie," I said.

Over the next few weeks, I stayed with Hans and sent out applications. I emailed Gucci Loafers about Cairo, to see if he might be able to help me get back in. I tried not to get eaten by a snake. I overheard Hans laugh and say, "Remember the bones phase? Maybe she'll go to medical school." And I tiptoed out of the apartment. There was nothing wrong with my other friends, but they weren't Amanda. They may have been as fun, as clever, as interesting as she was, but they weren't reliable. They didn't provide the same safety net. If I texted them, *Hey what's going on?* they didn't immediately call five seconds later and ask, *What's wrong?* At Hans's apartment, I felt like an intruder. Whereas Amanda's apartment had always been like a second, more well-organized home to me.

Often, I would grab my phone on instinct, to tell her something, and then I'd have to put it down. I spent a lot of time wondering if she felt the loss as much as I did. But she was busier. The busier person always wins. She didn't have time. I've never *not* had time.

At night, after Hans and Leonardas went to sleep, I worked on a few sketches about what can break you apart, but in a good way—time, water, sex, motion. I spent a lot of time at FedEx, shipping artwork to residency directors.

I tried to make sense of what Amanda had said to me. Her words followed me all day. Each insult felt like a secret I wish I hadn't been told. Fighting with men was easier. Fighting with men was like fighting with a less intelligent species. It's not that scary. It's pretty easy to control the flow of it. Female friends don't fight with each other very often because they are terrified of what the other might say. And with good reason. Because Amanda's words were stuck to me now, and whenever I thought of them, I paused whatever I was doing. Sometimes I ended up in a ball on the floor of a strange bathroom, crying my eyes out and wondering if my whole life has been a lie.

What if she's right?

Am I a horrible person?

What if everything I've ever done has been superficial and selfish?

These are the kinds of things you might ask yourself. For example: Maybe she was right. Maybe she knew something other people didn't. Maybe everyone else was lying. Maybe they'd be next. I started examining everything I'd done in the past, evaluating things in a new, more objective light. But eventually, I got tired. Eventually, I settled upon: *Maybe I am a monster, but I'm doing the best I can to be a small-*

ish monster. One with googly eyes, a backward cap, and a heart of gold. This may be a specific monster from a Pixar movie.

I didn't get out of bed before noon. I cooked Hans and Leonardas dinner at night. When their friends came over, I faked delight and then occupied myself with emptying the trash and doing the dishes, scrutinizing each stain, scrubbing the kitchen until it sparkled. Amanda was right. Anxiety cleaning? Actually quite effective.

And then, mid-detergent consolidating, I got a call from an international number and immediately I knew: the residency in Egypt was still possible.

That night, to celebrate, I took myself out for ice cream and then called my mother, my fingers sticky against the phone.

"I'm going to Cairo!" I declared. "There's a program there, and I just got accepted, and I'm actually going. It's taken me a long time to realize this, but what I want more than anything else is just time and space to . . . explore. And even though I might not want structure for my personal life, I actually do want it for my art."

"They want you to go there?"

"Yes, Mom. No. I tricked them."

"You didn't trick them. You're a very good artist."

"Thanks." She'd never said that before, but I rolled my eyes anyway, as a matter of course.

"Let me see if your grandmother is still awake."

"Wait! Can you talk to me about it for a minute?"

"I don't have time to talk to you! I have to tell everyone!"

I smiled a wide, wide smile.

I HAD A RENEWED SENSE OF PURPOSE. I went into the brownstone when I knew Amanda would be at work and put my things in boxes. The apartment looked much bigger without her there. I felt like a burglar in my own home, like I was casing the joint. I walked around quietly, carrying an empty duffel bag. *Should I tell her where I'm going?* A part of me still wanted her approval. As I filled the bag, I thought of ways to tell her without actually telling her. But even if I did, she'd have questions. She'd say, *Isn't the political situation there a little bit . . . questionable . . . right now? And what will the residency get you, in the end? Will you get a show at the gallery? Do they guarantee that to all their residents?* She did not understand what it was to need experiences. She did not understand what it was like to feel at home all over the world, to know that as long as you can connect to other people, in some small way, you'll be fine. Maybe Egypt on a moment's notice was not appealing to her. Not her style, as much as the occasional panic attack/existential crisis in the comfort of her own home. The problem with worrying about things that may or may not happen is that they don't exist. Amanda worried about so much that wasn't real. It was like that apple. *Dropped, but not forgotten.*

As I looked at her books on the shelves, aligned like trophies, I felt a tinge of affection for her. I thought of how we'd get up together, how the sound of her taking a shower accompanied me as I got dressed each morning. Then she read about sports while we ate breakfast and filled me in unnecessarily. Those days went by so fast. Sure, I missed her now, but soon I would be gone. I pulled a French-English dictionary off the shelf.

As soon as I was on that plane, this experience would be farther and farther behind me. I left the keys on the kitchen counter, then stared at them. The fact of it. I remembered getting them. I remembered ripping apart this kitchen and putting it back together and scouring the city for the perfect cabinets. I shook my head in disbelief. I wished that this was some amusing stunt that we could laugh about someday, that it could be easily transformed into an anecdote. But it couldn't. The only silver lining was that perhaps, after all, she'd done me a favor. Without our breakup, I might not have been able to leave. And I didn't belong here anymore. I wanted change. I wanted stories. I wanted . . . success.

They say your soul, not to mention your art, is nourished by all your experiences. I now understood that my desire to be an artist—in whatever form that had taken throughout my life—was the one thing that had always anchored me. When I lay color on a canvas, the whole world faded away. I was home. It was the quiet place where I, Sophie Warren, resided. Maybe I'd get married someday. Maybe I'd have children. Who knew? I just think that little girls trying on their mothers' wedding dresses should know they can wear that dress or they can buy a pair of fuck-you boots and leave for Egypt at five o'clock in the morning, and if anyone asks them why they're going, they can say, before a chorus of knives tapping on glasses: *To nourish my fucking soul.*

19

Amanda

I kept thinking: *I'm in my apartment and it looks completely different.* In a day, it had changed. I inspected everything, relics from the last moment of normalcy. I kept saying to myself: *It was an ordinary day.* Because I couldn't get over the difference between then and now. I ate by myself at our kitchen counter, with no memory of what took me from one moment to another. I was lost to it all, and then I got into bed like any other night, but it was so eerily quiet that I couldn't sleep. I felt lonely, and a wallop of dread caused me to sit up, stand, move about the house, and stretch my arms in the dark.

Everything that held meaning before seemed to have been emptied. Time could have been easily marked by my conversations with Sophie. Her words were so often circling in my head, before and after whatever else happened. So much of what I did was done not only for myself, but for her, too. It was better if I didn't look too closely, if I just got through my day-to-day routine. I had to get used to the way it was now. I went to sleep with her bedroom light on.

The past was my undoing. When I saw the kitchen table, I thought of our discussions there. Because maybe we wouldn't agree, and that had seemed like the worst possible problem. I looked at my bed and thought of how when we first moved here, I had missed Ethan, and that had seemed like the worst possible problem. I thought of the fights I had with my mother on the phone, how Sophie instructed me not to leave things on a bad note, and that had seemed like the worst possible problem. What you realize when something truly bad happens, when the bottom drops out, is that all those problems were . . . delightful. You yearn for those problems. You'd kill for them, actually. They seemed fun and lighthearted and like watching a television show. Yes, they were problems, but they weren't really yours. They didn't really unglue you. The happy moments with Sophie were the ones that really killed me. They caused me to stop dead in my tracks, to sit, to put my hand under my chin and think: *God, we were so happy and we didn't really appreciate anything at all.* The difference between then and now was where all the sadness resided.

This brownstone had history. Solidity. Permanence. And yet. I felt a terrible pain in the top of my chest, somewhere a little higher, knowing that Nick would never come here again. I might never see him again. Moments with him were coming back to me, and everywhere. A home was a sanctuary. It was meant to protect you from the outside world, but it could also turn on you. It could transform into a very painful place to be. It could take you in, flood you with relief, or it could destroy you from the inside out. It reminded you of what once was, or it told you what could have been, if only you had moved about it differently.

I texted Sophie a few times, to no avail. She didn't come home after our fight. Or the next day. Or the day after that. When I called, she didn't pick up. It didn't even ring, just went straight to voicemail. At one point, while I was away at work, she came to pick up more of her belongings. She left her keys on the counter. There were dusty wires where her laptop once was. I left her a message, finally: "We have to figure out what to do with our apartment." I figured, if nothing else, that would get her to call me back. It was also true.

But Sophie still didn't call. Jasper did. He and Sophie had discussed selling. I felt completely drained, apathetic, as we discussed the logistics of getting him a key. I was trying to put my mind on what should happen next, what the next logical step should be, but all I could think about was how she'd already made a decision. She was just waiting for me to comply.

Jasper talked about price, potential buyers, how to be competitive. He had a buyer within two weeks. Sophie was right. He was a good real estate agent.

I said goodbye to our apartment by walking around it with my arms folded across my chest, feeling something akin to grief, waves of grief that brought tears to my eyes, then just left me silent, with a leaden feeling, looking around for something that wasn't there. *Eventually, it will all feel better,* I thought, as I closed the front door, with my final box in hand, a cabdriver beeping in exasperation.

I NEEDED A RESTART. To teach myself how to be alone. It sounds simple, doesn't it? That's the thing about other people's fears. They sound very easy to get over, assuming that's not your particular issue. I started by seeing a therapist. I'm not *huge* on therapists because I don't trust anyone who is financially invested in my continuing to not feel well. I thought about actually going to yoga, as opposed to checking the class schedule, changing into yoga clothes, and then making myself a snack (I just felt like it satisfied me more). Whenever I found myself panicking, I followed the therapist's instructions and meditated. She explained that my fear of somebody breaking into my apartment probably had to do with my parents' divorce, how startled

I was by it, how it had felt like the problems appeared out of nowhere. I was afraid of silence transitioning, abruptly, into trouble. But I couldn't avoid silence. I couldn't avoid being alone. I had to make peace with it.

So I came home after a long workday and, instead of making plans to see someone, settled into the quiet. At first, it felt impossible. My mind was running at warp speed. To go home to an empty apartment and do nothing but read or watch television all night by myself? I couldn't hit the brakes like that. But then I thought: *What's the worst that can happen? You won't choke. You won't be murdered by a former defendant or a disgruntled garbage man. You will more likely than not be fine. Worst-case scenario: You'll be bored.*

Progress was slow. The first hour of being home alone was hard. But I was getting a little better, each time I pushed through. During the height of the trial, I put my own life aside for two weeks. I stayed so late at the office working on my closing that I accidentally fell asleep on the couch, and woke up to my coworker yelling, "We have to go to court in an hour!"

The call came on a Tuesday afternoon. My team was in the office that day, distracting ourselves from the tension by watching *Despicable Me*, which sounds counterproductive, but was far better than engaging in endless rounds of speculation about jury notes. After months of pouring everything I had into this case, I was so dead by the time my phone rang that I felt like someone could have knocked me over and I wouldn't have noticed.

"We have a verdict," the voice said. As I made my way to the courthouse, my heart was pounding. The defense came in with the defendants. The jury shuffled out and handed an envelope to the judge. The judge read it, handed the note back, and asked the bailiff to put the jury foreperson under oath. The foreperson of the jury announced the verdict. The jury found the coaches guilty on all counts. They received sentences. The sentences were fair. It was exactly what I wanted, but I couldn't react. I had to stay stone-faced. I waited until I was in the elevator to even crack a smile. And then, on my walk back to the office, I stopped in a parking lot to put my fist in the air and yell, *"Come on!"* One of the attendants saw me and must have thought I had either just won a big case, or I was a raving lunatic. Truthfully, at that point, it was a little of both.

When I got back to the office, everyone knew. I went to a bar that night with my coworkers. We always went to the same bar near the office when somebody won a case. Incidentally, this was also what we did when somebody lost one.

The next day, my team met with the US attorney so he could congratulate us. I left his office on a high, knowing I'd convinced a group of twelve people to do something. I was good at my job. It gave me confidence in all areas of my life. Each time I had that anxious feeling bubble up inside me, I reminded myself of this trial. My stock was rising in the eyes of everyone that I worked with. I had accomplished something concrete. I was intent on getting some mileage out of it. Maybe I had some of the answers some of the time. I didn't have to look quite so desperately to those around me, to friends and boyfriends. There would always be people to call, to help in a time of crisis. But for so long, I'd been discounting my biggest resource: myself.

A few months after the incident at the United Nations, I felt like a changed person. Greenland: Land of the free, home of the self-sufficient.

My first order of business, upon being reelected ambassador to the new, independent Greenland, was to get my friend back. I was prepared, now, to acknowledge the extent of the damage, not just the ways in which I'd been wronged. I called Sophie and the line rang in a strange way that meant one thing: she had left the country.

At first, I was angry. I didn't understand how she could cut ties with me like that. I questioned whether my friendship even meant that much to her in the first place. I questioned whether she had received my texts at all. Was she upset, or simply out of reach? There were times when I felt a resounding sadness, like when I opened my calendar and it said *Sophie's Birthday*. I composed a few birthday emails in my head but sent none of them. I didn't know what to say. I couldn't be cheery, exactly, but sending a melancholy note to someone on their birthday just seemed unpleasant. So I let the day pass. I told myself that birthdays weren't that important. She wasn't a big birthday person. She'd missed mine a bunch of times, even when we were the closest of friends. But then, Sophie didn't keep a calendar.

Eventually I settled upon the very Zen, very Buddhist notion that I couldn't force Sophie to be my friend. I had to let her go and hope that the winds of time would bring her back to me. Maybe she'd forgive me. Maybe she'd resurface, the way she used to. Maybe I'd never know.

Over the course of the winter, I called and texted Nick many times. He didn't respond. I thought about showing up in person. But all I could think of was this scenario where I showed up and he had nothing to say. He would shrug, with his hands in his pockets, and tell me that he wasn't sad anymore, that he was actually glad to be free of me. That voice that always envisioned the worst was still inside my head.

But then one Sunday morning, I woke up feeling lighter. Hopeful. As if I'd turned a corner. I turned on ESPN and I realized—it was baseball season. Spring. Winter was officially over. And I thought: *What have I got to lose?*

I started walking downtown, through the North Woods, down the cobblestone side of Central Park West, stopping at a bakery on Columbus. I made a turn on Eighty-First Street, passed a vendor selling candy and magazines, dodged a group of moms pushing strollers. Once I entered the park again, I felt the volume turn down on everything. I'd been avoiding this area because this particular path through the park, among the rolling hills of green and sun-flecked trees, made me think of him. I walked past the outdoor theater where they performed Shakespeare in the Park. By the time the pathway opened up to the Great Lawn, the traffic was distant, and it was just a vast blanket of green, dotted with sunbathers and baseball players, the grand buildings in the distance.

I thought about showing up at his apartment or at the hospital, but I felt like my chances of getting him back were vastly improved in a pastoral setting. His team wore green jerseys with white stripes on the arms, so I scanned the field until I saw a swarm of green players huddled together, the outline of a taller man that appeared to be Nick, or at least it seemed so, from a distance. I walked toward them, crossing the field, careful to avoid getting clocked by a baseball, which would have really put a damper on my plans.

The players were red-faced and perspiring as they chucked balls from the outfield back toward the pitcher. I watched as one player who was particularly small swung fiercely at a pitch, only to fall to the ground.

"Good swing," Nick said. The kid got up to his feet. "Stay in your shoes this time, okay?" He dug his cleats into the dirt. The next pitch came, and he had his feet planted firmly, his brow furrowed. Swing and a miss.

"Is that bat good for you, Billy?" Nick asked. "Do you want to try the white one?"

It was at this point that Nick noticed me standing behind the fence. He looked at me, and then immediately turned away. *Not a great start.*

Billy, white bat in hand, hit the ball and then went flying down the first-base line, kicking up a cloud of dust in his wake. I held back a cheer.

Before the next pitch, Nick waved at me, and I relaxed a little bit. There was no surprise in his face, but I was hoping that I caught a trace of pleasure. I kept standing. *Stay in your shoes,* I said to myself.

I scanned the bench, looking for a place to sit, but it was crowded with equipment, a clipboard, spare mitts and sneakers, a half-open bag of sunflower seeds. The team returned from the field, their heads turned down toward the grass as they walked. They gathered in a circle behind the bench and listened as Nick gave what I assumed was a motivational speech.

"Hey," I said, once Nick stepped out of the circle and the team dispersed. "Sorry to ambush you here."

He clapped dirt from his hands. "That's fine."

"How's it going?"

"It's okay. How are you?"

"I'm . . . fine."

"What are you doing here?"

"Oh, I just happened to be, you know, walking by . . ."

"Oh."

I smiled. "No. I wasn't."

I noticed that his hands were trembling. He turned to look at the kids. They were peering at him, waiting for instructions. He exclaimed: "Top of the order!" He took up a piece of paper and then shouted some names. He had his back to me. He looked at the paper and then attached his fingers to the batting cage. He swung his waist back and forth, looking out at the field. There was silence. I started to feel strange about being there. Unwanted.

"Should I go?" I said. "I can go."

He looked back. "I just— JASON! What are you doing?" He strode deliberately onto the field.

"There's a grasshopper on the field," said the second baseman.

"So?" Nick said.

Jason was kneeling down and trying to get something in the grass. "I think he's injured," he said. "He's not hopping."

"Kill it!" the first baseman yelled.

"NO!" shrieked a boy running toward them from the outfield.

"Can you give it CPR?" one of the boys said to Nick.

"CPR?" he said with a smile. "Let's just get him off the field. I'll call animal control after the game." He managed to get the grasshopper onto a glove and brought it to the bench.

"Are you really going to call animal control?" I said to him, when he was in earshot.

He shook his head. "No," as if it were obvious, which I suppose it was. "I mean. Maybe," he said. "How often do I get the chance to call animal control?" He still wasn't really looking at me.

"Is it okay if I stay?" I asked. He shook his head and said "unbelievable" under his breath. Was he talking about me . . . or the grasshopper?

He took up his glove and went back to the pitching mound. I cleared a spot for myself on the bench, next to the grasshopper, and we both watched the action on the field. Two intruders.

Pitches were hit. Most of the balls were thrown toward first base. A few were even caught. One boy appeared to get lost between first and second. Nick called the number of outs. The team migrated between the bench and the outfield. We were all squinting into the afternoon sun. Parents began to appear behind me, to collect their children. By the end of the seventh inning, the green jerseys were ahead 3–2, and they lined up and shook hands with the other team in the middle of the field. I was gearing up to talk to Nick after their post-game huddle, though I still wasn't sure what to say.

I was there to get him back. That was all I knew. I wasn't leaving there without him.

"Wait!" one of the boys called out, before the team dispersed.

"Oh, yes. I forgot. We have to hold a press conference," Nick said. The boys cheered and held up their hands, pleading with him. *Press conference?* It took me a bit to understand that they were fighting over who would be interviewed that day. Nick took out his phone, and a few of the parents handed over their phones, so the kids could hold them in front of the designated interviewee as if it were a real press conference in the major leagues. The kids without phones joined in, balling up their hands into fists and pretending they were microphones.

"Danny! Danny! Danny!" they all shouted.

"What do you think the keys were to today's victory?" Nick asked, and Danny did his best impression of the professional athletes he'd seen interviewed on television.

"I think overall it was a solid performance . . ." He tapped his finger to his cheek. "A real bounce-back victory."

They interviewed Nick. "The effort and grit that this team put in, especially at the end, in order to get the win . . ."

Parents corralled their children. The bases and cones were brought in from the field. Bats and balls were put into a bag. And the children staggered off the field, backpacks and water bottles bobbling against their backs. As the sun dipped behind a building, I was finally able to talk to Nick.

I stood before him and stated my case. "I'm sorry that I didn't tell you about Sophie. It was a really stupid and thoughtless thing to do. I didn't expect what happened between us to happen, and I just didn't want you to think that I was taken."

"But you were taken."

"No. I think I was just protecting myself."

"Okay . . ."

"I want you to know that I regret it, all the time, but especially at night, before I go to sleep. I lay there and feel nothing but regret, and like what took place was just . . . wrong. And I was hoping you might be able to . . ."

He stood, waiting. His eyebrows were raised as if to say, *yes?*

I said, "I was hoping you might be able to . . . get over it."

"Get over it?"

I smiled. "Yeah."

"I should get over it? That's the thing you came here to say?" He was trying to seem insulted, but he was more amused. My heart was beating fast, but I wasn't scared. I was feeling too good to be scared.

I nodded.

"That's it? That's all I get?"

"That's all you get."

"What about a big speech?"

"Nope. Sorry."

"An impromptu marriage proposal?"

"Don't think so."

"What about asking me out on a date?"

"Eh."

He threw his hands up in the air.

"Oh!" I said, and then walked over to my bag on the bench and pulled out a brownie covered in cellophane. Instead of going back to him, I stood behind the fence and pushed it through one of the holes. He stared at me briefly and then went over to the fence. He took it from my hands. He was smiling.

"Not bad," he said, through the fence. He walked toward me and wrapped his arms around my shoulders and everything inside me felt like it was coming loose.

"That was pretty cute. Come on."

"It's not bad! I said."

We walked along the path out of the park.

A FEW MONTHS LATER, I found myself in a familiar position: at a Japanese restaurant with Nick, thinking of Sophie.

I took a sip from my beer and ordered. I listened to Nick order. The lights were soft amber hues and one end of my chopsticks lay on a shiny, black pebble.

"Oh. Also. Can we have less rice?" I asked, interrupting him. "And can you please cut the rolls into eight pieces, not six?"

After the waitress left, I felt the sting of Sophie's absence.

"My soul hurts," I said to Nick.

"I don't understand what that means," he replied.

"You know." I gave him a look.

"Are you going to say this every time we order sushi?"

"Probably."

"You aren't friends with her anymore. I think you have to accept that."

I shook my head. "I can't."

When the appetizers arrived, I poked two holes in a dumpling and smiled. It looked like it had eyes. I took a photo of it and sent it to

Sophie because what the hell. There were a thousand unanswered texts above it. What was one more?

I put my phone on the table, screen-side down, so as not to be too optimistic about it. But then I heard it, even over the restaurant noise. It was the unmistakable sound of a text message coming through. I slammed my chopsticks down. I flipped over the phone.

Sophie. "She wrote back! She actually wrote back!"

My stomach was doing backflips and I was terrified the text was going to be something like, *Please do not contact me anymore.* Or something formal and to the point and devoid of all pleasantries. All the whimsy and impulsivity of a few seconds earlier was gone. I held my breath, and clicked.

He's cute.

Relief flooded through me. *She's playing ball. She doesn't hate me.* And then, there was a jolt of excitement. I wrote back immediately:

I know, right? We're dating.

I put my phone down, but held on to it, and looked up at Nick. "She's writing to me! She's writing me her thoughts!" My eyes welled up.

He widened his eyes and smiled. "Good," he said, raising his eyebrows, as if to say, *keep going.* I picked my phone back up. I wrote:

But he's so pale and plump.

The texts started rolling from there. I didn't know what else was happening in the restaurant or with Nick. I was in my own little universe. Our universe.

What can I say? He doesn't get out much!

That seems promising.

You'd think. He may be carrying on an
illicit affair with an egg roll.

All of that steam . . . it's gone to his head.

LOL.

Did you know that in Germany, a dumpling is
called a Knodel? Germany is also home to the
only potato dumpling museum in the world.

I was barely moving, barely breathing. Nick was chowing down on our sushi.

Question about the museum.

Yes?

Are there samples? Because I don't think I could handle
a museum about dumplings without samples.

I know! Can you imagine? You'd be so hungry by the end!

No. Unacceptable. There would have to be samples.

Agreed.

So you're in Germany then?

I'm in Egypt. With an Italian.

Have you guys knodeled?

Please! He's Italian!

Sorry. Ravioli'd?

She sent me an "LOL," and then there wasn't much else to say. There was no talk of the past and no plans made for the future. I put my phone away. I returned to Nick, feeling like I could do that now, like she had relieved him of something. I suppose that was the great power of our arrangement. There were no rules written down. Or said out loud. We just knew. Even tapping into it briefly was all I needed to get back to my life.

Outside, I reached for Nick's hand as we walked. He looked back at me and tightened his grip. And then we went home, to that place where you locked the door behind you, so that nobody else could come inside.

20

Sophie

We agreed to meet late, at a diner in Chelsea, which was more or less halfway between where she lived, with Nick, I gathered, and where I was staying for the weekend. I thought about canceling. Many times. A small voice inside me said: *I don't want to go. I really actually don't want to go at all.* But then another part of me imagined walking in and seeing her, what she would look like and what it might feel like to hug her, and felt a rush of anticipation. The good kind. There was so much to say and a lot to ignore and the whole thing required a lot of energy. We'd only texted once, a few months ago, and that was about a dumpling. But somehow, it had cleared some air between us.

Since then, she had gotten a new phone. She texted me her new number and I put it into my phone as: Amanda New. Not realizing that's exactly how I would feel when I texted her, like the old Amanda was gone, and I had to relearn how to talk to this new person. No longer the reliable safety net.

It was easy not to be up for this kind of experience. But the tempting part was always this: it just might make me feel better about everything.

When I got to the corner of Twenty-Third and Ninth, I was nervous. I was trying too hard, already, in my head. It felt, oddly, like I was going on a blind date. Except the stakes were much higher. I was already desperate to impress, with new clothes on and a slight tan. It started to rain, and I ran to take shelter under the diner's awning. I watched rain dripping from the edges, and collected myself, and by that I mean took a few breaths and counted my most recent accomplishments in my head.

Should I tell her about the white desert? I could say that it was one of the most beautiful places I'd ever been, and maybe that might sound like something. Should I say that I went to Sinai and smoked a lot of hash with some hippies? That Alexandria was nice, but more sterile? Would she like to know about the other artists, and how one of them always skipped out on the bill at Café Riche? What about his video installation about bread? Would she be interested to know that if you bought *koshari* on the street, you could save yourself a lot of money? That I might have an exhibit there, at the gallery, at the end, but I wasn't sure since the program was so deeply unstructured?

It wasn't the easiest place to have a moment, there in the middle of Ninth Avenue. There were horns blowing and people rushing by me, but through the glass, it looked very still. I peered inside at the familiar scene. I could hear the sounds of a cash register, the slight clanking of plates, a man jamming an umbrella into a canister of umbrellas.

Amanda and I went to this diner a lot in our twenties. It was just like any other diner in New York—maroon leather seats, Greek waiters dressed in black and white and carrying plates of yellow eggs,

Spanish flying between the busboys and the kitchen. Afterward, we would go off and do our separate things. But first, there was always breakfast.

Through the glass window, I saw her. She was in the same spot, in our same booth, but her face was a little different. She was always there first, but she used to sit nervously, eyeballing strangers, chugging water from her glass, prepared to recite to anyone who might ask: *I'm waiting for someone!* But now she looked calm. I swung open the door. I walked toward her. I'd moved to *Egypt,* and this was the most terrified I'd been in months. She perked up when she saw me. She stood. We hugged each other loosely. As soon as I felt her body against mine, I almost cried.

But no. *Don't.* I kept it together. I sat down and there was an awkwardness between us. It had been a while. What had happened was still sitting there with us. The words that had been exchanged. We didn't want to think about them now. We were blocking it out, but we both knew, deep down: It would be hard, maybe impossible, to get back to where we had been. It would be easier to find a new groove, to experience each other anew.

We said things like, *Good to see you. Glad we could find the time.* We commented on the weather. We turned to our menus for salvation.

"Are you going to get a tuna melt?" I said to her, to break the silence that was enveloping us like a swamp.

"I think so. What about you? Omelet?"

"I'm fine with anything as long as it doesn't involve chickpeas."

She smiled. "Chocolate chip pancakes to split?" she asked, a question in her eyes.

I gave it some thought, even though, what was there to think about?

"Sure."

She gathered the menus into a stack and placed them at the edge of the table. The waiter came over and Amanda repeated our whole order, glancing at me from time to time to see if I had any last-minute corrections. Once, I'd ordered tea and we'd split the bill, but she'd pretended to be very offended that we'd split it fifty-fifty, "*you* got the tea!" I had laughed, and it was exquisite. I realized now that even back then, we weren't perfect. We were kind of hiding from the outside world. But it wasn't that bad. It could never be that bad, because we had each other.

She opened with a few questions about my work. Apparently, I was to go first. I hated going first. But she was the more well-versed at this game. It's always best to hear the other side before presenting your case.

"How is Cairo? How long are you here for?"

These were the sort of questions that were asked.

I addressed them all as if being interviewed. *I was at an art fair and struck up a conversation with a gallerist. He said "I'd like to see your portfolio," and then he wanted to see pieces I'd left in New York.* But then I stumbled on the bridge between then and now and she seemed unsatisfied. *He has a gallery in Soho that's small and not particularly well-known, but I told him I'd show him more of my work in New York, and he said maybe they'd represent me, so here I am!* I'm not sure I'll ever impress her with my sense of direction. My answers were always too feathery for her, even now. She wanted to hear about the solo show, but I hadn't nailed it down yet. I didn't have anything concrete to show her. Maybe she was done waiting. You had to have a lot of patience with creative endeavors. More patience than Amanda possessed. But she didn't have to have it, I reminded myself. I did.

She was being a good sport about it. She was nodding and trying hard not to frown and doing her best. We were both working hard, actually, to be the very best versions of ourselves.

Which, by the way, is exhausting. So from the moment I sat down, there was a part of me that was dying to leave. Just to get away from her eyes beaming at me.

"At least he *seemed* interested when I met him in Cairo. I emailed him yesterday and got his out-of-office response, which I thought was promising because"—I started to smile—"usually he doesn't respond to my emails."

She smiled appreciatively. It was clear that something had shifted between us. We'd grown up in a way that made us further apart from each other.

"And what about the Italian?"

I made a slashing motion under my chin with my hand and said, "History."

"Not a social flosser?"

"Not nearly." And then, I thought of a way in.

"Oh! That reminds me. I have a New Year's resolution. Do you want to hear it?"

"Yes, please."

I held up my hand and closed my eyes as if about to say something profound, which I was.

"Always floss . . . like you've just gotten home from the dentist."

"That's a good one," she replied thoughtfully. "Impossible to maintain."

"Yeah."

"But good."

"It's . . . strictly aspirational."

The mood was warming. It was as if the lights had dimmed and the air molecules had separated somewhat. And so, I went for broke, and asked the question that had to be asked: "How are things with Nick?"

"Good . . ." Her eyes wandered. She looked at me and then back down at the table. I could tell that she didn't know quite what to say. I could tell that she was thinking, *What is the best approach?* Caught somewhere between not wanting to be too positive, or too negative.

And then, after a few more seconds, she appeared to give it up, to drop everything. She seemed to make a silent pact with herself to level with me, and just be the way we always were with each other. Honest.

"He's really great. He's sweet and funny and smart and . . ."

"Perfect? He sounds perfect!"

"No." She shook her head emphatically. "Not perfect. He's . . ." She rolled her eyes. "Annoying me, at the moment."

"Oh thank God." We smiled at each other briefly. "Why?"

"So, my grandmother passed away a few weeks ago, and I called him . . ."

"Oh. I'm really sorry." The mood was heavy again. Amanda's grandmother had died, and I'd missed it. I hadn't even known.

"Oh," she said, waving me off. "It's okay. She was ninety-seven."

"Still. I'm sorry. I'm sorry I didn't know."

"It's okay." She allowed herself a brief sulk. "Anyway . . . I was upset, obviously, and he was great about it, you know, very supportive, sat with me in bed while I sobbed, watched a four-hour special on Harry and Meghan's wedding . . ."

I raised an eyebrow.

"I don't know. It was oddly distracting."

I cocked my head. "I guess I could see that."

"A few weeks later, I was at my grandmother's house with my mom and they were taking her furniture away and it was *so sad* and I called

Nick and told him how I felt and he said, 'Why? You don't want it.' So I said it's *not about the furniture*. 'What would you do with it?' he kept asking me."

I shook my head in disbelief. "What else you got?"

"Well, whenever Nick eats a dessert, if he doesn't like it, he makes a face and says, 'It's so sweet,' which annoys me because . . . it's dessert! It's supposed to be sweet!"

"Yeah. Don't object to the premise."

"And when he has to fix something around the house, he gets dressed as if he's about to build something on a TV show."

She kept going.

"Oh! I'll ask him to do something and then an hour later he'll be on his phone and say, 'You know, there are some intense lip-sync battles out there.'"

"Easily distracted."

"*So easily.* And he leaves things around the apartment. I would get back at him by leaving my stuff everywhere, just to show him what our apartment would look like, if I didn't constantly put things away, except he would be *fine* and I would have a breakdown."

I nodded. "It would hurt you way more than it would hurt him."

"And he watches movies with subtitles."

"American movies?"

"Yes! He feels it helps him to fully absorb the plot."

"That's . . . odd."

"But he has taught me so much . . . like how to be more relaxed and live in the moment and that if you eat anything with orange juice, it instantly becomes breakfast. Once you decide that it's okay to eat pizza before eleven A.M., there's really no turning back."

"That's good. I think a big part of a relationship is being able to calm someone down more so than annoy them further."

"And to his credit, he's not the one up at three A.M. writing imaginary speeches that he'll never give so . . . he probably wins, generally, in the mental department."

"But I love your imaginary speeches!"

"I know! Wouldn't you say that I am the Barack Obama of emotional diatribes that I would never say out loud?"

"I would. I would say that."

"They'll never understand."

"Nobody I've ever dated understands how my neighbor's mail makes me feel."

"I understand it. I just think you should stop doing it."

"But it makes me feel like my life isn't full!"

"So stop checking it! You're basically giving yourself a burden."

"Okay," I said, giving her a long look. "If we don't count self-inflicted burdens . . ."

"We'd have almost nothing to complain about."

"Hey. How did the trial turn out? Did you win?"

"I won."

"That's amazing!"

"It nearly killed me, but yes. I needed caffeine and sugar almost all the time just to get through. I ate cookies instead of meals."

"What was in the rotation?"

"A few from bakeries but mostly boxed cookies in my office. I was desperate."

"Entenmann's?"

"No. I get the international boxed cookies because they seem healthier. An ingredient list in French cannot be questioned."

"By someone who can't speak French."

"Exactly. What's Cairo like?"

"It's sort of like New York, in that it's alive twenty-four seven. You could really throw yourself into the street life. I could spend an hour telling you about the politics behind these dueling coffee shops . . . Artists are always sitting on the street, trying to make sense of it all."

"How was your birthday?"

"Ah, it was okay. If you move somewhere new right before your birthday, you have to celebrate with strangers, which is always a little peculiar."

"Remember when you tried to get Allie to reschedule her thirtieth birthday party so that you could be there?"

"I just thought it would be bizarre for her to have it without me."

"You know Tomas from NYU? I went to his wedding in Arkansas. He was so dreamy, remember? You loved him."

"Except for the Tevas."

"The *Tevas*! I forgot about those!"

"I think Tevas might be making a comeback, by the way."

"No. Just no. Stop the comeback!"

"I saw Lauren O'Donnell at a museum in Germany. I thought we'd bond over a pfeffernuesse or something, but nooooo. She pretended not to see me. She was the worst! Remember her?"

"She *was* the worst. So unnecessarily bitchy."

"It was excessive."

"Oh! I met Nick's parents."

"And?"

"Sophie. These people. Do not. Stop. Talking. About cruises."

"Abe's parents were like that, too. They never listened! Just go into a meditative state. Do not engage."

"No. You don't understand. They'll spend, like, an hour talking to us about their latest cruise, which basically devolves into them explaining the concept of a vacation. Afterward, I googled 'lobotomy how much.'"

"What did Google say?"

"Seems complicated. I'll never impress his mother."

"Yeah, but I feel like there is an inherent contest between the mother and the wife, to see who can take better care of the son."

"I know. I've seen *Everybody Loves Raymond*. I just didn't realize how accurate it was until now."

"I know, right?"

"I mean. We're not living next door and competing over who can make the best lasagna, but the underlying antagonism is still there."

"I had coffee with Hans yesterday. He's a vegan now. Except he doesn't like vegetables. Do you know how hard it is to eat with a vegan who doesn't like vegetables? You basically have to go to a place that serves broth."

"So don't eat with him. Meet for coffee."

"Yeah, but coffee dates are bullshit. It makes me feel like we aren't friends. Oh! I heard Zoe bought a *huge* apartment."

"I guess her therapy business is going well. Are she and Giff still married?"

"Giff is obviously dead. Zoe strangled him with a pair of my jeans from college."

"I'm going to Miami with Nick for some conference he has there. Have you ever tried your bikinis on in the middle of winter? It makes you feel like the Marshmallow Man in a bikini."

"What Marshmallow Man?"

"You know the one."

"I bought these dresses online that would look so good on you! Here. Look. They look much better in real life."

"Ohhhh, I like these. Should I get it in white? Or black? Although I think my hips are too wide for this kind of thing. My shorts don't fit anymore."

"*Não acredito.*"

"I mean, I can wear them, technically, but they don't look as good as they used to."

"Do you ever feel like you can't focus for a few minutes because you have too many thoughts about things going badly?"

"Everyone feels that way sometimes."

"Really?"

"I think so. I do. And then it passes."

"I have to call my mom. I called her earlier and was really grouchy, so I have to call to apologize."

"I hate that feeling when I'm not nice to my mom."

"It wasn't her fault. I was just in a bad mood and took it out on her."

"I understand. My mom orders soup at a restaurant by telling the waiter what's gross about all the soups offered."

"Oh! Get *this.* I asked Cassandra about a Vietnamese restaurant that I wanted to try and if she's been and she said, 'NO, haven't you heard about the labor disputes? They have all these undocumented workers there!' So then I asked about good Thai food because remember she lived in Thailand for a summer? She said, 'Only in Queens. Don't even bother to look in Manhattan.'"

"Oh, please. She's such a poser. And I just busted out a word from middle school."

"Do you think I should email that gallery owner again? I hate to be too aggressive, but then again everyone is fucking aggressive."

"You want something? Go for it. Have no shame. Sometimes, when I'm trying to decide whether to send someone a follow-up email, I think of climate change and feel much better."

"Why?"

"Because everything is going to shit anyway."

"To me the most threatening part of climate change is that we'll all have to decide what to wear when it's sixty degrees."

"I don't know what to do except shield myself from all the bad news."

"Mostly I think the Internet is a horrible place, but every now and then I see a video of two monkeys who are brothers and were rescued and treated at different NGOs and then reunited and I think, thank God for the Internet."

"I tried following Cookie Monster on Twitter, but I just got fed up. He's so one-dimensional."

"Maybe try Oscar?"

"Too negative."

"Do you remember how your dad used to come visit and take us out to lunch all the time?"

"Yeah and he'd wear an NYU sweatshirt and NYU socks. He claimed he liked the purple."

"Such a dad move. Is your brother still dating that girl?"

"They're married, so yes."

"Have you seen Olivia lately?"

"Yeah. She's obsessed with her son. I'll text her on a Monday to get dinner that Saturday and she'll say, 'Well, Patrick naps today at noon . . .' As if I needed to know his whole schedule! So are you seeing anyone new?"

"No. I love being single. Unless it's nighttime."

"I know. That's when all the monsters come out."

"Do you ever lie in bed at night and think of all the things that you deeply regret doing or saying in your lifetime?"

"Do I *ever*?"

"I can't sleep on other people's couches anymore without waking up paralyzed. I'm going home to Rio for a bit."

"Really?"

"Three days. That's about how long I can take before I start to think, am I really home or am I just in another country being criticized?"

"Yeah. What was Thanksgiving like, back in the day? Like before the existence of alcohol?"

"Remember when we met up for brunch freshman year the morning after you lost your virginity and when you showed up I just *knew* something was different and I guessed what happened and then I started crying?"

"Which was a strange reaction."

"I know. I myself was confused. I kept saying, 'I don't know why I'm crying!'"

"I have this weird thing lately . . . where when I see a family of four, I find it comforting. If I'm feeling anxious or having a bad day and I see a mom and a dad and two children just casually eating dinner, it soothes me. What do you think it means?"

"I don't know. When I was younger, I used to keep track of how quickly everyone at the dinner table was eating so that I could always have the last bite. What does *that* mean?"

"It means . . . You know functioning alcoholics? I think we're all functioning neurotics."

"Who? Women?"

"Yeah. Women."

"Oh. Definitely. Without question."

"This may be a good time to tell you . . . in about seven months . . . Nick and I are going to have a daughter. So what should I tell her?"

"Tell her welcome. Welcome to the party."

Acknowledgments

Thank you to Alli Dyer at Temple Hill for coming to me with this project, and for being a guiding light throughout. Working with you has been so wonderful. Thank you to my editor, Elle Keck, for your kindness and patience and insightful edits, which made this book better.

My agent, Andrew Blauner, has fulfilled my lifelong dream of having an agent who speaks to me in sports analogies. Thanks for being on my team and for understanding my vision, even when it's slightly blurry.

Thank you to my friends, for cheering me on, for sharing your stories and being a part of mine: Madeleine Root (my first friend), Shelly Kellner (my soulmate), Anna Christodoulou (Greek goddess of having a very specific opinion on everything), Emma "Pajama Skirt" Zuroski, Erica Temel (still thinks I'm the number one tennis player in the world, despite all evidence to the contrary), Logan Fedder (always with a box of cookies in her car . . . always), Kevin Meredith (the Hobbes to my Calvin, the Darren to my Kramer, the Jim to my Andy), Nattha Chutinthranod, Carolina Cuervo, Marc Eskenazi, David Siffert (but *you* had the tea), Annie Plick, Kasey

Fechtor, Sandra Rose, Monica Sethi, Kristin Soong, Henry Ginna, Leyla Bilali, Christine Benedetti, Caroline Fairchild, Justin Galacki, Mariel Grossman, Jamie Joseph, Isabel Murphy, and Ellen Fedors. Everything I know about friendship I learned from you guys.

David Hochbaum, for helpful insights into the art world. Adam Eidelberg, for answering all of my contractor related queries. Fabiola Bloch and Pamela Trzesniowski for all things Brazil. Priya Levine and Noah Solowiejczyk, attorneys extraordinaire. My uncle, Phillip Rosen, part-time lawyer and full-time sneaker consultant. Simon Lipskar, Maja Nikolic, and Cecilia de la Campa at Writers House, for all of your work on my behalf.

My family: Roza, Yuly, Anya, Joe, Terry, Ryan, and Emmie. Cheryl, Frank, Lauren, and Doug.

My father and Diane, for your unwavering support.

My sister, Ali, for being my built-in best friend, and my brother-in-law, Danny. Thank you for being the most fun and most dedicated, and for giving me my baby nephew, Beau.

My husband, Dave, for being with me always and for giving me great suggestions, even when you know they will result in a lot of yelling and the occasional fistfight.

My mother tells me that on my first day of school, she followed the bus and hid in the bushes to make sure I was okay. I owe you and blame you for everything.

My daughter, Leyla, endured countless hours of cartoons and a wide variety of snacks while I wrote this book. Thank you, Nick Jr. and the makers of snacks everywhere, for getting us through this time.

About the Author

LESLIE COHEN was born and raised in New York. She studied English and creative writing at Columbia University. She is the author of *This Love Story Will Self-Destruct*.